The Dream Maker

COWBOY FOR HIRE

Alice Duncan

ZEBRA BOOKS

Kensington Publishing Corp.

http://www.zebrabooks.com

ZEBRA BOOKS are published by

Kensington Publishing Corp.
850 Third Avenue
New York, NY 10022

All Kensington titles, imprints and distributed lines are available at special quantity discounts for bulk purchases for sales promotion, premiums, fund raising, educational or institutional use.

Special book excerpts or customized printings can also be created to fit specific needs. For details, write or phone the office of the Kensington Special Sales Manager: Kensington Publishing Corp., 850 Third Avenue, New York, NY 10022. Attn. Special Sales Department. Phone: 1-800-221-2647.

First Printing: March, 2001
10 9 8 7 6 5 4 3 2 1

Printed in the United States of America

One

Pasadena, California.
May, 1905

Sunbeams filtered through the slatted ceiling of the Orange Rest Health Spa's elegant pavilion, casting a brilliant patchwork pattern of light and shadow on the white wicker tables and the people seated at them. The San Gabriel Mountains loomed in the near distance, looking remarkably green and friendly for a mountain range. The heavenly scent of orange blossoms and honeysuckle mingled with the robust aroma of roses to create an almost mystical atmosphere when combined with the variegated light and the overall beauty of the pavilion and its surroundings.

Amy Wilkes thought that if she were dealing with anyone other than the obnoxious human crocodile snarling at her from his white wicker chair, her spirits would be as bright and cheery as the sun itself. She wasn't, and they weren't. Horace Huxtable was the most recalcitrant, worst mannered, least respectful bully of a patient ever to sully the portals of her uncle Frank's health spa. What's more, he was a drunkard and a lecherous old goat. And he was rich. Rich, rich, rich. It wasn't fair, and Amy detested him.

"Mr. Huxtable," she said in her sternest tone, despising the task and wishing she could use less refined methods to make him behave—hammering him on the head with a blunt instrument, for instance—"you must drink your orange juice."

"Oh, must I?"

Amy imagined he'd practiced his sneer in front of a mirror in order to polish it to such a high gloss. "Yes."

"The stuff is vile." His sneer transformed into a glower, and he reminded her of a sulky child. "Damned if I will."

She glowered right back. "My uncle prefers that his guests refrain from the use of profanity on his premises, Mr. Huxtable."

"I don't give a crap what your uncle prefers, you damned little prude."

With her lips pressed together in a tight line, Amy frowned down at the man who was here at her uncle's health spa in Pasadena in order to dry himself out. He was here of his own volition. No one could force a person to take the cure.

Personally, Amy wished Huxtable would just go away and drown himself in a butt of malmsey—whatever that was—like that fellow in *Richard III*. He wasn't cooperating in his health regimen to the least degree, and Amy had thought from the moment he staggered through the front door that he was both horrid and egotistical.

Motion picture actors, she thought grimly, *ought to be locked away so they can't contaminate the rest of us.* They were a new breed, motion picture actors, but Amy had already encountered enough of the species to have formed a strong opinion about them.

"Orange juice is the elixir of life, Mr. Huxtable," she said primly, reciting a line from her uncle's colorful brochure.

"Elixir of life, my ass," rumbled the well-known actor in his deep and melodious voice which ought, in a just world, to have belonged to some fellow who deserved it.

Again, Amy recoiled from his language. "Well, really!"

He chuckled. "Now, now, girlie. You're too innocent for this world, do you know that?"

"I know no such thing, Mr. Huxtable. I do, however, know that you're paying a good bit of money to stay here and restore yourself to some kind of health."

"Who the hell are you, anyhow? Mary Baker Eddy?"

Amy drew in a deep breath, recalling the copy of *Science and Health* residing upstairs in her bedroom. Her aunt, an ardent disciple of Mrs. Baker Eddy, had given it to her, and Amy always felt guilty for not reading it more often. Today, however, she wished she'd brought it here with her. She'd thump Mr. Huxtable over his hard head with it. *That* might do him some good. It would make her feel better, at any rate. "It would do you no harm to read her book, sir."

"Pshaw." Huxtable waved that away. "My ass."

"It seems to me you should be trying to profit from this experience, not fight every attempt to help you recover."

"Recover, my ass."

Feeling savage, Amy said through gritted teeth, "I see you have a limited vocabulary."

He laughed.

"Anyhow, what about the money? Don't you care about wasting your money?"

If Amy had enough money to spend a month at her uncle's fancy health spa, she'd consider herself rich beyond avarice. It was her goal never to be insecure again in her lifetime, and she furiously resented people who wasted what she'd give her eyeteeth to possess. *She* wouldn't drink away a fortune. *She* wouldn't despise others' efforts on her behalf. *She,* unlike Horace Huxtable, was a reasonable and sensible human being.

He waved that one away, too. "I'm not paying. The Peerless Studio is."

"Then you ought to be cooperative. In fact, you ought to

be grateful. I'm sure they won't appreciate you wasting this opportunity and squandering their money."

"Balderdash. They need me."

Amy wrinkled her nose and refrained from making the statement she believed his words deserved.

Huxtable, caught up in his own thoughts and indifferent to anyone else's opinions, said, "If this bilgewater is so wonderful, I'll let *you* drink it, my adorable Miss Wilkes."

Amy gave up. She knew she shouldn't. Part of her job here was to see that the patients—she'd begun to think of them as inmates, actually—ate properly and drank their daily quota of orange juice. Most of them were suffering from the same excesses as was Huxtable—too much food and drink. That, to Amy's mind, was grossly unfair, considering how many people in the world went to bed hungry every day and had perishingly little with which to sustain themselves. Children died every day from starvation—Amy herself might have starved to death if her wonderful aunt and uncle hadn't rescued her—and Amy conceived of wastefulness as a crime.

But were her uncle's patients grateful? Did they cooperate in their own recovery and redemption? Did they take full advantage of this beautiful health spa? Did they eat their oatmeal and drink their orange juice with the appreciation it deserved? Did they study the health magazines Uncle Frank distributed in an effort to help them regain their well-being?

No. Most of them were defiant and uncooperative at least some of the time. Mr. Horace Huxtable, noted theatrical actor and lately to be seen on celluloid in nickelodeons across the country, seemed to go out of his way to be impossible.

She lifted her chin. "I shall leave you here, then, to contemplate the nature of your health. And I should advise you to begin looking kindly upon orange juice, Mr. Huxtable. If what I read in the newspapers is true, the whole nation will be liquor-free soon." Although she knew she shouldn't—after all, according to her uncle, the customer was always right no matter how wrong he was—she smirked.

"God, what a thought!" Huxtable gave a visible shudder.

"I think it's a perfectly splendid one." She whirled to go and almost bumped into a tall, slender, brown-haired man, modishly dressed in a light-colored summer motoring suit, with a driving scarf wound around his neck, and carrying a pair of motoring goggles. Amy chalked him up for another movie fellow, disliked him for it, nodded curtly, and marched off to deal with Mrs. Fellows, who might be fat, silly, and self-indulgent, but wasn't nearly as cantankerous as Horace Huxtable.

Martin Tafft, the fashionably dressed gentleman, whipped off his soft cap and said, "I'm very sorry, ma'am," to her stiff back, but she didn't turn around or acknowledge his apology. He sighed, deducing at once that Huxtable had said or done something to scandalize her. How typical of the overbearing brute. Nevertheless, Martin had a job to do, so he got at it.

"Huxtable," he said with a friendly smile. "You're looking well today."

He looked like a dipsomaniacal wastrel, actually, but Martin couldn't bring himself to say so aloud since Huxtable could cost the Peerless Motion Picture Studio a lot of money if he didn't dry out soon. Huxtable was only forty-two years old, for heaven's sake, and he had within his vanity-stuffed body a wealth of talent. It was a shame, both for Huxtable himself and for Peerless, the studio for which Martin labored, that he seemed determined to drink himself into an early grave.

"I feel like shit," Huxtable answered back, lifting his glass of orange juice. "Do you see this?"

"Yes."

"It's repellent stuff. Whoever invented the orange ought to be shot."

"I think God has that distinction," murmured Martin. "I doubt if a shot would do any good."

"A shot would do me good," the actor growled.

"Nonsense. Booze will be the death of you." Martin breathed deeply and sat when Huxtable waved him at a chair, looking around with interest. "It sure smells good around here. Orange blossoms, I presume. This place is very pretty."

"Hunh."

So much for beating around the bush. Martin got down to brass tacks. "I came to tell you the latest developments with *One and Only*."

At last Huxtable seemed to be interested. His bloodshot eyes focused on Martin. "Have you found a proper cowboy?"

"Yes. Or, rather, yup." Martin smiled. Huxtable didn't. Martin sighed again. "He's a young, gingery fellow named Charles Fox, and he's been working on a ranch in Arizona." Martin decided not to make any mention of what kind of ranch it was, feeling certain that Huxtable would sneer.

"Ah." Huxtable squinted narrowly. "A handsome lad, is he?"

This was tricky, mainly because Charlie Fox was *very* handsome. He sure took the shine out of Huxtable in his current condition. But the celluloid could hide many flaws, and so could theatrical makeup, and Huxtable was already a well-beloved character—thank God his many fans didn't know him personally—so Martin didn't anticipate any chance of Charlie making a better impression on the public than the leading man in the movie. "He's fairly good-looking," he said noncommittally.

Huxtable huffed with irritation. "God, I hate this stuff." He lifted his orange juice glass again and drained it. Then he gave an eloquent shudder and burped. "What they need to do is mix some gin in it. Make it palatable."

Martin, who had been dealing with actors for several years,

was not daunted by Huxtable's boorish manners. He plowed on. "We still need to find you a leading lady—"

Huxtable held up a hand. "Done."

His mouth already open to continue the leading lady line, Martin used his breath to say, "I beg your pardon?"

"I've done that part of your job for you, Martin old boy. I'm sure you noticed that pretty little filly you just bumped into?"

"We didn't actually touch," mumbled Martin.

"Pity, that, but you'll try harder next time, I'm sure." He gave Martin a lascivious wink, from which Martin did all he could not to shrink. "I want her to star with me."

Martin stared at Huxtable for a moment, then turned in his chair to see if he could catch sight of the young woman with whom he'd narrowly avoided contact. She was at present standing beside an elderly woman at a table on the other side of the room, smiling attractively. She was a striking girl, probably around eighteen or nineteen, with thick, reddish-brown hair piled on top of her head, and very nice eyes. Martin couldn't see their color from where he sat, but it didn't matter what color anything was since, on celluloid, it all came out black-and-white. Her lashes were thick, too, and wouldn't require much makeup.

She had a superb figure and looked dignified in her narrow black skirt and prim white shirtwaist with a high collar encircled by a tidy black bow tie. She actually fit the description of the leading lady in *One and Only* admirably. Still, Martin had grave doubts about asking her to act in a movie with Horace Huxtable, who would probably eat her alive and spit out the pieces.

"Her?" he asked dubiously.

"Her." Huxtable ran his fingers across his natty mustache. "I want her."

Martin didn't like the sound of this. "Has she any experience?"

"Not the kind you mean. Probably not the kind I mean, either." His chuckle rumbled out, an oily blot on the soft, sweet-smelling Pasadena air.

Deciding a firm hand was needed here, Martin said, "Now see here, Huxtable. You can't go about the country deflowering virgins. We have a picture to shoot, and Mr. Lovejoy is planning on making it the biggest and best one yet. Four reels, for heaven's sake. This picture will make Peerless Studio a name to be reckoned with in the industry. It's an expensive project, and we need a cast of professionals to act in it. I can't hire just anybody."

"You hired that cowboy."

"That's different. The public is clamoring for cowboy pictures and more cowboy pictures, and all the studios are using real cowboys nowadays. They add authenticity, and the movie-going public love it."

"Pshaw. Let me have that tidy bundle, and I'll give you all the authenticity you want."

The next time his studio head, Phineas Lovejoy, wanted to hire Horace Huxtable to act in a moving picture, Martin was going to object with all the energy in his body. He didn't care to have *pimp* added to his already overfull list of responsibilities at the studio.

"What about Ginny Mae Williams?"

Huxtable made a rude noise which Martin correctly interpreted as an objection.

"Mabel Gresham?" Another noise, ruder this time.

"Wilma Patecky?"

"Good God, man! What do you think I am?"

A sot, a reprobate, and a debauched cad, thought Martin instantly. He said, "You're a fine actor, Huxtable, and one with a loyal following." Otherwise, Peerless wouldn't have anything to do with him.

"You're damned right I am. I have instincts." He pounded his fist on the table. "And I know a good screen presence when I see one. I want *her.*"

"Very well." Martin resigned himself to tackle an unpleasant task. "I'll speak to her."

"You'll do more than speak to her. You'll hire her."

Irritated, Martin said, "I'll do my best."

"You'll succeed," Huxtable said complacently. "What girl wouldn't leap at the chance to act in a motion picture with Horace Huxtable?"

Any girl who possesses half a brain. Martin said, "Right. I'll talk to her now." He got up to leave, but thought it wouldn't hurt to give Huxtable a gentle warning. Actors and their exalted emotions and lofty opinions of themselves were a pain in the neck, but as Phineas had pointed out to Martin more than once, one had to pamper the blockheads. However, a hint wouldn't hurt.

He looked down at the Peerless star, who was preening himself. "Remember, Huxtable, the studio is paying for your stay here because we want you sober for the shooting. If you don't do your best in this picture, which will be the biggest, most expensive one made to date by any studio in the entire world, the chances are good that your reputation as a reliable actor will be ruined beyond recovery. You've had plenty of chances, and won't be given another."

Huxtable drew himself up as if Martin's words had mortally offended him. "Don't you talk to *me* like that, you impudent pup!"

Martin's temper snapped. "It's about time somebody did, because it's the truth. You aren't going to be able to live on your looks much longer. You're not only getting older, but you're ruining yourself with your drinking. If you must know the truth, you're beginning to look mighty liverish. Keep drinking orange juice, old man. It might just save your career."

Since he'd been associated with theatrics long enough to recognize a good exit line when he said one, Martin turned on his heels and walked toward the girl, leaving Huxtable in his chair, sputtering angrily.

If Amy Wilkes possessed a single defining personality trait, it was sensibleness. She'd learned long ago that the only way to get on in life was to make sensible plans and stick to them, no matter what obstacles people threw in her way.

At the tender age of seven, she'd lost her parents, a tragedy that had precipitated her descent into such a cauldron of grief, terror, and pain that she'd never forgotten it. She aimed never to experience such a catastrophe again and had made it a guiding principle never to allow insecurity so much as a toehold in her life.

Her gratitude toward her uncle Frank and aunt Julia was boundless. They'd taken her in when they'd learned of the dire straits into which she'd fallen, and loved her as if she'd been their own child.

For years now, Amy had been working for her aunt and uncle, starting during her summer vacations from school. Now she worked for them year-round. She enjoyed the work, although she didn't anticipate being employed at the Orange Rest Health Spa forever. She was only twenty years old, but already she'd experienced happiness and sadness, security and insecurity, and had been forced to put aside a child's rose-colored glasses and view the world as it was.

Amy had as many dreams for her future as any other young, modern woman, although her dreams might be considered by more romantic young women as awfully dull. And even Amy had to admit that her dreams weren't outrageous. She didn't long to become a hot-air balloonist, for instance. Nor did she want to conquer Mount Everest or swim the English Channel or join Buffalo Bill's Wild West Show.

Her dreams were much more reasonable than that. In fact, some people might call them prosaic. They didn't seem prosaic to Amy. They seemed golden, probably because her own family life with her mother and father had been cut so tragically short.

But she knew one thing for certain: Someday she was going to have a home and family of her own. That was all, the extent of her most precious and idyllic hopes for her future. Her friends thought she was remarkably shortsighted, but Amy knew what it was to lose life's most priceless gifts; she knew what was important in life and what was mere window dressing.

She even had a young man, Vernon Catesby, who appeared at this time to be the most likely means for Amy to achieve her dream. If he was the least bit stuffy, Amy didn't mind. She craved security. Predictability and security, to her at least, went hand in hand, and Vernon was nothing if not predictable.

At this particular moment, however, Amy wasn't contemplating her life's dream or Vernon Catesby. No. At this moment, she and Martin Tafft were seated in the snug lounge of the Orange Rest Health Spa, and Amy was staring at him, thinking he didn't fit into her dream-achieving pattern one tiny little trifling iota of an atom. In fact, she believed she'd misunderstood him and wondered if she could possibly be going deaf. Admittedly, she was rather young for that, but she couldn't conceive of what she'd heard any other way.

The lounge at the Orange Rest was furnished in a South Seas style with palm trees, Hawaiian prints on the sofa cushions, and woven grass matting on the floor. The afternoon heat had driven most of the inmates to their rooms, where electric fans added a modicum of comfort to the still air. This room, which was shaded by a row of stately pepper trees, was fairly comfortable.

With her hands folded modestly and resting on the table between herself and Martin, Amy stared at him, dumbfounded, unable to believe what her ears had just heard. She scarcely found the wit to say, "I beg your pardon?"

Martin repeated himself patiently and added, "I understand why you might be surprised, Miss Wilkes. After all, it isn't every day a young woman with no prior acting experience is invited to play a principal part in a motion picture opposite a famous star of stage and screen."

Unable to think of anything to say, Amy nodded.

"Mr. Huxtable would like you to act as his leading lady in the Peerless Studio's next production." Martin smiled pleasantly. "It's an ambitious prospect. Four whole reels, and it will take probably three weeks or more to shoot."

This was another surprise for Amy, because Martin's time scheme contradicted articles she'd read in newspapers and periodicals. She blurted out, "I thought people made moving pictures in a day or two."

Martin shook his head. "Not this one. This one's big. Mr. Lovejoy is counting on it to secure the studio's reputation. After this one is seen, when the public thinks of moving pictures, they'll think Vitagraph, Biograph, and Peerless, and of the three, only Peerless will be out here on the West Coast, where the sun shines year-round and pictures can be made in the dead of winter if they need to be."

"Oh."

Warming to his theme, Martin went on. "This picture will be what we're calling a 'feature.' It's a new term, and it's going to take off like wildfire. Folks will flock to theaters to see featured motion pictures along with a one-reel short or two."

"Theaters?" Amy's voice had dropped and was very small.

Martin nodded. "Oh, yes. Folks are building special theaters for moving pictures these days."

"Oh."

Amy noticed that Martin's eyes sparkled, and she thought it was nice that he enjoyed his work. But—act in a movie? Amy Wilkes? From Pasadena, California? She couldn't imagine herself doing anything so . . . so . . . so . . . bizarre. Amy craved continuity, not out-of-the-wayness.

She also couldn't feature her young gentleman banker friend Vernon Catesby, who had been paying her particular attentions of late, approving of this venture. She didn't approve, herself, if it came to that.

Martin went on. "It's a western picture, and it'll be called *One and Only.* Cowboys are very popular these days."

"One and Only," Amy said dully. "But why me?"

"Why not you?" He gave her a charming smile that Amy would bet a dozen of her uncle's oranges he'd practiced in front of a mirror, rather as Mr. Huxtable had practiced his sneer. "You're a lovely young woman. This will be a tremendous opportunity for you."

Glancing through the window to the patio, Amy spotted Horace Huxtable still there, the only inmate remaining outdoors, sprawled, glaring gloomily at his empty orange juice glass. "What kind of opportunity?"

"Why, to get in on the ground floor of a brand-new venture, to make money doing something enjoyable, and to see a little of the way in which motion pictures are made. Most of the industry is still located back East with Mr. Edison, but the Peerless Studio is at the forefront of Western production."

"Oh."

"Absolutely! Why, simply take a look around. We here in Southern California have wonderful weather and grand locations. The sun shines everywhere, all the time! Especially now, when the public fascination with cowboys is at its peak, why should movies be filmed in New York? It makes no sense."

"Oh."

"So you see, you'll be getting in at the beginning of a major innovation in a brand-new industry! And if you do well, you'll certainly get more work. You might even catch the public's fancy and become a star. There are monumental opportunities for money and fame in the movie business, Miss Wilkes."

Mercy sakes, wouldn't Vernon pitch a fit if she became a famous motion picture actress.

She shook her head to dislodge the notion. This was getting silly. She sat up straight and frowned slightly. "I've never been interested in fame, Mr. Tafft. I think it would be awful to be recognized by strangers on the street. And I don't want to make money if it means sacrificing my morals."

"Sacrificing your morals?" Martin Tafft looked positively shocked.

Amy, feeling uncomfortable, said, "Well, I've read things."

"Tosh. Miss Wilkes, the articles you've read have painted a faulty picture, if that's what you think. Why, the movies are supremely moral!"

"They are?"

"They are. Why, they're going to break down barriers between nations!"

"They are?"

"Absolutely! They're going to help us understand that we're all part of God's family. Nations will be able to view the way people in other nations live. They'll come to understand that people are alike the world over."

"Mercy."

"Pictures are marvelous! They're entertainment for the entire family. They promote community values and family togetherness."

"They do?"

"Of course! Why, fathers will be going to the movies with their families on Sunday afternoons instead of heading into pool palaces and gin mills! Pictures will be the salvation of our great country!"

"I . . . ah . . . hadn't heard that." She would, however, keep these arguments in mind should she need them when discussing this opportunity with Vernon.

Martin huffed. "You never need fear for the moral tone of a Peerless picture, Miss Wilkes. In fact, do you realize that when Peerless made a moving picture of *The Scarlet Letter*, Mr. Lovejoy made sure that Hester and Mr. Dimmesdale were married?"

Amy blinked, trying to take it in. "But—what was the story about, if they were a married couple? I mean, wasn't the whole plot—" She broke off, embarrassed to be talking about illegitimate children, adultery, and so forth with a stranger.

Martin waved her question away. "But, you see, don't you, that Peerless deals in nothing but material of the highest moral caliber."

Again peering through the window and taking in the spectacle of Horace Huxtable slouched at his table, Amy shook her head. "I'm sure Mr. Lovejoy's morals are of the highest caliber, but I don't care to be corrupted by anyone whose morals don't match his."

Martin glanced at Huxtable, too, and sighed. "Of course you don't. Believe me, I'll see that nothing bad happens to you. We even have matrons to assist our actresses on the set."

"What's a set?"

He looked at her blankly for a moment. Amy might have been embarrassed by her ignorance, except that she perceived this opportunity as too serious to gloss over. She needed to know everything in order to make an informed decision. Her future might depend upon her choice.

"The set is where the picture will be shot."

She squinted at him. "I'm afraid I still don't understand, Mr. Tafft. Don't you just set up a camera somewhere and paint a backdrop or something? As they do in the theater?"

His expression held a little condescension. Amy opted to overlook it for the moment in favor of gathering information. "Not any longer, Miss Wilkes. Not for this picture. The days of shooting moving pictures just any old where are gone for good. The public is demanding realism nowadays, and Peerless is going to give it to them with *One and Only*. That's why Peerless is setting up out here in California. Whoever heard of a cowboy in New York?"

He chuckled, but Amy didn't get the joke.

After clearing his throat, he went on. "One of my jobs is to scout out suitable locations. *One and Only* will be filmed not too far from here, in the desert outside a small community called El Monte."

She nodded. She knew El Monte; had even been there once. It was way out in the country and was full of cows. People grew an assortment of agricultural crops there as well. The rest of it was, well, desert. It was, in her limited experience, at the end of the earth.

Martin continued. "There are hundreds of movies being made every year now, and opportunities are better than ever for an ambitious young person to earn a good deal of money. Ever since *The Great Train Robbery*, the industry has taken off like a frightened rabbit."

An apt metaphor. Amy said with great reserve, "Thus far, I haven't found my association with moving picture folks a particularly happy one, Mr. Tafft."

She saw him heave another sigh. "Has Huxtable been a trial for you?"

"Yes." Although Amy was generally the most polite and

well-bred of young women, she saw no need to mince matters at present. "He's been perfectly awful."

"Well, but look here, Miss Wilkes, the rest of the cast is nice. The man who's been hired to play the love triangle interest is a real cowboy, and he's as polite and shy as anything."

"He is, is he?"

Martin nodded. "And think of the money. Where else can you earn so much by doing so little? And remember, you don't need to stay in the pictures forever. You can save your money and set yourself up anywhere. This is an opportunity that isn't offered to just anyone."

Having been brought up by relatives with strict ethical principles and old-fashioned ideals, Amy sniffed at that. "Making money for doing very little is not what I think of as suitable employment for an industrious, honest, hardworking young woman, Mr. Tafft."

He lifted his hands as if her starchy attitude was getting the better of him. "So you can work harder on the set if you want to. For heaven's sake, Miss Wilkes, we *need* you!"

She didn't like the turn this conversation was taking. Any time a person said he needed her, her immediate reaction was to leap in and help that person out. "Surely there must be other young women available to act the role."

He shook his head emphatically. "You're the one. You're the only one. The one and only. You fit the description of the heroine to a T."

Amy remained unimpressed. "Well . . . I'll have to discuss the matter with my aunt and uncle." *And Vernon.* She didn't mention him to Mr. Tafft. "They were kind enough to take me in and give me a position here at the Orange Rest when my parents passed on."

"I see." Martin paused to think for a minute. "There's another point right there," he said. "If you—a young woman alone in the world—have to make your own living, the movies are a good place to do it. As I've said over and over again, there's good money in the pictures."

"From all I've heard, there's a lot more than money in them," she said acidly. She read the newspapers and the magazines. She knew what shenanigans and scrapes some picture people got themselves into. Although, she had to admit, it would be pleasant to know she had money of her own tucked away in case of an emergency.

Martin evidently deduced what she was thinking because he repeated, "Believe me, Miss Wilkes, it's only a very small proportion of the motion picture community that misbehaves. Most of them are fine, upstanding people."

Amy's glance slid over to Huxtable and back to Martin, who shrugged helplessly. "He's really not so bad. Honestly. He overindulges sometimes, is all."

"Hmmm."

Nevertheless, Amy talked to Vernon Catesby about the opportunity when he paid a call upon her later in the afternoon. Vernon frowned. The expression was not unfamiliar to Amy, who heaved a silent, internal sigh. She was fond of Vernon, in a way, and she fully expected to marry him one day. He was dependable, sensible, and could offer her more security than anyone else in her present orbit. She could not, however, repress a tiny twinge of boredom every time she was in his company.

"I don't like it," he said flatly. "Motion pictures may be a way to make fast money, but you know very well that the morals of those people are suspect. Why, actors have been on the lowest echelon of society for hundreds of years."

"Mr. Tafft seemed quite pleasant and not at all immoral," Amy said, feeling suddenly stifled by Vernon's attitude.

Vernon shook his head. "I fear I must forbid you to do this thing, Amy. It's ludicrous and completely inappropriate."

Amy squinted at him. She would never go so far as to

announce to Vernon that he had no right to forbid her to do anything, but she didn't care for his tone. Or his words. "We'll see," she said in a voice that sounded more chilly than usual. "I shall speak to Aunt Julia and Uncle Frank about it."

Vernon's bloodless lips compressed and his thin, patrician features registered censure. Amy offered him orange juice and lemon bars to sweeten him up, and he was smiling again by the time he left.

When she spoke to her aunt and uncle later in the day, both of them were more eager for her to have this chance than she was.

"Just think, dear, your face will be up there on the screen in a picture palace! My niece!" Her aunt Julia clasped her hands to her bosom and beamed at her. "Oh, it's so exciting!"

"Sounds all right to me," her uncle Frank said with less enthusiasm, but no apparent misgivings. "You have to admit the money's swell."

Swell. Good heavens, Amy hadn't even started her career as an actress yet, and already her family's vocabulary was being corrupted. "Mr. Tafft says they'll want to change my name."

Her aunt looked puzzled. "Whatever for?"

She shrugged. "He says Amy might not be sophisticated enough for the movies."

"But," her aunt said, "they don't have the names of the players printed anywhere on the screen, do they?"

Amy was prepared for this question, and was pleased she'd asked Martin about it. "No, but interested members of the public sometimes write to the studios or to *Motion Picture Story* magazine, and they give out the names."

Both her aunt and uncle pondered this information for a moment or two. Finally her uncle said, "That actually might not be a bad idea. After all, you don't want everybody in the world to know your real name, do you?"

Gracious sakes. If even her easygoing uncle was ashamed of her possible association with the moving pictures, Amy didn't want anything to do with them herself.

Her aunt spoke next. "That's nonsense, Frank. I think it's a wonderful opportunity for Amy. It's the best way I can think of for her to gain some experience of the world—" She stopped speaking suddenly and looked worriedly at her niece. "There *will* be some kind of protection for you, won't there? I mean, the ladies and gentlemen in the picture won't mix socially, will they?"

With a touch of irony, Amy said, "Mr. Tafft said there are matrons and guards and so forth on all picture sets. I guess they need them to keep curiosity seekers away. And to protect the cast."

"Well, then," her aunt said with renewed enthusiasm. "I think you should do it."

After several more moments of deep thought, and after considering Vernon's objections and her aunt's excitement, Amy gave up her arguments. As Mr. Tafft had said, if she didn't like it, she never had to do it again—and the money was awfully good. "Very well. I'll give it a try."

Her aunt was ecstatic.

Her uncle was pleased.

Vernon was disgusted.

Martin was elated.

Huxtable immediately began plotting her seduction.

Two

The train chugged to a stop in a small station that looked
as if it had been dropped there, in the middle of nowhere, by
some maniacal devil trying to hide it from the world. As far
as his eyes could see, Charlie Fox detected no other sign of
life but that one small, dusty building. Did folks actually live
here?

A native of Arizona Territory, Charlie wasn't unfamiliar
with deserts, but this one looked a lot different from the deserts he was used to, near the beautiful rock formations around
Sedona. This California desert was ugly.

That was neither here nor there, however. He clutched his
one piece of luggage, a battered denim carpetbag his older
brother had used in '98 when he went off to Cuba to fight
in the Spanish-American War, and headed toward the exit.

He nodded at the Pullman porter and handed him a dime,
thinking it a suitable tip. From the look on the porter's face,
he disagreed. Charlie didn't much care. He wasn't one to fling
money around with abandon—mainly because he'd never had
much of it, and he respected it.

A horseless carriage—folks in the know called them simply
"machines" these days, or so Charlie had been told—awaited
him at the train depot. Charlie had seldom seen an automobile,
much less ridden in one, so this part of his adventure was
fun. The driver even pressed the rubber horn a couple of times

at Charlie's request. What a noise! A fellow could turn a stampeding herd with one of those things in no time flat.

It took them an hour of bumpy driving to get to the location where *One and Only* was to be filmed. Charlie snoozed most of the way since the scenery was so boring. The bumps didn't bother him, as he was used to sleeping when and where he could, including occasionally on horseback.

When the car rolled to a stop, he walked onto the set of *One and Only* with tolerable misgivings. This sissy moviemaking stuff didn't seem like a proper pursuit for a man like him, no matter what that nice fellow, Mr. Tafft, had told him.

On the other hand, he was sick to death of punching ostriches on his brother's ranch in Arizona Territory. Ostriches were in no respect akin to cattle, and Charlie had been born and bred into the cattle ranching business. In Charlie's opinion, those huge feathered monsters were a curse from above. He rued the day Sam, his brother, had won that ding-busted bird farm in a poker game.

He wasn't altogether sure playacting in a moving picture was the precise answer to ostriches, though. While Charlie was as game for a lark as the next fellow, acting didn't seem like a manly pursuit to him. All that standing around, strutting, waving your arms in the air, grimacing at the camera, being dramatic and silly. Shoot, that sort of stuff was for kids and saps.

But the money was good, and he wanted money badly. For years he'd dreamed of owning his own spread—stocked with cows, not ostriches. This nonsensical movie would pay him more money in a month than he could earn in a year on his brother's ranch, and Mr. Tafft had told him there was more work available for a good-looking cowboy like him. Charlie had blushed at the time, but he appreciated the information.

"Mr. Fox!" a voice called out.

Turning, Charlie saw Martin Tafft, the man who'd "discovered" him in Arizona. Tafft was a nice fellow and was giving him a friendly wave, so Charlie smiled and waved back. "How-de-do, Mr. Tafft. Right ugly place you got to shoot this here movie in."

Tafft, hurrying over to him, laughed. "Yes, I reckon El Monte is a little arid."

Whatever that meant. Charlie nodded because he figured it meant the place stank, which it did.

"It'll look better on film," Tafft assured him.

Frankly, Charlie didn't care how it looked on film as long as he got the money he'd been promised. He'd never even dreamed of having such a pile all at once.

Martin took his arm, a gesture Charlie wouldn't have tolerated in Arizona Territory, where you had to get to know a man before you took liberties. He didn't object, understanding from things he'd read that picture people were a peculiar and eccentric lot.

"Would you like to meet the rest of the cast?"

Martin's attitude was genial and outgoing, and Charlie appreciated it. He was downright nervous about this thing he was doing. Not, of course, that he believed he couldn't do it. After all, how hard could it be to strut around and look like a cowboy? He was a cowboy to begin with. It was only that he'd never stood in any sort of limelight before, and the notion of doing so made him itchy. "Sure," he said. "Glad to."

"Horace Huxtable hasn't arrived yet."

Charlie noted that Martin's smile faded when he said the actor's name. It came back, big and bright, however, when he added, "But Miss Wilkes is here. She's a delightful young lady, Charlie. I'm sure you two will hit it right off."

"Glad to hear it." Charlie hoped she was pretty. He was a little shy around women, but that was only because he'd met so few in his life up to now.

They strolled across the dusty ground toward what looked

like an Indian village—all white tents and clutter. These tents didn't have pretty pictures painted on them the way the Indians' tents did, though.

"We have to make do when we're shooting in the country," Martin explained. "And since this picture will take longer to film than most, we've built ourselves a sort of tent settlement here. We have most of the conveniences a person will need. Why, we even have a staff nurse on duty, in case of injuries. A restaurant in El Monte will deliver food three times a day. You'll have your own tent, of course, because you're one of the leading characters."

"That's right nice of you, Mr. Tafft."

Martin waved the thanks away. "Please call me Martin, and we have to take care of our actors," he said with a chuckle. "Otherwise, where would we be?"

Since Charlie didn't know, he didn't answer.

"Miss Wilkes has her own tent, too, of course. She's the female protagonist in our picture. She's the one you're going to lose to Horace Huxtable, who's playing the hero."

"Yeah?" Charlie didn't like the sound of that. He'd never been fond of losing, even in make-believe. "What did you say her name is?"

"It's Amy Wilkes really, but we've changed her first name to Amelia, because Mr. Lovejoy's wife thinks it sounds more romantic. Mr. Lovejoy is the head of the studio."

"Oh." Charlie wasn't in the habit of thinking of romance at all—except at certain times when he was susceptible, and then he took his needs to a discreet establishment in town— and he'd never even considered the possibility of one name being more "romantic" than another. Personally, he kind of liked Amy. He narrowed his eyes and contemplated the mess of tents up ahead, trying to locate a female who might be Amy—Amelia—Wilkes. Nobody caught his eye.

They arrived at the first tent, and Charlie noted with interest that the Peerless Studio hadn't spared any expenses. These temporary abodes were made out of good, heavy-duty canvas, and they looked as though they'd last for a century at least.

"Here's your new home, Charlie. You can stow your bag in there."

The inside of the tent was as impressive as the outside. "Why, it's got a whole lot of furniture in it," he exclaimed, surprised.

Martin chuckled and rubbed his hands together. "Nothing but the best for the Peerless cast. Our pictures have been very well received recently, and we're sharing the profits."

That was a happy circumstance for Charlie. He slung his carpetbag down next to a bed. Not a mere cot, mind you, but a bed with springs and a mattress and everything. Kerosene lamps were set about on small tables, an easy chair and ottoman had been provided, as well as a bureau, and a washstand complete with a bowl and pitcher for washing and shaving. Clean linen was stacked on a table next to the washstand, and a chamber pot had been provided for his overnight use.

He lifted his eyebrows. "Looks mighty good to me, Mr. Tafft." It was a hell of a lot better than what he usually bunked in on the ranch.

"Glad you think so. The studio maids will come and clean it every day. But come along now. Let me introduce you to Miss Wilkes."

Maids. Imagine that. Charlie guessed he could act the sissy for a while if he did it in such luxury. Wait until he told Sam about this.

He hitched up his trousers, glanced in the mirror attached to the bureau, adjusted his Stetson, decided he was fit to meet a lady, and followed Martin out of the tent. His eyes opened wide when Martin began to steer him to a woman seated under an umbrella in front of another white tent. She was dressed all in light blue, presumably in deference to the warm weather.

She wore a splendid, broad-brimmed straw hat with a blue flower on it, and she seemed to be engrossed in writing a letter.

"Holy cow," Charlie murmured, not having anticipated Miss Wilkes being such a lovely little thing. "Is that her? Look at all that hair." Her hair shone out from under her big hat like a halo.

"That's her," confirmed Martin.

Charlie whipped his stained Stetson from his head as they approached her. The girl looked up, squinting into the sun. When she saw Martin, she smiled. When she saw Charlie, she didn't.

"Miss Amelia Wilkes," Martin said with a great show of merriment, "please allow me to introduce you to Mr. Charlie Fox, who will be starring in *One and Only* with you and Mr. Huxtable."

She eyed him up and down, just like a city snob, held out her hand, which was, Charlie noted, gloved, and said in a chilly voice, "I'm very pleased to meet you, Mr. Fox."

Abashed and annoyed by her frigid demeanor, Charlie decided to lay on the cowboy act. Why not? The little prig. He'd had such high hopes for her, too. He grinned, took her hand, pumped it vigorously, and said, "Likewise. I'm *damned* glad to meet such a pretty gal as you, Miss Wilkes."

Miss Wilkes flinched and drew herself up straight, as if she'd taken offense. Since that was what Charlie had intended her to do, he was satisfied.

He didn't, however, understand why Mr. Tafft, who up until now had seemed happy, groaned softly under his breath.

Amy had taken one look at the tall, lanky man walking next to Mr. Tafft and known he was Charles Fox, the second leading man in *One and Only*. He had to be. Nobody could be that perfect for a part and not play it.

She instantly became heart-knockingly nervous, which rather surprised her, as she'd never experienced any particular attraction to cowboys before. Many of her friends had. One of them, Harriet Fulton, had even spent several weeks at a dude ranch in Wyoming one summer. Hettie had always been a bit of a flibbertigibbet with more money than sense, however, and Amy had secretly deplored such frivolous romantic fancies.

That was before she'd seen Charlie Fox, and her attitude toward cowboys underwent a sudden unanticipated and sensational change during which her heart sped up, her palms began to perspire, her mouth went dry, and she became inexplicably breathless. Also suddenly and unexpectedly, she felt a tremendous urge to impress him.

So really, she decided in an effort to explain her lamentable manners, if one boiled the phenomenon down to its barest essence, it was Mr. Fox's fault that she'd behaved like that, because he was the most stunning man she'd ever seen.

Innately honest, Amy knew she was shirking the truth.

What had really happened was that she'd taken one look at him, and her wits had flown straight out of her head. She'd pretended to be what Mr. Tafft had been trying to turn her into: a cultured, sophisticated woman of the world. Thus perhaps she had "put on airs," as her aunt often said of some of the inmates at the Orange Rest. In reality, the pose was nothing but an act. It was protective coloration, a silly effort on Amy's part not to be taken as an inexperienced boob.

Amy did not, however, appreciate Mr. Fox's language, even if she had come across as a tiny bit uppity. Amy Wilkes didn't approve of profanity, and wouldn't have even if the speaker had been ten times as good-looking as he. Not that such a thing was possible. She also didn't know what to say now.

Fortunately, Martin Tafft seemed adept at conciliating uncomfortable situations. He laughed easily and said, "I'm sure you two will get along just fine."

Amy considered his positive attitude both optimistic and quite sweet under the circumstances. Since she figured she ought to, she smiled, hoping her smile looked like a sophisticated one and not an inane one, which was what it felt like.

Martin rubbed his hands together and turned to survey the tent village that Peerless had created in the wilderness. He appeared extremely proud of his studio. "We've got all the luxuries of home here, by gum. It'll be a great movie, too."

"Sounds like it," Charlie said in a deep baritone that drawled deliciously and reminded Amy of her aunt's best and most expensive orange blossom honey.

Amy had never encountered a real drawl in the flesh before. She still didn't know what to say, so she tried to appear cool and collected. She noticed Charlie eyeing her slantwise, and hoped she was making a good impression. Above all things, she didn't want anyone to find out that she was an unworldly rube who'd never been anywhere or done anything.

Recalling Vernon Catesby's disapproval, she wondered if he'd been right, if this experience was going to damage her character. What a sobering thought. Charlie spoke then, forestalling further development upon that morose theme.

"I think this here moviemakin' thing'll be a whole lot of fun, Martin."

"I hope so." Martin's voice was a hearty, clipped counterpoint to Charlie's more lengthy, less grammatical syllables. He heaved a happy sigh. "We're going to have a cast meeting tomorrow morning, and I'll distribute the scripts."

"Scripts?" Amy could have kicked herself for sounding bewildered. She cleared her throat. "Er, isn't the picture silent?"

Martin laughed, but since it wasn't a condescending laugh, Amy didn't take exception. "Yes, indeedy, Miss Wilkes. The picture's silent, but we like the cast to have a script—more of a story line, really—to follow. So you'll know what the story's about and what to expect. You know, it helps everyone get into the emotional spirit of the thing. Wouldn't want you smiling when you're supposed to be crying, now, would we?"

She nodded and was pleased to see that Charlie did, too. Maybe she wasn't the only ignoramus on the Peerless lot.

Martin continued. "After a short rehearsal—just to let everyone get to know each other—Miss Wilkes will have her first costume fitting."

"My goodness! A costume fitting?" Again, Amy felt a spurt of annoyance at letting her ignorance show. Naturally, she'd wear costumes suitable for the cowboy picture; it was just that she hadn't anticipated all of these new aspects so abruptly accruing to a life that had, until a few days ago, been totally predictable from dawn to dark, every day. Even Vernon's visits, which were taken by all to be precursors to his and Amy's married life together, were predictable.

Which was exactly the way Amy wanted it. She didn't want or need excitement or spontaneity. The last unanticipated thing to happen in her life had been her parents' deaths, and that was plenty enough for her.

"Absolutely," Martin said with his beaming smile. "A dressmaker named Madame Dunbar, from your own home-town, has contracted to do the costumes for this picture."

"Oh. My goodness." She'd never heard of Madame Dunbar. That's probably because Amy, whose family was perfectly respectable but not lavishly wealthy, had always made her own clothes. She'd never admit it in front of Martin Tafft and Charlie Fox.

"She's a wonder, Madame Dunbar is. I'm sure you'll look stunning as a cowgirl."

A cowgirl. Oh, dear. Amy smiled gamely. "I do hope so." She noticed Charlie looking her up and down as if he were assessing the merits of her feminine charms. Feeling herself heating up and hating it, she drew upon her waning store of dignity and offered him a frosty stare.

"Aw, hell," Charlie said, making Amy blink. "I'll bet any damned man here a ten-spot that you'll look dandy in britches, Miss Wilkes. Jim-dandy!"

Horrified as much by what he'd said as the way he'd said it, Amy gasped. "Britches? You mean *trousers?*" She would die. She would positively *die* if she were forced to wear men's trousers in front of a camera.

Vernon was right. She was doomed. Vernon probably wouldn't want anything to do with her after this.

"No, no, no," Martin said hastily. "No trousers, Miss Wilkes. Our heroine is a lady. She wears skirts and dresses." He gave Charlie a dirty look.

Charlie grinned, as guileless as the new dawn. Amy, watching them both, wondered if Charlie had tried to upset her on purpose because she'd been behaving a teensy bit stuffy. She was too relieved about the trousers to ask him. She was so relieved, in fact, that she very nearly fainted from her sudden exhalation of breath.

Tomorrow, she vowed, she wouldn't lace her corset so tightly. This desert weather was less agreeable than the weather in Pasadena. Or perhaps she was feeling another effect from her attempts to appear cosmopolitan and fashionable.

At the moment, Amy didn't feel at all modish or urbane. In fact, she wished she were back at the Orange Rest Health Spa, drinking her uncle's orange juice, and doing something she understood.

A gong sounded in the distance, and Martin turned quickly. As if seizing an opportunity to extricate the three of them from a ticklish situation, he said, "There's the luncheon bell, Miss Wilkes. Please allow Mr. Fox and me to escort you to the chow tent."

"Thank you," she murmured. "I believe I'll freshen up first. I'll be along in a minute. You two go on ahead." She didn't want to try walking alongside Charlie Fox before she'd loosened her stays. She'd die of humiliation right here in the wilds of El Monte if she fainted in front of him.

"Hell's bells, ma'am," Charlie said with a big grin. "You already look as fresh as a damned daisy."

Amy gaped up at him for a moment, appalled. Whatever had she gotten herself into here? She feared for her sanity. Not to mention any claim she'd ever had to propriety.

Charlie strolled along next to Martin Tafft, whistling under his breath. He wondered if he'd overdone the cowboy routine with Miss Wilkes, and pondered whether to be ashamed of himself or not. His ma would have whupped him upside the head if she'd heard him cuss in front of a lady. Heck, any one of his brothers would have done the same thing if his ma hadn't been handy.

But, ding-bust-it, she'd been so unfriendly and cold, and she was so danged pretty, and those huge blue eyes of hers had opened so wide, and he'd wanted to kiss her so badly, and she'd irked him so much with her haughty manners, that his funny bone had taken over and he'd let her have it.

She'd probably never speak to him again. Fudge. Charlie kicked a clump of creosote, and the pungent, oily smell of the shrub kissed his nostrils, reminding him of Arizona, soothing his nerves a trace.

Martin cleared his throat. Charlie looked down at him and realized the shorter man was having to hotfoot it to keep up with Charlie's long, country-bred stride. He slowed down and smiled. He liked Martin Tafft, who seemed like a pleasant, down-to-earth sort of fellow, even if he did wear some mighty fancy city duds.

Today Martin sported gray plus fours and a Norfolk jacket with a polka-dotted four-in-hand tie and a tweed cap. Charlie supposed the movie man's sporty attire made Charlie's own denim trousers, plaid shirt, blue bandanna, sweat-stained Stetson hat, and faded sack jacket appear mighty shabby. Although Charlie had never cared much about clothes, today he wished he'd visited a tailor in town before he'd hopped that train to California.

"Um, you might want to slow down on the cussing a little, Charlie," Martin suggested. His voice was totally devoid of censure, and Charlie was impressed. He'd anticipated a lecture. He knew he deserved one. "I think Miss Wilkes has lived a pretty sheltered life." With a chuckle, Martin added, "I think you shocked her."

"That so?" As much as Charlie didn't want to disappoint Martin, who'd given him this chance, still less did he want Miss Wilkes to think she'd cowed him into complying with her personal notion of propriety.

"Yes. I don't suppose you've ever heard of Pasadena, but it's where she's from, and it's a pretty straitlaced place. I understand there's a church on every street corner, but it didn't have a single saloon until recently."

"Honest to God?"

"Honest to God. The Women's Christian Temperance Union's big there. I understand the *White Ribbon* is the biggest-selling newspaper in town."

"Shoot." Charlie was honestly impressed. Not to mention appalled.

Martin chuckled. "So you can imagine what Miss Wilkes thinks of folks who cuss."

"Mmmm."

"To tell the truth, I'm a little worried about how she'll get along with Horace Huxtable. He, er, drinks sometimes."

Charlie nodded. "I expect she won't like that." No wonder

Miss Wilkes acted so high and mighty. It was a shame, too, because Charlie'd seldom seen such a pretty girl. But if she lived in a town that didn't even let its citizens have a snort every now and then—Charlie could scarcely conceive of such a place—he feared there was probably no hope for her ever becoming human.

"So," Martin went on, "I guess you might want to take it easy on the cussing. Don't want to shock our leading lady, now, do we?" He laughed a full-bodied, happy laugh.

Charlie laughed with him. Why not? It was a kind of funny situation.

They entered the chow tent together. "Golly, Martin, I didn't know it took so many folks to shoot one of these here movie things."

Martin smiled with evident satisfaction. "This is the largest film crew ever assembled, Charlie. Why, this is the most ambitious project ever to be attempted in the industry."

"Honest?" Charlie was impressed. And he was part of it. Made a fellow kind of proud.

"Absolutely. Why, Charlie, *The Great Train Robbery* only ran for nine minutes. This movie will run for four whole reels, and will be a full forty-eight minutes long. We're even going to do one of those premiere things, like they do for stage plays."

"Shoot, really? Where?"

"Chicago. Chicago's a great place for moving pictures."

"Holy cow." Although Charlie couldn't conceive of who'd be willing to sit still for forty-eight minutes staring at a screen, he didn't say so. Hell, maybe folks in Chicago didn't have anything better to do with their time. Besides, it was nothing to him if the Peerless Studio folks wanted to throw their money around. They were throwing a good deal of it Charlie's way, and that was the only thing that mattered to him.

"Of course, the main players in the picture will be invited to the premiere. You'll like Chicago, I'm sure."

Only if Peerless paid. Charlie didn't say so, but he wasn't about to waste his money taking a train to Chicago to see a moving picture show. Hell, he could go to the nickelodeon in town if he ever wanted to see himself on film.

"Oh, there's Miss Wilkes." Martin nodded toward the front of the tent.

Turning, Charlie saw her, too. She looked mighty little, standing there at the opening of the tent, peering around with her hands folded politely in front of her as if she were sort of scared. Charlie's big heart got all warm and slushy, and he forgave her for being a prig and a cold fish. "I'll see if she'd like to sit with us."

"Good for you." Martin gave him an approving slap on the back, and Charlie strode over to her.

"Howdy, ma'am." He tipped his hat and smiled down at her.

She gave a jump of alarm, and some of Charlie's friendly feelings slid sideways. Slapping a hand to her starched white bosom, she gasped, "Oh, Mr. Fox, you startled me."

"Yeah? You might want to talk to a doctor about your nerves, ma'am. I hear they got all sorts of nerve specialists and other such truck out here in California."

"My nerves are fine, thank you, Mr. Fox." Her voice had taken on the frigid quality that rasped so disagreeably on Charlie's pride.

"Glad to hear it. Would you care to join Mr. Tafft and me, ma'am? I'll try not to eat with my knife." He probably should have attempted to suppress his sarcasm, but she was annoying the hell out of him with her fancy airs and graces.

"I'm sure your table manners are delightful," she said. It sounded to Charlie as if she'd chipped the words from a block of ice. "Thank you. I should be happy to sit with Mr. Tafft. And you."

Cold-hearted heifer. "We're over there," Charlie muttered. And, since he figured it would scandalize her, he pointed with a jabbing finger.

"Yes," she said—and she was clearly scandalized. "I see." She began moving ahead of Charlie, as if she hoped to lose him in the milling throng.

Fat chance. Not only was Charlie taller than almost every-body else in the tent, but he found himself resolving to stick to her like a flea on a hound dog until she either recognized him as a fellow human being on this green earth—well, brown earth here in this lousy desert—or he nettled her so much that she lost her temper and screamed at him. That would unnerve her completely. He knew he was being childish and couldn't seem to help himself.

She smiled at Martin as if she were relieved to see a civ-ilized human in a throng of wild savages.

Martin stood, smiled a charming smile, and held a chair out for her. "Here you go, Miss Wilkes. Nothing but the best for our stars."

"Thank you," she murmured. Then she sat as if she were a queen and Martin a courtier. She ignored Charlie absolutely, which grated on his self-image like a rusty file.

Feeling unaccountably huffy—what did he care about this female?—Charlie hauled a chair out for himself, making a lot of noise about it, and straddled it, being sure his long legs sprawled out on both sides. Let her deal with a *real* cowboy and see how she liked it.

Three

Amy gazed at Charlie's legs with some perplexity. She should deplore his abysmal deportment, but couldn't seem to get past admiring his musculature.

This was surely a bad sign. It probably signified the beginning of a slide down the perilous slope of moral rectitude into the swamp of sin and degradation. And all because she'd agreed to do something not quite right for money. Filthy lucre. Served her right. She should have stuck to what she knew. The familiar. It was safe. Pasadena was safe. Vernon was safe. This picture business was new and frightening and, therefore, extremely unsafe, and she was a silly fool to have agreed to do this job.

She sighed and folded her hands in her lap, unsure what to do now, but extremely glad that Vernon wasn't there to see the depths to which she'd sunk. Her heart thundered sickeningly, and her craving for the security of her old life rose up in her mind's eye like a shining, golden star.

Thank heavens for Martin Tafft, who seemed to have an uncanny knack for sensing when she was in distress. He smiled kindly and said, "The catering crew will be handing out sandwiches, Miss Wilkes. Peerless tries to give its cast and crew only the best, but sometimes the conditions don't allow for fancy meals. We'll probably be having sandwiches for lunch most days."

"Of course." She smiled at Martin and hoped her expression conveyed even a fraction of her appreciation. If she were made to deal with Charlie Fox and the whole new universe of moviemaking without Martin Tafft to ease her way, she was sure she'd fold up like a fan and run home to Pasadena, defeated and depressed. Wouldn't Vernon be happy then? Of course, she probably would be, too. She decided not to think about it.

"Here y'are," a female voice said at her back, and Amy started slightly when a waxed-paper-wrapped sandwich hit the table with a soft plop in front of her.

"Oh," she whispered. With a little more pep in her voice, she added, "Thank you." She smiled up at the girl who'd delivered the luncheon package and discovered herself being completely ignored. The sandwich girl was all but drooling over Charlie Fox. Amy quickly returned her attention to her sandwich.

"Thanks," Charlie said at her side. "I don't suppose I can have another one?" He grinned up at the girl who was handing out sandwiches. She grinned back and threw another sandwich onto the table in front of him.

Shocked out of contemplating her own sandwich, which looked large enough to feed a battalion or two, Amy turned to stare at Charlie, flabbergasted. "You're going to eat *two* of these things?" Good heavens, Amy was sure she'd never plow her way through even one of the enormous concoctions presently being flung hither and yon.

Charlie squinted down at her, and she wished she'd kept her mouth shut. "You got something against a feller eating a hearty meal, Miss Wilkes?"

"Of course not." Her voice, she noticed, sounded stifled. She felt stifled.

"I reckon," Charlie continued, "that you're not used to folks who toil for a livin', but some of us have to use our muscles and such, and we work up quite an appetite."

Indignation swelled in Amy's breast. Why did this man seem so all-fired eager to make fun of her? She resented it every bit as much as she deplored her own ignorance of the world. "I beg your pardon, Mr. Fox. I didn't mean to upset you."

"Hell, ma'am," Charlie said, "you didn't upset me."

He laughed. Amy noticed that Martin rolled his eyes. He, too, had a couple of sandwiches sitting in front of him.

Martin said, "Let's dig in, folks. I understand the roast beef sandwiches these folks prepare are quite good."

Fearing she would only put her foot in her mouth again if she tried to speak, Amy slowly unwrapped her sandwich. She was pretty sure she could get through a quarter of it if she tried hard. A thick ceramic mug of coffee appeared as if by magic in front of her, and she jumped again. Drat! Although she hated admitting it to herself, she guessed her nerves were somewhat rattled. Shooting a sideways glance at Charlie, she noticed him eyeing her with distaste. She lifted her chin, picked up her coffee mug, and sipped.

An involuntary shudder ran through her from tip to toe, and she set her mug down with a jerk, slopping the horrible-tasting beverage on the table. Good heavens, how did people drink this stuff? More to the point, *why* did they drink it? Amy had never tasted anything so vile in her life.

"You got something against coffee, too, Miss Wilkes?" Charlie's voice had taken on a sugary quality.

Swallowing convulsively, trying to get the bitter taste out of her mouth, Amy couldn't answer at first. When at last she managed to get her tongue uncurled she said, "I'm unused to coffee, Mr. Fox." Then she braced herself, wondering what unkind thing he'd say now.

"I imagine you're more accustomed to drinking orange juice," Martin said with one of his friendly chuckles.

Silently blessing him as a saint, Amy said, "Yes, I am, Mr.

Tafft. I—I've never tasted coffee before." What was more, if she could help it, she'd never taste it again.

"Orange juice?" Charlie stopped chewing and lifted an eyebrow. He had lovely eyes, Amy noticed with some dismay. They were ever so much prettier than Vernon's, which were rather squinty and small.

She nodded. "My uncle has a health resort in Pasadena where orange juice is served daily."

Amy's heart gave an enormous tug of nostalgia, and all at once she felt like crying. This was so foreign to her. She wanted her aunt and uncle here. She wanted Vernon. She wanted an orange. If she had to exist on huge meat sandwiches and coffee for as long as it took to finish this movie, she wasn't sure she could do it. She, who was accustomed to eating delicate meals replete with vegetables, fruit, and milk, and to drinking pure, sweet-tasting, unadulterated orange juice. Oh, dear.

"I'm sure we can get something else for you to drink," said Martin.

Amy silently blessed him again. She'd have thanked him, but feared for the steadiness of her voice. She did manage a smile.

Charlie said, "Hmmm," as if he didn't approve of people who had special, inconvenient, and probably arbitrary requirements in order to eat a meal or do a job. Amy shot him a frown.

"Do you care for milk, Miss Wilkes? I'm afraid we won't be able to get any orange juice." Martin, on the other hand, looked as if he understood completely and didn't consider Amy's unfamiliarity with coffee anything to be deplored.

Amy could have kissed him—were she another sort of woman. "Milk would be wonderful. Thank you so much, Mr. Tafft. You're very kind."

"Nonsense. Not everybody likes coffee."

Really? That made her feel better. She hoped he wasn't just trying to be nice. She compressed an end of her sandwich between her fingers so she could get her mouth around it, and took a bite. Thank the good Lord, it didn't taste bad. It was true that Amy was accustomed to eating light lunches composed primarily of cheese and fruit, but if she could have milk to drink, she might survive.

Charlie had finished his first sandwich and started in on the second before she'd taken three bites of hers. He was also guzzling the coffee as if it tasted like the nectar of the gods. Amy tried not to stare.

But, honestly, his legs still sprawled out in a most unseemly way, he was eating much too fast for gentility, and he'd even propped his elbows on the table. Amy was more shocked than disgusted.

As she'd never been exposed to coffee, she'd never been exposed to the manners which prevailed in a bunkhouse or a chuck wagon. At least she presumed these were those manners. They certainly weren't what she was used to. She was absolutely positive that Vernon would never allow himself to eat like that. Suddenly Vernon didn't seem boring at all, but merely civilized.

A glass of milk was plunked down in front of her, and Amy turned in her chair to smile at the girl who'd plunked it. It was the same girl who'd exchanged grins with Charlie, but she was now eyeing Amy as if she were a strange and unwelcome species of animal life. Amy gulped and maintained her smile. "Thank you very much." The girl sniffed and flounced off, and Amy wondered what she'd done to irritate her.

Life outside Pasadena was a strange and mysterious affair, and Amy feared she was going to have a hard time adjusting. She heard Charlie mutter something and turned to him.

"I beg your pardon?" she asked politely.

"Nothin'."

"Oh. I thought you said something."

"Naw. Not really. Just thinking about the airs some folks give themselves is all."

Martin Tafft muttered, "Charlie!"

Amy's mouth pursed. "I don't believe I know what you mean, Mr. Fox." She knew exactly what he meant, the cretinous blockhead.

He shrugged. "Probably not."

But, thanks to the milk and Martin Tafft, Amy was regaining some of her fighting spirit. Charlie Fox wasn't being fair to her, and his attitude irked her. "Merely because a person is accustomed to polite manners and milk, I don't believe that person should be accused of putting on airs."

"Yeah?" Charlie grinned at her and stuffed the last of his sandwich into his mouth. Then he licked his fingers.

Amy felt her lips prune up and made an effort to smooth them out again. She didn't approve of ladies wearing makeup and powder. In an effort to negate the need for such paint, she'd vowed to avoid wrinkles if she could. "Yes," she said firmly.

"Then maybe you'll just have to teach me some manners. Hell, I wouldn't want to upset such a dignified little lady."

She thought she heard Martin groan, but wasn't sure. "I'd be delighted to try to teach you some manners." She placed some emphasis on the word *try*. "The efficacy of such an educational undertaking will depend primarily upon the ability of the student to learn." There, she thought savagely as she opened her mouth as wide as it would go and tried to fit a corner of her sandwich in it, let him figure *that* one out if he can.

To her astonishment, Charlie Fox threw back his head and laughed. She scowled at him, gave up on eating her sandwich as it was, and opened it up. If you can't beat them, she thought ferociously, join them. It was horribly impolite and probably unsanitary as well, but it seemed that nobody else cared about manners. Why should she?

Oh, dear, she was truly being corrupted. Thank heavens Vernon couldn't see her now. Even as she deplored her incipient fall, Amy picked up a piece of roast beef from a piece of bread with her fingers and popped it into her mouth. Then she glared defiantly at Charlie Fox as she chewed. She might be going straight to hell, but she wasn't going to starve to death in order to get there, Vernon or no Vernon.

"Here, Miss Wilkes," Charlie said after he'd stopped laughing and wiped his eyes. "Maybe you can use this." He unsnapped a leather scabbard, which Amy hadn't noticed was buckled to his belt, and withdrew a knife that was larger than any Amy had ever seen outside of a kitchen. She blinked at it. "Maybe it'll help you carve through some of that meat and bread."

He withdrew a clean handkerchief from his pocket, dipped it in his mug of coffee, wiped the blade of the knife with it, and handed the knife to Amy, haft first. Amy eyed it warily for a minute, decided he was right, even though he probably meant the gesture as one of contempt, and took the knife. She handled it gingerly. "Thank you very much."

"You're welcome."

Sweet pickles, his eyes were sparkling like some kind of gemstones. Amy wished they wouldn't do that, as they affected the speed of her heartbeat alarmingly. She took out her own clean hankie and wiped the coffee from the blade of the knife. Then, concentrating on her sandwich, she carved a bit of roast beef and bread with Charlie's knife and forked it into her mouth. The knife was very sharp. After she'd swallowed— her code of conduct might have slipped some, but she hadn't sunk far enough to talk with her mouth full—she turned to Charlie again.

"Thank you, Mr. Fox. Your knife works very well. It's quite sharp. You must take great pains to keep the edge well honed."

Charlie nodded. He'd propped his chin on his folded hands, which were supported by his elbows, and was watching every move she made. Amy heaved a small internal sigh and wondered if most of the world was like him, or if most people behaved as she and her Pasadena friends and family did. If she herself was unique, and not Charlie Fox, she expected she'd have a lot of adjusting to do as she moved through life. Or perhaps she could merely return to Pasadena and not have to face the world again.

"Yes, ma'am. Got to keep 'em sharp or they don't do no good."

"I see."

"But it ain't hard to do. A honin' strop, a piece of rock, and bear grease does the job right fine."

"Bear grease?" Amy eyed her sandwich. But she hadn't tasted anything amiss, so she guessed the napkin and coffee had eliminated any telltale traces. Probably it had been the coffee. Amy couldn't imagine even bear grease surviving coffee.

"Yes, ma'am. Them bears, they's good for lots of things besides eatin'."

She squinted up at him sideways, curious as to why he sounded so much more ungrammatical now than when she'd first met him. Eyeing the remains of her sandwich, she wondered if she should take another bite or two. She was feeling full, but didn't know when her next meal would be served—or what it would be. She hadn't anticipated eating foreign food when she'd agreed to play a part in this picture.

"Losin' yer appetite?"

When she glanced at Charlie again, his grin was in place, his eyes were twinkling, and Amy decided that if one were forced to face trials in life in order to temper one's character, which was what she'd always been told was the way of the world, Charlie Fox was setting up to be a huge trial. "Yes." She smiled. It had been a somewhat pleasant little joke. "I do believe I am."

"You got a whole lot of sandwich left," Charlie pointed out.

Immediately, Amy thought of the poor starving orphan children in China and India, as she'd been taught to do as a child. She wished she had a starving orphan right here right now; she'd gladly relinquish the rest of her sandwich. On the other hand . . .

She smiled sweetly at Charlie. "Since you're such a hard-working fellow and need lots of fuel to keep your energy up, perhaps you can help me finish it, Mr. Fox."

He looked startled for a moment, then grinned back. "Why, that's a very nice offer, Miss Wilkes. Don't mind if I do."

So he did. Amy watched him polish off the last three-quarters of her sandwich with amazement. He really did have a prodigious appetite, didn't he?

Thinking about Charlie's appetite started a whole new train of speculation about him in her head. She started out by wondering if he'd enjoy her cooking. Amy had always believed herself to be quite a hand in the kitchen. Then she considered his accent and changeable grammatical leanings. He was an awfully handsome man; he'd appear to advantage in a suit and tie of a Sunday morning, say, on his way to church. With his neatly dressed children and his pretty wife.

Amy couldn't help thinking that Charlie Fox could be quite a respectable member of society if someone were to take him in hand—clean him up, as her uncle might say. If someone were to, oh, for instance, teach him grammar and table manners and not to swear in public, Amy had a feeling he'd fool anyone into thinking he was a perfectly refined gentleman.

She was distilling her image of Charlie as a civilized human being when a commotion broke out at the front flap of the tent. She heard someone shouting, then heard a woman scream, and turned to see what was happening.

Charlie turned, too. Martin, who, Amy realized, had been sitting as still as a stone and watching Charlie and her banter back and forth, stood, shaded his eyes, and stared in the direction of the ruckus. Amy heard him mutter under his breath, but couldn't make out what he said, which was probably just as well. Although Martin Tafft would never, she felt sure, sink so low as to curse in a room full of people, she could clearly see that he was upset.

With growing uneasiness, she asked, "What is it, Mr. Tafft?"

Charlie, too, seemed concerned, and glanced at Martin sharply. "Need any help, Martin?"

"I'm not sure," Martin said. He extricated himself from his chair, skirted their table, and headed like a bee to its hive toward the front of the tent.

Amy watched, apprehensive. "I hope nothing's the matter."

"Yeah," said Charlie. "Me, too." He rose and, because of his height, didn't have as much trouble as Martin had in discerning the cause of the commotion. He frowned. "Hellfire."

Amy, alarmed in earnest now, jumped from her chair. "Oh, Mr. Fox, what is it?"

"Some drunk, it looks like from here."

"Oh." Some drunk? Amy's nose wrinkled.

"Yeah. Looks to be carrying on something fearful."

"How disgusting."

She shouldn't have said that; she could tell as soon as she noticed the expression on Charlie's face. "Well, it is," she averred with some spirit. "I think it's deplorable for men to drink themselves senseless and then cause problems for others."

Shrugging, Charlie said, "I reckon you're right."

He didn't sound as if he believed it. Amy felt considerably deflated and said darkly, "One of the people in this picture is a man who drinks too much. He spent a month at my uncle's health spa, but I don't believe he profited from the experience." She sniffed her disapproval.

"That so?" Still watching the melee, his eyes thinned for better vision, Charlie said, "Would that be Mr. Horace Huxtable, by any chance? The man who spent time at your uncle's place, I mean."

"Yes. Yes, it was Mr. Huxtable." A sinking sensation crept into Amy's breast; a feeling of premonition, of dire anticipation. If that man making all the fuss was Horace Huxtable—

"That's him, all right," Charlie said cheerfully, confirming Amy's worst fears. "Drunk as a skunk and roarin' something comical."

Amy, speechless, pressed a hand to her bosom. She'd die. She'd absolutely *die* if she had to put up with Horace Huxtable after he'd been drinking. The man was insufferable sober, for heaven's sake.

"Shooty tooty, he's raisin' hell for sure. I think Martin needs a hand." Charlie took off at a lope.

Amy watched him go with a plummeting heart.

There was nothing the least bit comical about this situation as far as Martin Tafft was concerned.

"For God's sake, Huxtable, they only let you loose yesterday." He tried to take Huxtable's arm, but the actor flung Martin's hand away.

"Unhand me, vassal," Huxtable slurred as if he were king of the world and Martin a lowly servant.

"For the love of Mike," Martin muttered. "Let me get you put away someplace. You've got to get sobered up before tomorrow. We rehearse in the morning."

"I," Huxtable said, swinging his arms about and narrowly avoiding collisions with several spectators, "am a profesh—profesh—a sheasoned performer."

"You're seasoned, all right. Pickled is more like it."

Several people snickered, and Huxtable attempted to draw himself up majestically. He succeeded in overbalancing himself and staggering backwards, bumping into a table and a man who'd been watching.

About at his wits' end, Martin was ecstatic when Charlie showed up.

"Need some help, Martin?" the big cowboy asked as if the problem were nothing to him.

"I sure do. Thanks, Charlie. We've got to get him out of here and to his tent. We'll have to dry him out somehow."

"Tie him up," Charlie suggested. "That's what we had to do with Pete Thatcher at the ranch. He'd be okay tied up. Loose, he was hell on fire."

Although so drastic a measure hadn't occurred to Martin, the circumstances were such that he grabbed at it instantly. "Good idea."

Charlie seemed to survey the wobbly actor with a judicious eye for a moment. Then he said, "Reckon I'll catch him up top, Martin. I've had more practice rassling wild animals than you have, I 'spect."

In spite of the catastrophic entrance of Horace Huxtable onto the scene, stinking drunk in the face of dire warnings from Phineas Lovejoy and Martin himself, Charlie's easygoing, practical assessment of the task ahead of them tickled Martin. He approved wholeheartedly. "Thanks, Charlie."

Charlie seemed to catch sight of Amy Wilkes a moment after Martin himself did. He hitched himself up for a second, then rubbed his hands together and said, "Aw, hell, Martin. 'Tain't nothin'."

Good God, the man was deliberately making himself sound

like an oaf in front of Miss Wilkes! Martin had no time to contemplate this weird phenomenon before Charlie, who really did look as if he'd performed this operation more than once in his life, slipped behind Huxtable and snaked his arms around him, pinning the actor's arms to his sides and immobilizing him. Huxtable spluttered for a second, then bellowed obscenely. Spectators flinched from the noise and began to laugh. Amy blushed and pressed a hand to her cheek.

"Fetch up his legs, Martin. Maybe somebody will have to help, since he's got two of 'em—although they ain't workin' too good at the moment."

This was true. However, Huxtable was still able to kick, and Martin was glad to see a man—he thought it was the chief cameraman, but couldn't take the time to make sure—step out from the crowd. "I'll get the left leg, Tafft. You take the right."

"Thanks." Martin waited until Huxtable had lifted his right knee and grabbed him by the calf and stuck the leg under his arm tightly, subduing Huxtable's struggles. The cameraman grabbed the actor's other leg.

"There we go." Charlie nodded and grinned at his helpers. "Point the way, Martin, and we can carry him there. I got me a rope in my bag, if somebody'll fetch it out of my tent."

Glancing around wildly, Martin's attention landed on Amy, the one person on hand in whose common sense he trusted implicitly. "Miss Wilkes?" he asked, lending a tone of pleading to his voice.

She swallowed. "I—why, of course, Mr. Tafft."

"Thanks a lot, Miss Wilkes. Charlie's tent is the first one on the left next to the one where the cameras are stored."

"Very well." She gave what looked like a valiant smile, and Martin appreciated her a lot. "I'll be there as soon as possible." She started briskly off, then stopped in her tracks. "Er, where shall I bring it?"

"You won't have no trouble findin' us," Charlie assured her with a wink. "You'll hear this here hoss bellerin' like a stuck hog."

Martin wasn't surprised when Amy's eyebrows arched nearly into her prettily piled hairdo. He couldn't fault her for her reaction. Charlie in cowboy mode was an astonishing thing to behold. And to be-heard.

Intensely glad that she'd taken the time to loosen her corset, Amy ran to Charlie Fox's tent. She felt a pang of indecision—after all, it was dreadfully improper to go through a gentleman's bag—which she overcame quickly. She'd been sent on an important errand, and she'd been given permission by the bag's owner to rifle through it.

She had to force herself not to dawdle, because she'd never had the opportunity to inspect a gentleman's things before. He wore very large shirts, she noticed. And his underthings were clean and mended, if not of the highest quality. Amy supposed a cowboy had considerations other than luxury when purchasing such items.

"Good heavens, Amy Wilkes, you're behaving badly." She quit contemplating Charlie's underwear and searched for the rope, making sure she didn't wrinkle anything. Ah, there it was. She snatched it up, replaced the clothes in the carpetbag and fastened it, and hastened back to Huxtable's tent.

Charlie had been right. If Amy had any doubts about which tent was the right one, Huxtable's bellows would have led her on the proper path. The man was a disgrace to humankind. And Amy was supposed to fall in love with him on-screen. She wasn't sure she had any acting talent, but if she did, she was pretty certain it didn't extend that far.

Thrusting her apprehension about *One and Only* aside, she entered the tent. The sight that greeted her wasn't an attractive one. Huxtable was on his back on his bed, shouting vile curses as he bucked and kicked, and Charlie, the cameraman, and Martin tried to hold him down. Amy gazed upon the spectacle, frowning, trying to figure out what to do now. Charlie couldn't very well leave off holding the beast down, because Martin was surely not strong enough to hold him by himself, and the cameraman looked exhausted already.

"Hurry up with the rope!" Charlie hollered at her.

She transferred her frown to him. "In a minute. I'm thinking."

"Kee-rist," Charlie muttered, offending Amy.

Huxtable let go of a string of words, half of which Amy had never heard before. She had no trouble at all in discerning their meanings, however.

She shook her head once, decisively, said, "This is ridiculous," and headed straight for Huxtable's dressing table. There she picked up the flowered water pitcher, which some underling had filled earlier in the day, and carried it to the bed.

"For God's sake, give me the rope!" Charlie cried. He sounded as if he were tiring some himself.

"Oh, hold your horses." Amy was quite pleased with the tone of voice she achieved, which was both peeved and steadfast. She paused only long enough to observe the deplorable spectacle in order to judge trajectories. Then she said, "Please close your eyes, Mr. Fox. Prepare yourself, Mr. Tafft," and she emptied the entire pitcher of water on Huxtable's face.

"Aaaarrrrrgh!" bubbled out from Huxtable's throat. After the one terrified yell, he was too busy coughing and choking to make any more noise. Amy stepped back, pleased with her work.

Charlie, who had been splattered, as Amy had expected, in the face and front of his shirt, grinned broadly at her. "Quick thinking, Miss Wilkes," he said. "May I have the rope now?"

My, wasn't he polite and grammatical all of a sudden? Amy

was beginning to think Mr. Charlie Fox was something of a fraud. Which would probably make him a superb actor. She said, "Certainly," and handed over the rope.

Quick as a wink, Charlie had Horace Huxtable wrapped and tied. "Hog-tied," Charlie said with a pleased expression on his face.

Amy was pleased, too.

Martin laughed. "I swear, you two make quite a team. I must say, Miss Wilkes, I never expected you to do anything so enterprising."

"Neither did I," said Charlie.

Amy smiled at Martin, lifted her chin, and turned to Charlie. "I'm sure you didn't. But it worked, didn't it?"

"It sure did." For the first time since she'd met him several hours earlier, Charlie looked as if he approved of her. Amy tried not to bask.

"God damn you!" Huxtable bellowed from the bed. "What did you do that for?" He was glaring at Amy. He was also dripping all over the floor of his tent.

Amy picked up her skirt so its hem wouldn't get wet. She walked over and stared down at Huxtable, not bothering to hide her contempt. "I did that because you were behaving in a vile and abominable way. A body would think these men were dealing with a baby, the way you carried on. You ought to be ashamed of yourself!" And, although Amy had no experience with good exit lines, she turned on her heel and headed for the flap of Huxtable's tent.

"So there," Charlie laughed.

After sputtering in impotent fury for a moment, Huxtable scowled up at him. "Shut up, you damned bastard."

"Got a rag?" Charlie asked Martin.

"Um, I don't know. Why?" Martin sounded puzzled.

"We'd probably better gag this stinker so he can't call anybody else any dirty names."

Amy hoped the men in the tent wouldn't hear the giggle that burst out of her mouth. My goodness, in spite of their differences, she *did* like Charlie Fox.

The rest of Amy's day was spent in accustoming herself to the rigors of on-site motion picture making. Martin gave her and Charlie a tour of the tent settlement. Amy was vastly interested in the cameras. She'd never seen anything like them, and wondered if the cameraman's arm didn't get tired from all the cranking it had to do. Believing the question too naive to voice aloud, she didn't.

She went to bed that night, after a tolerable supper of soup and bread and butter and cheese, in her own little tent, and hoped she'd be able to acquit herself well in this new and dangerous endeavor.

She also vowed she'd never be lured into making another moving picture again as long as she lived. She even said as much to Vernon in the letter she wrote to him that night. She missed him terribly. She told him that, too.

Four

Horace Huxtable arrived at rehearsal the next morning looking sick and with a greenish cast to his skin. His eyes were streaked with red veins, and their lids were puffy. He scowled horribly at Charlie Fox and eyed Amy with evident loathing. Which was fine with her. She loathed him, too.

Martin, observing his cast with misgiving, put on a cheerful mien in spite of it all. "All right, everyone!" he called out in a chipper voice. "Let's assemble for the first scene."

Huxtable groaned and said bitterly, "Can you keep your voice down, Tafft? None of us are deaf."

"None of us are hungover, either, except you," Amy muttered under her breath, hoping nobody would hear.

Huxtable did. He grimaced at her—Amy thought it was supposed to be a smile—and said, "Oh, but perhaps we can help you overcome that flaw, my dear."

Detestable animal, Amy thought, although she kept that one to herself. Charlie, she noticed, was grinning at her as if he thought she'd said something witty. She thought she had, too, actually.

Martin said in a voice not quite so loud or cheerful, "All right. Take your places, everyone. Miss Wilkes, you'll note in this first scene that you've been told by Charlie here that his boss, Mr. McAllister, is going to buy up your father's loan on the ranch you've been trying to keep since his death. Charlie's convinced you that McAllister is an evil fellow, although he's really a noble hero."

"That's me, all right," said Huxtable from the sidelines. Amy's nose wrinkled spontaneously.

Speaking a little louder, Martin went on. "You're afraid that if McAllister gets his hands on the notes, he'll either drive you from your home or exact an improper payment from you."

Huxtable muttered, "Improper, my ass."

Amy pressed a sweaty palm to her cheek and prayed that a lightning bolt from heaven would rid the world of Horace Huxtable. At least until she'd finished this job. He could come back after that, as long as he didn't plague her any longer. She was *so* nervous about this moving picture nonsense.

Martin said, "Huxtable, please. We don't need that sort of thing." He smiled kindly upon Amy. "Ready? Your marks are chalked on the ground, so you'll know where to stand."

Thank God for that, at any rate. At least she'd know where to stand, if she didn't know another single thing about this idiotic picture.

Amy nodded at Martin, feeling more shy than she could ever recall. She'd never even acted in a school play, for heaven's sake, and now she was supposed to emote in front of a bunch of strangers and, eventually, a bunch of strangers with cameras. Not to mention Horace Huxtable, who had taken to leering at her, in what she was sure was a studied campaign to discompose her.

Little did he know that his efforts were unnecessary, as she was so unnerved already that it was all she could do to keep herself from trembling like a Pasadena poppy field in a breeze. She tried with every fiber of her being not to let her lack of experience show.

With that in mind, and trying to keep Vernon's face in her mind's eye as a stabilizing influence, she stepped forward, holding her script steady. Martin had been right about the script. It was merely a story outline, and there was no dialogue printed therein. She was glad to know what the story was, however. Charlie walked up to her and turned to Martin.

"This all right, Martin? Should I be closer?" He demonstrated, almost bumping into Amy, who fought the urge to take a step back. She was supposed to be a sophisticate, for the love of glory. She wasn't supposed to be shy around her second leading man. She tried to remember if she had ever been this close to Vernon, physically, and decided she'd not been.

"Back up a little bit," Martin suggested. "There. That's good. All right. Miss Wilkes? Remember, you're worried about what you perceive as an impending disaster. After all, this ranch has been your only home your whole life."

"Right," Amy said, and licked her lips. Determined not to fail, and drawing upon what she remembered of the few moving pictures she'd seen, she adopted what she hoped was a desperately worried expression. She remembered to wring her hands, as she'd seen other distressed-looking females do in pictures, and was pleased with herself.

Charlie said, "I'm sorry to have to tell you this, Miss Wilkes, but my boss, the evil Mr. McAllister, is going to buy up the loan on your daddy's ranch. I'm afraid you're going to be tossed out into the cold."

Since the temperature had been hovering in the upper nineties ever since Amy had arrived in El Monte, this seemed singularly inapt phrasing. She did not point it out to Charlie, being way too shaky to say anything at all. Instead, she pressed the back of her left hand to her forehead, tilted her head back, closed her eyes, as she'd seen an actress do in a nickelodeon once, and tried to convey the impression of a young woman who was both horrified and delicate.

"Say something, Miss Wilkes. You have to move your mouth."

Pickles. Amy didn't want to say anything, partly because her mouth was dry and her tongue was stuck to the roof of it, but mostly because she was undergoing a moment of exquisite embarrassment and had no idea what to say. Struggling to maintain her composure, she managed to blurt out, "Oh, dear."

From the sidelines, Huxtable snorted. " 'Oh, dear,' " he repeated in a mocking tone. "Good God, Tafft. You have to give the girl something to say. She's obviously been stricken dumb by the thrill of starring in a picture with me."

Amy dropped her hand from her forehead and straightened. "I have not! That's the most ridiculous thing I've ever heard!"

"Better," Martin said with pleasure. "Much better! Only, you should probably look a little scared, too. It's good to be angry, but you need to show that you're worried, as well." He tilted his head and frowned, his benign expression not wavering. "Er, perhaps you should forgo the dramatic gesture with your hand to your forehead."

Amy gazed at him, bewildered.

"And, Charlie, try to look sly. You're a bit of a villain, you know, trying to get the girl away from Huxtable by devious tricks."

"I'm sure he wouldn't need any devious tricks to do *that*," Amy grumbled under her breath. She'd been thinking mainly of Huxtable, but blushed when Charlie gave her a wicked grin.

"No?" he said softly. "Is that so, Miss Wilkes? I had no idea."

She huffed, beginning to wonder if all men were beasts and not just Horace Huxtable. "It's because of him," she said sharply. "Not you."

He sighed dramatically. "I was afraid of that."

"Okay," Martin called. "Let's try again." He'd forgotten

Huxtable's condition and spoken too loudly. He realized his error when Huxtable spat out an expletive. Amy gave him a good scowl to let him know she didn't approve of profanity. He sneered at her.

"Miss Wilkes," Charlie said, starting over, this time with a sly twinkle in his eyes, "I'm trying to win you away from Horace Huxtable by devious stratagems. Think I have a chance?"

Fighting a sudden urge to giggle, Amy took a step back and tried her best to appear totally aghast. She was assisted in the endeavor by recollections of how she'd had to deal with Huxtable at her uncle's health spa. The further recollection that she'd soon have to be playing scenes with the actor himself erased any desire to giggle. "I sincerely doubt that either one of you stands a chance," she said with a snap in her voice. She opened her eyes wide and made a stab at looking scared.

"Good!" Martin called. "Why don't you squeeze your hands together, too, like you did before? Give the scene a touch of sentiment. We want the public to be worried for you."

Sentiment? Worry? Good heavens, it was a moving picture, not an episode from life. Nevertheless, Amy did as he'd suggested, clasping her hands to her bosom and attempting with all her might to appear pathetic.

"Better," she heard Huxtable mumble. "Not much better, but better."

She stopped emoting instantly and turned on him. *"Will* you be quiet? You're distracting me, and this is hard enough to begin with." When she heard herself, she was fairly stunned. Good glory, she was turning into a shrew. Her mother, who had taught her ladylike behavior before she could walk, would have been horrified. Vernon would be horrified. Amy was a little horrified herself.

Huxtable snorted and growled, "Temperamental bitch, ain't she?"

Charlie scratched his chin and looked as if he were trying not to laugh.

Martin cried, "That's it! That's perfect! Use that exact expression, Miss Wilkes!"

"Gracious," murmured Amy, and decided on the spot that acting in the moving pictures was a lot more complicated than one might expect if one only saw the end result. Then her brain registered what Huxtable had called her, and she whipped around, slamming her fists on her hips. "How *dare* you! You drunken sot! Don't you dare call me that word again!"

Charlie lost the battle he'd been waging with his funny bone and burst out laughing. Martin blinked, surprised. Amy stamped her foot and didn't know if she was more angry with Horace Huxtable, with herself for allowing him to get under her skin, or with Charlie Fox for laughing at her.

With bitterness in her heart, Amy returned her whole attention to the rehearsal. She tried hard to perform as Mr. Tafft desired her to and to ignore Huxtable's many snide asides. She told herself she didn't care what anyone else thought of her acting. She had to act in truth when the time came for her to perform with Horace Huxtable.

He lumbered onto the set, still looking green and bloodshot, and smirking up a storm. Amy frowned at him. Charlie, she noticed, was watching curiously from the sidelines, a grin on his face. She'd like to wipe that grin away but didn't know how to accomplish it.

"All right," said Huxtable. "Let's get this over with."

Martin's voice had evidently become strained, because he'd picked up a megaphone to help himself project. He looked slightly nervous about this latest pairing, although he sounded buoyant when he called out, "Take your places, Horace and Miss Wilkes. Miss Wilkes, I think you should be at the fence, staring off into the distance, worrying about how you're going to hold on to your father's legacy."

"Certainly." Moving to the fence, Amy thought that, had her own father been so careless as to stake the family homestead as equity with so obviously undesirable a person as Horace Huxtable, he would have deserved to lose it. With her handkerchief she wiped dust off the top rail and folded her arms on it. Huxtable huffed in the background, but she didn't turn around to see what he was huffing about.

"Prude," he said. "Afraid of a little dirt."

She heard that one, but opted not to respond. If it was prudish to care about keeping her shirtwaist clean, then she was a prude.

"All right," Martin said hurriedly. "Let's get on with it. Miss Wilkes, you don't know Huxtable has entered the yard. You're over there mooning into space, and when he speaks, you're startled and whirl around. Got it?"

"Got it." She was pleased she sounded so sporty.

"Action!" called Martin.

Amy stared off into the unlovely distance, missing the orange groves and poppy fields of her Pasadena home. She tried to feel bad about losing a ranch in the desert outside of El Monte, but couldn't make herself do it because the scenery was so ugly. She figured the orange trees and poppies would do quite nicely as substitutes, so she mourned losing them instead.

Huxtable wasn't exactly light on his feet. He stomped onto the marked-off set border, and Amy turned, trying to look startled.

"No, no, Miss Wilkes." Martin set his megaphone down and walked over to her. "You turned too soon. You don't turn until he speaks. Until then, you don't hear him."

"But I did hear him. He walks like an elephant."

Huxtable cast a long-suffering glance into the heavens. Amy resented it like thunder.

"But, you see," Martin told her gently, "nobody but you can hear him. The audience watching the picture in the theater won't. The picture's silent."

Fiddle. That's right. "I beg your pardon. May we try it again?"

"Of course."

She felt better about her error when Martin smiled and patted her shoulder. Charlie was smiling, too, with what looked like sympathy. She tried not to begrudge his expression as she'd begrudged Huxtable's, since she didn't think Charlie's smile should be cast into the same mold as Huxtable's long-suffering, insulting glance. She smiled back at Martin. "Very well. I'll get set again."

Huxtable sighed long and loud, and Martin whispered, "Pay no attention to him, Miss Wilkes. He doesn't feel well today."

"Small wonder," she said darkly, and resumed her pose at the fence.

Again she heard Huxtable shuffle onto the set. The big boor. But she didn't turn, awaiting his words. They weren't long in coming.

"Well, bless my soul, if it ain't Miss Prissy Wilkes. Do you suppose I can wrangle a kiss from her? Most women can't resist me once I turn on the old charm."

She turned at that, horrified. "You beastly man! How dare you say things like that to me?"

"No, no, no," said Martin, sounding faintly exasperated this time. "Miss Wilkes, you're not supposed to be angry, only surprised."

She turned to Martin, furious. "Did you hear what he said to me?"

"Yes." Martin frowned at Huxtable, who was snickering like a naughty schoolboy. "But you have to ignore his words,

Miss Wilkes. I know you're not used to this." His smile appeared a wee bit tight. "And you're doing remarkably well. You only need to keep in mind that this is a silent picture, and that the audience probably isn't adept at lipreading. Act your part, and forget Huxtable."

"I wish I could!"

He rounded on Huxtable. "Will you at least try to behave yourself, Horace? You're not helping any, you know."

Huxtable chuffed irritably. "I feel like shit, and she's doing a very bad job."

Amy gasped.

"You're the one who told me to hire her," Martin said.

She gasped again, dismayed. Was that the truth?

Huxtable shrugged. "She's pretty. I figured I could probably woo her into my bed before the end of the picture—"

Amy shrieked, *"What did he say?"*

"—but I don't think I even want her anymore."

Whirling, Amy shouted again, *"What* did he say?"

Huxtable, ignoring her, shouts and all, went on, "She's pretty enough, and she has a luscious figure. But she's also got a ghastly personality, and she's a terrible prig."

Before Amy knew what was happening, Charlie had come over to the little group. She was shaking with rage and humiliation, felt like crying, refused to give in to the urge, but didn't know what to say or do instead. At least Martin appeared chagrined, which was something. Huxtable, needless to say, sneered at her.

Charlie had been chewing on a straw, but when Huxtable's vile comment smote his ears, he chucked the straw aside. He didn't approve of men talking about women that way, even when the women weren't around to hear it. Miss Wilkes was standing right there, hearing every word. And Miss Amy Wilkes, while assuredly priggish and a shade too sharp, was sure as the devil no match for Horace Huxtable when it came to bandying words. Charlie disapproved mightily of Huxtable's taking advantage of her lack of experience.

"I don't think you want to be talkin' like that in front of a lady, Mr. Huxtable." He kept his voice low and soft, as if he were merely offering a suggestion.

Huxtable eyed him up and down as if he were an unwelcome species of desert reptile. "What do you have to say about it, pray tell?"

"Oh, I ain't much of a one for words." Charlie smiled, giving the oaf a chance.

"You ain't much of a one for grammar, neither," sneered Huxtable.

Charlie only smiled some more.

Huxtable flipped a hand at him. "Off with you, bumpkin. I won't be dictated to by the likes of you."

Amy gasped.

Charlie's expression didn't alter a whit.

"Horace," Martin muttered miserably. "Can it, will you?"

"Pshaw," murmured Huxtable, preening. "The ignorance of folks from the sticks is insupportable." Turning to Amy, he leered and waggled his eyebrows. "Ready for another stab at it, my little dove?"

As she sucked in a huge breath of desert air, Charlie thought she didn't look as if she'd ever be ready for this. Before she could either say so or lie, Charlie spoke again.

"I think you ought to mind your manners, Mr. Huxtable." He kept his tone friendly. "And cut out the suggestive comments to Miss Wilkes. She don't like them."

Huxtable sighed deeply. "Go to hell, Mr. Fox. You're an intolerable bore."

"Probably," Charlie agreed amiably. "But I still don't aim to listen to you talk dirty to Miss Wilkes."

"Then plug your ears. The wench is a handful, but if I

have my way, I'll know her inside and out before this picture is—"

He didn't get to finish the sentence, because Charlie, with remarkably little effort, socked him in the jaw. Horace toppled like a felled oak.

"Oh, my God," Martin said, goggling at the scene, slapping a hand to his head, and beginning to tug on a lock of hair.

"Oh, my goodness!" cried Amy.

Huxtable was out like a light. Charlie reached down and hauled him up by the front of his fashionable sack suit coat. The actor's head lolled about like a pumpkin on a vine. Presenting him to Martin, Charlie said, "Sorry about that, Martin, but I can't tolerate men abusing women in my hearing."

Patently unhappy about this latest turn of events, Martin said, "I know he's difficult to take, Charlie, but did you have to punch him?"

Charlie shrugged. "Reckon I did. He wouldn't've shut up otherwise."

Amy, at a loss for words, only stared at them.

"I suppose that's so." Martin turned and yelled into the crowd of movie people who'd begun gathering when they'd smelled a fight brewing. "Somebody come over here and get Huxtable to his tent. Give him some . . . give him some water or something. Keep him away from the booze, for the love of God." A sour glance at his star prompted him to add, "And better get some cold rags on his jaw. It's going to swell or I'm a monkey's uncle."

"Oh, dear," murmured Amy.

"Didn't mean to cause you grief, Miss Wilkes," Charlie told her, fearing she was one of those city girls who couldn't tolerate violence even if it was perpetrated for their sake.

Her eyes were as big as saucers and as blue as the sky when she looked up at him. "Oh, no, Mr. Fox! Please don't think anything of it. I'm glad you hit him." She sounded quite fierce, and Charlie wondered if she'd have hit Huxtable herself after a few more of his nasty comments. Maybe she had more spunk than he'd given her credit for.

Martin muttered, "This is going to slow things down. We'll have to wait to do any camera work until that jaw goes down." He rubbed his chin and thought hard. "Maybe we can shoot him from the right side."

"You can shoot him in the head, for all I care," Amy said, and Martin looked alarmed.

Yes, she definitely had more spunk than Charlie had originally believed.

"I'm very sorry, Miss Wilkes. I know Huxtable can be a terrible tease."

"He's more than a tease," she said with energy. "He's a vulgar, licentious reprobate."

Martin sighed deeply. "I'm afraid you may be right. I don't know why Lovejoy wanted him for this picture."

"If he talks to Miss Wilkes like that again, I'll do the same thing," Charlie said, keeping his tone mild. "I'm sorry, Martin, but there it is." He wanted Martin to know what was what. Maybe Martin could talk some sense into Huxtable, although it seemed unlikely. Huxtable's ego was huge, and his head seemed hard and impenetrable.

Charlie was both pleased and surprised when Amy laid a hand on his arm. "Oh, Mr. Fox, please don't. It's partly my fault for reacting to his taunts. I'm sure that's what he wants. I should have ignored him. He's such a . . . pig."

"He is that." Charlie liked the feel of her hand on his arm. Unfortunately, she didn't leave it there.

"You're very understanding, Miss Wilkes," Martin told her with a smile that looked as if it were nine-tenths relief. "I'm sure you're right."

"I don't know about this." Charlie didn't care for the turn

the conversation was taking. "It ain't right for a fellow to talk to a lady the way Mr. Huxtable talked to Miss Wilkes."

"I know it's not," said Martin.

Amy nodded. "Yes, but you see, I don't think there's any changing Mr. Huxtable. He was a beast at my uncle's health spa, and he's a beast here. I think he's simply a beast, and there's no doing anything with him."

"I did something with him," Charlie pointed out, beginning to feel slightly peeved.

"Yes, you did." Amy beamed up at him, making him light-headed for a second. "And I truly do appreciate it. But you really can't continue to hit him every time he says something awful, because the only time he isn't saying awful things is when he's asleep. If you hit him all the time, we'll never get this picture made."

"Exactly!" Martin looked happy with her sensible attitude.

"I don't know. I don't like it." Charlie kicked at the dirt, beginning to get the uncomfortable idea that he'd done something silly. Only a moment before, he'd been feeling kind of heroic. Ding-bust-it, females and movies were a purely baffling combination. He'd enjoyed watching both individually in the past, but dealing with them in person and together was another matter entirely.

"Believe me," said Amy, "I don't like it when he's rude and awful to me. It's humiliating to be baited by such a man. And he deserves to be hit for being such a swine. But the sooner we get this picture over and done with, the sooner we can all go home again."

"Yes, indeed," said Martin, again with clear appreciation of Amy's good sense. "For the time being, why don't we take a break from rehearsal. I'm sure everyone's nerves need to settle a bit. I'll go see how the costumes are coming. They might be ready for your first fitting, Miss Wilkes."

"Thank you, Mr. Tafft." She gazed at Charlie. "And thank

you, Mr. Fox. It's nice to know that not all men are like that . . . that . . . awful Mr. Huxtable."

"Sure thing, ma'am."

Charlie peered down at her, noticing all over again how pretty she was, how her hair glinted with red and gold highlights in the sunlight, how big her blue eyes were, how fresh her complexion, how elegant her figure. She was quite a package. Some of the boys on the ranch might even call her a dish. Charlie would never do anything so disrespectful, but he was beginning to like her better than he had at first. Maybe he'd been a little hard on her, even. Just because a person had never drunk coffee was no reason to—

"Oh, my goodness!"

At Amy's sharp cry, he jerked his head up so fast he all but broke his neck. "What is it? What's wrong?" He was ready, whatever it was. He didn't have a gun, but he could heave a knife as well as anybody in Arizona Territory. He scanned the scene, from right to left and back again, searching for whatever it was that had alarmed her. From the tone of her voice, he expected to see anything from a rattlesnake to a rabid polecat to Horace Huxtable with a gun.

Her voice had sunk to a whisper when she spoke again, and she'd pressed a palm to a cheek that had suddenly gone as white as a snowdrift. "Is that woman actually"—she inhaled a big breath—*"smoking?"*

Charlie blinked at her, then blinked into the distance. A young woman stood outside one of the crew tents. And, yes, she was smoking a cigarette. The way Miss Wilkes had said it, he'd thought the girl had caught fire, at least.

"I think so," he said, not sure what she expected him to say—or what she expected him to do about it. While he was as happy as a lark to belt Horace Huxtable for making improper suggestions to a female member of the cast, he sure as heck wasn't going to punch that lady for smoking.

"My goodness."

When he peered at Amy again, he saw that her cheeks remained pale, and that the expression of horror he'd thought he'd imagined, he hadn't. It was there; no doubt about it.

All righty, then, Charlie presumed that folks in Pasadena, California, didn't cotton to females smoking. He didn't either, really, although his grounds weren't moral—as he felt sure Amy's were—but protective. It was dang dry in the Arizona desert, and smoldering cigarette butts had set off more than one wildfire.

Curious, he asked, "You got something against folks smoking, Miss Wilkes?" He tried to keep his tone friendly.

Her head jerked up and she stared at him for a moment. Charlie all but got lost in those big, limpid pools of blue. Then her gaze fell, and the pink returned to her cheeks. "I suppose," she said tightly, "that you think I'm an unconscionable snob for being shocked to see a woman smoking a cigarette."

Well, yeah, kinda. Charlie said, "Er, I don't know about that, ma'am. Just wondered why you cared, is all. I'm sort of a live-and-let-live kind of feller myself."

She made a clicking noise with her tongue, and Charlie thought he glimpsed the ragged edge of her frustration. With a gesture of her hand, she said, "Oh, I don't *care*. Exactly. Not really. But . . ." She tilted her head and stared up at him some more.

Charlie had to swallow an oath. He wished she wouldn't do that. It made him prey to all sorts of impulses he was sure she'd just hate, and which made him feel sort of like Horace Huxtable, which was an awful way to feel.

"But this is all so new to me, Mr. Fox. I know you think I'm a straitlaced priss, but I've . . . well, I suppose I've been sheltered in my life."

Since he didn't know what to say to that, and sensing she wouldn't appreciate agreement, Charlie kept mum.

She went on with a choppy wave of her arm that spoke eloquently of the state of her nerves. "Since I was seven years old, I've never been anywhere but Pasadena or done anything but what . . . well, what people in Pasadena do. And all of us at home do the same things—and *none* of us do anything I'm being expected to do in this picture. A woman in Pasadena wouldn't be caught dead smoking or drinking." She hung her head. "I suppose you think that's intolerably stodgy."

Charlie, who had been appreciating the way Miss Wilkes's lithe body moved and the way her rosebud mouth tilted at the corners, pried his mind away from baser matters and thought about it for a minute. When he answered, he told the truth. "Well, ma'am, I don't rightly think it's stodgy. It's . . . well, it's kinda irritating when somebody keeps exclaiming about what other folks do. It's not as if anybody asked for your opinion or anything."

The pink in her cheeks deepened significantly. "Oh, dear, you must dislike me intensely, Mr. Fox."

"Good God, no! I don't dislike you at all." Her little rose-bud mouth quivered, and Charlie went gooey inside.

Amy hung her head. "Thank you for saying that, even if you don't really mean it. I honestly didn't mean to give you the impression that I disapprove of everything everybody who doesn't live in Pasadena does. It's only that this is all so new to me."

"I understand," Charlie said, nodding. And he did. Sort of.

The poor thing looked as if she were suffering acute humiliation, and Charlie hadn't meant her to. He was shuffling through the rubbish heap in his brain, trying to dust off some words that might both soothe her and keep her from slapping his face, when Martin's voice came to them. Reprieve, thank

God! Charlie turned with a real, live, honest-to-God happy smile. "Well, howdy, Martin. How're things?"

Martin eyed him as if he wondered if Charlie, too, had taken to drink, and Charlie realized that Martin had only left Amy and him five minutes before. He broadened his smile to show that he was in full possession of his senses.

He wasn't, though. Staring into Amy Wilkes's eyes had done something serious to his senses, although Charlie wasn't sure what it was. They were heaving and spluttering like crazy, though, and making him wonder if he'd taken sick.

She, too, appeared comforted to have Martin interrupt what she evidently considered the scene of her embarrassment. She shot one last glance at the cigarette-smoking woman over by the crew's tent. Charlie thought he detected a little reproach—and a whole lot of bewilderment—in her expression.

Her smile for Martin Tafft was a winner, though. Charlie wouldn't mind her tossing a couple of those smiles his way. Not that she would, since she thought he was lower than snake spit—and she thought he thought she was, too. It was tough maintaining his smile with that notion rattling around in his brain pan.

"Miss Wilkes!" Martin called while he was still several yards off. "The costumes are ready for your first fitting, and I think they'll be wonderful."

"Thank you. That sounds like a nice—er—thing to do."

What it sounded like to Charlie was that she was guarding her tongue to within an inch of its life and was trying like thunder not to allow another spontaneous comment past her lips. Charlie wished he'd kept his danged mouth shut earlier. He kind of enjoyed hearing about all the things that perturbed her and made her ever-so-dainty feelings recoil. A body couldn't haul back his spoken words like he could a runaway calf, though. Fine time to remember that, he thought glumly.

Martin shook Charlie's hand when they were close enough

to reach each other. Charlie wasn't used to shaking hands every single time he came across a fellow he worked with, but guessed he could stand it.

"Let me show you to the fitting tent," Martin said to Amy. "It'll probably be lunchtime when you're through there. When the bell rings, why don't I drop by and walk you to the chow tent?"

"Thank you very much, Mr. Tafft."

Turning to Charlie, Martin said, "Why don't you—ah—study your script or something, Charlie? We'll have another rehearsal after lunch, since this morning's was—er—shortened unexpectedly."

If that wasn't a polite way of putting it, Charlie didn't know what was. He said, "Sure thing, Martin. Will do."

And as he watched Martin and Amy walk away, Charlie noticed that the constraint Amy exhibited when she was in his own vicinity had slipped away. He frowned. She was cozy as kittens with Martin Tafft. With Charlie Fox, she was like a frozen millpond. He figured it was because he'd teased her a wee tiny bit when they'd first met.

Well, and then he'd told her that nobody cared to hear her opinions about things.

And maybe he'd hinted that she might be a drop too fussy.

Oh, all right, and he supposed he'd treated her as if he thought she was a stuffy prig.

Aw, hell, what he'd done was make her feel like a pile of horse poop. He heard his uncle Bill, clear as a bell, telling him, "Never miss the chance to keep mum, Charlie."

Uncle Bill, as usual, was right. Charlie hadn't kept mum when he'd had the chance, and he'd managed to hurt Miss Wilkes's feelings. Shoot.

As he shoved his hands into his pockets, hunched up his shoulders, and headed to his tent, another one of his uncle Bill's favorite sayings tiptoed into his head. "There's two ways to deal with women, Charlie, and don't neither one of 'em work."

Charlie could almost hear his Aunt Bess's hollered reaction to Bill's words from the kitchen of their ranch house.

He had a feeling Uncle Bill was right. Damn it.

Five

Amy felt pretty awful by the time she and Martin arrived at the tent where the costume fittings were to be done. That wretched Charlie Fox always seemed to make the worst possible interpretations of the things she said.

She couldn't help it if she'd been surprised—oh, very well, scandalized—to see a young female, and a respectable-looking one, at that, smoking a cigarette. Everything Amy had ever been taught told her that smoking was a masculine pastime and not one to be indulged in by women. In Pasadena, even *men* who smoked cigarettes were looked upon with disapproval unless they were otherwise judged worthy citizens. For some reason, cigars and pipes weren't looked upon with such intense disapproval. In men. No amount of good works, in Pasadena, could ever nullify the evil of smoking in a woman.

Why, the minister at the First Presbyterian Church in Pasadena, to which church Amy went every Sunday of her life, had as much as said that females who smoked were going straight to hell. *Amy* hadn't said it; a minister of the Gospel had said it. So there.

So why did she now feel as if she'd been wrong to disclose her shock?

Nobody'd asked her for her opinion, Charlie Fox had told her. Humph. Horrid man. He'd asked her what was wrong, and she'd told him. Then he'd as much as told *her* that she was a stiff-necked, judgmental fusspot. Anyhow, where would the world be if it depended on people being asked before they told other people what they thought?

That didn't make sense even to herself, and she was frowning at it and trying to reconfigure it when Martin's voice dragged her out of the dumps.

"Miss Wilkes," he said, "please let me introduce you to Miss Karen Crenshaw. Miss Crenshaw is Madame Dunbar's assistant, and has been more than helpful to our cast members for some time now."

Looking up, for her eyes had been downcast and focused on the ground while her brain had toiled with her discomposure, Amy discovered herself staring straight into the face of the woman who'd been smoking. She felt herself blush. *Fiddle!*

Miss Crenshaw curtsied prettily. Not having anticipated such a courtesy from a woman who smoked cigarettes, Amy stuttered, "Oh! Oh, well, I'm pleased to meet you, Miss Crenshaw." Heavenly days, Amy was accustomed to curtsying to her uncle's inmates. She couldn't recall ever having been curtsied to, herself.

"Likewise," said Miss Crenshaw, gazing at her askance, as if she didn't understand why Amy was rattled.

Why should she? Amy asked herself bitterly.

Because Charlie's words seemed to be ringing in her ears and scoffing at her, Amy held out her hand. "It's so good of you to do this, Miss Crenshaw."

Miss Crenshaw transferred her puzzled gaze to Amy's hand and held it there for a moment before taking the hand in her own and shaking it. Martin cleared his throat behind her, and Amy feared she'd made a fool of herself. Again.

Well, that was just too bad. She lifted her chin, determined to maintain her good manners no matter what. She was no better than Miss Crenshaw—even though Miss Crenshaw did smoke cigarettes—and she wouldn't try to pretend that she was, as she'd read some moving picture actresses did. Amy, too, had to work for a living. Until she'd met Mr. Tafft, she'd done it at her uncle's health spa. Now she was supposed to be acting. All things considered, Amy wished she'd stayed in Pasadena and refused this offer.

But that was how quitters talked, she lectured herself sternly. She was a Wilkes, and Wilkeses didn't quit. They fulfilled their promises and finished their jobs. Then they quit.

Very well. She would do her job. She smiled at Martin. "Thank you, Mr. Tafft."

Beaming and rubbing his hands together, Martin said, "Certainly, certainly. I'm sure you two will get along just fine. I—er—had better check up on some things."

Horace Huxtable, unless Amy missed her guess. She managed not to wrinkle her nose and purse up her lips, and was proud of herself.

After he'd left the tent, Miss Crenshaw went to the flap and tied it. With a smile for Amy, she said, "Don't want anybody waltzing in while you're in your knickers and chemise, do we?"

Horrified, Amy cried, "Good heavens, no!"

Fiddle. She knew she'd misspoken when Miss Crenshaw lifted her eyebrows and said, "There's no need to carry on. The flap's tied shut."

Oh, dear, now she thinks I'm a prig, too. Amy was beginning to get awfully discouraged. Miss Crenshaw had lovely eyes, Amy noticed—probably because they were opened so wide. Big and pansy brown. Amy would wager that Charlie Fox would consider Miss Crenshaw quite pretty. That made her feel even more discouraged.

With a sigh, she said, "I beg your pardon, Miss Crenshaw. I didn't mean to speak so loudly."

"Nonsense, don't even think about it." Miss Crenshaw flipped Amy's apology away with her hand. "But let's get you undressed now so we can try on your costume for the first scene. I hope you'll like it."

"I'm sure I shall," murmured Amy, praying she was right.

She undressed, uneasy about it. Not that she feared Miss Crenshaw would do anything untoward, or that anyone else would enter the tent during her fitting. But she'd never undressed in front of another person, and she was shy about it. She also had a feeling Vernon would disapprove. She disapproved, herself, if it came to that. She kept her back to Miss Crenshaw, worried as she did so that the costumer would believe her to be a big prude.

With a heavy sigh, Amy came to the conclusion that she *was* a big prude. And since that was the case, she might as well behave as she wanted to. The good Lord knew, she reflected darkly as she gave a thought to Horace Huxtable, that everyone else around here seemed to do so.

When she turned around again, she realized Miss Crenshaw had not been looking at her at all but had turned her back and was working at a large table set against the far side of the tent. Amy sighed, and the other woman turned.

"All ready now?" asked Miss Crenshaw pleasantly.

She guessed so. "Yes." She tried to sound pleasant, too.

"All right, let's take a look first."

Amy felt like a china doll on display in a department store window.

"Yes," said Miss Crenshaw, eyeing her critically. "I think we'll need very few alterations."

Assuming that was a good thing, Amy smiled. Her smile tipped a bit when Miss Crenshaw, treating her as Amy expected she might treat a dressmaker's dummy, put two fingers against Amy's shoulder and pushed it in an effort to get her to turn around. The seamstress frowned and stared at every inch of Amy's figure, reminding Amy of Horace Huxtable in one of his shocking displays of salacious rudeness, except that Miss Crenshaw's expression was much more critical.

But this wasn't rude. This was business, and Amy tried hard to keep her embarrassment from creeping out into the open.

"We'll have to shorten the skirts," Miss Crenshaw said after Amy had just about decided she couldn't take any more.

"Oh."

"But that won't be difficult."

"Good."

"Madame Dunbar is very adept at designing costumes for the pictures," Miss Crenshaw said. "She has an eye for it. You're lucky to have her." She turned and waltzed over to a rack against the west tent wall where several ladies' and gentlemen's costumes hung.

"Oh. Good."

Great grief, she couldn't go on saying "Oh" and "Good" all day, could she? Scrambling madly to think of something else to say, she suddenly lit on Pasadena. Thank heavens! Something she knew about!

"Um, I understand Madame Dunbar has her business in Pasadena."

"It's actually in Altadena, but it's close by to Pasadena."

"Oh." Irked with herself for succumbing to another "Oh," Amy said, "Yes. Altadena's just north of us. In Pasadena."

Miss Crenshaw, her mouth full of pins and her hands full of clothes, nodded. She handed Amy a pretty blue shirtwaist. Amy assumed she was supposed to put it on, so she did. Without speaking, Miss Crenshaw yanked Amy around to face her and buttoned the waist up the front. Amy blinked, rather surprised that this was all such a businesslike operation. Miss Crenshaw stabbed pins into the material here and there, taking up folds of excess fabric.

"Er, whereabouts does Madame Dunbar have her establishment?"

Speaking around a mouthful of pins, Miss Crenshaw said, "Foothill Boulevard and Maiden Lane. She had the house built last year."

Foothill Boulevard and Maiden Lane. Amy consulted her mental map of the area until she found the proper location. Then she was taken aback. "My goodness, that's a very big house!"

Miss Crenshaw nodded. Amy knew it was probably impolite to talk to someone who couldn't talk back very well due to having her mouth full of pins, but she couldn't account for Madame Dunbar's house unless the woman was phenomenally wealthy. Could a dressmaker become so wealthy simply by designing costumes for the moving pictures? It didn't seem possible.

Still and all, that house was gigantic. It must have cost a fortune. Avidly curious, she decided to plunge ahead and ask questions, in spite of Miss Crenshaw's pins. Heaven knew, everyone else in this stupid moving picture village seemed exempt from proper behavior. "Er, does she make a large amount of money from the pictures? I mean, so that she could afford to build that huge house?"

Again Miss Crenshaw nodded. Greatly impressed and feeling a trifle more kindly disposed toward her new pursuit, Amy said, "My goodness." The notion of becoming morally corrupt didn't sound so awful if a great deal of wealth was provided as compensation. She'd never say so to Vernon. Or anyone else, for that matter.

Swirling around, Miss Crenshaw took the pins out of her mouth and headed back to the rack of clothing. "Oh, yes, ever since she started working for the pictures, she's been making gobs of money."

Gobs. How nice. "I see. I—er—had no idea working in the pictures was so profitable."

"You'll find out." Grabbing a fringed skirt from the rack, Miss Crenshaw whirled again and returned to Amy.

She moved quickly. And gracefully. Again, Amy thought about how Charlie Fox would probably admire Miss Crenshaw, and again she felt a little blue.

"Here, hold up your arms and I'll slip this over your head."

Without speaking, Amy did as she'd been bidden. She felt sort of like a department store mannequin. The skirt slid over her shoulders, and Miss Crenshaw caught it at her waist so it wouldn't fall to the floor. The fabric seemed to be some kind of soft and supple chamois or animal hide. It felt nice and soft to the touch as Amy fingered it.

"Please don't touch," Miss Crenshaw admonished, making Amy jerk her hand away from the fabric as if she'd been slapped. "It's buckskin, and the oil on your fingers will discolor it. We try to keep them in pristine condition, at least until the shooting's over. Then they'll probably use them again and again and again. Peerless is frugal about sets and costumes."

"I see." There was no reason on earth, Amy told herself, why she should be suffering from embarrassment. There was no crime attached to not knowing something until you'd been told.

She was embarrassed anyway.

"I didn't mean to bark," Miss Crenshaw said with a laugh in her voice. "I tend to get involved in my work and forget to be polite when I'm working with people instead of dressmakers' dummies. I'm sorry if I startled you."

Much mollified, Amy said, "Oh, no, that's quite all right. I didn't know about the buckskin discoloring."

They got along well, considering that Amy was almost too afraid to open her mouth during most of the fitting. Miss

Crenshaw seemed like a pleasant person, though, a fact that slightly altered Amy's opinion about females who smoked cigarettes. She still deplored the activity, but she was relatively certain that not every single female who smoked was heading straight to hell.

In other words, she disagreed with her minister. Oh, dear. That meant, she supposed, that either she herself was headed straight to hell, or the minister was too harsh in his judgments. She decided not to worry about this particular conundrum at the moment because she had plenty of other things to worry about. She concentrated on them, and on trying not to appear too awfully foolish in front of Miss Crenshaw

"Damn, blast, and hell." Huxtable had escaped again.

So Martin swore out loud—something he seldom did—when he peeked into Horace Huxtable's tent, expecting to find the actor nursing a sore jaw. Instead, he didn't find the actor at all.

Immediately Martin set out to find him. On the way, he met Charlie ambling along, and he perked up. Charlie was a good egg, even if he did seem to possess a violent streak and variable grammatical leanings. Martin was sure he'd help in this instance.

"Charlie!" he called.

Charlie, a slow-moving cowpoke from head to toe, Martin noticed with an internal chuckle, stopped moseying and turned. When he spotted Martin, he smiled and gave a small salute.

"I'm glad I saw you." Martin hurried up to him and held out his hand. He noticed that Charlie gazed at his hand for a moment before taking and shaking it. Must be unused to such a civilized custom as shaking hands, Martin presumed.

"Listen, Charlie, I just dropped Miss Wilkes off at the costume tent and went to see how Huxtable's getting on."

Charlie's expression clouded. "I know I probably shouldn't've plugged him, Martin, but he made me mad. No man should talk to a woman the way he talked to Miss Wilkes."

"I know, I know. Horace makes everyone mad. But, listen, Charlie. He wasn't in his tent when I looked. I'm afraid he's gotten loose and is looking for booze. Will you help me find him?"

With narrowing eyes, Charlie muttered, "That guy's got a real problem with the booze, doesn't he?"

"I'm afraid he does."

"You might want to see about usin' other folks in future pictures, Martin. Once folks get to drinking all the time, there's no doing anything with them. But I'll be glad to help you look for him."

"Thanks a lot, Charlie. You're a trump. And I'm sure you're right about using other people in future films. But it's an awful shame. Huxtable is a wonderful actor, and he has a great presence on the screen."

His companion regarded Martin as if he didn't have a clue to what he was talking about. Which he probably didn't.

Martin continued, "We'd better check in at the chow tent. Chances are, if he went looking for alcohol, he'd look there first."

"Doesn't he have any of his own? He got a snootful last night somehow or other."

Martin shook his head. "I made him give it all to me, and then I searched his tent on my own. Didn't want any more of these things to happen." He snorted. "For all the good it did."

"A man can only do what he can do," Charlie said philosophically. "It isn't your fault the man's a pain in the ass and a drunk."

"I suppose not." It would be his problem if his star got plastered and delayed the shooting of the picture, though. And it would be his problem if Huxtable harassed Amy Wilkes so much she quit, too. It would also be his problem if he insulted someone who took exception to one of his diatribes and beat him up and broke his arm or neck or something, as well.

Every now and again, he wished Peerless had enough money to hire a few more people. Phineas Lovejoy, the owner of the studio and Martin's best friend from childhood, was a whiz at finding money and backers for his pictures. Unfortunately, finding money and backers took a lot of time. And that left all the legwork and most of the other work to Martin.

As if he'd read Martin's mind, Charlie said, "You sure have a lot to do with this picture-making business, Martin."

Discovering it pleasant to be talking to someone who understood, if only a little bit, what his work entailed, Martin nodded. "Yes, I do. I don't mind, really, and I enjoy the variety, but looking after Horace Huxtable isn't one of my favorite pastimes."

"You ought to get some assistants. Or chain him to a wall or something."

"I'm hoping to do that very thing—hire assistants, that is—if this picture is the success we think it will be. Assistants cost money, and you can see already how large a crew it takes to make a picture."

"Yeah. I was kind of surprised."

"We need cameramen, people to write the musical score, people to write and paint the subtitles, people to create scenery, costumes, all sorts of things like that. Not to mention people to scout out locations and set the scenes and pick up and clean the tents and other stuff. When we use animals, as we do in this picture, we need to find them, and the people to take care of them, too. And don't forget food service when we're on location, as we are this time."

"That must cost a bundle."

"It does, believe me. So I don't begrudge Mr. Lovejoy his job, believe me. He's a whiz at finding money."

"Now, there's a fine, useful quality in a man," said Charlie with approval.

"It is indeed. But it leaves everything else to me. One of these days, though, we'll be able to hire assistants."

"Good luck to you. I hope you make a fortune."

Charlie sounded as if he meant it, and Martin was glad to accept his good wishes. "Thanks, Charlie."

They had to look into every tent they passed. It pleased Martin that Charlie was so eager to help. Unless it was because he wanted to punch Huxtable again. He decided not to dwell on that unlikely possibility. After all, Charlie was a sensible fellow. He'd only hit Huxtable the first time because the man had been an insufferable boor. In Huxtable's last picture for Peerless, an assistant cameraman had popped him with much less cause.

Which brought to mind a whole slew of scenarios in which they might find Peerless's errant star. Lord, what if Huxtable had insulted a native and been shot for his efforts? This was El Monte, after all, where Wild Western sensibilities might yet prevail.

Opening a trunk and peering inside, in case Huxtable was sleeping it off in there, Charlie asked, "What-all kinds of jobs do you have to do for these pictures, Martin?"

Silently blessing Charlie for taking his mind away from the mental image of Horace Huxtable with a bullet hole in his egotistical head, Martin said, "Oh, I'm the one who has to search out locations and so forth. That's the first job to be done when a picture is in the planning stages."

"You mean like here?"

"That's right. We do a lot of cowboy stuff, so I hang around deserts a good deal."

"Hope they aren't all as ugly as this one," Charlie opined.

With a soft laugh, Martin said, "Deserts aren't my favorite places. And we usually have to shoot during the hottest part of the year, because of the sunlight, so it's not awfully pleasant sometimes."

Charlie, an Arizonan, nodded as if he understood completely.

"Of course, I search out new talent, too. I found you, remember."

"I remember."

Shooting a sharp glance at him, Martin wondered why Charlie didn't sound more cheerful about it. Figuring he should deal with one crisis at a time, he opted to ask later.

"And I often direct, as I'm doing on this picture. I'm part owner of the studio, but I generally leave the business side of it to my partner, Mr. Lovejoy. He's better at it than I am."

"You trust him not to cheat you?"

"Absolutely." Martin was shocked that anyone would question Phineas Lovejoy's integrity. Then again, Charlie had never met him, so he couldn't know that Phineas would sooner cut his own throat than perpetrate a swindle. That was the only reason Martin had felt comfortable in joining his moviemaking enterprise. That and the fact that he had no money of his own and Lovejoy was rolling in it.

Charlie simply nodded complacently, as if he'd only wanted to know.

Martin guessed it was a cowboy thing, and went on explaining his role in Peerless as he and Charlie lifted tent flaps and searched under benches and chairs. Damn Huxtable anyway.

"I have to line up extra people if we need crowd scenes and so forth. If we're filming near a town or city, the local folks are generally happy to oblige for five dollars or so."

"You mean you'd pay them five bucks a day to stand around and be part of a crowd?"

"Oh, yes. When we filmed *Betsy of the Badlands,* we needed a whole bunch of people milling around during the lynching scene."

Again, Charlie nodded. "Not bad. Five bucks is a lot of money for some of us."

"Right. Then there are the animals."

"Animals?"

"Yes. If we need horses or cows or something, I have to find them. For instance, in this picture, we have several horses, and we'll be using a lot of cattle eventually. Those are some of the horses." He pointed to a fenced-in area where six horses grazed lazily beneath some trees.

"I see. Better go over there and see if he's got himself kicked by a horse and had his head stove in."

"Don't even *say* something like that!" Martin cried, horrified by the mere thought of his star being killed by a horse.

Chuckling, Charlie said, "I don't think you need to worry about it. Huxtable don't seem to me to be the horsy type." He climbed the fence and strode over to the horses.

Martin bit his fingernails and watched in great anxiety, expelling a huge gust of breath when Charlie ambled back, shaking his head. "He isn't there."

"Thank God," breathed Martin, thinking he wasn't up to this sort of nonsense, and that if Phineas *did* want to use Horace Huxtable in another picture, he'd have to pay Martin triple his regular salary for putting up with the big ham and seeing that he stayed out of trouble.

"So that's a whole lot of stuff you have to do, Martin," Charlie said, making Martin's mind veer back to their earlier conversation. "Do you have to do other stuff, too?"

"Yes indeed. I have to make sure the cast is fed and housed. Sometimes we can rent rooms in a hotel. Often we can make an entire moving picture in a single day of filming. The short stuff, you know. We'll take the cast and the camera, head to the park, and voila! We have a single-reeler all set to go."

"I didn't know that. How come this one's takin' so long?"

"This one's different." Martin couldn't keep the swell of pride he felt from leaking into his voice. "This is going to be a major motion picture. A feature. It's not just one of those cheap shorts. It's going to make people sit up and take notice. Why, Charlie, pretty soon the moving pictures will be the biggest thing in the whole U.S. of A."

"That so?" They'd finished with the Peerless village and the outlying pastures, and now headed out to the desert. Charlie vaulted over a fence and jogged over to inspect a pile of boulders.

Martin raised his voice so Charlie could hear him. "Oh, yes. Why, you can send a can of celluloid anywhere. It's not like the theater, where a person has to travel to New York or Chicago or San Francisco to see a good stage production. Pictures have the potential of reaching everyone in the world eventually. They're already building picture palaces in some of our bigger cities. That's why the premiere performance of *One and Only* is going to be held in Chicago." He was disappointed when he saw Charlie head back empty-handed.

As he vaulted back over the fence, Charlie said, "I guess I never thought about it before, but I expect you're right."

"The industry is growing by leaps and bounds," Martin said firmly. "And you're fortunate to be in it at the beginning."

"I suppose so." Charlie didn't sound as thrilled as Martin thought he should. Charlie stopped next to Martin, hooked his thumbs in his belt, and surveyed the desert. "I don't know, Martin. It doesn't look too promising."

"No," Martin agreed unhappily. "It doesn't. Where on earth can the man have gotten himself off to?"

Charlie had opened his mouth, presumably to offer a suggestion, when both men stiffened as if the finger of God had smote them into pillars of salt. A high-pitched, terrified scream pierced the air around them.

Martin said, "Huxtable."

Charlie said, "Aw, hell."

They both took off at a gallop to see what the star of their picture had done this time.

Amy, trying hard not to be mortified, had just stepped out of her own plain chemise and donned the undergarments she'd have to wear for the picture. She now stood before Miss Crenshaw in a waist-length chemise and stiff-boned corset with a type of garters Amy had never used before. They dangled from the bottom of the corset and exposed a good deal of the bare skin of her thighs. Amy felt extremely uncomfortable thus clad, as she was accustomed to wearing more demure underwear. And always covered by outer clothing if she was going to be seen by anyone.

She'd just straightened up from attaching, via the garters, the pair of white silk stockings, also provided by Miss Crenshaw and undoubtedly much more fashionable than the dark cotton stockings she generally wore. She inspected herself surreptitiously in the full-length mirror on its stand in a corner—surreptitiously because she didn't want Miss Crenshaw to think she was vain.

Although she knew it was a meaningless conceit, she was glad that—although she was embarrassed to admit it to herself—she looked quite well thus clad. Or unclad. *Shocking, Amy Wilkes. You're becoming a perfectly shocking hussy.* She believed, however, that Vernon might be jarred out of his general superior serenity if he could see her now, and she smiled inside.

Worse than that, she had the scandalous notion that she'd like Charlie Fox to see her. She was sure he'd find her every bit as attractive as he found Miss Crenshaw. And, what was more, Amy didn't smoke cigarettes, so her breath would be sweeter than Miss Crenshaw's.

Great heaven, she was slipping fast.

Fortunately, Miss Crenshaw had begun to speak again, so Amy was compelled to haul her mind out of the sewer.

"Does that fit too tightly, Miss Wilkes? I can loosen it if you want me to, although we need to keep it fairly snug so the costume will fit properly."

Amy swiveled this way and that, testing the garment. "I don't think this is too tight, depending on what I'll have to do in it."

"Oh, don't worry about that. The ladies never have to do too much unless you're in one of those *Perilous Polly* pictures or something. In this one, you're going to be rescued, so you won't need to be doing anything very strenuous. I think they're going to tie you to a log in a sawmill, and you'll have to struggle to get the bonds loose before the saw can cut you in half, but you'll be lying down for that."

Amy snorted and then felt silly.

Miss Crenshaw glanced up at her. "What is it? Is something wrong?"

Fiddlesticks. Would she never learn to keep her big mouth shut? "I beg your pardon, Miss Crenshaw. I was contemplating being rescued by Mr. Huxtable, and I couldn't seem to help myself."

Miss Crenshaw's laugh sounded genuine and spontaneous, and Amy felt better. "I know *exactly* what you mean," Miss Crenshaw said. "That man is horrible. I don't think there's a woman on the set whom he hasn't pestered at one time or another. He's terrible when he's not drinking, and he's insufferable when he's drunk."

"Oh, you're so right! I really can't stand him."

"He's awful." She poked Amy's shoulder. Amy, having learned shortly after she'd arrived in the costume tent what that meant, obediently turned, and Miss Crenshaw began doing whatever it was she did to the right side of the garment. After a moment, she muttered, "Oh, piffle, I forgot the tape. Can you stand there, just like that, for another little minute? Don't let your arm drop or the fit will change. I'll be right back."

"Certainly."

Amy was facing the back of the tent, and peered over her shoulder to watch Miss Crenshaw as she headed to the table littered with scissors, tapes, pincushions, needles, and pins, and lorded over by one of those brand-new portable sewing machines. They were portable, that is, if one were a gorilla. Amy, curious about the modern phenomenon, had tried to lift it and nearly broke her back.

"I know it's here somewhere," Miss Crenshaw muttered, lifting and discarding pieces of fabric, cardboard, and sewing lint. "I just had it a minute ago."

Suddenly, as Amy watched, Miss Crenshaw squealed in fright and fell over backwards as an enormous body shoved against the closed flap of the tent, knocking into her and the table. The tent swayed as if in the clutches of a hurricane for a moment, as whatever it was that was trying to get in battered against the flap again.

Amy cried, "Miss Crenshaw!" and ran to help her.

A roar from outside the tent frightened her nearly to death. She reached Miss Crenshaw and grabbed the trembling hand the dressmaker was holding out to her. Miss Crenshaw stumbled up, and the two women threw their arms around each other, terror propelling them.

"What is it?" Miss Crenshaw cried.

"Something's trying to get in!" Amy cried back.

"Is it an animal?"

"I don't know."

Another terrible bellow smote the air, the women gasped in unison, and the center tent pole began to sway and tilt precariously. After one more violent blow to its side, the tent gave up the battle and folded up like a concertina, with Amy and Miss Crenshaw inside it, clinging to each other in horror.

Six

"It wasn't I who screamed," Amy grumbled. "And you can put me down now, if you please. I'm perfectly fine."

She was that. Charlie's eyes had almost started from his head when he'd seen her flounder out from underneath all that jumbled canvas. The last time he'd seen a female in so few clothes, she'd been a picture on a cigarette card. And she hadn't looked a tenth as good as Amy Wilkes.

"We need to get you away from the mess there," Charlie told her, lying through his teeth. "There might still be some danger."

In truth, the reason he still held her was that he couldn't get his arms to perform any of the commands he was mentally giving them. They wanted to stay wrapped around the lovely, supple, warm flesh of Amy Wilkes.

"But I need to know if Miss Crenshaw is all right!" Amy tried to struggle, which only made Charlie grit his teeth in erotic anguish as her delicious skin rubbed against him. Lord, Lord, she was really something.

"Martin got her out safe and sound. She's okay." He could barely squeeze the words out of his tight throat.

"Are you sure?"

Charlie knew she was scared, and that was why she was doing all those wiggly things, but when she managed to twist her body around, press her bosom against his chest and her bottom against his arms, and gaze over his shoulder, he blamed near died anyway. He'd never dreamed, when he'd agreed to do this picture, that he'd be holding a near-naked Amy Wilkes. Hell, if he'd known, he'd have paid them. His britches were near to busting their buttons already, and he'd only been carrying her for a few seconds.

"I'm sure. I saw him. And her."

"But where are they?" She wriggled again, sending jolts of lust through Charlie's entire long body, and stared over his other shoulder. "I can't see them! Oh, please, Mr. Fox! I must know that she's not hurt."

It took every ounce of self-will Charlie possessed to make himself stop and turn around. Ding-bust-it, he wanted to carry her off somewhere private and ravish her; to sling her behind his saddle and gallop off into the sunset with her and ravish her some more.

Since his horse was currently being stabled at an ostrich ranch in Arizona Territory, that was foolish and he knew it. Besides, Miss Wilkes might be naive, but she wasn't any shrinking violet. Charlie imagined she'd have something to say about being made away with.

Which was a real shame, in his opinion.

Nevertheless, he turned. They were far enough away from the melee that he didn't suppose it mattered—except to him. "There," he said. "You can see from here." He turned sideways so she could have a better view.

"Oh, yes, I see her. She doesn't seem to be limping, does she?" Her voice conveyed a good deal of worry, and Charlie was pleased to know she was capable of feeling concern for a female who smoked cigarettes.

"No, ma'am. I'm sure she's all right. Just scared."

"It was terrifying." She shuddered, delighting Charlie and causing him to experience further tortures of an unfulfilled sexual nature.

"I really need to get back there and see what's going on, Mr. Fox."

"I think you'd better wait a bit, ma'am." He knew he couldn't hold out too much longer and would have to relinquish his delightful burden sooner or later, but he was going to do his best to prolong the event. Charlie Fox wasn't a man to back down on a good deal without a fight.

"But this is silly. You can't stand here and hold me all day."

He could too. He didn't say so, but said instead, "You've had a shock, ma'am. You ought to take it easy."

"Please put me down, Mr. Fox." She was beginning to sound severe, as she did when she was deploring something.

Charlie sighed and gave up. Very gently, he began lowering her to the desert floor, when a brilliant thought struck him and he stood upright again, Amy still clutched in his arms. "Er, ma'am, you don't have very many clothes on. Don't you think it would be better to get some duds on first?"

"What?" She glanced wildly around, as if searching for her clothes. Then—and Charlie could feel it as it happened, since he'd made sure his hands were still placed on spots that weren't covered by anything—she blushed from her toes to her head. "Oh, my sweet Lord in heaven! I've got nothing *on!* Oh, please! *Do* something!"

Charlie'd like to do something. However, she'd probably slap him from here to Sunday if he so much as suggested it. "Um, how about I give you my shirt, ma'am? It'll be long enough to cover you."

"Your *shirt?*"

She had a powerfully shrill voice when she got going. Charlie was surprised he didn't hate it more than he did, and chalked up his tolerance to his aroused state. Lust could get a fellow in trouble if he didn't watch out. In spite of knowing it, he continued, "My tent's nearby. I'll get you a clean shirt to wear. It'll be big enough, I'm sure."

"*Your* tent?" she squealed. "What about *my* tent?"

"Yours is mighty near the action, ma'am. I thought you didn't want folks to see you."

She said something, but Charlie couldn't make it out because the words were a little high-pitched and jammed together.

He shrugged. "It's better than standing around in . . . well, the way you are now." He wondered if his nose would grow if he told any more whoppers like that one. That's what his ma used to say happened to little boys who fibbed.

"Oh, my land," she moaned, and buried her face against Charlie's shirtfront.

He had, therefore, a very large smile on his face when he carried Amy to his tent.

This was the last straw. It was the grand finale. Amy had taken just about enough of this nonsense. Never in all her born days—as her great-grandmother Wilkes, who hailed from Virginia, used to say—had she ever been so upset and humiliated. Just wait until she wrote to Vernon this evening.

As she walked back to what used to be the costumer's tent, trying to keep up with Charlie and clad in one of his huge shirts that dangled clear to her ankles—thank God—she already had a pretty good idea what had happened to make the tent collapse.

Horace Huxtable. That's what had happened.

She was so mad she could ignite sparks from gnashing her teeth together. "He might have hurt somebody, the cad." He might have hurt *her*, in fact! Or Miss Crenshaw, she added guiltily after a second or two.

"Yes, ma'am. It's pure-D dumb luck that neither you nor

Miss Crenshaw got hit by that center pole when it went down."

Miss Crenshaw. Amy shot a glance up to Charlie's face. He knew her name. How had he learned it?

Bother! That was none of her concern. She didn't care if Charlie Fox and Karen Crenshaw got married and had a hundred children. She, Amy Wilkes, was going to marry Vernon Catesby and live in a comfortable home and be secure for ever and ever and never experience another moment of insecurity in her life.

Forcing herself back to the here and now, she said, "I hope she's all right. She didn't look as if she'd been hurt, from a distance, but—"

"I think she's fine, ma'am. There she is, standing with Martin. Looks like they got Huxtable under control."

Amy was glad to hear the note of disapproval in Charlie's voice when he spoke of Horace Huxtable. At least he didn't seem to find Mr. Huxtable's antics amusing, as some young men of low character might have done.

She ran the last few yards up to Miss Crenshaw. "Oh, Miss Crenshaw! Are you all right? I was so worried about you!"

Miss Crenshaw and Martin turned and immediately began gaping at her. Amy stopped, embarrassed. "I—er—didn't have anything on . . . well, I didn't have *much* on, I mean . . . so Mr. Fox was kind enough to lend me a shirt." When she peeked around, she noticed that several other people, who had already begun to raise the costume tent from its state of collapse, were also staring at her. Mortified, she lifted her chin. "I think it was very nice of him."

"Er . . . yes indeed," said Martin.

Miss Crenshaw, who had been considering Amy intently, turned suddenly to Martin, a strangely intense expression on her face. "What a wonderful idea! Martin, what if we were to have something happen to the heroine in the fourth reel after the rescue scene at the sawmill, and have her be forced to don the hero's shirt? She looks charming dressed like that!"

Another abrupt swirl brought Miss Crenshaw face to face again with Amy, who could feel the heat stain her cheeks. *Charming? Good heavens.* "Um . . ."

"I mean, *look* at her!" cried Miss Crenshaw. "Isn't that the sweetest thing you've ever seen?"

Good glory, now they were *all* gawking at her. Amy wished her internal heater, which was pumping furiously, would ignite her entirely and save her from this humiliation.

"Hmmm," said Martin judiciously. "You may be right." He smiled at Amy. "Would you mind turning so that I can see you from the back, Miss Wilkes?"

She was going to die. That was all there was to it. She was going to die from shame and the disgrace of it all right this minute. She turned around and didn't catch fire. Fiddle.

"I do believe you're right, Karen."

Good heavens, thought Amy, *he calls Miss Crenshaw* Karen. *Picture people are such a loose lot.*

Martin gestured for Charlie. "Come here, Charlie. What do you think?"

Charlie came there, and Amy was subjected to his scrutiny, too. If she *didn't* die, she'd never be able to show her face in public again. She decided she'd leave this part out of her letter to Vernon; he'd never understand. *She* didn't understand.

"Looks good to me," said Charlie with considerable warmth. Since fire had failed, Amy prayed for a bolt from heaven to strike her dead on the spot.

Nothing happened, which made her wonder if she'd wasted her time going to church all these years. If the good Lord wouldn't help a poor woman in these circumstances, what good was He? She knew she'd just blasphemed, and was ashamed of herself. Not that she wasn't ashamed already. Bother.

Tapping her chin with a finger, Karen Crenshaw gazed fixedly at Amy in Charlie's shirt. "After we get the tent upright again, we can determine how to work it out. We'll need to decide whether the shirt should be plain or plaid, and if a darker color would look better on film."

"Right," agreed Martin, also staring at Amy, who was beginning to feel like a painting in an art gallery. Or a side of beef in a butcher's shop. "I think Huxtable's considerably smaller than Charlie, so we'll have to figure out how to make it look as if she's wearing Huxtable's shirt."

Both Miss Crenshaw and Amy huffed at once, and Amy broke through the paralysis of her embarrassment. "Speaking of Mr. Huxtable," she said in a voice she hoped sounded as infuriated as she felt, "I presume *he* was the author of this particular travesty?"

She swept her arm out to indicate the wreckage of the costume tent. Unfortunately, Charlie had moved up behind her and was now standing very close to her. She whacked his stomach with the back of her hand. She spun around. "Oh, my goodness, Mr. Fox. I'm so sorry!"

His smile could warm the coldest winter day. "It's nothing, Miss Wilkes. You can hit me any old time."

If it was nothing, how come her hand stung so badly? She shook it, amazed. His stomach was as hard as a rock. Amy tried not to be too impressed, since she couldn't afford to get distracted from her complaint about Horace Huxtable. She did, however, wonder if Vernon was in such good condition. She didn't think so.

"I fear it was Huxtable, all right, Miss Wilkes."

At least her question seemed to have taken everyone's attention away from her scanty costume and fixed it where it belonged: On Horace Huxtable and his abysmal behavior.

"I honestly don't think it's fair to the rest of us for him to be let loose to perpetrate these horrors, Mr. Tafft." Her tone was stern, rather surprising her since her state of mortification was still acute.

"I know, I know. Two of the bigger grips have wrestled him down and tied him up." Martin shook his head as if he wished he had an answer to the Huxtable problem. "I've got to figure out how to keep him away from the booze and out of trouble from now on. He evidently drank all the vanilla extract in the kitchen and managed to get drunk on that."

Amy huffed in disgust. "I believe you ought to set a guard on him," she said severely. "He shouldn't be let out alone, because he can't be trusted."

"Isn't *that* the truth," Miss Crenshaw chimed in.

"I know, I know."

Since Amy liked Mr. Tafft a good deal, she was sorry she'd caused the expression of concern to settle on his face. Still and all, facts had to be faced. If one man could cause this much damage, he really needed to be kept confined. "How about leg shackles?" she suggested, not entirely facetiously.

"Leg shackles?" cried Martin, evidently not recognizing even the tiny bit of humor Amy had intended to convey in her suggestion. He started tugging on a lock of hair.

"Why not?" asked Miss Crenshaw acidly. "Shackles would slow him down, at least."

Martin turned to stare at her in patent consternation.

Charlie laughed outright, then said, "Aw, shoot, Martin, I think he only needs to be watched carefully. The trouble always seems to start when he's left alone."

Amy nodded and smiled at Charlie. "That's it! He needs a keeper. Maybe a collar and a leash."

"Good Lord," whispered Martin, clearly appalled. "He'd never stand for that."

"What difference does that make?" asked Miss Crenshaw, her words remarkably curt. Amy decided she liked Miss Crenshaw a lot, cigarettes or no cigarettes, and no matter how attractive Charlie Fox found her. "The man's a menace. It's getting to the point where you're going to have to decide if you're here to make a picture or are simply providing a playground for the drunken lout."

Amy nodded her agreement.

"Oh, dear," Martin moaned. It looked to Amy as if that poor lock of hair was in danger of being pulled out of his skull.

"I'll help keep watch on him," Charlie offered.

Amy thought that was very nice of him, considering Mr. Huxtable didn't like him at all since he'd punched him in the jaw, God bless him. She gave him another smile to show her appreciation, and was rewarded by a warm twinkle in his lovely brown eyes. She turned to gaze at Martin at once, fearing for her consciousness. It was the corset, she told herself. It was laced tightly on account of the picture. She wasn't sure she believed herself.

"Well . . . I hate to ask you to do that, Charlie."

"You didn't ask," Charlie pointed out. "I offered."

"And you *do* need an around-the-clock watch put on him," Miss Crenshaw declared. "You know you do, Martin. He can't be trusted."

"Right. I'm afraid you're right." He let go of his hair and sighed. "Very well, then. Charlie, you've got a good deal to do in the picture, so you can't be forever trailing Huxtable around. I'll see if I can't get a couple of burly fellows to watch him most of the time. You try to keep an eye on him when the shooting starts."

The shooting? Amy felt her eyes go wide until she recollected that was what the movie folks called filming. This business was so odd.

Miss Crenshaw turned to gaze at her former workroom. "What a wreck," she muttered. Turning back to Amy, she said, "I'm afraid we won't be able to work on your fittings any more today. We could work in your tent, but all of the fabrics, implements, and costume pieces are under there somewhere."

Amy felt sorry for Martin Tafft, who stared disconsolately at the rubble before him and again started pulling on that tuft of hair and muttering to himself. She put a hand on his arm. He jumped in startled reaction.

"Please don't despair, Mr. Tafft," she said, sorry she'd frightened him. "I'm sure things will go more smoothly now that you've figured out how to manage Mr. Huxtable."

"*Manage* him?" Martin exclaimed. "I'm sure no one will ever be able to *manage* him, Miss Wilkes." It seemed to take a good deal of effort for him to pull himself back from melancholy and into some sort of order. "But I do appreciate your forbearance. I know your first picturemaking venture hasn't been exactly smooth sailing so far."

He could say that again. And it wasn't merely her *first* picture-making venture, either, Amy thought sourly. It was assuredly to be her last, as well. Rather than saying anything so mean-spirited while Martin was plainly in distress, Amy smiled and said, "I'm sure I shall survive."

The luncheon gong sounded. Martin said, "Thank you very much, Miss Wilkes. Karen," he said, glancing at Miss Crenshaw, "would you please see that Miss Wilkes has something to wear to lunch, and then join us there?"

"I'd be happy to." Miss Crenshaw smiled at Amy. "Where's your tent, Miss Wilkes? I'll help you get out of that corset. I know it's a devil."

In a stifled voice—why did picture people speak so freely about underthings and talk of the devil in front of everybody, as if they were talking about the weather? she wondered— Amy said, "Thank you very much, Miss Crenshaw."

"Oh, please call me Karen. Everyone does."

Did they indeed? Well, Amy guessed she could do so too, even though it seemed a remarkably casual thing to do on such short acquaintance. On the other hand, she was in the pictures now, and picture people, as she'd been noticing for days, were unlike any other people Amy had ever met.

Nevertheless, she bowed to the exigencies of her situation. She truly didn't want the people with whom she worked to think she was a stuffed shirt. So to speak. She almost giggled when she remembered she was at this moment stuffed into one of Charlie Fox's shirts. What was more, she was experiencing an alarming reluctance to remove it and give it back to him.

Oh, dear. Forcing herself to deal with the present, she said, "Thank you. Please call me Amy." They started walking toward Amy's tent.

"Amy?"

Miss Crenshaw sounded surprised. Amy glanced at her, puzzled. "Yes. My name is Amy Wilkes."

"Oh." A frown furrowed Karen Crenshaw's brow. "But I thought your name was Amelia. Is Amy short for Amelia?"

"Oh, yes. I forgot." Amy sighed windily. "Somebody decided Amy wasn't romantic enough, so they changed it to Amelia for the picture."

"Ah." Karen nodded wisely, as if such things happened all the time and she ought to have expected it.

Out of curiosity, Amy asked, "Do you think Amelia is more romantic than Amy?"

Her companion shrugged. "I don't find anything romantic in either one of them, actually."

"Oh." Daunted, Amy had no idea what to say now.

"I'm sorry," Karen said quickly. "I'm always saying stupid things without thinking first. Please forgive me. Will it help if I tell you I think both Amy and Amelia are more romantic than Karen? It's true, you know."

The two young women looked at each other for a moment, and laughed. They chatted merrily the rest of the way to Amy's tent, and were fast friends by the time they entered the chow tent together, Amy clad in an unexceptionable pink flowered day dress and a much more comfortable corset.

Horace Huxtable, Charlie was pleased to note, was not only tied up and lashed to his bed, but he'd been gagged as well, so he couldn't rant and rave at anyone. He was as furious as a maddened bull.

Charlie and Martin had detoured to Huxtable's tent to check on his progress toward sobriety before they went to lunch.

"Because, you know, Charlie, he *is* the star of the picture. If I let him kill himself or somebody else, it's liable to reflect badly on the Peerless Studio, and that would be a catastrophe. We're just beginning to make a name for ourselves. We don't need any scandal attached to the studio's name."

"Mmmm," replied Charlie, who had no other comment to offer. He knew precisely nothing about pictures, although he could understand Peerless's attitude about this particular problem. If word got out that one of Peerless's actors was a raging drunk who tore tents apart and tried to ravish innocent young women, the picture-going public would never pay to see another Peerless picture. Hell, a man had to watch out for his reputation and keep it clean even if he wasn't starring in moving pictures.

A huge mountain of a fellow sat in a chair beside the bed to which Huxtable was bound. He'd been reading an issue of *Motion Picture Story,* but when Charlie and Martin entered the tent, he put the magazine aside and stood up. "How-do, Mr. Tafft." He nodded at Charlie. "Mr. Fox."

Wasn't that nice? Everybody in the little tent city knew who he was. Charlie was impressed and told himself not to get swell-headed.

"I appreciate your help, Gus," Martin said. The two men

shook hands, an event Charlie had anticipated. Maybe he was getting a handle on these strange California manners.

"It's nothin'," said Gus.

A muffled roar issued from the bed. Huxtable obviously didn't think it was nothing.

An exasperated huff leaked from Martin. He slewed around to glare at his obstreperous star, who looked not at all starlike at the moment. "It's your own fault, darn it, Horace. If you'd only behave yourself, we wouldn't be forced to take these extreme measures."

Another sound came from the bed.

"You're not only causing all sorts of trouble with the ladies in the cast," Martin went on, heedless of Huxtable's discomfort and anger, "but you're beginning to cost Peerless a lot of money, what with destroying tents and delaying the shooting schedule and all. I don't know if anything can be salvaged from the costume tent, but I know good and well that Mr. Lovejoy will take the cost of repairs out of your salary."

"Grmmph," grunted Huxtable. "Mmmraguh."

"It's not fair to the rest of the cast, who are here to work. I can assure you that neither the cast nor the crew think your antics are funny."

"Mrrrraw!"

"And I can also guarantee that if you don't stop behaving badly, you'll never do another Peerless picture."

Charlie felt like applauding.

More sounds spewed up from the bed.

"What's more, if you jeopardize this production any more than you already have, I'll make sure every major motion picture studio in the United States, from New York to California, knows what happened and who was responsible. And theatrical companies, as well."

This time Charlie felt like cheering and stamping his feet and whistling.

Martin chuffed impatiently. "I'm not putting up with any more nonsense from you. In order to be sure you keep to the line, and as much as I don't want to do it, I'm going to have to post men to watch you, Horace."

"Hrrrrrooogh!" Huxtable's face turned brick red with fury.

Clearly at the end of his tether, Martin snapped, "It's your own damned fault! You refuse to be responsible for yourself, so we're going to assign men to nursemaid you and make sure you don't get into any more trouble." He went so far as to shake a finger at the infuriated actor. "If you're going to misbehave like a spoiled brat, you're going to be treated like one, Horace Huxtable, and you might as well get used to it."

Because he disliked the man a whole lot, Charlie said amicably, "I'm gonna help watch over you, Huxtable. I'm sure I can keep you out of trouble." He smiled and winked at the star.

"Rrrrrrraaaah!"

"You might as well stop trying to yell at us," Martin told Huxtable grumpily. "We can't understand a word, and I've told Gus not to remove that gag until you're under control. We won't tolerate any more nonsense from you."

And with that, Martin turned on his heel and headed out of the tent. Charlie nodded affably at Huxtable, who, he was sure, would have spat at him if he'd been able, and followed Martin. He was feeling fine as he entered the chow tent.

It had been an eventful day, and by rights, Amy should have been exhausted. That evening after supper, though, when the sun had set and several crew members had built a nice big outdoor fire, she discovered herself sitting between Karen Crenshaw and Charlie Fox on a big log in front of the fire.

"It's just like camp," declared Karen.

"Is it?" asked Amy. "I've never been to camp."

"Oh, it was such fun. We used to build fires just like this, and sit around them, singing songs."

It sounded like fun to Amy, who wished her aunt had been more daring and had sent her to some of the summer camps for girls that were run by the suffragists and other organizations. The mere idea of making a spectacle of herself by demanding the vote—or anything at all, for that matter—horrified Amy's aunt, however, and Amy had never gone to camp.

"It's like home to me," Charlie opined, gazing into the fire.

"Is it really?" breathed Amy, who couldn't imagine such a thing. "You mean, you have campfires like this in Arizona Territory?"

He grinned down at her. The firelight picked out the planes and angles of his face, and made him even more handsome than usual. Amy found herself staring, and turned abruptly to look into the fire.

"Sure," he said. "We're on a ranch, and we have to drive the stock to market. It takes time to get from the ranch to the rail heads, and we camp out on the way."

"My goodness. It sounds so . . . so . . ."

"It's like something out of the Wild West," supplied Karen, who didn't sound as entranced by the tale as Amy was.

"I reckon it kind of is the Wild West. Sort of."

Amy dared to glance at him again, since that "sort of" had been somewhat dry. Charlie, who had continued to regard her even after she'd looked away from him, said, "My brother's ranch isn't like a lot of ranches."

"No?"

He shook his head. Since Amy knew nothing at all about ranching, she hardly knew enough to ask questions. She figured a "Why?" was appropriate, so she gave him one.

Charlie shrugged. "Well, it's . . . different, is all. A different kind of ranch, so to speak."

Amy couldn't think of a single question to ask. She didn't

know a solitary thing about regular ranches, much less different kinds of ranches.

"Martin said your brother raises ostriches," said Karen with a laugh. "I thought he must have been making it up."

"Ostriches?" cried Amy. She, too, laughed. "My goodness, what an idea!"

The lengthy silence from Charlie made her laughter dry up, and she stared at him, oblivious to his masculine beauty for the first time since they'd been introduced. "Ostriches?" she repeated. "Honestly?"

"Well, hang it, it's an experiment. I grew up on a cattle ranch, and I think ostriches are a damn fool thing to raise." He shot Amy a guilty look. "Sorry for cussing, ma'am."

She waved his apology aside. Ostriches. Merciful heavens. Mirth bubbled up in her bosom, and she had a time of it not to allow it to hit the air. But Charlie had looked disconcerted about his brother's ostriches, and Amy found in herself a great reluctance to make him more uncomfortable.

After a few moments of silence, Karen sighed and stood up. "I guess I'll be off to bed. I hope the crew has the tent repaired tomorrow so we can finish your costumes, Amy."

"I do, too. Thanks so much for your help today."

Karen smiled down at her. "It's my job."

Amy felt a little silly. "Well, but it's not your job to be nice to actresses who don't know what they're doing, and I appreciate it."

The two women smiled at each other, Karen waved at Charlie and was off, leaving Amy and Charlie side by side on the log. Suddenly Amy felt ill at ease. She'd never been alone with a personable young man for whom she felt some stirrings of emotion. She and Vernon understood each other so completely that she never felt any emotions at all with him. She didn't know what to do about Charlie Fox.

"You can sure see the stars out here," Charlie said after a moment or two.

Silently blessing him for bringing up an innocuous topic, Amy said, "Yes, you can. They're ever so much brighter out here on the desert than they are in Pasadena, even though we aren't a very big city."

"I reckon city lights and smoke and so forth get in the way of the stars, even in small cities."

"I suppose so. Er . . . I imagine you can see them very well in Arizona Territory."

"Yup. They're like diamonds shining in the sky sometimes."

Diamonds in the sky. Wasn't that a poetic analogy? Or did she mean metaphor? Fiddle, she didn't care. "I'd love to see Arizona Territory someday." She was surprised when she heard what she'd said, but when she tested the words, she discovered they were the truth.

"You would?" Charlie sounded surprised too, and Amy didn't appreciate his skepticism.

"Indeed I would. Just because I grew up in a city doesn't mean I haven't often craved wide-open spaces. In fact, I'd love to see more of the world." Good heavens, did she mean *that,* too? By heaven, she did. How astonishing. Perhaps she and Vernon could travel abroad one day.

"Well," Charlie said in his slow drawl after several seconds. "Maybe we can see 'em together someday."

Amy felt her eyes widen enormously. Since she didn't have a clue as to what to say, she remained silent. Her insides, though, bubbled like champagne. When she finally went to her tent—to which Charlie walked her—and pulled the blankets up to her chin, she had a very hard time getting to sleep for the excitement in her soul.

Since she couldn't sleep, she got up and dutifully wrote her letter to Vernon, but the image of Charlie Fox kept sneaking into her brain and she tried to shake it loose. Charlie Fox was an unknown quantity, but Amy knew good and well that he wasn't established securely, like Vernon was. Amy didn't need any mysteries in her life. Mysteries had always meant misery to her. She did notice that she didn't mention Charlie Fox in her letter, although it was filled to the brim with tales of Horace Huxtable.

She didn't mention Charlie's shirt, either.

After she sealed the envelope and affixed a stamp, she still didn't feel sleepy. Instead, she lay under her quilt and thought about what it might be like to live on a ranch in Arizona Territory. With Charlie Fox, the happy-go-lucky cowboy.

And when the occasional disruptive ostrich thrust its ungainly head into her pleasant fantasy, her brain immediately turned it into a cow. While Amy'd had almost as little to do with live cows as she'd had live ostriches, they weren't as disquieting somehow.

The image of Vernon Catesby in cowboy garb, riding a horse and chasing an ostrich, galloped into her head right before her eyelids finally grew heavy, and she went to sleep giggling.

Seven

The guards who had been assigned to dog Horace Hux-table's footsteps were right there beside him when he showed up for the next day's rehearsal. Charlie could clearly tell that Huxtable was trying to make the best of a bad situation. He even felt a little sorry for the obnoxious old coot.

He could also tell that Huxtable was feeling none too chip-per today, due to yesterday's excesses. Served him right.

Of course, Charlie himself wasn't too well rested this morn-ing, either. Which served him right, too, for lying there in his bed, spinning impossible daydreams about Amy Wilkes.

He thought it was a dirty shame that he should have had the opportunity both to see and to feel Amy in so few clothes the day before. Things like that rattled a man's balance. Hell, the finest, most upright fellow might allow his thoughts to slip from the straight and narrow when forced not merely to confront, but to touch, such blatant and lovely femininity.

Charlie considered it right unkind of God to have thrust him into that situation. Maybe it was a test, although if it was, he couldn't conceive why the good Lord was testing him so blamed hard. What possible purpose could it serve God to have Charlie Fox in a state of frustrated sexual arousal for the next few weeks? Charlie resented it.

Martin had called this rehearsal for nine o'clock, and it was to have been a dress rehearsal. Charlie had heard of dress rehearsals. Since Huxtable had ruined the costume tent, a dress rehearsal wasn't possible this morning, so they'd had to delay the shooting schedule for a day, although Martin said he had hopes they could make things go faster after they achieved smooth sailing. Charlie thought that was a diplomatic way of phrasing it, not to mention highly optimistic, all things considered.

Actually, this movie crew was working amazingly hard to get everything put back together again. They were efficient at it, too. The costume tent had been righted already, and now poor Miss Crenshaw was rooting around in it, with assistants, trying to get it back into some kind of shape. Charlie had heard folks voice concerns about some newfangled sewing machine that had got knocked around some. He hoped that, if the machine was broken and needed to be replaced, the cost would come out of Huxtable's pocket. The man was a confounded carbuncle on the seat of society, if you asked Charlie.

"Places, everyone," Martin called through his megaphone. He looked haggard this morning, too, and Charlie vowed to do his best to make Martin's life easier. This was the opening scene, so he had to be in the shot. His job here was to stare soulfully at Amy.

No problem there, dagnabbit.

This morning Amy was clad in a sensible white shirtwaist and a sensible brown skirt. Someone had convinced her that her collar didn't really need to be buttoned up to her chin, and she didn't *have* to wear her tie with it since the weather was hot and there was a lot of standing-around-in-the-sun-and-waiting to be done on a movie set. Charlie suspected that Miss Crenshaw, who seemed like a pragmatic sort even if she did smoke cigarettes—Charlie, too, had been a tiny bit shocked to see a lady smoke, since up until now he'd only seen sporting girls light up—was the one who'd suggested that Amy go a little easier on herself, clothingwise.

He also suspected that Amy still wore a corset, even though

the day promised weather in the 100's. Hot on that thought's heels came the idea that he'd like to investigate her underpinnings and find out for himself.

"Shoot, man, you're hopeless." He chucked his toothpick aside and strode onto the set.

Huxtable didn't even look at him—ashamed of himself, Charlie hoped—but Amy gave him a nice smile. She appeared a bit shy, but her eyes were shining like stars. Charlie swallowed, removed his Stetson, and said, "Howdy, ma'am."

She said "Howdy" back, but she wasn't comfortable with the word. Charlie didn't know whether to consider such a lack of sophistication about the language of his world sweet or unfortunate. His romantic side endorsed the former, but his larger, no-nonsense side leaned toward the latter.

He jumped when he heard his name called and realized he'd been mooning at Amy and not paying attention to Martin. Huxtable snickered. Amy blushed. Charlie, knowing from experience that there was no gainsaying Providence and it was foolish to deny an error that twenty persons had seen, grinned sheepishly. "Sorry, Martin. Got a little moonshine in my eyes this morning and my mind went gallivanting."

"This morning?" Huxtable said under his breath but fully loud enough for Charlie to hear.

"Stop that, Mr. Huxtable," Amy said sharply, scowling at the man.

"No problem, Charlie," said Martin, who either didn't hear Huxtable or chose to ignore him. "Would you move a little closer to the fence? That will make a more artistic shot."

"Artistic, faugh. Not with that big lummox in it." Huxtable sneered.

"Mr. Huxtable, *will* you be quiet?" Amy scowled.

Hmmm. It sounded to Charlie as if his two co-stars weren't ready to toss out their grievances yet. He feared their mutual dislike might affect the rehearsal. While he wouldn't mind being in Amy's company for hours or even days, he'd rather do it somewhere that wasn't so blasted hot and public—and so filled with strife and animosity. He smiled at her and mouthed, "Don't get riled. He's just an old poop."

He wasn't sure if his assessment of Huxtable shocked or amused her, but she did give him an answering smile, so that was fine and dandy. He moseyed to the fence and turned. "This okay?"

"The pose is fine. Look casual," instructed Martin.

Charlie decided the best way to do that was to adopt a pose familiar to everyone on an Arizona ranch. He hitched his elbow over the top rail, lifted his left boot and rested it on the lowest fence board, and sort of draped himself. In Charlie's experience, which was considerable, that was the most comfortable posture a man could assume while standing.

"All right," said Martin. "Perfect. Horace, you come into the picture from the left and go over to talk to Charlie. He's your foreman, remember, and you trust him."

"The more fool, I," Huxtable growled.

Charlie had to give the great oaf credit. As soon as he set foot onto the set, he was his character. Damned if he didn't look exactly like this Luke McAllister fellow whom he was supposed to be. Since Charlie's character was supposed to be trying to undermine McAllister's ranching operation while attempting to steal McAllister's girl from him, Charlie guessed it wouldn't be amiss to try to look the part. He recalled a fellow named Eli Grant who had turned out to be a thoroughgoing scoundrel although everyone, at first, had believed him to be a nice man. Charlie did his best to emulate old Eli.

"Don't look so sinister, Charlie. At this point, nobody knows you're a snake in the grass."

"I do," said Huxtable—to no one's surprise, evidently, because nobody called him to task. Amy humphed off-screen, but that was all right. Charlie'd talk to her later.

"But the guy is sinister, isn't he?" Charlie would never argue with Martin, who knew what he was doing, but he thought the question wouldn't be out of place since he wanted to do a good job here and he really needed to know.

"Right. But nobody knows it yet except you. Remember, the audience hasn't read the script."

"Right." That made sense to Charlie.

Huxtable gave him a superior smirk. That made sense to Charlie, too, since Huxtable was a miserable, low-life, belly-crawling polecat. He didn't react, but smoothed his sinister expression out to reflect nothing but blandness and goodwill. The way Eli Grant had appeared when he'd first arrived on the scene and before he'd proven his snakishness beyond all doubt.

"Oh, I get it!" he cried, enlightenment having stricken him hard.

"Good," said Martin with a smile.

"God," muttered Huxtable. Charlie decided to pretend Horace had left out the second *o* by accident. Life was less troublesome that way.

Amy hissed, "Honestly!" from the wings.

He'd definitely have to talk with her at lunchtime. The way Charlie had it figured, the more people reacted to Huxtable, the worse he got. What with bodyguards standing around everywhere, Charlie imagined Horace would not be able to get himself off alone and get drunk. Besides, he'd drunk all the vanilla extract in the kitchen quarters yesterday.

If, in addition to the bodyguards, folks stopped reacting to his offensive asides and smirking looks, maybe he'd get tired of being such a hound dog. Charlie tossed Amy a smile, hoping it conveyed at least part of his message. Since she was at present glaring at Horace Huxtable, the smile went for naught. Charlie sighed and resumed his pose.

"I imagine I'm supposed to ask you if you've seen Miss

Priscilla—Miss Wilkes to you, if your brain hasn't figured out her name's supposed to be Priscilla in this picture," Huxtable said as he approached Charlie.

Charlie peered at him and was astounded to see that his facial expression was perfect for a boss merely asking a subordinate a civil question. This acting stuff was weird. Trying to play his part, he said, "I reckon you are, Mr. Huxtable."

"No, no, no!" Huxtable stopped walking and looked aggrieved. He even put his fists on his hips. "For the love of Christ, man, don't say my name. If the audience has never seen a motion picture before, they've at least seen people say my name. The slowest person in the world will be able to lipread that much."

The conceited bastard. Charlie heard Amy growl, "Vanity. All is vanity in that man," and he decided that for today at least, it would be best for him not to react to Huxtable's provocations, no matter how severe. "Reckon you're right, Mr. H." He even managed a fairly good imitation of a smile.

"Mr. H. is just as bad," Huxtable snarled.

"That so? I wonder. After all, an H could stand for horse's ass just as easily as Huxtable." Charlie's smile didn't waver, but he did mentally kick himself in the butt. Poor Martin would never get this picture made if the cast took to feuding. As it was, Huxtable's jaw was a livid yellow-green and still swollen. Charlie felt kind of guilty about that—but not very.

Through gritted teeth, Huxtable muttered, "Just say the name as it's supposed to be in the script if you can't think of anything else to say, you unmitigated oaf."

Fortunately, Charlie wasn't sure what unmitigated meant, so he managed to shrug off the oaf part without much trouble.

"You'd better just call him McAllister," Martin suggested from his director's chair. He smiled sympathetically, so Charlie decided to do it that way. As much fun as it might be to provoke Huxtable, he didn't want to make Martin's life any rougher than it already was. Or delay shooting, which Huxtable was doing quite nicely all by himself.

Charlie gave Martin a salute. "Will do."

"All right, let's start again." Martin's relief was visible.

Huxtable stalked off the set, looking pained. Charlie didn't perceive any reason for Horace to be peeved, as he must know that Charlie and Amy both were new at this moviemaking business. Nevertheless, Charlie assumed his former insouciant pose and gazed off into the distance—which was at present full of tents and people and didn't look at all ranchlike.

With a smile that seemed absolutely genuine, Huxtable again walked onto the set. "I see you're gazing at the tents. Planning a nap, are we?"

Charlie turned and plastered an almost-genuine smile on his own face. "No, sir, Mr. McAllister. Just wondering how much it's costing to make this picture."

"More money than you'll ever see, no doubt."

Since it was meant as a low blow, Charlie countered with a fake. "You're probably right, Mr. McAllister. Some of us work hard for not much pay, unlike you picture folks."

"Unlike those of us with talent in our bones, you mean?"

"If you take that to mean acting talent and experience, I reckon you're right."

"It takes little skill to use one's muscles." Huxtable brushed a dot of dust from his shoulder.

"Oh, this is ridiculous!" Amy cried. "Can't you make him stop taunting the other actors, Mr. Tafft? He's being hateful!"

Charlie heard Martin's enormous sigh from where he stood. He turned and shook his head at Amy, but she wasn't looking at him. She looked charmingly indignant, actually, and all of that precious female indignation was being expended on his account. Charlie thought that was sweet. He also wished she'd kept her rosy lips shut.

"It's all right, Martin," he said pleasantly. "I'm used to it.

Poor Mr. Huxtable here hasn't got any manners, and I reckon the whole crew knows it by this time."

"You're very understanding, Charlie," Martin told him. He turned to Huxtable. "Horace, can't you please forget your differences and follow the script? You're making this very difficult for all of us."

Huxtable drew himself up tall. He was still five or so inches shorter than Charlie, which gave Charlie a deplorable sense of pride, but at present Huxtable was looking as vain as the very devil. Charlie thought the comparison as apt as any he could have come up with if he'd thought about it for a week.

"*I,*" Huxtable intoned in his best stage actor's voice, "am the star of this motion picture. Without *me,* the thing will be a total flop."

"That's nonsense and you know it," Martin said, finally losing his temper. "Folks will flock to see anything nowadays. I have a good mind to throw you out on your ear and let Charlie take the hero's role. He'd look a darned sight better in the role than you do."

Aw, horse turds. Charlie wished Martin hadn't said that. It was difficult enough dealing with Huxtable without the man getting jealous, too. "He don't mean that, Mr. H.," Charlie said gently. "Everybody knows you're the star of this thing."

Huxtable had started to nod regally when Amy's voice sang out from the sidelines. "What a wonderful idea, Mr. Tafft! Wouldn't that be grand? No more salacious innuendos. No more drunken rampages. No more ruined tents. No more delays and so forth. Why, I think it's a *splendid* notion!"

Crap. Charlie turned and gave Amy a very small frown. Not that he didn't appreciate her sentiments on the issue; he simply wanted to get this picture finished some day in this century. She caught his glance this time, and blinked at him as if she couldn't understand his attitude. He'd be happy to explain it over lunch. Right now he wanted her to shut up.

Turning back to Huxtable, he said, "She don't mean it either, Mr. H. They're both a little put off by your shenanigans, is all. Miss Wilkes doesn't understand that there's more to this acting business than standing around and looking silly in front of a camera. I'm sure she'd see the difference if I was to take over your role." He choked out a fairly successful laugh of self-deprecation. "Why, can you feature it?"

Huxtable eyed him from Stetson to boots. "No," he said haughtily. "I cannot."

"Well, then," Charlie said, giving Huxtable a sizable pat on his shoulder. "There we go."

Staggering slightly, Huxtable glared at him. "Keep your dirty hands to yourself, *if* you please."

"Yes, sir." Because his anger had begun to rise and he feared he'd pop the star again if he didn't watch himself, Charlie smiled innocently and turned away. Because he didn't trust himself within slugging range of Huxtable, he moseyed over to where Amy stood.

Her pretty eyebrows were lowered, and she looked as if she were mad at him now. With an internal sigh, Charlie decided he just couldn't win this game.

"I don't know why you're trying to be so nice to that big bully!"

"Well, ma'am," Charlie said reasonably. "I sure don't like him."

"I should say not!"

"But I *do* want to get home one of these days."

She glanced sharply at him, her frown in place. "What do you mean?"

"I think we ought to try to ignore him. He's only saying these things to get a rise out of us, and that only delays the process of making this picture. Poor Mr. Tafft would probably appreciate it if we'd just get on with business."

Her lips pressed together and she appeared unconvinced.

"Well, I don't see *him* trying to cooperate with Mr. Tafft." She jerked her head in the direction of Huxtable.

Charlie sighed. "No, ma'am. He seems to be doing everything he can to make everybody miserable." Sudden insight made him add, "I sure don't want to be anything like him, though, so I believe I'll just go along with Mr. Tafft's instructions and try to ignore Huxtable's meanness."

"Oh." Amy's frown eased some. "I see what you mean. No, one doesn't want to be anything at all like *him,* does one?"

"No, ma'am. One sure doesn't." Charlie wasn't accustomed to speaking of himself in the third person, but he acknowledged himself to be innocent of city manners.

Amy huffed, which lifted her bosom deliciously under her frothy white blouse. Charlie, remembering the pressure of that delightful bosom against his chest, tried not to stare. "You're right, of course. I understand. It's galling, though."

"It sure is."

"Places!" Martin called.

With a smile for Amy, Charlie strolled back onto the set. They managed to get through the morning without too many more delays. By the time the luncheon gong sounded, Karen Crenshaw had arrived at the set, looking as if she'd spent a trying and tiring morning. Charlie saw her conferring with Martin, who seemed happy with whatever news she'd brought him. He supposed the sewing machine had survived yesterday's crash.

As soon as he heard the bell, Charlie hurried over to Amy. She'd accredited herself admirably during the morning's rehearsal, refusing to give in to her impulse to react to Huxtable or to scold him. Charlie knew, because her face so vividly expressed her emotions, that it had been a struggle for her to maintain her composure. He wanted to express his appreciation.

"Can I walk you to lunch, Miss Wilkes?" he asked politely.

She smiled at him. "Thank you, Mr. Fox. That would be nice. I think I'd better visit my tent first, if you don't mind."

"Not at all."

It was hot as a firecracker today and there was no shade under which he could wait for Amy, but he waited patiently anyway, mopping his brow with his big red bandanna every three seconds or so. She didn't take long, thank God.

When she exited her tent, she was folding a paper and replacing it into an envelope. Charlie knew that the mail pouch was generally delivered from El Monte around lunchtime, and he imagined Amy had received a letter. He didn't like the frown on her face, or the way her brow was wrinkled. In fact, she looked kind of distressed, and he experienced a mad urge to slay whoever it was whose letter had distressed her.

"Everything all right, ma'am?" he asked solicitously.

Her head lifted quickly, and she seemed to make an effort to smile. "Oh, yes. Thank you." She waved the envelope. "I just received a letter from Pasadena."

From Pasadena. Not from home? "Who's it from?" He wondered if it was impolite to ask.

"My fiancé, Mr. Vernon Catesby. He's a banker in Pasadena," Amy said distractedly.

Her fiancé. Shoot. "I—er—didn't know you had a fiancé," he mumbled, feeling a sickish sensation spread in his middle.

"Well," she equivocated, "we're not formally engaged, but we've had an understanding for some time now."

Whatever that meant. Charlie allowed himself to wonder if Amy's beau had written something disagreeable. He felt a fierce compulsion to beat Mr. Vernon, the banker, Catesby about the head and shoulders. "I hope the letter contained good news," he ventured, knowing already that his hope was for naught.

He noticed that her lips grimmed up for a second before she said, "Yes. Fine. Thank you."

As much as he'd have liked to pump her for information, Charlie knew it wasn't his place to do so. If, however, he ever learned that Mr. Catesby had written anything unkind to Amy, Charlie'd do something about it. He didn't know what, but he knew he'd have to do *something*.

"Ready for the chow tent?"

"All ready," she said brightly. Charlie saw that she'd brushed her hair and washed her face. He wished he'd thought to do that. He felt kind of grubby.

They sat with Martin and Karen at lunch. Charlie noticed that Amy was doing better with the luncheon sandwiches provided for the cast and crew of the picture. She no longer hesitated to open the sandwich up and pick out its contents. Her pretty little mouth was too delicate to bite into such a gigantic sandwich whole. With a sigh, he thought he'd like to investigate her mouth for himself. He knew, although he didn't know how he knew, that Mr. Catesby would never appreciate it properly.

"We'll rehearse the sawmill scene tomorrow, Amy," Charlie heard Martin say, and he turned to listen. Far better to listen to Martin than to daydream about kissing Amy Wilkes or punching Vernon Catesby. More profitable, too, since he'd assuredly need to follow Martin's instructions long before he ever got around to Amy's lips, if such a delightful prospect ever did come to him.

"Where will that take place?" Amy asked, her eyes bright with interest. She seemed to have put the letter out of her mind, a circumstance of which Charlie approved wholeheartedly. Doggone, she had pretty eyes.

"We've managed to find a tumbledown building farther out

on the desert. I suspect it was used by prospectors in the old days. It's a mess, but it will serve our purpose beautifully."

Amy fiddled with her milk glass. "Er—will there be a real saw?"

With a laugh, Martin said, "No. We won't risk our star's skin on a real saw."

She laughed, too. "I must say I'm very glad to hear it."

Charlie suppressed his agreement. He didn't like to think of Amy in peril, even fake peril for a motion picture.

"It'll probably be uncomfortable, though," Martin went on. "The weather's insufferable, and inside the building it will be even hotter, even though we've removed one wall because we have to set up lights and so forth. I fear it's going to be awfully hot and stuffy, but we'll try not to take too long in rehearsal. Then we can shoot the scene and get it over with, and we won't have to work indoors any longer. Karen can take your costume out to the set with us in the morning, and you can change there."

"I see."

Amy nodded, although Charlie perceived she still wasn't sure what the morrow would bring. Neither was he, for that matter. All of this moviemaking stuff was alien to his experience of life. Hers too, he realized, and he felt suddenly closer to her.

Which was stupid, and he'd better not dwell on it, since their lives were, in reality, worlds apart, with precious little chance of them ever coming together.

"This will be the first scene we'll shoot." Martin shared a glance with Amy and Charlie. "I'm sure you'll both find the experience interesting."

"I'm sure," Amy said uncertainly.

"I'm looking forward to it." Charlie, on the other hand, meant it. He enjoyed new experiences, even if they weren't awfully comfortable while they were happening. He liked learning stuff. And it would be lots of fun to tell stories later, to his brothers and pals on the ranch.

Amy, he deduced, would rather be back home in Pasadena and forget all about picturemaking. She didn't seem keen on new experiences. Which was another huge difference between them. The notion didn't cheer him. Neither did the notion of her and the banker settling down together. It sounded like a mortally dull life to him. He'd rather take his chances with the ranching business.

The afternoon's rehearsal went more smoothly than the morning's had. Charlie thought the relative ease of the afternoon was due in large part to Horace Huxtable's state of health. He appeared to feel rotten, and he was obviously very weary. Behaving badly evidently took a good deal of energy, and Charlie was glad he'd never decided to play the part of a bad boy.

Martin cut the rehearsal short when an unexpected caravan entered the encampment, stirring up dust and excitement. He could scarcely believe his eyes when Phineas Lovejoy, his best friend and the monetary brain behind the Peerless Studio, chugged into the tent city in his Pierce Arrow Special shortly after two in the afternoon. Hot as it was, Martin raced toward the automobile.

"Phin!" He didn't have to feign his joy. This picture had been rough so far, and it was less than a week old. He really wanted to talk to Phineas about it.

"Martin, old chum!"

The two men embraced. Martin saw his second leading man eyeing them oddly, and deduced therefrom that men did not hug each other in Arizona Territory.

"I've brought Ricardo with me, Marty," Phineas said, sweeping his arm out to indicate a swarthy gent with bowed legs. "He finished the stunts for *Arabian Nights,* and we need him for *Marching Along* next week. Thought I'd drive him up today. That way he can teach Miss Wilkes how to ride a horse, and we can talk. I guess things haven't gone too well so far." He glanced slantways at Horace Huxtable.

"I'm really glad you're here, Phin." Martin smiled at Ricardo Archuleta, whom he'd known for several years. Ricardo was a superlative horseman, a pretty good teacher, and an old grump. Martin liked him. "Hello, Rick. How are you?"

Archuleta nodded without smiling, which was typical. "Fine, fine. I'm supposed to teach the lady in this picture how to ride a horse." He squinted at the set. "Which one is she?"

"Miss Wilkes is the one with the reddish hair, standing next to the tall cowboy."

Archuleta grunted as if he wasn't impressed.

"Right." Martin pondered for a moment. Horace Huxtable was seated in a camp chair under a scrubby tree, looking sulky. Amy Wilkes and Charlie Fox were both watching the goings-on with interest. Martin realized that the two seemed to gravitate toward each other when nothing else was going on, and was pleased. Maybe they were beginning to get along better than they had at first. "I suppose you want to work fast."

Archuleta nodded.

Phineas said, "Yes. I'm afraid we won't be able to stay long. I'm hoping Miss Wilkes will be a quick study." He gave Martin an inquiring look, which Martin chose to ignore. They could talk later.

Archuleta huffed, as if to say he didn't believe Amy Wilkes could learn to ride a horse if she tried for the rest of her life.

Martin came to a decision. "Why don't we begin lessons now? I'm sure Miss Wilkes would appreciate taking a break in the rehearsal." He gestured for Amy to join them. After shooting an apprehensive glance at Charlie, she walked over. "Yes, Mr. Tafft?"

Martin hoped that before the picture was wrapped up and in the can, she'd unbend enough to call him Martin, although he wasn't going to hold his breath. He gave her a warm smile. Given the state of the weather, it was the only kind he could drum up. "Amy, please allow me to introduce you to Mr. Ricardo Archuleta, the finest riding instructor in Southern California. Mr. Archuleta's going to teach you how to ride a horse for the picture."

"Oh." She gazed at him blankly, then transferred her vacant gaze to Archuleta. Recovering her composure slightly, she held out her hand to him. "How do you do?"

Archuleta frowned at her and gave her hand a grudging shake. "Fine, fine." He eyed her up and down, scowling critically the whole time.

Amy noticed his critical stare, clearly disliked it, and frowned back.

Rats. Martin, who had known Ricardo Archuleta for a long time, feared the man had already assessed Amy's ability to ride a horse as being less than spectacular—and he hadn't even begun giving her lessons. Unfortunately, Archuleta was almost uncannily correct in his evaluations of people and their skill with horses. When the wrinkled old Mexican heaved a lusty, dispirited sigh, Martin's fears were confirmed.

"This," said Archuleta in a gloomy accent, "will take some time. I hope there's enough."

Amy smiled brightly. Martin exchanged an anxious glance with Phineas Lovejoy. Horace Huxtable snorted loudly from his chair under the tree. Charlie Fox moseyed over and grinned at Archuleta, who didn't grin back.

Just this once, Martin thought, he'd really like for things regarding *One and Only* to go right.

"I won't have no cowboy interfering with my instructions," Archuleta announced to nobody in particular.

In that instant, Martin knew, if he hadn't before, that Amy's riding lessons weren't going to be that once.

Eight

While it was true that Amy'd never had much to do with horses, it was also true that she wasn't afraid of them. At least she hadn't been before now.

She hadn't realized, as she'd watched them plod sedately along, pulling wagons and surreys and so forth on the pleasantly shady streets of Pasadena, that horses were such large animals. They'd always looked rather sweet and graceful to Amy as she observed them from a sidewalk or a porch.

But when one got right up next to a horse, one realized that horses were large. Very large. Really, Amy didn't think a horse needed to be quite so big.

This one didn't seem like a particularly pleasant example of the equine race, either. At the moment it was giving her a steady, beady stare—more of a scowl, actually—and Amy sensed that it didn't like her. She also feared that the expression of antipathy on the horse's face boded ill for her success as a horsewoman.

Whatever would Charlie Fox think of her if she fell off of this excessively tall animal? Dismal thought. She thrust it aside, much as she'd thrust aside Vernon's letter earlier in the day. Drat Vernon Catesby to goodness. He had no business writing her such upsetting letters. Thrusting him aside yet again, Amy regarded the horse.

She swallowed. "I've—er—never been this close to a horse

before." She offered Mr. Archuleta a shaky smile. He glowered back. Oh, dear. "I, ah, had no idea horses were so large."

"This is a pony," he said. "A baby. A tiny thing."

She gaped at him for a moment. "It looks quite large to me."

He shrugged, said, "No. Small horse," and turned to do something to the animal's saddle.

Amy thought she detected contempt in his tone, and she resented it. It wasn't her fault she was born into a civilized community and had always had more to do with streetcars and trolleys than with horses.

She glanced around, trying to find Charlie Fox. She didn't see him and wasn't sure if she was glad or not. Overall, she supposed she'd as soon he not witness her humiliation. On the other hand, she thought she'd detected some rather flattering interest in her person on his part, and she was disappointed that he hadn't cared enough to watch this farce.

This lesson. She meant this lesson.

She squared her shoulders. Amy Wilkes was as capable as the next person. Surely she could learn to ride a horse. The horse continued to eye her unblinkingly, and her confidence, not awfully strong to begin with, sank further.

Thank heaven Karen had come over to watch. Simply knowing that Karen was her friend, and that she was there for her, gave Amy courage.

Karen had helped Amy change into the split skirt she now wore. Amy liked the skirt; it was really rather dashing, and she looked good in it. She only hoped it would preserve her modesty if she ever managed to mount this beast.

"Don't be afraid of the animal," Archuleta, who'd finished with the saddle, commanded. As if she had a choice in the matter. "You're his master, he's not your master."

Technically, she was supposed to be the horse's *mistress,* but Amy decided not to correct the little Spanish fellow's English. She sensed he wouldn't appreciate it, and she already had a strong suspicion that he didn't approve of her. It was an odd sensation to Amy, who'd always been thoroughly respectable and had never experienced this sort of blatant disapproval before.

Well, except for Vernon, who disapproved of her current endeavor. He'd made that perfectly clear in his letter, if she'd had any doubt.

At any rate, she didn't like the feeling of being disapproved of one teensy bit.

Where was Charlie Fox, blast it? She shook her head, ridding it of irrelevant side issues. She had a horse to conquer at the moment, and Vernon wasn't here. Neither was Charlie Fox. Blast it.

"Right. Don't be afraid." She licked her lips and lifted her chin. She could do this.

Archuleta gave her a short illustrated lesson in mounting, then said, "Put your hand on the saddle horn like I showed you."

He squinted at her with small dark eyes that reminded Amy of ripe olives. His skin was dark, too, and he had about a zillion crows' feet radiating from around his eyes. Obviously, he'd spent lots of time in the sun, presumably bending horses' wills to his own.

Which was not important at the moment. What was important was to learn to ride this wretched giant. The realization that Mr. Archuleta was no taller than she comforted her, and she braced herself. If a short gentleman could ride a horse, surely a short lady could. Sucking in another big breath and praying silently that she wouldn't kill herself, she put her hand, protected by a worn leather glove Karen had found in the costume tent, on the saddle horn.

Archuleta handed her the reins, and she took them the way

he'd demonstrated. He nodded, Amy assumed for encouragement's sake, then said, "Put your foot in the stirrup."

She lifted her foot.

"No!"

The instructor's harsh cry startled her, which startled the horse, which made them both shuffle awkwardly. Archuleta rolled his eyes. "Your other foot."

"Oh." Good heavens, he was speaking to her through gritted teeth. Was she *that* incompetent? Swallowing again, she vowed to try harder. "The other foot. Right."

"Right. Otherwise you'd be riding backwards."

"Oh. Of course." She felt like an idiot. "Sorry."

It took Archuleta a moment or two to settle the horse. Amy could have sworn the animal was now sneering at her. Its expression reminded her of Horace Huxtable's when he was being naughty.

"Try again." Archuleta's expression was grim. Amy believed that a truly superior teacher wouldn't allow doubt in his student's ability to show.

She attempted to ignore her instructor's expression as she again placed her hand on the saddle horn and lifted her foot—the correct foot this time—to the stirrup. The horse moved sideways. She lost her balance and fell against it.

A horse smelled very—horsy—when one's nose was pressed against its belly. She withdrew her nose from the horse's hide and attempted to straighten up. Since her heel seemed to be caught in the stirrup, this entailed quite a bit of jumping up and down on her other foot. She heard someone—she assumed it was Mr. Archuleta—sigh heavily, and tried not to hate him for it.

Thank God he stopped sighing and restrained the horse from prancing about. She was out of breath and panting when she finally regained her balance. She cleared her throat. "Um, the horse moved before I could leap up."

There he went again, into that eye-rolling routine. Amy frowned at him. Disregarding her frown, he growled, "You don't *leap* up. You lift your body into the saddle. You don't have to leap."

She wished he wouldn't talk about bodies in that casual way. Amy wasn't used to such loose language. She also didn't understand how she was supposed to *lift* her body into the saddle without leaping. Nonetheless, she'd agreed to do this picture, and she aimed to see it through, no matter how horrible the experience was. "I'm trying, Mr. Archuleta. I truly am."

"Sí." He nodded gloomily. "You're trying, all right."

She squinted at him, wondering if he'd meant that the way she suspected he did. She decided not to press the issue. "Shall we try again?"

Archuleta shrugged, as if it didn't matter to him what she did. "I get paid. Sure."

Although his attitude echoed her own, it somehow seemed to contain an element of exasperation which Amy didn't appreciate. Before she could brace up her courage and tackle the reins and saddle and animal again, she and Archuleta were interrupted.

"Howdy, folks."

Amy's heart gave a gigantic leap when she heard Charlie Fox's voice behind her. She glanced up quickly, saw that he was smiling kindly upon her, and wished he'd take over her horsemanship lessons. She had a feeling he was more kindly disposed toward her than Mr. Archuleta, who was impatient with her naivete regarding horses as well as with her awkwardness around them. And, since neither of those attributes were her fault, she thought he was being needlessly unpleasant.

Archuleta said, "I don't need no cowboy telling her things

I don't want her to know." His tone was flat, as if he expected Charlie to comply with his edict at once and go away.

Charlie scratched his head and grinned down at the much smaller man. Amy was impressed, both by Charlie's size and by his congeniality. Mr. Archuleta hadn't spoken nicely at all. As for her, she seized her moment of reprieve to back away from the monstrous horse—thank God, thank God—fold her hands at her waist, and watch.

"Well, now, Mr. Archuleta, Martin's told me that you're one of the finest riding instructors in California, and I sure don't want to interfere."

Archuleta nodded sharply. "Good."

"But, you see, Miss Wilkes here has never been close to a horse before, and she's a little nervous."

"Yes, exactly," Amy said at once, gratified that Charlie understood, even if her teacher didn't.

Archuleta shrugged. "Horses are easy." He gave Amy a crabby look. "Like most women."

Amy felt her eyes go wide, but opted not to voice her protest, believing silence in this instance to be the better part of prudence. She didn't like him very well, though. In fact, she didn't like him at all. Why were motion picture people so difficult?

"It appears to me," Charlie continued in his easy, friendly drawl, "that Miss Wilkes might be better off getting to know the horse first, and then maybe how it feels to sit in the saddle, before you teach her how to climb up onto one."

Archuleta's eyes squinched up as he thought about it. Amy, too, thought about it and decided Charlie was brilliant. "My goodness, yes!" she cried. "What a famous idea. That way I'll know what I'm aiming for." She noticed Archuleta's expression of sour bewilderment and smiled at him. "So to speak."

"Just for a minute or two," urged Charlie gently. "Until she's comfortable on the horse."

"This is stupid," Archuleta declared, and turned to search the encampment, Amy presumed for Martin Tafft. Karen caught her eye, grinned at her, and gave her a thumbs-up signal, and she appreciated her new friend a lot.

"Why don't you go find Martin?" Charlie suggested. "We can see what he thinks about the idea."

"Yeah, I better," Archuleta growled, and turned to slouch away.

Charlie winked at Amy, then turned to watch the riding instructor as he made his extremely bowlegged way to the tent village.

Amy put her hand on Charlie's arm. "Thanks so much, Mr. Fox. That man was making me wildly nervous." She glanced at the horse, who had taken to snuffling the ground in search, she presumed, of comestibles. It didn't look to her as if it was going to have much luck in the endeavor. "And," she confessed after a second, "I'm nervous about the horse, too."

He nodded kindly. "I understand."

She gazed up into his lovely brown eyes. "Do you really? Mr. Archuleta didn't."

"You're not used to horses."

"No," she said on a relieved sigh. "I'm not."

"You've never been on one before?"

It was a legitimate question, and Amy shook her head. "No. I've never even been this close to one before."

"Well, why don't we try to get you used to this one while Archuleta is complaining to Martin?"

"Oh, dear, do you think he's going to complain?"

His lazy grin warmed her already warm heart. "I 'spect so. He don't seem to like cowboys much."

"He don't—doesn't like me much, either," Amy said.

With a start, she realized that she'd stuffed Mr. Archuleta

and Vernon Catesby into the same compartment in her mind—the one labeled "fusspots." How odd.

"So how's about I lift you up onto this thing's back, and you can see how it feels to sit a horse?"

Charlie's sensible suggestion drew Amy's thoughts back to the problem at hand. She eyed the horse again. "All right." She wasn't looking forward to viewing the world from on top of that brute. She didn't care for heights.

"Turn around, please."

She turned around and a second later felt Charlie's big, competent hands go around her waist. Unprepared for the thrill that shot through her at his touch, she shut her eyes and held her breath until he'd settled her in the saddle. It wasn't ladylike to ride astride, she guessed, but Karen had told her that modern women often did. Otherwise, nobody would have invented split skirts. Besides, horseback riding was safer and more comfortable that way.

On that sensible and practical thought, she dared to open her eyes—and gasped.

Charlie was right there beside her, holding the horse's reins with one hand. He'd settled his other hand on the horse's neck. Amy's hands were clutching the saddle horn as if it were her only link to life.

"You all right, ma'am?"

She tried to swallow, but all of her spit had dried up, so she nodded instead. Then she shook her head, closed her eyes, tried to slow her breathing, and opened them again. "Um . . . I'm not sure."

"It's a long way up there, isn't it?"

His easy smile, silky drawl, and twinkly eyes were all that currently kept Amy from breaking into shrieks of terror, so she stared into his face, petrified. "Yes." It was a mere whisper of air, and she almost didn't hear it herself.

"Just take it easy," he suggested. "Horses are pretty dumb

animals. This old boy wants his pasture, I reckon, and isn't happy to be in school this afternoon."

"Neither am I."

Charlie chuckled softly. "We'll try to make your experience not too rough. Okay?"

She nodded again, unable to make herself say "Okay" in response, but unwilling to say anything less casual. Her heart was beating a crazy tattoo against her ribs, her tongue was trying to cleave to the roof of her mouth, and she feared she was in imminent danger of fainting from sheer fright. Her head felt swimmy from the altitude.

"Here," Charlie said, never altering the tone of his voice. "Why don't you hold on to these for a second or two? Just to get used to them." He held the reins out to her.

Amy stared at them, petrified. Merciful God, he was going to leave her to her own devices on top of this enormous beast. He was relinquishing the reins to her. Did he *want* her to die? Too unnerved to speak, she managed to unstick one of her hands from the saddle horn long enough to grab the reins. Immediately, her hand went back to the saddle horn, reins and all. She heard Charlie sigh, even as another voice came to them from several yards off.

"Oh, yes, I see."

She dared to turn her head slightly at the sound and saw Martin, whose voice it was. He was approaching with Mr. Archuleta limping at his side. Why was he limping? Was it because a horse had injured him? If so, why hadn't anyone told Amy about it? After all, if horses were so dangerous that they created limps in competent riders, somebody ought to have warned her.

"Howdy, Martin," Charlie said in his usual amiable drawl. "We're getting Miss Wilkes accustomed to this here animal."

After trying thrice, Amy managed to swallow and say, "Yes." Her voice was high-pitched and somewhat squeaky.

She tried to clear her throat, but couldn't summon enough spit.

Martin, who didn't seem at all put out, a circumstance for which Amy was extremely thankful, smiled and nodded. "So I see. How's it going, Amy?"

"All right," she squeezed out. She realized that both of her hands were still clamped like talons to the saddle horn, and she made an effort to unclamp them. They didn't want to be unclamped. Failing in the endeavor, she attempted a smile for Martin. That didn't work, either. Fiddle.

"I think she needs to get used to the horse for a few minutes before she tries to mount," Charlie told Martin. "I lifted her up so she could see how it feels to sit in the saddle."

Archuleta huffed, but Martin said, "Sounds reasonable." He eyed Amy critically.

Amy, who was now experiencing a mortifying impulse to burst into tears, gave a jerky nod and hoped she didn't look as pitiful as she felt.

"In fact," Martin said, and there was a trace of concern in his expression, "maybe it would be better if Charlie took over for a little while here. Would that be all right with you, Amy?"

She managed another short nod, but couldn't form words. Martin smiled at her encouragingly.

"I don't want no cowboy interfering with my lessons," Archuleta said stubbornly.

With a placating gesture and a gentle smile, Martin said, "I'm sure Charlie doesn't want to interfere. But Miss Wilkes and he know each other already, and maybe he can get her accustomed to the horse before you begin teaching her the finer points of riding."

"Finer points?" Archuleta's voice rose. "What finer points? She don't even know how to mount!"

"She'll be able to learn better when she's comfortable with the animal."

That was Charlie, and, though he spoke reasonably, Amy thought she detected a note of steel in his voice. She hoped so, because if she were left to the tender mercies of Mr. Archuleta, she feared she'd collapse from fright. She was about to pass out now, if it came to that. She couldn't recall another single time in her life when she'd been more afraid—not even when her parents had left her. She'd been too young to understand then, but she wasn't any longer.

"I don't like it," Archuleta declared. "It don't make no sense. I'm supposed to be the teacher."

"You're still the teacher," Charlie assured him.

To Amy's horror, he withdrew his hand from the horse's neck and took a step closer to Martin and Mr. Archuleta. She would have cried out but couldn't get her mouth, lips, and tongue coordinated. She wanted to shriek at him not to leave her. The horse moved, and everything in her froze into a solid lump of panic.

"I don't want to be nobody's teacher if I got to have a cowboy interfering."

Charlie moved another step away from Amy and the monster. She tried to protest, but the horse moved under her, and her protest was drowned in a haze of terror. Good God in heaven, the thing was beginning to walk! Unable to think—her thought processes had congealed along with everything else within her—she held on to the saddle horn for dear life.

As Charlie, Martin, and Mr. Archuleta conversed—Charlie and Martin amiably, Mr. Archuleta with much hand-waving and angry shouting—Amy and her mount ambled along. Only it didn't feel like an amble to Amy. It felt like a death march. A funeral dirge. An elegy to Amy Wilkes, whose life on this green earth had been short, but sweet for the most part.

She'd miss her aunt and uncle. She'd miss Charlie Fox—she wished she'd been able to get to know him better; she believed they might have found they had a good deal in common underneath their surface differences. She'd miss her friends in Pasadena. She'd miss Martin Tafft. She'd miss Karen Crenshaw, even if she did smoke cigarettes.

She wasn't altogether sure she'd miss Vernon Catesby, because she was annoyed with him and wished she'd had more time to deal with her feelings about that wretched letter. She was pretty sure he'd miss her.

A sob broke from her as the horse reached the fence. Was it going to try to leap over it? If it did, Amy knew she'd fall off.

But wait. Didn't horses have to take running starts before they jumped over things? Amy prayed it was so. Her relief was incalculable—and inexpressible, since she still couldn't talk—when instead of leaping, the horse turned and moved along the fence, as if it were looking for a gate. Thank God, thank God. Maybe it wasn't as stupid as Charlie thought if it was looking for a gate.

After what seemed like thirteen days but could only have been a minute at most, Amy realized that she wasn't falling off of the horse's back. Not only that, but the horse, although entirely too tall for any useful purpose in life, didn't seem to have a truly evil spirit in it, as Amy had at first feared. Actually, it seemed . . . well . . . sort of relaxed. Placid. Lazy, even. It halted every few steps to nuzzle the ground in search of green stuff to eat. There wasn't any, since this was the middle of the desert in the middle of summer.

With that realization came the understanding that she, who held the reins, might actually be able to control this equine fiend. She wasn't about to take any chances, but she did allow her body to relax its solid rigidity. She even dared to turn her head an inch or so, and was ecstatic to see that they were not too many yards away from Charlie, Martin, and Mr. Archuleta, who were still in animated conversation.

She licked her lips, pleased to note that she also had some

spit to spare, although not quite enough to swallow with. Taking a deep breath, she released it slowly and said, "All right, horse."

It was a start, although it didn't get her very far. The horse, however, seemed intent on getting her farther, and she decided that such a circumstance was probably not advisable. Which, she figured, drawing upon scenes witnessed during her lifetime, was where the reins came in. She lifted them in one hand—she still couldn't quite bring herself to release the saddle horn entirely.

Taking another deep breath, she pulled back on the reins very lightly—she didn't want the horse to object—and said, "Whoa." Even she could hear the lack of sincerity in the one syllable, so she spoke more firmly.

"Whoa!" There. That was better.

It wasn't better enough, however, because the horse didn't stop its slow walk away from the people who were supposed to be taking care of her. But were they? No-o-o-o. They were chatting. Arguing with each other. Discussing Mr. Archuleta's bruised ego. Amy turned her head a little further this time and aimed a frown at the trio, who still hadn't even noticed she wasn't there any longer.

Bother. Amy was beginning to understand her aunt's sometimes caustic strictures against the male of the species. Her temper began to get the better of her terror. She spoke sharply to the horse. "Stop it!" Along with her command, she pulled more strongly on the reins.

She could have sworn the horse heaved a big, dispirited sigh, but at least it stopped walking. Amy was very pleased with herself.

"That's better. Now why don't you turn around and go back to where we came from?" Still clutching the saddle horn with her right hand, Amy pulled the reins in her left hand across her chest and over her right shoulder. It was an awkward position, but she didn't dare let go of the saddle horn in order to rearrange the reins in her hands. If the horse didn't like it, that was just too bad. She didn't like it, either.

The horse might well not have liked it, but it did as Amy directed. She wanted to cheer, but still didn't have enough spit.

Her annoyance did not abate as she neared the three men, who were as yet unaware of her at all—not her presence, her absence, or her abject fear and terror. Amy resented them mightily and wished them all at the devil. Since she was far too refined and delicately reared ever to say such a thing aloud, she decided to bump into them with the horse and see how *they* liked it. Fortunately for her, the horse was either also annoyed or very obedient, because it did just as she directed it to do, and thrust its big horsy head smack into the middle of the three gentlemen.

Charlie and Martin had begun to shout at Mr. Archuleta by this time, but the intrusion of the horse effectively stopped their conversation cold. All three men stared dumbly up at Amy, who frowned down at them.

"Amy!" cried Martin.

"Mr. Tafft," she said coldly. Turning her attention to Charlie, she said, "I think this animal and I understand each other now, Mr. Fox. Would you care to continue the lesson?" Eyeing Mr. Archuleta arctically, she added, "I prefer to take lessons from Mr. Fox, who possesses far more patience than you do, sir."

Martin's eyes went as round as doughnuts. Charlie grinned. Archuleta scowled hideously, threw up his hands, turned on his heel, and marched off toward the tent village. Amy, who wasn't nearly as unfazed by recent events as she wanted everyone to believe, glanced over to find Karen Crenshaw holding her clasped hands over her head in a gesture of victory and smiling broadly at her.

The starch went out of Amy's sails instantly, and she felt only very tired and very, very glad she had Karen Crenshaw as a friend.

Thank the good Lord *that* was over. After her initial problems with horseback riding, Amy's lesson had proceeded fairly well, with Charlie teaching her. She had no idea what had happened to Mr. Archuleta and didn't care if she ever found out.

At the moment, she was frowning over the letter from Vernon Catesby which she'd received that noontime. She hadn't liked it the first time she'd scanned it; she liked it even less now.

"My dearest Amy," the letter read, "I must admit to feeling great consternation about the conditions that appear to obtain on the Peerless moving picture set."

"Hmmm," mused Amy, trying to decide whether or not to be angry about that first sentence and deciding not to be. "He sounds awfully pompous, though." She wondered why she'd never noticed Vernon's tendency toward pomposity before.

"I must again express my disapproval," Vernon continued in the same stuffy prose, in his same stuffy hand, "of this folly of yours."

"Well, I like that! Folly, indeed!" Amy was doing a job of work and earning money, and she resented Vernon's attitude like anything. She chose to forget that she herself had possessed grave doubts about the venture in the beginning. Vernon had no right to approve or disapprove of anything she did. They weren't married, after all. Or even officially engaged. There had been an agreement, of sorts, between them for some time, but that was all it was: a sort-of agreement.

"I don't like to know," Vernon's letter went on, "that my future wife is doing something of which I disapprove so strongly. You know, my dear Amy, that the acting profession has been practiced among the lowest classes for generations. Even in the great Bard's day, actors were considered far from upstanding citizens."

"Fiddlesticks," muttered Amy. "I don't need this." So saying, she thrust the letter aside, intending to ignore it until her attitude improved. It had been a trying day, and she wasn't up to fighting Horace Huxtable, Mr. Archuleta, a horse, *and* Vernon Catesby. What she realized she really wanted to do was to hold a quiet, civilized conversation with Charlie Fox.

Or Karen Crenshaw, of course.

But, really, there was something so comforting about Mr. Fox. He was such a sensible fellow. So calm. *He* wasn't stuffy and disapproving of everything that didn't fit neatly into his boxed-in life. *He* didn't write bothersome letters expressing his doubts about Amy's common sense and intelligence. *He* could even ride a horse.

Amy would bet anything she owned that Vernon could ride a horse no better than she could. And, actually, after today's lesson, she'd bet she could ride better than he.

So there.

On that childish note, the supper gong sounded, and Amy had to rush to wash her face and hands and get to the chow tent before the soup got cold. She sat with Karen, Martin, and Charlie, forgot all about Vernon Catesby, and enjoyed herself. Hugely.

Nine

"It must be a hundred and fifteen out there," Amy told Karen, who was holding out a limp shirtwaist for her to put on. Amy was every bit as limp as the shirtwaist. What was more, she was dripping with sweat—she refused to think of it as perspiration as a lady should, because she was too hot and miserable and crabby. "And the air's as thick as cream."

They were in a hastily set-up tent way out on the desert near the dilapidated cabin being used as the sawmill.

"More like a hundred and twenty," Karen said. "And I suspect that thickness is a prelude to rain. It looks like we're in for a summer storm."

"Wonderful. Maybe I won't have to wash the sweat off. Maybe the rain will do it for me."

Karen laughed. "Nothing ever works out that well." She, too, was dripping and uncomfortable. "I'm sorry you'll have to wear that awful makeup. It'll make you even more uncomfortable, or I miss my guess."

"Makeup?" Amy stared at Karen, slightly befuddled by her words although she knew she shouldn't be. It was the heat making her fuddle-headed.

With a nod, Karen said, "Oh, yes. This is the first scene to be shot, and you and everybody else will have to be made up. The cameras are unkind to unmade-up faces. The stuff is thick and sort of greasy."

"Oh." What an unhappy reflection. Amy's moral attitudes

toward makeup weren't strong enough to poke their uncomfortable heads through the heat of the day and out into the open, but the notion of slapping greasepaint over her sweaty brow held no appeal whatsoever. Nor did the knowledge that, if Vernon ever saw this picture, or a photograph of Amy in theatrical makeup, he'd assuredly pitch a fit.

Her attitude toward Vernon had improved overnight. It was still true that he was relatively fussy, but when Amy considered the options in her life, Vernon looked pretty good. He was absolutely reliable and solid. Rather boulderlike, in truth. And that was exactly what Amy needed. Never again, if she could help it, would her life be insecure. Never. Ever. She wouldn't even entertain the possibility.

She stuck her arms in the sleeves of her costume, and Karen buttoned her up the back. Amy's body was sleek with sweat, and she hoped perspiration stains wouldn't show on celluloid. How icky to have the whole world view her sweaty armpits in a nickelodeon or theater.

"With luck, the process won't take long. The rehearsal went surprisingly well."

"Yes, it did." Amy had been as surprised as Karen. Horace Huxtable had been as docile as a lamb all morning long. Amy hoped it meant a mended attitude on his part, although she acknowledged that it was too soon to count any chickens. If she knew Huxtable, he'd wait until the chicks were ready to hatch and then smash them flat.

"Hope it keeps up."

"Oh, so do I!"

She groaned when Karen pulled the sash at her waist tight and tied a bow in the back. "This is very uncomfortable."

"I'm sure it is," Karen said sympathetically. "But I'll have water for you if you need it, and a towel to blot your face, and you can change again as soon as the shot's in the can."

What strange terminology these people used. Amy smiled

at her new friend, and they walked out to the adopted sawmill together. In truth, it was a large, ramshackle cabin that had probably been used as a prospector's home in the last century, although nobody knew for sure. Martin had scouted it out—Amy didn't know how he kept all aspects of his job straight—and decided to use it, and here they were.

The building sat alone on the bare landscape, brown and dilapidated, and listing to port. The wind and earthquakes, Martin had confided to Charlie and Amy, tilted most structures in California that weren't tended regularly. Amy, who was familiar with earthquakes, had nodded. Charlie had swallowed and muttered something she didn't catch, but she got the impression that Charlie'd as soon not hang around California long enough to experience an earthquake for himself. She was vaguely disappointed, although she couldn't have said why.

There wasn't a speck of green on the ground anywhere. Amy wished these motion picture people possessed the sense God gave a gnat and had decided to film their famous feature picture in the springtime rather than in midsummer. Midsummer on the desert was extremely uncomfortable. Spring, on the other hand, could be rather pleasant, fraught as it was with sufficient rain, grass, and wildflowers. But had they? Heavens, no. They had to follow the sun. Like a sunflower. Or a buzzard.

She tried to console herself with the thought of all the money she was making, but sweat kept dripping down her arms and legs and trickling down her back and between her breasts and annoying her.

"Fiddle," she grumbled.

"Beg pardon?" Karen turned from wiping her forehead with a handkerchief and lifted her eyebrows.

"Nothing," mumbled Amy. "Just talking to myself."

"Better watch out," cautioned Karen. "If Huxtable catches you talking to yourself, he'll never let you live it down."

She was right. Amy shut her mouth and intended to keep it shut until she had to say a line. Or pretend to say a line. Making a motion picture could be awfully silly sometimes.

"Ready to be tied to the log, Miss Wilkes?"

Charlie's friendly, humorous voice did something to banish Amy's hot, black thoughts. When she turned, she beheld him walking toward her, lean and lanky, clean and handsome, and cool as a cucumber. How did he do that?

"You don't look nearly as hot as you ought to, given the weather, Mr. Fox," she said, only partly teasing.

He grinned. "Don't tell anybody, but I just dumped a bucket of water on my head."

She and Karen laughed. "What a splendid idea," Amy said. "I wish I could do that."

"No such luck," Karen said. "In fact, we'd better get you made up."

Amy sighed and capitulated. Charlie walked with them over to the makeup table, where several tall, short-backed stools stood with people behind them under some shady umbrellas that didn't do anything to reduce the heat but would probably prevent sunburn. Amy presumed the people were the Peerless Studio's makeup artists.

Horace Huxtable sat on one stool, and was in the process of having his handsome face plastered with dead-white grease-paint by a young woman who didn't appear to be enjoying the job. Forgetting for a moment that she knew better than to say or do anything that might stir Huxtable to sarcasm, Amy stared at him, aghast.

He eyed her malevolently. "What's the matter, my dear Miss Wilkes? You'll look every bit as charming as I when you're made up."

Amy swallowed, wishing she'd guarded her reaction to the hideous white makeup more closely. But it was truly awful.

Ghostly. Eerie. She hated it. "I beg your pardon," she said in a smothered voice.

"Don't beg, sweetheart. It's demeaning."

Karen tapped Amy on the arm and shook her head, as if to warn her not to answer the fiendish Huxtable. Amy didn't need the warning; she already knew that Huxtable could twist anything anybody said into something vile. So she smiled at Charlie, tried to stifle her distaste for the icky makeup, and went to the tall stool that was farthest away from Huxtable. She knew he followed her with his eyes, and wished he'd just go away.

Fat chance.

Fortunately, Charlie walked with her and helped her climb onto the stool. He, of course, was tall enough so that he had no trouble sitting on the high stool. Amy's legs dangled several inches from the ground, making her feel unsophisticated and more like a child playing dress-up than an actress in a major motion picture.

The makeup artist assigned to Amy tucked a towel into the neck of her shirtwaist—which made her even hotter than she already was—and brushed her hair back from her face. Amy almost protested before she recalled that she knew nothing—*nothing*—about this process and she'd do well to keep her mouth shut.

She was glad she'd caught herself before she could rile Horace Huxtable. He was still watching her, his gaze sharp, hoping to catch her doing something he could malign, impugn, or otherwise belittle.

She had a mad impulse to stick her tongue out at him. And then introduce him to Vernon Catesby.

Which was silly. "Mph."

"Sorry," the makeup artist said, handing Amy a handkerchief. "Here, you can wipe it with this."

"Ew. Thank you." Pfew, makeup tasted vile. She wiped her

lips and shuddered, wondering if one could be poisoned by theatrical makeup. Probably not. One never read about actors and actresses dying of imbibing makeup.

Although she couldn't imagine how the greasepaint could stick to her sweaty skin, the artist seemed to be having no problem in making her up. As the woman worked, Amy observed the set. The cabin itself was nondescript, but one wall had been removed so that the cameras could maneuver more easily. Indoors, the place had been transformed.

Members of the movie crew had made up a huge cardboard sawlike structure that was operated by a crank. A bucket of sawdust had been placed beneath the saw, where another crew member would be positioned. He would toss up handfuls of sawdust when the saw was cranked, in order to simulate the process of cutting logs. Amy was supposed to be tied to a log by Charlie Fox's character, and rescued by Horace Huxtable's before she could be sawn in half by the cardboard saw. It seemed to Amy that the chances of her being tickled to death by the serrated cardboard were more likely.

The whole setup had seemed comical to her earlier in the day. Now it all seemed like work. Hot work. And she had no desire to be rescued by Horace Huxtable. In fact, she wanted nothing whatever to do with Huxtable for the rest of her life.

But she'd agreed to do this picture, and she'd keep her word. She felt as if she had a blanket plastered to her face by the time the artist was finished with her. She was hot, cranky, and felt smothered. A glance at Charlie Fox garnered her a grin, which perked her up a little bit, but not much. It was too hot to be perky. He, too, looked ghastly in the makeup, although not nearly as ghastly as she did.

She did, however, feel as though she was among friends when she walked back to the pseudo-sawmill, what with Charlie on one side and Karen on the other. Even Horace Huxtable and the heat couldn't defeat her if she had such nice people on her side.

That thought carried her through Horace Huxtable's first snide comments when she walked onto the set. Martin's friendly smile and considerate manner helped her through Huxtable's next several vicious verbal thrusts, and by that time Martin was ready to start the scene.

"I know you've not acted in front of the camera before, Amy, but just think of it as an extension of me, if you want to. Then you won't be worried about it."

Oh, really? Little did he know. She smiled. "Certainly. Thank you."

Huxtable huffed.

Charlie said, "Shall I tie her up now, Martin?"

"My, my, the cowboy is eager to tie the girl up, isn't he?" muttered Huxtable, buffing his nails on his plaid shirtfront. "One never knows what odd fancies other folks enjoy, does one?"

Amy ignored him. So did Charlie. Martin thought about Charlie's question. "Let's rehearse the scene once first. Up to the tying-up part."

They rehearsed the scene. As they did so, Amy, remembering Karen's comment about the prospect of rain, thought she heard the rumble of distant thunder. So unfamiliar was she with thunder, however—Pasadena was too proper to allow any but the very rarest of thunderstorms to invade its precincts—that she wasn't sure. Since she was lying on a lumpy log, staring into Charlie's eyes, and doing her best to look terrified, she didn't comment on the possibility of a storm in the distance.

"Good, Amy, good. You should probably scream now," Martin coached. "Remember, this man is aiming to kill you."

Scream? Good Lord, if she screamed in reality, she'd deafen the poor man. It was annoying, too, that the heat was so intense. If it weren't for the insufferable stuffiness and sweltering heat inside this awful building, she'd likely enjoy being tied up by Charlie Fox. As it was, her skin was so slick the rope kept slipping. She sighed heavily, wondering again if Vernon was right and her morals were in jeopardy of being compromised.

With an effort, she opened her mouth and pretended to scream. She also struggled, as Martin had requested. Both she and Charlie were so drippy that, if he'd been trying to restrain her in earnest, she'd have slithered from his grasp in an instant, but they tried to make it look good for the picture's sake.

"Good!" Martin called. "That's good! Let's take our places and shoot the scene now. Do it just that way! Let's get it in one take."

"Grph." Amy knew it was unladylike to grunt, but she couldn't help it. The stupid log was grotesquely uncomfortable to lie upon.

"Here, Miss Wilkes, let me help you up."

She took Charlie's hand and appreciated his tugging her to her feet. "Thank you."

Horace Huxtable was standing a few feet off, glaring at her as she straightened her skirt. Although she felt like making a face at him, she didn't, and was proud of her restraint.

"Here, Amy, blot your face with this."

She turned to find Karen holding out a fresh towel. She'd rather have a drink of water. Nevertheless, she blotted the sweat from her face, being careful not to smear her paint. "Thanks, Karen."

"Sure. We have to take care of our stars."

Amy wasn't sure, but she thought Karen was making a joke. She didn't have energy enough to laugh, but drank greedily when another crew member handed her a glass of water. It wasn't cold, but it was wet. Since Amy felt sort of like a squeezed sponge at the moment, it was pleasant to fill up her empty spots.

"Places!"

Martin's cry drew the cast back to the sawmill. Amy found her mark chalked on the floor where she was to begin the scene, struggling with Charlie. Again she wished it weren't so blasted hot. It got hotter—and much noisier—when a crew member touched a match to the gas jets, lights flared up on the set, and the cameraman began cranking.

The camera seemed an ominous instrument. Amy tried to ignore it, but it was as noisy as the very devil, and it kept spitting out sprockets as it churned. She envisioned some kind of rodent inside the box, running wildly on a wheel that kept the thing going. As the sprockets hit the floor, they sounded like discarded rifle casings, and she hoped the rodent wouldn't get hurt. She knew she was being fanciful and chalked it up to the heat.

"I've heard people say they might make talking pictures someday," Charlie shouted as he pretended to rough her up. "It doesn't seem likely to me."

"Impossible," Amy shouted back. "You'd never be able to hear the actors talking over the noise of the camera."

"Maybe they'll invent quieter cameras eventually."

"I hope so, if only to protect the ears of the—Ack!"

"Whoops. Sorry."

"Don't apologize, Charlie!" Martin cried from the sidelines. "Somebody might read your lips."

"Right," said Charlie, remarkably unabashed. How nice that he didn't get upset when he made a mistake. Amy wished she were more like that.

Amy would like to read his lips. By hand.

Good heavens, if she got any more shocking notions in her head, she'd have to retire from picturemaking and enter a nunnery. And she wasn't even Catholic.

"Make it look good!" hollered Martin. "Struggle, Amy!"

Amy thought she had been struggling. However, she increased her energy output until she thought for sure she'd faint from heat prostration. "Anyway, I've heard some of the cast members talking about how they think adding talk to the movies will destroy their artistic merit," she shrieked, hoping she looked scared for the camera. She felt thoroughly rotten, if that counted.

"Do they have any artistic merit?" Charlie asked. He sounded honestly intrigued by the thought, and not at all as if he were making a joke.

"Well," she hollered, "I don't think so, but I don't know much about them."

"That makes two of us."

And wasn't *that* a pleasant thought?—the two of them. Oh, dear, she had to stop thinking such things. Vernon would be shocked. Even she was a little shocked.

"Struggle!" shouted Martin.

With a sigh, Amy increased her struggle output. Thank God Charlie was strong and able to subdue her in not too many more moments. She was panting like a winded racehorse by the time he got her back against the log—the bumpy, uncomfortable log—and began lashing her limbs down.

"Good heavens, this thing tastes awful," she sputtered when the rope accidentally ended up in her mouth.

"Sorry. Whoops! I'm not supposed to apologize."

Amy did her best not to giggle. Fortunately, she was so miserably uncomfortable that her impulse to laugh was short-lived.

"Good! Good!" Martin hollered from the sidelines. "Make it look good Charlie. Good! Perfect! Now throw the lever on the sawmill. Do it from behind so the audience will see what you're doing! Look mean and evil. Good!"

With her mouth still open, and feigning cries of terror and

rage, Amy watched Charlie rush to the big metal lever that was supposed to start the cardboard saw whirling. In truth, a man beneath the raised set would begin cranking as soon as Charlie threw the lever.

He was really quite good. He looked positively wicked as, with a huge gesture, he flung the lever up and grimaced horribly. The timing was perfect, and the man with the crank started the saw to spinning. The other man, the one with the sawdust in a bucket, threw a handful of dust into the air.

"Wait on the sawdust until the log gets closer!" Martin yelled.

Amy was glad of that, since she didn't need any more stuff falling onto her greasy makeup or into her mouth. As it was, she had to spit out a mouthful of sawdust, and flakes of it stuck to her sweaty body. "Pthht. Ew."

"All right!" Martin said with an anxious overtone to his voice. "We're about ready to . . . Now! Horace! Rush in and save her!"

It continued to amaze Amy that Horace Huxtable, who was about the most deplorable human being she'd ever had the misfortune to meet, should be such a superb actor. He burst into the supposed sawmill as if he were truly bent upon the salvation of his own true love. Charlie, still standing by the lever, managed a creditable expression of shock and dismay and, like the sneaky snake he was supposed to be, tried to slink away. Huxtable drew out his trusty six-gun, which, Amy prayed, he'd loaded with trusty blanks—she personally wouldn't trust Huxtable to brush his own hair if he didn't want to—and fired at Charlie.

As it had been scripted, Charlie staggered and clutched his arm. He shook a fist at Huxtable and ran from the set. Huxtable paused, as if torn between chasing the villain Charlie and rescuing the lovely Amy. Then, exhibiting a good deal of frustration, as he was supposed to do, he cast one last baleful look at the place where Charlie had been, shook his fist, shouted, "To hell with you, Fox!" and charged toward Amy.

While the scene had been going forward, the log to which she was strapped continued what probably looked like its relentless progress toward the vicious blades of—a cardboard saw. Amy was sure audiences would be thrilled. Really, the scene looked pretty good to her, although her vantage point—flat on her back and tied to a log—wasn't the best. She was glad she'd be freed from her uncomfortable situation soon.

"Thank goodness. Now you can get me untied from this bumpy log."

"Oh, I don't know," returned Huxtable, who still looked the part of a hero, although he didn't sound like one at all. "I think it wouldn't hurt you to get sawed in half. It would be awfully damned bloody, though."

"You're perfectly disgusting, Mr. Huxtable."

"I'm flattered, my lovely Miss Wilkes. I didn't think anyone was perfect."

"You're impossible."

He laughed one of his oily, ugly laughs, and proceeded to the side of the conveyor belt where, with great dramatic gusto, he threw the lever to what was supposed to be its "off" position. The man underneath the set stopped cranking the saw, the other man stopped flinging sawdust, and Amy's log halted within an inch or two of a wicked-looking set of cardboard saw teeth.

With even more dramatic gusto, Huxtable drew out what looked like a very sharp knife and began hacking through her bonds. She eyed him with concern, although she tried not to show it. "Be careful with that, if you will."

"Don't worry, sweetheart. I won't nick your precious skin."

"I'm glad of that." She was proud of the acidic quality she managed to pour into her voice.

"Good! Good!" Martin encouraged from his director's

chair. "That's the ticket! As soon as the last knot is cut through, haul her into your arms and kiss her! This is going to be wonderful! Perfect!"

Yuck, thought Amy, who wouldn't have cared to be kissed by Horace Huxtable even if he had rescued her in truth. She wished Charlie were the hero of this piece. She'd much rather be kissed by him.

But that was only because she wouldn't find it revolting to be kissed by him—she told her better nature when it recoiled at her faltering moral resolve—as she would to be kissed by Huxtable. No wonder actors had such dreadful reputations. They were always required to kiss people to whom they weren't married. She knew that Vernon hadn't merely been fussy when he'd written his letter.

Her attitude toward Vernon Catesby softened still further when Horace Huxtable, flinging aside a host of rope ends and his knife, drew her up from the log and embraced her tightly.

"Aha," he said into her ear. "Now I've got you. And I'm going to enjoy myself, too."

Good heavens! He was actually *kissing* her! Amy, who'd had to force herself to struggle earlier in the scene, started struggling like a wildcat.

"No! No, Amy! Don't try to get away from him! He's your lover! He's the man you're madly in love with! Kiss him back!"

Fortunately for the scene, Martin's commonsensical words penetrated Amy's seething brain in time for her to stop her instinctual attempt to escape. She pretended to melt into Huxtable's embrace—the melting part was easy—but she decided Martin was just going to have to be disappointed about the kissing-him-back part. She'd be fricasseed and served with dumplings before she'd kiss Mr. Horace, the most awful man she'd ever met, Huxtable.

"I'm so glad you haven't been able to drink lately, Mr.

Huxtable," she hissed into his ear. "Your breath is not nearly so foul as it is when you've been drinking."

"Bitch," Huxtable growled. "You're a pretty little bitch, though, and I wouldn't want you to think you've won your game, sweetheart."

And with that, he whirled around so that they both faced the camera, dipped her in a manner Amy had only seen illustrated in magazines, and kissed her with what she might have sworn was genuine mad passion if she'd seen it on the screen. She undertook manfully to hide her revulsion—and she succeeded for the first thirty or forty seconds. Unfortunately, the kiss went on. And on.

Finally, Amy decided she'd taken enough. Wrenching her lips from Huxtable's, she whispered furiously, "That's enough, Mr. Huxtable!"

He didn't alter his position one iota except to chuckle hatefully and say, "We go until the director cuts the scene, my lovely Miss Wilkes. It's our job."

Fiddle. He was right. "You don't have to bend me over so far. My back is hurting."

"What a shame." He dipped her lower.

"Fiend!"

"Bitch!"

"Cut!" cried Martin at long, long last.

Amy breathed a relieved sigh that lasted long enough for her to feel Huxtable withdraw his hands from her back. He didn't bother to lift her up first, but let her fall, whack on her back, onto the bumpy log from which he'd just "rescued" her. She banged her head and elbow on the log, scrambled madly for a purchase on the conveyor belt, didn't find any, and rolled off of the raised set.

She landed with a thud on the floor with her skirt up around her knees, her bottom bruised, and her mortification complete. When she raised her head to see what had happened, she viewed Huxtable's ironically smiling face peering down at her. What was more, he was twirling his mustache like a real celluloid villain.

"Oh, I say, how terribly clumsy of me."

Amy's temper flared up like a skyrocket. "You wicked brute! You did that on purpose!"

"Horace, if you've hurt her . . ."

Amy heard Martin's angry voice trail off as his feet began pelting toward her.

"You lousy son of a bitch."

That was Charlie, and as soon as Amy heard the words, she saw Huxtable's face vanish from above. She clambered to her feet and tried to run around the set to see what the two men were doing. She hoped Charlie was beating the horrible actor to a pulp.

Her effort to run was hampered by her muscles, which didn't seem to want to cooperate. First they'd been cramped into an uncomfortable position on the log, then they'd been flung from a high precipice—well, a semihigh precipice—and they rebelled now. So she limped around the set, hoping there would still be some excitement going on.

She heard lots of noises. She heard what sounded like flesh meeting flesh, several muttered curses, and the grunts of men who were, with luck, pounding each other to dust. Or, she amended, with luck, Charlie was pounding Horace Huxtable to dust.

It occurred to her that she'd never experienced bloodthirsty impulses before she'd taken to acting. This job of hers was definitely damaging her character. She resolved to write a conciliatory letter to Vernon this evening after supper.

In the meantime it was gratifying, when she finally struggled to the front of the set, to find that Charlie had taken Huxtable by the front of his shirt and was shaking him violently. Martin and several crew members tried to pull the men apart.

"Stop him!" Huxtable screamed, his words falling like corrugated cardboard from his mouth. "He's trying to kill me!"

"It's what you deserve, you filthy bastard," declared the valiant Charlie, who was resisting interference fiercely.

"I didn't mean to drop her!" Huxtable screamed. "Honest."

"Don't make me laugh," said Charlie, who sounded far from laughter.

"You did, too, mean to drop me," Amy cried, indignant that Huxtable should voice so blatant a lie. She'd seen his face. She knew he'd planned exactly what would happen at the end of their kiss. "You're lucky you didn't hurt me badly, you horrible man!"

"There! Did you hear that?" roared Charlie. He hauled his bunched fist back, intending, Amy was sure, to crush Huxtable's jaw with it. Fortunately for her, the problems associated with the star's broken jaw paraded across her mind's eye in the split second she had to think about things, and she leaped for Charlie's fist, grabbing it with both of her hands.

He was certainly a strong man. Amy could hardly credit the fact that, even with all of her weight dangling from his fist, he still managed to hit Horace Huxtable. It was her misfortune that it was the back of her head that connected with Huxtable's jaw.

"Aaaaaah!" bellowed Huxtable in what sounded very much like excruciating pain.

"Aaaaaah!" cried Amy in what was certainly awful pain.

"Oh, shit," hollered Charlie, who seemed to understand all at once what had happened. "Amy! Amy, are you all right?"

He dropped Horace Huxtable like a hot rock and drew Amy into his arms. Amy caught the merest flash of Martin Tafft before her face was buried in Charlie's shirtfront. Martin was tugging at his hair, and his expression conveyed his consternation.

"Oh, God, Amy, did I hurt you?" Charlie cried.

She tried to shake her head, but Charlie's hand was pressing the back of her head too firmly against his chest for her to do so. She feared she might smother if this kept up much longer, so she made a big effort and got her nose free. Her mouth was another matter, but she did succeed in uttering a muffled, "Nomph."

It was enough for Charlie, who breathed, "Thank God, thank God," in what sounded like a truly heartfelt prayer of relief.

As much as she appreciated Charlie Fox's acting as her champion—again—Amy was awfully tired of being mauled and manhandled on such a miserably hot day in such a hellishly hot building. She ground out, "Please let me go, Mr. Fox. I'm fine now."

Charlie must have heard an edgy quality in her voice, because he let her go. He blinked down at her, though, and looked worried. "You sure you're all right?"

She pulled her shirtwaist down and made a stab at straightening her skirt. She was certain her makeup had been smeared beyond redemption when she saw the mess it had made of Charlie's shirtfront. "Yes. Thank you."

Karen rushed up and began helping her tidy up. The two women exchanged a smile. Amy couldn't recall another time in her life when she'd appreciated a person's friendship more. She wished foolishly that Karen had been around when her parents died.

Martin hurried over to her. "I guess he'll be all right once he calms down."

Amy assumed he was referring to Horace Huxtable, and she didn't care. She frowned at Martin to let him know it. As far as she was concerned, Martin ought to be spending his thoughts on her.

Martin still appeared flustered. He'd stopped pulling at his hair, but it stuck out all over his head. He was chewing his lower lip as he gazed at Amy, critically surveying her person. "Are you all right, Miss Wilkes. I'm terribly sorry about what happened. I'm sure it was an accident."

"It wasn't an accident," Amy told him flatly. "He did it on purpose."

She almost wished she'd lied when Martin started tugging at his hair again. Charlie and Karen helped her off the set and outside, where, even though the weather still hovered in the upper nineties, it was relatively cool compared to the sawmill.

But, according to the crew, the scene had gone very well. Amy supposed that counted for something. She'd never been so happy to see a day end in her life.

Ten

The first fat droplets of rain spattered down on the exhausted cast and crew of *One and Only* as the crew members were packing up to return to the Peerless Studio's tent village. The air smelled of rain, which was a refreshing change from smelling like dust.

When Charlie glanced around, he saw Martin Tafft peering at the lowering sky. He was surprised that Martin was now looking even more worried than when he'd been dealing with Horace Huxtable earlier in the day. As far as Charlie was concerned, weather was no problem at all compared to Huxtable.

"What's wrong?"

Martin, still squinting at the sky, chewed on his lower lip. "It's raining."

Charlie squinted at the sky, too. A couple of drops of rain, in his estimation, didn't mean it was raining, but he wasn't accustomed to California ways. Perhaps this was considered "raining" in California.

Amy Wilkes walked up to them. She looked hot and tired and bruised, although her spirits were good and she'd finally washed the rest of her makeup off. She looked much better without it. Fresh. Pretty. More lovable than any other girl Charlie'd ever met.

He'd apologized at least fifty times for hitting Huxtable with her head, and she'd accepted his apologies, but he was still worried about her. Huxtable was a tough customer. Charlie feared for internal damage inside of Amy's lovely head. Huxtable himself hadn't spoken a word to either Charlie or Amy since the incident occurred. That was fine and dandy with Charlie. He suspected that Amy wasn't offended by Huxtable's silence either.

"Will the cameras be all right, Mr. Tafft?" Amy asked. "I think you ought to put them in the covered wagon and let the cast ride in the rain. We won't rust like they will."

Martin squinted at the sky, then at Amy, and then at Charlie, who shrugged and said, "Sounds reasonable to me. The cameras are likely to get ruined if it starts raining any harder. We humans can dry off and not suffer any consequences, I reckon."

"Exactly." Amy nodded.

She looked totally exhausted, and Charlie experienced a fierce urge to take her in his arms and cuddle her until she slept. She needed somebody to care for her. Why the devil was a woman like Amy Wilkes working out here in a stupid moving picture when she ought to be married to some nice man—himself, for instance—who would support her and care for her and not let her tangle with the likes of Horace Huxtable. She'd be better occupied in keeping house and raising kids than in making movies, in his opinion.

As soon as those notions tiptoed through his head, Charlie stopped thinking and mentally shook himself.

What in the name of holy hell was he thinking things like that for? He couldn't believe it of himself. He, who didn't have a single thing in the universe to call his own, except some money in the bank, had no business even contemplating setting up housekeeping with a delicate damsel like Amy Wilkes. Maybe if he was secure; owned his own ranch, or was rolling in riches or something . . . But he wasn't. Damn it.

"I'm not sure," Martin said, still chewing on his lip and

beginning to pull that tuft of hair he seemed so fond of. "I don't want anybody to get sick if we have a downpour."

"Don't worry about us," said Amy stoutly. Charlie was as proud of her as if he had a right to be. "We'd be much safer in a rainstorm than the cameras would be."

Martin made up his mind. "You're right, of course, Amy. Thank you for your consideration."

"Don't be silly," she said, coloring slightly. "It's the only sensible thing to do."

And that was another thing. While, when he'd first met her, he'd pretty much thought she was a stuck-up prude, Charlie had come to understand that she was only trying to present a fearless front to the world. Underneath the act, she was soft and vulnerable and as sweet as a ripe peach. He sighed inside and wished he'd never discovered the truth. His life would be much less complicated if he didn't have these tender, mushy feelings for Amy Wilkes that seemed to have taken possession of him recently.

"Are you sure you'll be all right riding a horse?" Martin asked her. "I know you're not . . . ah . . . used to horseback riding."

"You mean I'm a terrible horsewoman," Amy said with a smile. "I know it, but that's all right. The Peerless village is only two or three miles off, and if the horse doesn't run away or anything, I'm sure I'll be fine."

"I'll ride with her and make sure nothing bad happens," Charlie offered instantly.

Martin eyed him thoughtfully for a second or two, then nodded. "Good. That's fine, then. I'll entrust Miss Wilkes and the rest of the cast who ride the horses to your care, if that's all right with you, Charlie. You've got more experience riding herd on animals and people than anybody else." Martin smiled, but Charlie knew what he meant.

Shoot, Charlie had been sort of hoping he'd have Amy to

himself for an hour or so as they rode back to the tent city. But he guessed it couldn't be helped. "Sure thing, Martin. I'll try to make sure nobody drowns."

He laughed and looked at the sky, which was still spitting a raindrop or two every few minutes. It was a tolerably lazy-looking sky to Charlie. Reminded him of Horace Huxtable, actually. Huxtable, except when he was drinking, seemed to prefer the exercise of sitting on his butt and criticizing everyone else than doing anything useful.

Speaking of Huxtable, the actor stormed over to Martin before Charlie had turned away, sputtering and shouting about the possibility of a rainstorm. Charlie watched, just in case Huxtable got carried away. Although he was pretty sure Martin could deck the star, Charlie didn't think it was worth it to take a chance.

"I'm the star of this picture!" Huxtable roared. "I'm not used to being treated like this! I'm accustomed to being taken care of."

"Pampered," muttered Charlie under his breath. Huxtable turned and glared at him, and he wished he'd been more discreet. No sense in riling the salty old hamhock now, no matter how much Huxtable deserved to be riled.

Huxtable pointed a trembling finger at Charlie. "I'll talk to *you* later. I have a bone to pick with you. You're a violent, unpredictable villain, and you're a menace to the civilized members of the cast!"

Charlie bridled even though he knew Huxtable wasn't worth getting mad at. People like him needed to be ignored almost more than they needed shooting. "Right," he said sarcastically. "Unlike you, who only pick on tiny little ladies and throw them off of raised platforms."

"I did no such thing!"

"Stop it!" Martin yelled, sounding as near to fierce as Charlie expected he could sound. He was also yanking hard on his hair, which Charlie was sorry to see, since it meant the poor fellow was at his wits' end. "Please, don't fight! We've got to think about the cameras now!"

Charlie felt guilty about provoking Huxtable. Making Huxtable mad was pathetically easy to do, and Charlie knew it upset Martin. He said, "I'll leave you to take care of your star, Martin. I'll go help the ladies saddle up."

"Thanks, Charlie," Martin said with patent relief. "Huxtable, you can ride in the covered wagon with the cameras."

"A covered wagon?" Huxtable roared. "What do you think I am? A pioneer? I've never heard of such a thing!"

So Charlie strolled off in search of Amy and Karen, leaving Martin to soothe Horace Huxtable's tender sensibilities, a prospect from which he himself shrank as if from a pack of wild boars. He heard the two men squabbling at his back, Huxtable indignant, Martin sensible and very weary. As for Charlie, he still considered the chance of any problems resulting from the rain as remote as the possibility of Horace Huxtable going to heaven when he died.

He was wrong. They'd only been riding for about ten minutes when the sky opened up and the deluge began. Huge forks of lightning lit up the sky, which had gone as dark as midnight, and booms of thunder rattled Charlie's bones and the earth around him. Rain came down in sheets so thick he couldn't see the ground in front of his horse's hooves, much less the other people in his small party of riders.

Pulling his collar up around his chin and yanking his Stetson down on his forehead, he muttered, "Shoot, it's gone on toward a regular gully-buster."

"Beg pardon?"

That was another thing. The racket from the storm was so great that voices had to be raised in order to be heard. "It's turned into a big storm," he shouted to Amy, who had asked the question. He pulled his horse up next to hers and gazed at her in some concern. "You all right, ma'am?"

"I'll be fine."

He didn't believe her. She was soaked to the skin already, and the day had been so insufferably hot that she hadn't thought to bring any sort of wrap out to the sawmill. Neither had Charlie, for that matter, nor anyone else. She looked kind of like a drowned kitten, and Charlie's protective impulses soared like the mercury in a thermometer on a blistering summer's day.

"Wish I had a jacket to lend you," he told her. "You look mighty cold and uncomfortable."

She glanced up at him for a moment before ducking her head to avoid getting drowned by breathing in rain. "I'm no worse off than anyone else," she said shortly.

He guessed that was true. Glancing about at the five others in their little band of horseback riders, he saw that Karen Crenshaw was every bit as wet and miserable as Amy. For some reason, while he wished he could do something for Karen, he wasn't paralyzed with worry about her, as he was for Amy. That probably meant something really stupid on his part, but he couldn't seem to help himself.

He didn't know where the wagons were. Behind them somewhere. Martin had insisted the riders go on ahead in an effort to beat the storm. The crew had to remain behind and secure the cameras and other equipment in the wagons, and make sure the waterproof covers were strapped down tightly. Cameras were expensive. More expensive than, say, Charlie and Amy, who could be replaced with ease.

"Glad Martin knows more about California weather than I do," he shouted. "I didn't think those few drops of rain meant a thing. In the territory, we usually can spot a storm coming for hours in advance. I didn't even see any clouds to predict this one. The air was just sort of thick and heavy."

"I guess Mr. Tafft has experience with these things," said Amy.

Charlie's heart turned over when he realized her teeth had begun to chatter. Shoot, he wished he could think of—wait a minute. Maybe he could.

"Just a minute, ma'am. I think there's a blanket rolled up behind this saddle. Let me unstrap it, and you can wrap yourself up in it."

"Don't be silly, Mr. Fox," Amy snapped. "I'm in no worse shape than you or Miss Crenshaw. If the two of you don't have blankets, I certainly won't use one."

Damn. She would have to go all noble on him now, of all unhealthy times, wouldn't she? A rumble from in back of them made Charlie turn in his saddle. "There are the wagons." He wondered how those heavily laden wagons were going to traverse the rocky road to the tent city. Already water was running over the rocks and potholes like a river, and swirling mud was sucking at his horse's feet. He was pretty sure he could keep his own mount upright and hoped the other horses wouldn't flounder.

Through the curtain of rain, he saw that one of the mules pulling the lead wagon had stumbled. He pulled his horse around. "I think they might need some help back there."

Amy turned, too. "Oh, the poor horse."

He didn't tell her that the poor horse was a mule, figuring it didn't matter.

She went on, "Yes, please try to help them, Mr. Fox. I'm sure you have more experience with such things than they do."

"Yeah." Charlie didn't know how she'd gained that impression—after all, his experience with cameras dated back no further than his arrival on the Peerless lot—but he didn't argue about that, either. Instead, he guided his horse back to the supply wagon. After a shouted conversation with the driver, he nodded and went to the mules' heads, where he could be of some use in directing them around the biggest potholes.

It was a bedraggled motion picture company that eventually stumbled into the Peerless lot a couple of hours later. Charlie, far from having been private with Amy Wilkes during that time, had spent the better part of it keeping the mules from breaking their legs. He wasn't a happy man when he left Martin and the wagons and went off in search of Amy. If he hadn't been of use to her on the ride home, he might at least help her settle in now.

There would be no settling in that night, he soon discovered. Several of the tents had already been flooded, including the tent provided for female crew members. When he sloshed back through the muddy encampment, Charlie found Martin in the tent reserved for the cameras, trying to build temporary platforms in case the rain should get worse during the night. He asked about Amy.

"Lord, I don't know where anybody is," a frenzied Martin told him. "We're still trying to secure the cameras." Martin waved a hand in the air and looked as if he might never recover from this particular rainstorm. "Check out the chow tent. I don't think that one's flooded. I know I saw Karen heading there with her suitcase a few minutes ago."

Shoot. The notion of Amy and Karen, and however many other ladies might be working on this picture, fending for themselves while everybody else worried about cameras didn't appeal to Charlie. He thought women deserved to be taken care of. At the very least, somebody ought to be watching out for them.

Because he thought it was important to Amy's peace of mind—perhaps even to her safety—he asked Martin one other question before he set out for the chow tent. "What about Huxtable? Is his tent flooded?"

"Good Lord, I hope not," Martin said. "He's too much trouble when conditions are ideal. If we have to suffer a flood and Huxtable's temperament, too, I'm not sure I won't go clean out of my mind."

Two crew members carrying a heavy burden swathed in oilskin struggled up to Martin then, and his attention was diverted from Charlie. What was more, it didn't look to Charlie as if it would come back to him any time soon.

With a worried mind and a heavy heart, Charlie set out for the chow tent. He knew he should stay and help, but some compulsion with which he was totally unfamiliar drove him to find Amy before he did another single thing.

The first person he saw when he entered the chow tent was Amy Wilkes. The worry lifted from his heart instantly, and he smiled at her. She smiled back—rather shyly, Charlie thought.

"You're all right?" He hurried up to her, holding out his hands before he realized what he was doing.

"Yes, thank you. We're only a little bit wet." She ignored his outstretched hands and gestured at the rest of the company, who were in various stages of toweling themselves dry.

Charlie dropped his hands to his sides, embarrassed at having been caught in a spontaneous and, he feared, unwelcome gesture of intimacy. Shoot. When would he learn? He and Amy Wilkes were poles apart, both socially and historically, and it would take more than a single motion picture to draw them together. Ding-bust-it.

Trying to recover a modicum of his dignity, Charlie said, "Yes, so I see." Karen Crenshaw, he noticed with gratitude, smiled and winked at him, as if she knew exactly what agonies of embarrassment he was experiencing. He smiled back. "Is there anything I can do to help you folks out?"

Dang, there was Horace Huxtable. Charlie frowned at the miserable old ham, who was, naturally, making a fuss.

"I can't endure this!" Huxtable whined. Then he sneezed.

Good. Maybe he'd catch some deadly disease and do the world a favor by croaking. Charlie supposed he ought to feel guilty for entertaining the mean-spirited thought, but he couldn't drum up an ounce of guilt to save himself.

Amy peered over her shoulder at the commotion, wrinkled her nose, and stuck out her tongue, surprising Charlie, who hadn't anticipated anything of such a spontaneous nature from this source. "That man ought to be forced to live like other people for a few days and see how he likes it."

Surprised by Amy's comment, Charlie couldn't think of a response. Amy eyed him and frowned.

"Oh, I know," she said, brushing her hair out with angry vigor. She had gorgeous hair. Charlie wished she'd let him brush it for a while. Silly Charlie. "You think I'm a spoiled rich girl, but I'm not. I've had a rather sheltered life since I came to live with my aunt and uncle, but, believe me, before that I was far from sheltered."

"Yeah?" Fascinated by this unexpected aspect of Amy's life, Charlie hoped she'd expound upon her background. In truth, he had believed her to be a spoiled rich girl before he'd gotten to know her. He was kind of afraid to ask her about it because he sensed such questions would be considered impolite by a lady from Pasadena.

In Arizona Territory, life was a good deal more casual than it seemed to be here, and nobody minded others asking stuff like that. If a man didn't want anybody to know his background, he'd either say so, make up another one, or shoot you for asking, and most folks honored him for it. There was more than one fellow who'd started over from a bad East Coast beginning in the Western territories.

"Charlie!"

Charlie turned at his name, and realized Karen had walked up to him. He tipped his drenched Stetson and smiled at her.

"Would you mind helping us set up cots and bedrolls in this tent so we can sleep here tonight? I guess the cooks are going to fix some kind of soup and sandwiches for supper in the kitchen area, but most of us are going to have to camp out here since our tents are all wet."

"We're going to be camping out!" Amy exclaimed.

Both Charlie and Karen looked at her, and Charlie was charmed when she flushed.

"I've never camped out before," Amy explained, lifting her chin in a gesture Charlie had come to recognize as one of defiance. He thought she was cute as a button.

"By gum, that's so," he said, mainly to encourage her. "This will be just like camping out, only we'll all be in a big tent instead of out under the stars."

"If we were out under the stars," Karen said wryly, "I don't suppose we'd, any of us, get any sleep."

"True," said Amy, whose spirit had returned. "We'd be too busy swimming."

Both Charlie and Karen laughed, and Charlie could tell that Amy was pleased with herself for being witty in trying circumstances. He was pleased with her, too. In fact, he realized, there was very little about Amy Wilkes that didn't please him these days. He sighed, thinking he was a danged fool to fall for a city girl.

Nevertheless, he set about arranging things so that as many people as possible could fit into the chow tent to sleep. He even rigged up a curtain behind which the ladies could change their clothes, providing they could find warm dry clothes to swap for their sopping ones.

"This is just like camp," Karen said at one point. She seemed mighty cheerful about it.

"Oh, how fun. I always wanted to go to a camp in the wilderness somewhere." Amy sounded cheerful, too.

Charlie watched them curiously. "It's like a storm on the trail, too," he murmured, wondering what they'd make of that.

"Oh, is it really? How interesting." That was Amy, and Charlie felt a potent combination of enchantment and surprise mingling in his chest area.

"Yes, ma'am. Sometimes when we're driving cattle to market, it'll storm. Thunder and lightning scares the willies out of cattle."

"My goodness." She sounded breathless, as if she'd never heard anything so fascinating in her life.

Wondering if she was pretending or if she really found tales of ranch life interesting, Charlie went on cautiously, ready to stop talking immediately if she began to look the least bit bored. Maybe the dreams he'd begun to spin weren't as nonsensical as he'd believed them to be. "Yes, ma'am. It's hard to get a herd settled when there's thunder in the air."

"Is it the noise, do you suppose? I imagine a cow wouldn't know what thunder was and might be startled."

Charlie grinned, but didn't laugh, sensing that Amy wouldn't appreciate it but would believe that he was laughing at her ignorance. And it wasn't that, exactly. It was only that she was so danged darling. "That is true, ma'am. Cattle are pretty stupid. But there's also something in the air that riles them, even before the rain starts. Something they can sense that we humans can't. Reckon it might be the electricity or something."

"My goodness."

"Oh, yes," Karen said. "My cat always gets a little strange before a rainstorm. Although," she added as if bent upon telling nothing but the truth, "we don't often get thunder and lightning in the Pasadena area."

"That's true," said Amy.

She didn't sound as if she were as terrified of thunder and

lightning as Charlie'd been led to believe city ladies were. He asked with interest, "Do you mind the storm, ma'am?"

He stood on a chair, grabbed the rope Amy tossed to him, and wrapped it around a tent beam. He tied a square knot in the rope so he'd be able to untie it again come morning if they didn't need it any longer.

Amy shrugged. "Not really. I mean, I'm not scared, if that is what you mean. It would be rather more pleasant to be listening to it from inside a nice, warm house, I guess."

"You can say that again," said Karen. "With a cup of hot cocoa and a big fire in a fireplace." She sighed.

"On a soft bearskin rug," Amy said dreamily.

"With a plate of macaroons to nibble on."

"That sounds lovely," Amy said, and Charlie noted a hint of wistfulness in her voice.

"It sounds a whole lot more comfortable than being rained on while you're driving a herd of cattle to market," he said, uncoiling the rope as he walked across the chow tent floor. Amy followed with the chair. "And trying to keep the critters from getting spooked by the thunder is no fun, either."

"I suppose not." Amy looked thoughtful, and Charlie got the impression she didn't mean it, that she believed she'd enjoy the excitement of driving cattle through a storm. She set the chair down on the other side of the tent. Charlie climbed on it and tied the rope to a tent pole on that side. Karen, with her arms full of blankets, stood next to Amy. She handed Charlie a blanket, which he arranged over the rope, securing it with a clothespin Amy handed him.

He went on, testing Amy and her interest in things outside her frame of reference. Maybe she honestly wouldn't mind life on a cattle ranch. "Sometimes you'll see lightning do weird things. It'll flash on the cattle horns and roll from steer to steer. It'll look like blue balls of electricity running through the herd."

"My goodness!" Amy's eyes were as round as robins' eggs. She'd taken up the bucket full of clothespins, and she handed another one to Charlie.

"Really?" Karen was interested, too. Somehow, Charlie didn't care.

"Yup." He shoved a clothespin onto the blanket to hold it in place, and took another one from Amy's delicate fingers. He peered at those fingers hard, wondering if they were capable of doing the kind of work a ranch wife had to do.

"Doesn't the lightning kill the cows?" Amy asked, handing him yet another clothespin.

"Sometimes." He jabbed that clothespin at the end of the blanket and reached for another blanket from Karen, which he swung over the rope. Their goal was to create separate sleeping quarters for the men and the women. Inelegant, perhaps, but more proper than having all of them sleep together. "But not that blue-ball lightning. It's the bolts of lightning hitting an animal that will kill it. The ball lightning only plays with their horns. I saw it happen with a herd of longhorns once. It was something to see, you bet."

Amy and Karen looked at each other while Charlie clipped another couple of clothespins onto the latest blanket. Karen said, "Do you suppose he's teasing us, Amy?"

"I'm not sure."

"I'm not!" Charlie cried, stung. "Honest Injun, it happens all the time. Well," he amended, honesty having overcome him, "not all the time. But it happens. You can ask anybody."

"I suppose we could ask anybody," said Amy with a grin. "But I doubt that would help any, since nobody from around here would know what we're talking about."

Both girls laughed. Charlie joined them, but he didn't mean it. He didn't like having his word doubted.

"I'd love to see that blue-ball lightning," Amy murmured. Charlie eyed her. "Maybe you will someday." She gazed at him, his eyes stuck in place staring into hers, and Karen had to clear her throat twice to unlock the spell. Amy jerked and looked into her clothespin bucket. Charlie cleared *his* throat and turned away to secure another blanket.

They finished hanging the blanket curtain shortly before the cooking crew hollered out that chow was ready to be dished up. The seating arrangements were casual and crowded, but since Amy and Karen didn't seem inclined to leave him, Charlie didn't mind that. In fact, he offered to fetch both young ladies their soup and sandwiches, an offer they declined.

"You couldn't hold three bowls of soup and however many sandwiches you aim to eat tonight, Charlie Fox, much less a couple for us, too."

The look Amy gave him—coquettish and full of humor—nearly felled Charlie. He didn't argue, because he wasn't sure what would come out of his mouth if he let it operate while his brain was in such a muddle. He feared he'd say something really idiotic, like "Please marry me." Considering silence prudent, he laughed and let the two ladies precede him in the chow line.

They found a bench not too far from a warm stove where there was room for the three of them, and sat together there. Charlie hadn't realized quite how hungry he was, and all but inhaled his soup and sandwiches. Both Karen and Amy offered him half of theirs, which he took with many thanks. "I'm used to eating a lot," he said simply.

"I imagine so," said Amy. "You must work very hard at ranching."

"Yes," Karen put in. "I guess it's a harder life than we who live in the city have. Well, unless you're one of those poor unfortunate people crowded together in a New York slum or something."

"My goodness, yes!" Amy exclaimed. "Why, I've read articles describing the terrible conditions some of those poor immigrant families endure. It's awful."

"Sure is," Charlie agreed after he'd swallowed. He knew that Amy didn't approve of people talking with their mouths full. Which was only good manners, as his mother had tried to teach him and his brothers for years. This was the first time Charlie'd ever had reason to be thankful that his mother was a strict woman who didn't let her sons get away with stuff. "I don't think I'd like to live in a big city like that."

"Pasadena's not bad," Amy ventured, sounding sort of tentative about it. "It's small and pleasant."

"Oh, yes," agreed Karen. "Pasadena is lovely. It's nothing like some of those horrible cities back East where everything's dirty and crowded."

"I'm not much of a one for crowds," Charlie admitted.

"I suppose you're accustomed to the wide-open spaces," Amy said. Again, Charlie thought he detected a hint of wistfulness in her voice.

"I suppose so," he said. "Arizona Territory's not like this, though. Where I'm from, it's beautiful."

"I'd like to see it someday," Amy said upon a sigh.

"Really?"

She looked at him as if his question surprised her. "Why, of course I would. I'd love to travel."

"Hmmm."

"Um, do ostriches get bothered by thunderstorms?"

Charlie huffed. He wished she hadn't brought up those fool ostriches. "I suppose they do. I don't reckon very many animals much like thunder and lightning."

"Hmmm."

"But, you know, it's my brother who's got the ostrich ranch." He elected not to mention the poker game in which Sam had won the ranch, sensing Amy Wilkes wouldn't approve of gambling. "The family has a cattle ranch near Sedona. That was where I've spent most of my life."

"Oh?"

Was it his imagination, or did she perk up at that? He couldn't really blame her for not cottoning to the thought of ostriches.

"Sure. My granddaddy moved to the territory after the war, and my daddy took over the ranch after that. It's been in the family for a long time."

"My goodness."

"It's a prosperous place," Charlie added, feeling a little defiant. He really didn't like Amy thinking of him as an itinerant ostrich-rancher.

"I didn't realize."

"Didn't think so."

They talked—whispering mostly—far into the night. Karen drifted off after an hour or so, and they kept talking. Long after everyone else had settled down to sleep, Charlie and Amy talked while rain pounded down, sliding off the canvas siding of the chow tent and splashing into the lake growing outside.

Charlie told Amy all sorts of stories about life on the ranch. He was happy to note that she not only seemed interested, but he thought he detected some longing, too, perhaps for a life that had a little more to it than drinking orange juice. His impression that she wasn't such an outrageous candidate for territorial living as he'd first supposed grew as the night progressed.

He knew better than to set his heart on anything, but he was encouraged, and he didn't mind admitting it. To himself.

Eleven

The rain continued all night and into the following morning, making the atmosphere outdoors cool and muggy and indoors steamy. For the first time in her life, Amy smelled the aroma of many bodies huddled together. She didn't like it. Charlie's wide-open spaces began to sound more appealing as the rain continued.

The desert was covered in water, reminding Amy of a weird, flat ocean with prickly plant tops sticking out of it. Rain splashed in sheets and then in sprinkles and then in sheets again. The thunder subsided during the day, but the sky was as gray as her aunt Julia's hair. There wasn't a jot of blue or a flash of sunlight anywhere. When she let her imagination motor ahead on its own, it seemed to Amy as if the whole world had turned sullen and dangerous.

She didn't get her letter to Vernon written the night of the flood. Nor did she have a chance to write it the following day, most of which was spent by the cast and crew of *One and Only* in digging trenches around the chow tent and trying to repair leaks. The chow tent eventually ended up the only domicile in the temporary Peerless lot that remained relatively undamaged and free from water.

"Heave!" Charlie yelled at Martin and Horace Huxtable, who were struggling with a flat board that looked like a door to Amy, although she wouldn't have sworn to it.

The two men heaved, Huxtable without even whining or

complaining about having to do some real work for once in his life. He was apparently as worried about the picture lot and the completion of *One and Only* as anyone else on the set. The reason they were heaving unattached doors was to create a bridge across the trench, and thereby connect the chow tent to the rest of the world. At present, the chow tent bore a slight resemblance to a very small, very unstable medieval castle with a moat around it.

The wooden door—or whatever it was—was slapped into place, sending up a spray of mud that coated Huxtable and Martin. Martin leaped back and laughed. Huxtable leaped back and swore.

Amy shook her head, thinking the two reactions could have been predicted by anyone with an ounce of understanding in his soul. If she were writing a script of this episode, she'd write it just this way, with Charlie leading the pack. The dialogue would have to be cleaned up a little, since Huxtable's penchant for cursing was both shocking and revolting. Amy was certain the picture-watching public would never countenance such vile language.

She sighed as she stirred the soup. She'd volunteered to work in the kitchen since the kitchen crew had been unable, presumably, to traverse the flooded roads from El Monte after they'd gone home the night before. Whatever their reasons, they hadn't appeared this morning. Most of the resident male crew members had been recruited to work in pursuits more muscular than cooking. Therefore, Amy and Karen were pulling kitchen duty, while other female crew members had been set to mending things that needed it, tent flaps and so forth.

At the moment, Amy and Karen were engaged in fixing lunch. Breakfast had consisted of biscuits and coffee. Since everyone in the crew understood, by this time, how much Amy knew about coffee, she'd made the biscuits. Charlie had told her that he and his brothers generally ate biscuits and coffee for breakfast on the trail.

The trail. Amy stirred dreamily, remembering his comment and thinking about life on a ranch and how peaceful it probably was. Most of the time.

Perhaps it was even too peaceful sometimes. Amy always tried to pepper her dreams with doses of reality in order to keep her feet on solid ground. She had to admit, however, that the ranching life sounded lovely. A little boredom never hurt anyone, and it beat the tar out of the kinds of excitement she'd lived through in her earlier days.

"What are they doing out there?" Karen wiped hair from her sweaty forehead and resumed beating the cornmeal mixture she'd been assigned to put together.

Her attention recaptured and plunked down slap in the middle of the waterlogged Peerless Studio set, Amy said, "I think they're trying to secure the rest of the tents so the water won't get inside and ruin everybody's clothing and so forth. They went around earlier today and made sure everyone's luggage was placed on top of the beds." She tasted the soup, decided it needed more oomph, and tossed in another cut-up onion and some salt and pepper. She liked well-seasoned food.

"How are they doing that? Securing the tents, I mean."

Amy shook her head. "I'm not sure. I think it involves folding up the edges of the canvas so that water can't leak in through the seams." She thought about it and shrugged. "I have no idea, really."

"I imagine we'll find out eventually. If we live through this rain. It reminds me of Noah and the flood."

"It does indeed." Amy squinted at the roof of the tent, wondering if it would hold. The chow tent was the largest and most elaborate of the tents, and had cross-beams supporting it. Cross-beams wouldn't be of much help if the canvas decided to collapse around them.

But, as her aunt told her with regularity, it was no use borrowing trouble. "The good Lord knows what he's doing, Amy. He doesn't need you to guide His hand," Aunt Julia would say when Amy got to fretting and fuming.

Amy knew her aunt spoke the truth. Amy's life, which in late years had been remarkably free from insecurity and doubt, had not always been thus, and she still worried. When she was a little girl, insecurity was all she'd known. Worry, when it was so deeply entrenched in a person's heart, was a hard habit to break.

At least the cameras were safe for the time being. They still resided in the wagon, and had been tucked all around with oilskin and canvas coverings. Martin had been going outside every time he thought about them—which seemed to Amy every fifteen seconds or thereabouts—to check on them.

Amy found it amusing, in a cynical sort of way, that Martin, who was really a very nice man, should be much more worried about the cameras than about the cast and crew. Of course, cameras, as Martin had told her with some show of irritation when she'd voiced her observations, couldn't swim.

Horace Huxtable had finally been coerced into helping Charlie and Martin build the bridge over the moat, but he'd had to be bribed with the promise of liquor after the storm was over. Amy deplored such tactics but had to admit they'd worked on Huxtable.

"I hope I won't be around when they give him his reward," she huffed, changing hands because her right arm was beginning to ache from stirring.

Karen sniffed. "I expect they'll take him to a roadhouse to tank up."

The way she'd expressed it tickled Amy, and she giggled. "I hope he drowns on the way."

"I fear there's little chance of that happy prospect coming to pass." Karen's cornbread mixture was ready to dump into two large greased tins which were awaiting their turn at usefulness. "Would you mind holding these things down while I pour?"

"Don't mind at all." Amy removed the huge wooden spoon from the soup pot, tasted the soup again, decided the onion, salt, and pepper had helped a good deal, and laid the spoon aside. "It's a miracle there was enough wood to fire up the stove this morning. I'd expected it all to be soaked through."

"I guess they have a lot of wood put aside for just such emergencies. The people who run picture studios don't like to take many chances." Karen shook out her arms and prepared to lift the huge bowl of batter.

"You mean they anticipated a flood?" In an effort to help her friend, Amy shoved one of the tins closer to the bowl.

"I don't know if they anticipated *this,* exactly, but picture-making can be a rough sort of business when you leave town for the country. I'm sure Peerless has run into troubles of a similar nature before this."

"I suppose they must have. Making a picture is quite an undertaking."

Karen didn't speak while she concentrated on pouring out her batter, giving Amy time to think about leaving town for the country. Arizona Territory, for instance.

Charlie had told her all about his ranching operation. It had sounded like some kind of remote and gorgeous heaven to Amy. She chided herself for being foolish. She knew good and well that it was dangerous to leap into things without checking them out first. For heaven's sake, leaping before they looked was what had sickened and eventually killed her father and mother.

She didn't want to think about her parents, since doing so always made her sad. Instead, she thought about Vernon Catesby. She needed to write a response to his letter. It wasn't kind of her to be spending all of her thoughts on Charlie Fox, whom she really didn't know very well.

Vernon was a known and therefore a comfortable commodity in her life. It was true that he had no tales to relate about blue lightning balls passing back and forth on cattle horns, and he had no experience with wildfires or flash floods, both of which phenomena Charlie had explained to her last night, but Vernon was stable. Stability was good. Stability was a most desirable quality in a man.

Stability might be sort of boring, but Amy would much rather be bored than scared and in danger. She'd been both of those things, and she didn't intend to be again if she could help it.

On the other hand, the Fox family's ranch had been a thriving concern, according to Charlie—whom she had no reason to doubt—for nearly fifty years. That was a long time. It sounded almost frightfully stable.

The ranching life also appealed to Amy for other reasons. She adored her aunt and uncle, but she wasn't keen on pampering the whims of self-indulgent inmates of the Orange Rest Health Spa, like Horace Huxtable, for the rest of her life. Although she knew she'd do that in a minute rather than suffer the disquietude of insecurity.

But having her own home and family on a thriving ranch in the Arizona Territory or in California—especially in California, actually, where there were lots of them already—sounded nice to her. She knew her aspirations seemed dull and uninspired to many young women her age, but they were hers, and she cherished them. A home of her own. A loving husband. Lots of children. Wide-open spaces and fresh country air. Maybe an orange grove, if the ranch was in California. Why, it all sounded like some idyllic Eden to her.

"Ooof!" Karen plopped the heavy mixing bowl on the

counter, again brushed hair from her forehead, and eyed the other greased tin with a frown.

Amy quickly opened the oven door, picked up the batter-filled tin, and thrust it into the oven. The stove was a modern one, thank goodness, and boasted a regulated heating element. Modern conveniences. The world was making great strides in appliances. Amy expected a well-to-do ranching family would have such a stove. Maybe. If the wife of the rancher was lucky.

She turned and placed the other greased tin next to the mixing bowl. "Would you like me to pour this time? Are your arms tired?"

"No, thanks. I can do it." Karen sighed. "I've never been much of a hand in the kitchen. I'm much more comfortable with a needle and thread."

"I like to cook," said Amy. "I think it's fun to feed people."

"I'll hire you to cook for me when I'm rich."

Both women laughed, and Karen dumped the rest of the cornmeal batter into the second greased tin. Amy scraped out the last of the batter and put the tin in the oven. "There." She dusted off her hands and went back to her soup.

The crew, when they came in for lunch, were a sorry-looking band of water-soaked men. The women who'd been sewing patches onto canvas and mending tent flaps didn't look very good, either.

"Good heavens, they look like refugees from some strife-torn European country," Karen muttered as she took up a ladle and prepared to serve the crew cafeteria-style.

"They certainly do." Amy positioned her tongs over a huge mound of cut-up cornbread. She supposed this wasn't the best lunch in the world, but it would be warm and nourishing. And if Horace Huxtable complained, she might just whack him with her tongs.

He didn't. Actually, he looked too bushed to whine. Amy

might have felt sorry for him if he were an otherwise decent human being. He wasn't. He was a contemptible, miserable, selfish, and ghastly animal. She didn't even react to his sneer as he passed, but plopped a piece of cornbread on his plate without comment.

Next in line was Charlie, to whom she offered what she hoped was an engaging smile and two slabs of cornbread.

"When you're through serving, would you come sit by me, Miss Wilkes?" He nodded at Karen. "You too, Karen. You two have done a lot of work in the kitchen. You deserve to rest while you eat."

"Thank you. I'm sure we'd enjoy that." Amy was charmed.

"Absolutely," agreed Karen. "I'm feeling sort of bedraggled."

"You don't look bedraggled," Charlie told her gallantly. "You both look as perky as ever."

Amy thought that was charming, too, even if it was a blatant lie. Both Karen and she were dripping with sweat, undoubtedly redolent of onions and other vegetable matter, and feeling filthy and uncomfortable. She'd be mortally glad when the rain stopped and they could use some of the excess water to bathe with.

The rain kept up for the rest of the day, forcing the cast and crew to spend another night in the chow tent. The atmosphere began to take on the aroma of a cave dwelling—or what Amy expected a cave dwelling might smell like. It was full of unwashed people and the odors of old cooking, and it wasn't pleasant.

The next day, although the sun came out, the mud was so deep there wasn't much hope of getting any filming done. The mud was as thick and sticky as tar, and it covered the desert for as far as the eye could see. Amy and Karen opened all the window flaps on the chow tent to allow the air to come

in and blow out the smell of too many people too long confined in too small a space.

Martin and the cameramen spent a good deal of time testing
the cameras and making sure the equipment was in working
order. Amy and Karen spent that day, too, in the kitchen, since
nothing, not even a mule train, could traverse the muddy river
that used to be the road to town.

Charlie and most of the other men spent their time shov-
eling mud from tents and trying to clean up the village. Care
had to be taken in the tents, since a rattlesnake had been found
curled up in a corner of one of them. Evidently, as some wag
said, even snakes knew enough to come in out of the rain.

Perhaps it was the same wit who said, as he looked around
the mud-ravaged village, that the scene was a "royal mess,"
and suitable for the star of the picture. Everyone but Horace
Huxtable laughed. He only turned up his nose and went to
his tent, which he'd insisted be cleaned out first, to lie down
and rest his royal bones. Amy thought justice would be served
if he encountered a rattlesnake there, but he didn't.

She eyed the pile of potatoes in front of her with some
misgiving. "What are we supposed to do with a hundred
pounds of potatoes and nothing else?"

Karen, her hands on her hips, looked at the potatoes, too.
"I don't know. You're the one who's supposed to know how
to cook."

"I do, but generally one has something to put with potatoes—
like meat stock for soup or something."

"Oh."

"I wonder if there are any onions left. And maybe some
bacon or ham or something."

Karen shrugged. "I'll help you look."

Both women started when a series of popping noises came
from outside. They ran to the front of the chow tent and

looked cautiously out. Neither fancied getting run over by a loose wagon or a rolling log, or drowned by a mud slide.

"I don't see anything," Amy said after a moment or two.

"Neither do I," said Karen.

They stepped cautiously onto the temporary bridge that was still the only means of getting from the chow tent to the rest of the encampment, unless one wanted to wade in mud up to one's knees. They stood together at the other end of the bridge, their arms about each other's waists, gazing into the tent village.

"The tents look clean and washed after the storm," Karen said.

"They certainly do. On the outside at least." They'd spent hours discussing how horrid it would be to discover one's home—even one's temporary tent home—filled with mud. Since they hadn't ventured farther than the chow tent for two days, they didn't know if either of their tents had suffered such a dire consequence of the rainstorm.

Amy spotted Martin some yards off and waved at him. "Mr. Tafft!" she called.

Karen huffed, said, "Honestly, Amy, you're *so* polite," and hollered, "Martin!"

Amy clapped her hands over her ears and laughed. Martin, who'd heard Karen's cry, looked over at the two women, waved, and began slogging their way.

"Where do you suppose he got those hip boots?" Amy asked.

"He probably brought them along in case there was any fishing to do anywhere. He likes to fish."

"Fish? Are there fish around here?" Amy surveyed the desert. At the moment, she supposed that any number of fish might find places to swim out here, but before the deluge it had seemed dry as a bone.

Karen laughed. "I understand there's a lake not too far off. I expect he was hoping he'd have a chance to get over there."

"Oh. I never would have suspected such a thing."

"No, it doesn't look very much like there'd be lakes tucked away anywhere around here, does it?"

Martin was close enough now that he could make himself heard without shouting. "I've got some good news for you, ladies."

Offhand, Amy could think of several things that might constitute good news, the primary one of which would be word from the outside world. She felt cut off and isolated, and she didn't like it. Suddenly she wondered if ranch life would engender such a feeling of isolation and loneliness, and she frowned, not liking the train of that particular thought.

"Did Mr. Huxtable drown?" Karen asked innocently.

Amy, startled by her friend's verbal jab, laughed aloud and slapped a hand over her mouth.

Martin didn't look particularly amused. "No, he did not, Karen Crenshaw, you terrible woman you."

"I'm so ashamed of myself," said Karen in a voice that held not a trace of penitence.

"What was the good news?" Amy asked. She, unlike Karen, did feel somewhat abashed about laughing at so unkind a joke.

"Charlie's been hunting, and he's got some meat for a meal."

The women looked at each other, then at Martin. Amy said uncertainly, "He's been hunting?"

"Yes indeed. He's a real outdoorsman, he is. A little flooding doesn't slow him down any." Martin rubbed his hands together as if he couldn't wait to eat whatever it was Charlie had been hunting.

Amy wasn't so sure. She'd never had anything to do with wild game, since she lived in the city of Pasadena where people ate things like chickens and cows and pigs and so forth.

If he brought her a dead deer, she feared she might even be sick. And how in the world was a body supposed to get at the meat of such a large dead beast?

She wasn't equipped to skin a deer. Or a bear. Good heavens, what if it was a bear? Or—heaven forbid—a rattlesnake. Amy had read novels in which cowboys had cooked and eaten rattlesnakes. The notion made her feel queasy, even if the books did equate the taste of snake meat with that of chicken. Amy figured that if the good Lord had wanted people to eat rattlesnakes, he'd have made them into chickens in the first place.

Karen, with her usual bluntness, said, "What's he been hunting? If he's got a great big dead animal slung over his horse, *I'm* not cooking it."

God bless Karen Crenshaw, Amy thought to herself. How nice it must be to feel free to ask any old thing of anyone, no matter how unrefined the question might seem.

Martin laughed. "Ha! I can see the headlines now: 'Motion picture actor saves cast and crew from starvation on the desert of Southern California by shooting a herd of antelopes.' "

Karen laughed. Amy didn't think it was very funny, but she smiled. The notion of having to shoot one of those pretty little creatures she'd seen pictured in *The National Geographic* for meat didn't appeal to her. There was a lot to be said for civilization.

"No, I don't think he's shot anything awfully big. I think he managed to bag a couple of rabbits. Do you ladies think you can cook up a rabbit stew if you tried real hard?"

The light dawned in Amy's brain. "Oh. Those noises were from Mr. Fox shooting rabbits?"

"They were. I think he bagged three of them."

"Um, what kind of rabbits, do you know?" Amy didn't know much about the wonders of the camping life, but she clearly recalled her uncle laughing about how he and Amy's father had tried to eat a jackrabbit they'd shot once. It had not been a successful venture.

"What kind?" Martin looked at her blankly, and Amy realized that he was as much a child of civilization as she.

"I understand cottontails are good for eating, but jackrabbits aren't," she explained.

"Oh."

"Really? I didn't know that." Karen beamed at her, as if Amy had demonstrated some kind of esoteric frontier knowledge that had impressed her greatly.

Another child of the city, Amy realized at once. Perhaps she wasn't such an odd duck after all. The thought gave her an odd feeling of kinship with Karen and Martin that she hadn't had before. She murmured, "I'm sure Mr. Fox already knows that."

"Hey there!" another voice called to them, and Amy's heart warmed instantly. Charlie Fox. She'd never forget that lovely deep drawl.

The trio turned, and Amy saw Charlie walking toward them, having very little trouble in the mud—and he had on no hip boots, but only his usual, everyday cowboy boots. She admired his athletic grace.

Bother. She'd forgotten to write to Vernon again. Tonight, she promised herself, she'd see to it.

In the meantime, she enjoyed the sight of Charlie Fox walking to the chow tent. He was quite a manly sort of fellow, Charlie was. Not soft and pallid and citylike, like Vernon, but rugged. Tanned. Westernish. She sighed before she could stop herself.

Karen peered at her slantwise for a second, and Amy felt her cheeks warm. Fortunately, Martin was waving at Charlie and missed the exchange.

"What have you brought to our cooks here, Charlie?" he

called, sounding happy. Amy thought it was nice that the motion picture fellow had such a friendly personality.

"Three nice plump rabbits," Charlie sang out. He sounded cheerful, too.

Amy appreciated people with bright, sunny natures. Her own nature tended to be gloomy when she didn't watch it. She knew her aunt and uncle used to worry about her a good deal, and for good reason. When they'd taken her in, Amy had been a pathetic specimen. Not any longer. These days, she was quite satisfied and secure.

She *had* to write to Vernon. It wasn't fair of her to ignore his letter as she'd been doing. Not, of course, that she hadn't had cause to fail to write him. After all, floods didn't happen every day of one's life. She wondered if Vernon would worry when she wrote about the flood, and realized she hoped he would.

Vernon was a very nice gentleman, and he was enormously proper and refined, but Amy wouldn't have minded if he were a teensy bit more demonstrative of his devotion to her. If he were, say, to pine to be with her, she wouldn't mind. A woman liked to know she was cherished. At least, she thought, *she* wouldn't mind being cherished.

Charlie strode up to them and held out his rabbits. Amy took a step back and wrinkled her nose before she could stop herself. He said, "I skinned 'em for you. Didn't think you ladies would like to have to skin rabbits."

"God, no!" Karen said. She sounded as if she were appalled by the sight of the naked, helpless-looking rabbit corpses.

Amy was glad. She was also glad she hadn't gasped or said anything to suggest that she didn't appreciate Charlie's thoughtfulness. She really did appreciate it. *She* wouldn't want to skin a sweet little bunny rabbit.

"They're cottontails," Charlie went on blithely, "so they'll be tasty."

Poor little things. Amy took herself to task for worrying about rabbits when a whole crew of people needed to be fed. That's what rabbits were for—eating. She said, "Thank you," and hoped she sounded as merry as he.

"Yes. And thanks very much for skinning them. I'd have been sick all over the chow tent if I'd had to do that," Karen said in her downright fashion. Amy grimaced, and wished she hadn't been quite so downright in this instance.

Charlie laughed. "I saved you that, anyway. Want me to cut 'em up for you, too? You can make a good stew with these babies."

"Oh, would you?" Feeling reprieve in the air—and from a man who had become her very favorite cowboy in the whole wide world—Amy beamed at him.

He swallowed, as if her beam were more than he could take with equanimity. "Sure. Got any potatoes and onions?"

"We've got lots of potatoes." Amy turned and led the way into the tent. She was feeling sort of light-headed all of a sudden, and feared it had something to do with the look Charlie Fox had just given her.

"You start peeling the potatoes," Karen said. "I'll look for onions."

"See if there are any carrots and celery and stuff like that, too," Charlie called after her.

"Will do."

Charlie and Amy smiled at each other, Amy a little uncomfortably. She found Charlie *so* attractive and appealing. She didn't want to show him exactly how appealing, because she sensed that that would be not merely disloyal to Vernon but unwise, fantasies about being a ranch wife notwithstanding. "Well, ah, I suppose I'd better get started on these potatoes."

"Right. And I'll get started on the rabbits."

Amy couldn't seem to look away from him. His gorgeous eyes held her there for what seemed like hours. It was silly, she thought later. There he was, with his hands full of strings wound around skinned rabbits, and there she was, in her big stained apron and holding two huge Irish potatoes, and they were staring at each other as if some invisible bond connected them. At that moment, the bond was a palpable thing, and it seemed to attach her heart to his.

It was all make-believe, Amy told herself later. She was a practical person and not given to whimsical fantasies. She didn't believe in deathless love or fated passions. All of the operas she'd seen in which soul-deep love was featured ended tragically. Look at *Carmen,* for heaven's sake. Or *La Traviata.*

Anyway, all of that was fiction. Amy had learned young to be hardheaded when it came to her own welfare. No fanciful dreams for her. No sirree.

And she couldn't look away from Charlie Fox at that moment to save her immortal soul.

It wasn't until they heard Karen's cheerful cry of "I found the onions!" that the spell broke, and they turned away from each other as if their movements had been choreographed. Amy's heart didn't stop whacking at her ribs until she'd peeled at least ten pounds of potatoes.

Charlie didn't say another word, but chopped up the rabbits as if doing so was going to save his life.

She absolutely *had* to write to Vernon. And the sooner, the better.

Twelve

The air was as clean as if God had scrubbed it with soap and water, and the pungent scents of the desert kissed Amy's nostrils pleasantly. The sky was as blue as her own eyes—a coincidence Charlie had pointed out to her earlier in the day—and Amy had a delicious sense of belonging and of being an integral part of a new enterprise that appealed to her. Her mood of satisfaction didn't quite last through the first paragraph of Vernon's letter.

> *Dearest Amy,*
>   *I am sorely distressed to read about the miserable conditions in which you have been living and working, and I pray that you will come back to Pasadena, safe and sound, soon. I also trust you will never agree to participate in another motion picture production.*

Amy sighed heavily. On the third day after the rain stopped, the ground had been dry enough to renew work on the picture. She and Karen had also been able to cease being camp cooks, for which she was enormously grateful, and the roads were traversable. She had, therefore, sent a letter to Vernon by the first available transport.

Today she received his reply, and she was perusing it as Horace Huxtable and Charlie Fox had a fistfight. For the picture. Amy was relatively sure that both men would just as soon fight in earnest, but Charlie, at least, was too much of a gentleman to do such a thing unless he were defending a lady's honor or something equally gallant.

She suspected that Huxtable might try to get in a low blow or two, but she didn't believe he'd succeed. She had developed infinite trust in Charlie's finer instincts and was sure he'd not allow a blow to land, or to retaliate should Huxtable succumb to his baser urges. He was too good for that.

And she'd better stop thinking about Charlie's merits and concentrate on Vernon's letter or she'd become as depraved and uncivilized as Horace Huxtable, perish the thought. She wrenched her gaze away from the scene being filmed and focused anew on the missive she held.

We all miss you very much, my dear. Your aunt and uncle are doing tolerably well without your help. This circumstance has been of interest to me, since you will certainly cease working at the Orange Rest after we are married.

Amy supposed that was true. Respectable ladies in Pasadena, California, whose husbands held good jobs—and Vernon's position with the bank was *very* good—did not hold outside employment. No. They might work like galley slaves in their own homes, but they didn't get paid for it.

Now where, she wondered, had that errant and unlovely thought sprung from? It must have sprouted since she and Karen had become such good friends. Karen was very practical and down-to-earth about all things, and she was definitely a feminist and an ardent suffragist. At present, Karen was in the costume tent, mending the shirt Amy was to wear in the next scene to be filmed. When they'd rehearsed earlier in the day, Huxtable had managed to take out a seam when he'd flung her too energetically to the ground. He'd apologized, but Amy didn't believe he hadn't intended to hurt her.

When they filmed the scene later today, if he behaved badly again, she planned to retaliate. She didn't have to be a gentleman, and she good and well refused to take any more abuse from Horace, the Horrible Ham, Huxtable.

Oh, dear, she'd allowed her mind to wander again. With another sigh, she went back to Vernon's letter.

I attended a meeting of the Valley Hunt Club yesterday. The Tournament of Roses Committee is debating whether a series of chariot races or a football game would be the more appropriate entertainment after the parade in 1906. I am privileged to be among those chosen to decide this important aspect of our city's most prestigious annual event.

Again Amy sighed. A chariot race or a football game? Neither one held much appeal to her, although she imagined gentlemen might appreciate either. She suspected, although Vernon did not say, that he would prefer the football game. Vernon might be as stuffy as a taxidermist's window display, but he liked to consider himself a modern fellow. Football was modern, Amy guessed.

Perhaps, Vernon's letter continued, *you might again be persuaded to ride on the Hunt Club's float on the event of the coming new year. The members are seeking three or four attractive young ladies to adorn the float, and I can think of no more lovely an addition to our float than you, my dear. You might well be selected to serve as the Queen, as Miss Hallie Wood was this year. Selecting a Queen seems to heighten people's interest in the parade, and I believe you would make a most admirable one.*

Oh, how sweet. Amy waited for her heart to flutter or do something else of an appreciative nature, but it didn't. It just sat there, beating as usual. How strange. On January first of this year, when she'd ridden on the Valley Hunt Club's float, pulled by six gorgeous white horses and decorated by any number of lovely flowers, she'd been thrilled. Hallie Wood was a good friend of Amy's, and she'd been happy for Hallie, too.

Surely she should be excited about repeating the pleasurable experience—perhaps even having the experience enhanced by being crowned Queen of the Tournament of Roses herself. That was definitely a stimulating prospect. She should be jumping up and down with enthusiasm and anticipation.

Probably. That is to say, she undoubtedly *should* be enthusiastic about it. The prospect of having Vernon Catesby assist her onto and off of the float, however, did nothing at all for her. Now, if Charlie Fox were to be there . . . Yes, indeedy. Amy frowned, disappointed that the mere thought of Charlie Fox did to her heart what the mere thought of Vernon Catesby was supposed to do.

She hoped she'd get over this infatuation with Charlie Fox before the conclusion of this picture, or she was going to be in trouble. As long as Vernon never found out how leaden her heart remained in reaction to him, she didn't imagine it would matter much.

Except to her. Frowning, she considered this strange and unpleasant phenomenon and tried to decide whether it would be awful to be married to a man who left her heart cold, or if it would be worth it in order never to experience vulnerability to the world's cruelty and uncertainty again. Glancing at Vernon's letter, she took note of his firm, even hand; of his firm, even attitudes; and his firm, even emotions; and she shuddered.

"Gad, I can't keep reading this thing or I'll fall into a decline." She folded the letter and stuffed it in her pocket.

It was almost time for her scene in the shirt, and she turned to see if Karen was anywhere nearby. She wasn't, so Amy decided to go to the costume tent. Maybe Karen would allow her to help somehow. Doing anything at all would be better than worrying about her future with Vernon Catesby.

"Hi there," Karen called cheerfully when Amy poked her head into the tent. "Almost ready here. Do you want to change in the tent?"

"Might as well. Thank you."

So Karen helped Amy out of the costume she'd worn that morning, her split skirt and blue blouse with buckskin vest— very fashionable, according to Karen, and quite attractive, according to Charlie. Amy agreed, and was pleased that he'd noticed. Which was all wrong, blast it.

She donned the mended shirt in a jiffy. "I'm really not comfortable appearing in public like this," Amy said as she scrutinized herself in the mirror.

"It's not the public," Karen protested. "It's the set of a motion picture. Take it off. I have to fix one of those buttons. It looks loose, and we wouldn't want you losing a button on the set."

Amy took the shirt off. As she handed it to Karen, she muttered, "Yes, yes, I know it's a picture set, but it's public enough."

With nimble fingers, Karen reinforced the button. "Pooh. It's all been arranged in the script, and everybody else likes the scene," she pointed out. "Anyway, this thing covers you every bit as much as any of the dresses you wear."

"I know it, but it's a man's shirt. It's—well, it's not very respectable."

"I know," Karen said with a laugh. "Whatever will Vernon think?"

Amy felt herself flush. She should have known Karen would say something like that. Ever since Amy had told Karen about Vernon, her friend had considered him insufferably dull. What was worse, she was always saying so to Amy.

"You can't really blame him," she said in justification of Vernon's attitude. "He wasn't keen on my appearing in this picture to begin with. When he finds out I've been parading around in nothing but a man's shirt, he'll like it even less."

"Yes, dear. I know. But there's nothing the least bit risqué in this shirt. It's huge, it's flannel, and it covers you from your neck to your toes. A body couldn't find one of your curves if he looked forever."

"But it's a *man's shirt,* Karen!" Amy's protest was muffled in a swath of flannel as Karen again flung the shirt over her head.

Karen tugged the shirt down and laughed again. "Yes, Amy. It's a man's shirt. You know what I think?"

"No."

"*I* think Vernon's a fusspot."

"He's not. Not really." A sudden burst of affection for stuffy old Vernon made Amy defensive on his behalf. "He's a kind man and will be a good provider."

It was Karen's turn to sigh. "That's something in his favor, I suppose. Better a boring good provider than a boring bad provider. But what I don't understand is why you can't find an *interesting* good provider."

"Vernon isn't boring," Amy said stoutly. "He's . . . a little conventional, I guess."

"I guess." Karen stood back and surveyed Amy critically. "There. I think you're all set. I'll go out to the set with you."

"Thank you. I appreciate your help." She appreciated her accompanying her to the set, too, although she knew Karen would pooh-pooh her saying so. Karen, unlike Amy, didn't believe in being embarrassed about anything as long as one was engaged in a job of honest work. If Peerless wanted Amy to disrobe completely and bathe naked in a stream, Karen would undoubtedly see nothing wrong with it.

"I don't know why you can't go after Charlie Fox," Karen said as they left the costume tent.

Her statement was so exactly along the lines of Amy's own thoughts, although she didn't want it to be, that Amy jumped a little. "I don't know what you mean," she lied stiffly.

"Piffle." Karen picked up a rock and threw it at a bluejay that was about to settle on a line of clothes she'd hung out to dry. "You do, too. He's wild about you, you know."

"He's not!" Sweet pickles, was she blushing again? Fortunately, since she'd been here on the Peerless lot in the middle of the desert for several weeks now, her cheeks had been blooming with color even when she didn't blush. "Anyway, I don't believe I could ever *go after* a man, no matter what."

"I'm sure you couldn't. You're pretty darned conventional yourself."

Karen giggled, and Amy huffed. "You're awful. You know that, don't you?"

"Piffle," Karen said again. "Charlie is crazy about you, and I think he'd make a wonderful husband."

Drat it! So did Amy, and she didn't need her new best friend's confirmation of her own feelings on the matter, because she was confused enough already.

Amy's future had been settled before she came here. Amy detested, loathed, despised, and abominated anything upsetting her plans. Unfortunately, this time it was Charlie Fox who'd upset them, and she couldn't find it in herself to hate him. She could and did, however, hate the fact that he was currently causing her to feel unsettled. She said, "Nonsense!" It was inadequate, but she didn't feel up to arguing with Karen.

It was interesting, though, that Karen had noticed a certain warmth in Charlie's dealings with Amy. It confirmed Amy's own observations. Which made her rather proud, actually, since it was pleasant to be considered desirable, although it also played hob with her plans.

Stop being a nitwit, Amy Wilkes. Charlie Fox has nothing whatever to do with your plans. It's not as if he's asked you to marry him or anything.

Good Lord, what if he did? What would she do? What would she say?

She'd say she was engaged to marry another, was what she'd say, she thought grumpily. At the moment, she wished all thoughts of Charlie Fox to Perdition.

"Mercy sakes, what are they doing?"

Karen's startled question plucked Amy's thoughts from the muddle they were in, and she was glad of it. She glanced over to where Karen's attention seemed to be fixed, and even found a grin somewhere inside herself. "They're fighting for the movie."

"Oh. I was hoping they were fighting for real. I'm sure Charlie would win."

"No doubt."

Karen eyed her for a moment. Amy pretended not to notice. She would *not,* she swore to herself, indicate by so much as a flicker of an eyelash that she found Charlie Fox the most wildly attractive man she'd ever met in her life. That road led straight to disaster.

If—and it was a great big huge fat if—he began paying her special attention, and *if* he proved to her that he was fully able and willing to support a wife and family—Amy would never, if she could help it, be in the position she'd been in as a little girl—she might reconsider her resolution to marry Vernon Catesby. She and Vernon weren't officially engaged, no matter how much Vernon seemed to think theirs was a fixed engagement. Amy was no jilt. She hadn't given Vernon a definite yes yet because she wasn't entirely sure of her own mind.

Unfortunately, the longer she worked on this ridiculous moving picture, the less sure she became. Bother. She hated it when circumstances disturbed her firm ideas about things.

"Cut! Great job, gentlemen!"

Amy and Karen both looked at the scene of the pretend fight.

The two men on the set, who had been struggling quite realistically, turned away from each other so abruptly that a laugh was startled out of Karen. Even Amy, who was in no mood to laugh, grinned. Huxtable brushed himself off. The ground, thank heavens, was no longer muddy but had turned dusty once more. It hadn't taken long for excess water to be sucked up under the relentless sun.

Today the sky was as blue as her aunt Julia's Spode china teapot, and sported clouds like cotton fluff. They reminded Amy of lambs cavorting in a blue meadow, and she wondered if the sky in Arizona Territory was as pretty as this.

Fiddlesticks. She really had to stop thinking in a such a romantic way about Arizona Territory. It was probably hot and dirty and full of desperadoes and illiterates. And bugs and snakes. And prickly cacti. It wasn't even a *state,* for the love of heaven!

She walked over to where Martin stood, discussing something with one of his minions. She didn't interrupt. Nor did she react when she saw, out of the corner of her eye, Charlie Fox spot her, change the course of his travels, and begin to stride over to her. She wished his attention didn't thrill her so, but it did.

She was a fallen woman, and she ought to be ashamed of herself. Unfortunately, she was ever so much more pleased than ashamed.

Bother.

"Howdy, Miss Wilkes." Charlie removed his hat politely and smiled one of his wonderful, heart-stopping smiles at her.

She smiled back, mainly because she couldn't help herself. "Hello, Mr. Fox. I watched most of the fight. It looked very realistic."

"It ought to have." He didn't sound as if he appreciated it, either.

Surprised, Amy said, "Oh, dear, what happened? Did Mr. Huxtable do something awful again?"

Evidently he found her instant supposition that Huxtable had been at fault amusing, because he chuckled. "No. He was all right. But it was hot and uncomfortable, and . . . well, I don't like him, and he doesn't like me, and it's not fun being all wrapped up with someone you don't like."

"I should say not!" Amy laughed, too, until she understood the meaning behind Charlie's words. It shouldn't have taken her as long as it did, really, since he was gazing at her with the most abject longing she'd ever seen on a person's face. Oh, dear. He shouldn't do that; he was embarrassing her. She looked away, and he sighed.

"Ah, Amy. You're here. Good. We can get started on the next scene," said Martin. Amy blessed him for his perfect timing.

The next scene featured Amy running away from Charlie and being rescued by Huxtable, who was supposed to throw her onto a horse's back.

That was how her shirt had become torn in rehearsal, because his throw had been too energetic. He said he hadn't meant it, but Amy didn't believe him. Nor did she trust him, and she was a little worried about the scene, although she was almost sure that Huxtable wouldn't do anything too dreadful. Not with Martin Tafft watching. Not to mention Charlie Fox, who could break Huxtable in two without half trying.

If he did do something rotten, at least his actions would

be captured by the camera. When he was arrested and tried for her murder, he wouldn't be able to wriggle out of it, the fiend.

She scolded herself for even thinking such a thing.

"Places, everyone!" Martin called. "We don't have much daylight left, so let's make the most of it. I'm sure we can get this next scene filmed." He rubbed his hands together and smiled an all-together-boys-let's-do-this-right smile. "Try to make it in one take, all right?"

When they'd first begun to film the picture, Amy hadn't known what a "take" was. Now she knew. And she also knew that Martin was keen on doing everything only once—in one take, as he said constantly. Amy understood. After all, it must take much less film if each scene only had to be shot once. Which would also help keep expenses down.

So she always did her best to assist Martin in achieving perfect scenes in one take. This one would be no different. She told herself so even as she experienced a mad desire to rush toward Charlie rather than away from him. She had a sinking feeling that if Vernon Catesby were playing Charlie's role, she wouldn't have any trouble at all making herself run away from him. She told herself to stop thinking such thoughts at once.

"Everyone ready?" Martin hollered through his megaphone. "Charlie, try to look meaner."

Charlie, who had been gazing at Amy not meanly at all, scowled and turned into a ferocious animal. Amy was impressed.

"Amy, you have to look terrified. Remember, this man wants to kill you and steal your ranch!"

"Right," Amy said, and saluted. It was remarkable how much easier this whole picturemaking endeavor was these days. Which only made sense. She looked at Charlie and plastered an expression of horror and fright on her face.

"Good! Perfect! And . . . action!"

At the cry from Martin, Charlie began moving toward Amy as if he were a panther stalking a defenseless bird. Amy backed up, as Martin had told her to do, with her hands up as if she were pushing Charlie away. If she'd truly been in danger, she would have bolted away from her pursuer without pausing to back up as her character was doing. But that wasn't art; it was sensible. This was art. Therefore, she did her best to appear panic-stricken and aghast—and extremely slow-moving.

"Perfect!"

Martin's approbation pleased her.

"All right," Martin went on. "It's almost time to turn and run. One, two, three, turn!"

Amy turned and, as she'd rehearsed that morning, ran like a frightened animal away from Charlie, who let out a roar of what sounded awfully like rage, and ran after her.

"Perfect!" Martin jumped up from his director's chair, excited. "Keep going! Perfect! And . . . *cut!*" He rushed over to Amy and Charlie. "Great job! You two are really taking to this picturemaking stuff. By gad, I wouldn't be surprised if Mr. Lovejoy wanted you in lots more pictures!"

"Hmmm," said Charlie.

Amy wrinkled her nose. "Thanks, but I don't think so."

Martin laughed. "I guess we can discuss that option later. One thing at a time." He turned and scanned the group of people standing on the sidelines. "Huxtable!"

"Here," said the star, who was looking pouty.

From his expression, Amy deduced he didn't appreciate other people getting praise for their work. The miserable egoist. She looked him straight in the eye. "Please be careful when you lift me onto the horse, Mr. Huxtable."

"Yeah, Huxtable," Charlie said, and there was some threat in his tone. "Be careful. If you hurt her, you'll pay for it."

Martin tugged on his hair. Amy was sorry to see the gesture, because she liked Martin a lot and didn't want to fuss him. In an effort to ease the situation, she said, "I'm sure everything will go smoothly." Eyeing Huxtable with narrowed eyes, she added, "Won't it, Mr. Huxtable?"

Huxtable huffed irritably. "Of course it will. I'm a professional, for heaven's sake. I know what I'm doing!"

"Yes, I'm sure you do," Amy said with some asperity. "And as long as you don't try to get back at me for not liking you, I'm sure the scene will go well."

"Don't be an utter fool!" Huxtable stalked away to take his place on the set.

Martin sighed lustily. "Places, everyone." He didn't sound as happy as he had the last few times he'd given the same order.

Amy exchanged a glance with Charlie, who appeared unappeased. She hoped he wouldn't do anything—unless, of course, Huxtable tried to hurt her. Then, she hoped Charlie would pound the ham bone's head to pulp.

Goodness, she hadn't realized that one could become hateful with so little effort. Small wonder people waged wars all the time.

Charlie wasn't in this scene, but his presence was felt all the same. Amy was glad to see him standing with his arms crossed and his legs splayed—looking rather piratelike, actually—watching like a hawk from the sidelines and ready to exact retribution if required to do so by any underhanded stunt Huxtable might pull. It comforted Amy to know he was there and overseeing her welfare.

The first part of the scene was the most difficult for her, because she had to appear overjoyed when she ran out of a door and into Huxtable's arms. She was supposed to be still fleeing from Charlie. In other words, the script had it exactly backwards.

Nevertheless, Amy did her job. Still pretending terror, she dashed through the door—attached to the false front of what was supposed to be a ranch house—and saw Huxtable. His character was supposed to have just dismounted from his horse and begun running toward the ranch house in order to rescue Amy's character. The two met outside the door in a huge embrace. Thank God the embrace didn't last long, since Charlie's character was still supposed to be in hot pursuit.

"Be gentle when you put me on that horse, Mr. Huxtable," Amy said sternly, although her expression of rapture didn't alter. Why any woman would be rapturous if she'd just run into Horace Huxtable, Amy couldn't imagine, but she was doing her best.

"Oh, for Christ's sake, shut up," Huxtable barked. "You're supposed to be acting!"

"I may be acting—Ooof! Be careful!"

"Shut up."

"I may be acting, but I don't care to be hurt!" Amy finally got out, although she couldn't talk very well since she was at present being carried to a horse by a very bouncy Horace Huxtable.

"Watch it, Huxtable," Charlie growled from the sidelines.

Amy thought she heard Martin groan, but she couldn't be sure. She was bracing herself for the upcoming ordeal. Even when she mounted that blasted horse on her own, she didn't enjoy the experience. Being tossed into a saddle by a man who wished she were dead was not exactly her cup of tea. Not to mention the fact that she didn't trust Huxtable. At all.

"All right. Upsy-daisy!" Huxtable sounded devilishly gleeful when he heaved Amy.

She shrieked when she felt how hard he was shoving her, but she managed to grasp the saddle horn in spite of Huxtable's best efforts to throw her clean over the horse's back.

"You rat! Are you trying to kill me?" She said it with a smile, because she could hear that the camera was still cranking away.

"Don't be such a baby!" Huxtable mounted his own horse with an ease Amy resented.

"That was it!" Charlie bellowed. "I'm gonna kill him."

"No!" hollered Martin. "Wait until I call cut!"

Somebody grabbed Charlie's arms to hold him back from rushing over to the horses and hauling Huxtable out of his saddle.

"You rotten louse!" Amy yelled furiously as she pulled on her horse's reins. They snapped, and she was left holding two strips of leather, in real horror this time.

The horse, upset by all the jostling and screaming, started off at a gallop, and Amy could do no more than cling like a barnacle to the saddle horn. Later, she couldn't recall another time in her life when she'd been so scared. Even when her parents had died and she'd been left alone in the world, she hadn't feared for her immediate life. It would, after all, have taken several days to die of starvation. Dying by falling off a horse and breaking her neck seemed perilously imminent.

"Oh, my God!"

After it was all over, Amy was told by Karen, Martin, and at least a dozen other people that Charlie stormed over to Horace Huxtable, who was trying to escape on his horse, grabbed him by the leg, hauled him out of the saddle, dropped him on the ground, and, without even looking to see if he was out of the way of the horse's hooves, leaped up into the saddle and raced after Amy as if all the demons in hell were after him. Actually, most of the observers joked, the only demon around was scrambling in the dust to avoid being kicked to death by the horse Charlie had mounted.

At the time, Amy had no idea that rescue was close at hand. She was frozen with fear, trying with every ounce of her strength to maintain her seat in the saddle, and losing the battle inch by inch. She knew she couldn't stay mounted for many more seconds, but everything happened so fast that she couldn't think of anything to do. She did yell "Stop!" at the top of her lungs several times, but the horse didn't seem to be paying attention. Or perhaps it understood only Spanish, since it was one of the horses Mr. Archuleta had brought to the set.

When she saw Charlie and his horse gallop into sight, she would have taken heart if her heart hadn't been occupied at that moment in jumping around in her chest like a demented jackrabbit. When he leaned over and his hand reached out to grab the bridle, she wanted to squeeze her eyes shut because she feared for his balance. When she realized that the horse that had run away with her was slowing down, she felt a smidgen of hope. When the horse finally came to a stop, panting and wheezing, and Charlie lifted her out of the saddle and onto his, she did something she couldn't help, but which embarrassed her to death. She burst into tears.

He held her tight, right there in front of him on the saddle, and spoke sweet words into her hair. Amy tried to stop crying, but couldn't. She was making an awful noise, but Charlie didn't seem to mind. He stroked her hair—her hat had blown off somewhere during her headlong ride—and rocked her gently, crooning softly all the while, "It's all right, honey. You're all right now."

Somehow or other, being called "honey" by Charlie Fox made her cry harder. She clung to him as she'd been clinging to her saddle horn only seconds earlier—but she felt ever so much more secure than she had then.

She managed to choke out, "I'm sorry," although she wasn't sure exactly what she was sorry for. Crying, probably.

"It'll be all right, sweetheart. It'll be fine in a minute."

"Sweetheart" had the same effect on her that "honey" had, and Amy, who was trying to gulp breaths of air in an effort to stop this unladylike display of tears, made a horrid choking noise and cried harder.

"You're okay now, Amy darlin'. You'll be fine. I'm going to kill Horace Huxtable as soon as we get back to the set, and he'll never be able to hurt you again."

That stopped her tears instantly. She whipped her head up, bumping Charlie's chin. She stroked it with her hand to soothe the bump, and stared at him, terrified that he'd meant what he'd just said. "No!" she cried. "You can't hurt him!"

"He hurt you." Charlie took the hand she'd stroked his chin with and kissed its palm. "Any man who hurts you needs killin', darlin'."

If that wasn't the sweetest thing anyone had ever said to her, Amy didn't know what was. She was sure as anything that Vernon would never, ever say such a sweet thing. Not even if he rescued her from a runaway horse. Not that he could. Which was totally beside the point. "But, no, Charlie. Please don't hurt him. You'll get into trouble if you do, and that would be awful."

"Would it?"

His eyes held an expression that was as soft and warm as cocoa on a winter day, and Amy melted like a marshmallow as she gazed into them. Unable to get her mouth and tongue coordinated enough to form words, she nodded.

"Well, then, maybe I won't kill him. Maybe I'll just hurt him. It'll go against the grain, though. He needs killin' bad."

His face was blurring. Amy had only a second or two to consider this phenomenon when his lips touched hers and she understood that the blurring had been because he was leaning toward her.

She kissed him back passionately. Thoroughly. With love.

Thirteen

The following night, a Friday, the entire cast and crew were promised a trip to the city of El Monte to have a good dinner in a restaurant, visit a nightclub, and spend the night in a hotel. Martin estimated that the picture would wrap up in another three or four days' shooting, and this was a precelebration.

"It's not much of a treat, but after the flood and all the hard work we've all done, I think we deserve it," Martin said as he made the announcement later on the day of the horse incident.

Everyone in the throng gathered around Martin turned to stare at Horace Huxtable. Huxtable, as everyone knew, had been promised a trip to town in return for helping out during the flood.

Charlie, who'd been keeping particular tabs on Huxtable since Amy's latest accident, noticed that the majority of the stares trained at the actor were disapproving. Which, he thought, was absolutely appropriate.

It wasn't Horace Huxtable's fault that Amy Wilkes hadn't been killed today when her horse had bolted. Charlie was pretty sure he was the only one on the set who'd seen Huxtable flick the rump of her horse with a twig. And, although Charlie couldn't prove it, he was morally certain it had been Huxtable who'd cut Amy's reins so that she couldn't stop the horse when she tried. The lousy bastard. He might be a murderer this minute if Charlie hadn't saved Amy's gorgeous hide.

It wasn't Charlie's fault that Huxtable was still alive, either. His intentions post-rescue had been directed at homicide, and in his opinion had been valid.

It was the way Amy had kissed him that had distracted him from his purpose. By the time she'd finally pulled away from him he'd been fit for only one thing—procreation—and that was about as opposite to murder as it could be.

Unfortunately, the act of procreation was denied him, too. Not only were they on top of a horse in the middle of a motion picture set, but he and Amy Wilkes weren't married. Shoot, they weren't even promised.

And *that,* Charlie swore to himself as he, too, glared at Huxtable, was a situation he aimed to fix tonight. The evening would be given over to relaxation and fun, and he was sure to find an opportunity to have Amy to himself for a little while. It wouldn't take long, he hoped, to convince her that, no matter how remote the possibility seemed when they'd first met, he knew—and he'd convince her of it or die trying—they were made for each other.

Charlie had been to saloons in Arizona Territory. He expected that any nightclub in El Monte, California, would be comparable. Maybe a little fancier. But there would be music and laughter, and maybe he could get Amy to dance with him. And then maybe he could get her to walk outside with him. And then maybe they could get to talking, and he could tell her how well fixed he was to begin married life.

Or, he amended, since he needed to be honest with himself and with her, he would be well fixed after this picture was finished and he added his pay to the money he had in the bank. Charlie had been saving for years. With the big pile of cash he'd earn from this picture, he'd be ready to make his move.

He aimed to have himself a real, honest-to-God cattle ranch. No ostriches or any other silly thing for him. No, sir. He was going to have himself the finest herd of Jersey cows west of Texas. He was particularly fond of Jerseys because they produced the richest milk, and Charlie aimed to have at least a dozen kids, all of whom would need that good, rich milk.

Cattle ranching was the life he knew and loved. Shoot, he might even branch out into dairy farming if such a move seemed profitable. He'd been reading up on both industries, and they were absolutely compatible. Dairy farming might be better for California, which Amy might prefer. Charlie had been reading up about California, too.

After all, he had Amy's wishes to consider as well as his own. If Amy had a particular attachment to California, well, then, they could settle in California. He wouldn't mind California. He liked it here. He'd even plant her an orange tree, if she wanted one. Or a whole danged grove of the things. Oranges were good for kids, too.

Of course, first he had to talk her into marrying him. He saw her standing next to Karen Crenshaw across the way from him. She and Karen seemed to be real chummy lately, a circumstance Charlie found amusing. She'd been so upset when she'd first seen Karen smoking.

But she wasn't as much of a prig as Charlie'd at first believed her to be, and she'd been willing to overlook Karen's smoking habit because Karen was a nice girl. Charlie approved of such flexibility in personal relationships, because it made life easier. Anytime a body required folks to behave in a prescribed manner, a body got to losing friends. Charlie knew from experience that a man could never have too many friends.

Martin called the casual meeting to a halt, and dismissed the cast and crew to prepare for a trip to town. He cornered

Charlie before he was able to lope over to Amy and make arrangements to have dinner with her.

"Charlie, will you try to keep an eye on Amy this evening?" Martin asked. He looked a little worried.

Startled that Martin should ask him to do exactly what he'd planned to do, Charlie nodded his assent. "Sure. How come?"

"Well . . ." Martin took a glance around the clearing that had lately been full of people. "I hate to say this, but I think Huxtable has it in for Amy. He resents her for not falling in love with him. He thinks he's God's gift to women, you know, and doesn't like it when women don't agree with him. Also . . ." He broke off abruptly and looked embarrassed.

Charlie tried to appear kind and approachable because he wanted to hear what other interesting tidbits of information or speculation Martin had to divulge. He knew he himself was being less than forthcoming—after all, if Martin added any more fuel to Charlie's already huge heap of Huxtable detritus, Charlie probably wouldn't be able to restrain himself from killing the bastard—but he wanted to know the worst. "Also what?" he asked encouragingly.

"Well," Martin said, and he seemed very uncomfortable to be speaking so, "I wouldn't want to accuse anybody unjustly, you understand, but I have a hunch Huxtable might have been behind that runaway horse incident this morning."

Charlie stared at him, unable to imagine even the kind-hearted, sweet-natured Martin Tafft being so naive as to feel any reluctance to blame Huxtable for so Huxtable-like a maneuver. "He was behind it, all right. I saw him hit the horse with a twig."

Martin's eyes went huge. "You *what?*"

Charlie shrugged. "I saw him. He might have killed her."

"Good God, I think the man's lost his mind."

"He's going to lose more than that if I can get him alone."

He smiled amiably to let Martin know he didn't hold him responsible for any of Huxtable's antics.

"Good God," Martin repeated, as if bereft of more cogent speech.

"At first I thought I might just break one of his arms, but I think he'd learn more from a couple of broken legs."

Martin's eyes looked as if they might bug out of his head. "I can't believe you're actually saying this."

"Believe it," Charlie suggested. He warmed to his subject, glad that Martin knew Huxtable had spooked Amy's horse. "I saw him. I'm going to break both his legs for spooking Miss Wilkes's horse as soon as I can get him alone."

"Good God," Martin said for the third time.

Charlie was sorry to see the horrified look on his face. He liked Martin Tafft and didn't want to upset him. But enough was enough. "Sorry, Martin, but that's the way it is. Somebody's got to teach the man a lesson, and if nothing else will work, I expect I can at least lay him up so that he can't get around for a while."

"You can't do that. Lord above, you can't do that, Charlie! Think about what you're saying! The police will arrest you. You'll be thrown in jail!"

Charlie obligingly thought about it for approximately five seconds, which was all the time he needed. He shrugged again. "It'll be worth it."

If he did get thrown in jail for performing such a worthwhile public service—and he supposed it could happen. After all, he was in California now and not Arizona Territory, where people looked upon justice in a more practical light than they did here. Still, he was sure he'd be let out in plenty of time to get ready for his wedding.

"No. No, you can't do it. It's . . . it's . . ." Martin broke off and looked up at Charlie. He smiled tentatively. "Oh, I get it. You're joking, right?"

Charlie shook his head. "Nope. The man deserves to have his legs broken. He could have killed her."

"Good God."

"I'm real sorry, Martin. I've held back for this long, but this morning he really could have killed Miss Wilkes. He's hurt her before, but that was a long ways from killing somebody. He deserves whatever he gets, and if I can help it, he's going to get hurt bad."

"Can't you at least wait until the filming's over?" Martin's level of stress was making his voice hoarse.

Charlie thought about it and shook his head. "I don't think so. Sorry, Martin. The man's dangerous."

"Lord, Charlie, you can't do this. Think of what it will mean to Peerless! It will be the end of the studio!"

Damn. Charlie frowned, disliking the possibility just presented. He didn't want to cause Martin any further trouble. His whole aim in ridding the world of Horace Huxtable was to prevent him from doing any more evil deeds. "Well . . . I'm sure I could make it look like an accident."

"No!" Martin began tugging at his hair.

Feeling frustrated, Charlie muttered, "Can I break one of his legs?"

"No."

"How about an arm?"

"No."

"Not even one?"

"No."

"Dammit, Martin, the man's a menace. He's hurt her before, and this morning he might have killed her! I mean, how much more is the poor lady supposed to endure? Is it going to take Huxtable laying her out on a slab in order for these things to stop happening?"

"No, no. I'll think of something. I've *got* to think of something."

"You've already set guards on him. And tonight he's going to be drinking again, and you know what that means."

"There are only two days left of filming. Surely he won't do anything in two days' time."

"It only took him a second this morning."

Martin let out a low groan and began pacing in front of Charlie. Charlie was sorry to see how worried and distracted Martin was, but certain facts had to be faced.

To spur Martin on to greater inspirational thought, he said, "It's both of his legs or you think of something, Martin. I can't keep worrying about Miss Wilkes. It's driving me nuts, wondering what Huxtable's going to do to her next and trying to anticipate him. It was pure dumb luck that I saw what he did this morning, so I could go after her before the horse threw her. She could have landed on any of those boulders out there." He shuddered at the thought.

So did Martin. "Gus. I'll set Gus to watch him closely tonight."

"It's going to take more than Gus. It's going to take somebody who knows what Huxtable's capable of."

Martin snapped his fingers as if he'd been struck with a brilliant idea. "You! You can watch him! You're the best man for the job, because you hate his guts and won't let him get away with anything."

His smile faded when Charlie shook his head. "Nope. I've got other plans for the evening."

"I'll pay you a bonus." Martin must have sensed the finality of Charlie's decision, because his voice carried no conviction.

"Nope. Sorry, Martin."

"Hmmm. Well, I'll still send Gus to watch him."

"You'd better send someone with him. Sam's pretty big. If you go with Gus and Sam, the three of you ought to be able to ride herd on one lousy actor."

"Me?" Martin looked as if he'd rather do just about anything else on earth—even have a tooth pulled or a broken arm set—than babysit Horace Huxtable.

"Well . . ." Charlie lifted his hands, as if to say he was sorry but there didn't seem to be much choice. "There's Eddie."

"Eddie's good. You sure you aren't interested?"

"No way."

Martin deflated like a pricked balloon. "All right. Anyhow, it's my responsibility." He scowled horribly. "But it'll never happen again." He turned and began walking away, talking to himself. "If Phineas Lovejoy ever, *ever* wants Horace Huxtable to play in another picture, he'll have to direct the damned thing himself and that's all there is to it."

Charlie was sorry to have added to Martin's burdens, but he wasn't going to let this evening's opportunity pass him by. Somehow or other, he was going to get Amy Wilkes to agree to marry him.

Amy was looking forward to her evening out with the cast and crew of *One and Only*. She'd never been to a real nightclub before, although there was one in Pasadena, and she knew that Vernon went there occasionally. It had never occurred to her that ladies could go to nightclubs. She said as much to Karen, who was helping her find evening things to wear.

"Why not? Women need recreation every bit as much as men do," Karen declared as she adjusted her hair ornament, a beautiful evening creation of jet beads and fabric roses that went superbly with her evening's ensemble.

Amy eyed her, trying not to be envious. After all, Karen's trade was fashion. Of course she'd have lots of lovely clothes. "I've always been told that gentlemen need to relax away from home, while women are supposed to sit home and knit or something." She told herself to forget about Karen's gorgeous costume and squinted into the mirror. Perhaps she could use a little dab of rouge on her lips.

And if this wasn't another indication of her impending downfall, she didn't know what was. If Vernon knew she was contemplating the wearing of lip rouge, he would have a hissy fit. The notion of Vernon going so far as to have any kind of fit made her giggle.

Karen eyed her slantways. "What? Is my ribbon crooked?"

"Not at all. You look lovely. That's a marvelous dress. I'm wildly jealous."

"Thank you." Karen beamed with justifiable pride, and Amy decided it was sort of fun to be open and honest and not absolutely tied to convention all the time. Sometimes when one blurted out what one felt, one not only made oneself feel good, but others, too.

Karen turned suddenly as if she'd just remembered something. "Oh! I forgot!" she cried, confirming Amy's impression. "I have a perfectly stunning gown that would look wonderful on you. I'll have to take up the front a tiny little bit so it won't drag."

"Oh! Well, really, I don't think . . ."

"Oh, come on," urged Karen, darting to a huge pile of boxes stacked in a corner of the costume tent. She rummaged through the stack until she found a cherry-red box with white polka dots. She pulled it from the pile and thrust it aside, as if she knew there was something in it she'd need later.

Amy eyed the box doubtfully. She'd never seen anything good come from polka dots. "Really, Karen, I don't mind not wearing anything stunning. I'd probably feel stupid in anything stunning, actually."

"Don't be a goose," her friend said firmly. "You're a beautiful woman and deserve nice clothes. Especially since you've never been to a nightclub before. You'll want to wear something suitable for dancing."

Dancing? Merciful heavens. The evening sounded delicious already. Amy loved to dance. Unfortunately, Vernon didn't. She'd bet any amount of money—except that she wasn't so abandoned as to gamble, yet—that Martin Tafft could take a turn on the dance floor and not stumble over his feet. She wondered about Charlie Fox. Then she sighed as she got lost in the pleasant fantasies that thoughts of him always produced in her.

"Now, where is that thing? I thought it was here."

The only part of Karen that Amy could see at present was her satin-clad bottom, which was sticking out of a rack of gowns in the corner next to the stack of boxes. Amy wasn't at all sure about this. Yet she discovered within herself an enormous well of trust in Karen, which was cheering. Amy was certain that her friend wouldn't make her wear anything scandalous.

Idiot, Amy. She can't force *you to wear anything at all!*

Which conjured up all sorts of other wildly improbable— not to mention shockingly improper—images in her mind and made her laugh again. She saw Karen's rump disappear, and a moment later saw her head poke out of the rack of clothes.

"Now what?" Karen asked. "Are you laughing at me?"

"No. I'm laughing at myself. I'm sitting here fearing that you'll make me wear red-and-white polka dots."

"Polka dots!" Karen's lovely brown eyes widened. "Don't be a goose!" She disappeared into the rack of clothes again. "Aha!" she shouted a moment later. "Here it is!"

When she pushed her way out of the rack of clothes and Amy saw the gown she was holding up on its padded silk hanger, Amy gasped. "Oh, my!" She pressed her hands to her cheeks. Never in her entire life had she even so much as dreamed she'd wear anything so lovely.

"It's absolutely up to crack," Karen said triumphantly. "And it will look perfect on you! It was *made* for you." She tossed the skirt of the gown over her free arm and walked to Amy's side. "Not literally, of course, but I'm sure it will fit with a judicious tuck here and there."

"It's beautiful," Amy said simply.

"Yes, it is. It's one of Madame Dunbar's finest. Gray silk chiffon mounted over dark blue silk. The bodice is fitted, and may need to be taken in a little bit, but not much. It probably won't matter. Nobody will look at it that closely."

"I'd just as soon not wear anything too tight anyway," Amy said. "I detest tight corsets." When she heard herself, she smiled at how much her taste had changed in a few short weeks.

Or perhaps they hadn't changed, exactly. This was the first time in her life she'd ever actually thought about things that she'd merely accepted without question. She'd never once, for instance, believed that a respectable woman might smoke cigarettes. Or that one didn't have to wear a corset so tight it cut off one's air and made it impossible for one to sing in church, for another example. My, but life was an interesting proposition when one spent a few weeks outside of Pasadena, wasn't it?

Karen had adopted her working mien and was all business. "Take that thing off and slip this on, and we'll see what needs to be done."

So Amy slipped "that thing"—formerly, her most daring and exciting evening ensemble—over her head and placed it carefully on the back of a ladder-back chair. The blue silk and gray chiffon felt like a cloud slipping over her skin. She sighed with pleasure.

"If I have to take any tucks at the waist in order to keep it from dragging in the front, this black velvet cummerbund will hide the evidence." Karen's mouth was full of pins, but by this time Amy'd had lots of practice interpreting her speech when she was so encumbered.

"This," Amy said, and she could hear the awe in her own voice, "is magnificent."

"Isn't it?" Karen sounded merely delighted. "I love it. Wilma Patecky's going to wear it in another Peerless flicker that they're going to shoot right after this one."

"Wilma Patecky?" Amy could hardly believe she was, at this very moment, wearing a gown crafted for Wilma Patecky, one of the major stars of the Broadway stage. "I didn't know she played in the pictures."

"Sure. They all do," Karen said simply. "They make lots of money, and nobody knows their names."

It made perfect sense when said in Karen's blunt manner. "I see. Yes, I can understand the appeal." Amy didn't particularly care for being in the limelight, but if one was accustomed to it, as a stage actress must be, she supposed the moving pictures would be a logical step. Especially since no one who hadn't seen you on the stage would know it was you there on celluloid.

"Yes," Karen mumbled. "I'll have to gather the skirt up in front. But it has this long train, so the back is okay."

It always inspired Amy to watch Karen work. She was so capable, and her hands seemed to fly when working with fabric. She was an artist in her own arena. Amy sighed, feeling small and unimportant all at once.

"That polka-dot box, by the way, contains the gray pearls you're going to wear."

"Pearls?" Good heavens, Amy wasn't sure about this. She'd be wearing clothes and jewels worth more than she was. What a lowering reflection that was.

"They aren't real," Karen mumbled, alleviating Amy's doubts somewhat. "But they're perfect for this gown."

What a relief. Rather than say so, Amy gave a judicious "Hmmm." She thought of something else that gave her a thrill of apprehension. "Um, did you say there will be dancing at the nightclub, Karen?"

"Yes, I did."

Something in Amy's voice must have alerted Karen that Amy was apprehensive about dancing. She stopped sticking pins in the gown Amy wore and glanced at her. "Don't you dance?"

She sounded neither disapproving nor surprised; only curious. Nevertheless, Amy felt a little foolish. "Well, not a lot. I love to waltz. And one of my friends tried to teach me some steps to the new ragtime music people are always playing, but we didn't have enough time for me to learn very well."

"Ragtime's easy," Karen declared. "And it's lots of fun. Here. Look at this." She backed away from Amy, held her arms out as if she were holding on to a gentleman, leaned a little forward, and scooted across the floor of the tent.

Amy blinked at where her friend's feet were supposed to be. She saw nothing but Karen's gown, swishing around her evening slippers. "Um, I can't see a thing."

"Oh." Karen stopped and glanced at her feet. "Of course not." She picked up her skirt and moved her feet again in a series of quick but uncomplicated steps. Amy peered at Karen's moving feet closely, then lifted her own skirt and imitated her.

"That was the way!" Karen said, smiling.

"It's not too hard, is it?" Amy said doubtfully.

"Not at all. And don't forget. You'll probably be asked to dance by Martin, who's an excellent dancer."

"Oh, dear."

But Karen shook her head. "Nonsense. If a man's a good dancer—and Martin is splendid—he'll carry you along as if you were a dandelion puff. Martin makes dancing easy."

"Really?"

"I know you don't believe me." Karen stopped dancing and

came back to Amy, armed with pins once more. "But it's the truth. And you'll certainly dance with Charlie Fox. Now, I don't have any idea whether or not Charlie can dance, but I have a feeling it won't matter." She poked Amy's shoulder to get her to turn around and lifted the train of her dress.

Honestly curious, Amy peered over her shoulder to watch Karen do something mysterious with her train. "Why not?"

"Because," Karen said as she gave the train a tug, almost toppling Amy, "he's in love with you and will probably just stand there in a daze with you in his arms."

"Karen!" Amy was really quite shocked—and extremely gratified. After her initial astonishment subsided, which took approximately three seconds, she said with a hesitant hitch to her voice, "Do you really think he admires me?"

Karen did something extremely unladylike: She rolled her eyes. "Good Lord, child, are you that innocent?"

"I guess I must be," Amy mumbled.

"I guess so. Of course he admires you! He's in love with you! And you're in love with him. And the sooner you write and tell your precious Vernon so, the better off all three of you will be."

"Mercy sakes." Amy wished life were that simple.

Did she love Charlie Fox? Was Karen correct?

She feared so.

Did Charlie Fox love her, Amy Wilkes, from Pasadena, California?

Oh, wouldn't that be wonderful? Amy wasn't vain enough to take Karen's word on the matter, but it might be so.

But whatever would Vernon think? And her aunt and uncle? And Vernon's parents, who were stuffier even than Vernon, and ever so proper? They summered in New York and wintered in Pasadena, and had more money than they knew what to do with—which was why Vernon had gone into banking, actually, because a position with a bank gave him opportunities for investment that he wouldn't otherwise have. Among them, Vernon and his parents must own three-quarters of the city of Pasadena, not to mention entire towns back East.

In other words, if Amy married Vernon Catesby, she'd be set for life. If she married Charlie Fox, she'd be . . . what? She had no idea.

"Oh, stop it," she told herself aloud.

Karen jumped. "Beg pardon?"

"I'm sorry, Karen." Amy shook her head, trying to clear it of the fuddle that seemed to envelop her every time she considered marriage to Charlie Fox. "I was just thinking."

"About Vernon, I'm sure," Karen said caustically.

Amy sighed. "I fear you're right."

"Fiddlesticks!"

Amy feared she was right about that, too.

Fourteen

Amy couldn't recall another evening in her life when she'd felt so perfectly gowned and shod. The evening dress Karen had found for her was stunning, the shoes she'd dug out of that polka-dot box were perfect, the gray silk stockings felt like eiderdown against her skin, and the gray pearls and eardrops were ideal.

She'd seen elegance when she'd finally peered at herself in the mirror in the costume tent. She knew she hadn't been mistaken in her judgment when Charlie Fox and Martin Tafft stopped dead in their tracks and stared at her. And at Karen. Amy was not so vain that she didn't know Karen looked wonderful tonight, too, and she was happy to share the limelight with her good friend.

"My goodness, ladies," Martin, who recovered first, said. "I fear El Monte won't be grand enough for the likes of you two. You're both very beautiful this evening."

Amy noticed that Charlie, who had stood there gaping during Martin's chivalrous speech, finally shut his mouth and nodded. "Yes, sir." His voice was low and throaty, as if he didn't have enough air to use it properly.

She smiled graciously and peeked at Karen, who was grinning like Mr. Carroll's Cheshire Cat. Amy climbed down from her high horse fast and grinned, too, sensing that Karen had the right idea. This was sort of like a little girl's dress-up party, and she and Karen were playing at being sophisticated

and worldly grown-up ladies out for a night on the town—
even if the town was El Monte.

Martin took Karen's overnight bag, and Charlie took Amy's.
They put the bags in the tonneau of the big car and returned
to open the doors for the two ladies.

"You're both looking pretty swank yourselves," Karen told
the two men as she lifted her skirt and allowed Martin to
assist her into his automobile, a Pierce Great Arrow, which
was about the most splendid motorcar Amy had ever seen,
much less ridden in.

The flickers, as Karen liked to call them, were certainly a
profitable enterprise. Karen was adept at slang. *Swank* and
flickers were but two of the new words Amy had learned since
being in Karen's company. Why, she might go home to
Pasadena having learned a whole new language.

Vernon would never stop scolding her if she ever forgot
herself and spoke her newly acquired vocabulary in his company.

She heaved a huge sigh—almost as big as the Pierce Great
Arrow—and realized how boring life with Vernon was going
to be. Why, he probably wouldn't even approve of Amy taking
their children to the park, but would assuredly prefer having
a nanny for them. Amy had always rather looked forward to
the prospect of caring for her own children.

Not that she'd ever wanted to be one of those pitifully poor
creatures she'd read about in Mr. Jacob Riis's *How the Other
Half Lives*. That would be too ghastly. But surely there must
be a happy medium.

Perhaps, in fact, life as a rancher's wife.

Oh, dear, there she went again.

"You look good enough to eat this evening, Miss Wilkes,"
Charlie said softly after he'd settled in next to her.

She and he were in the backseat, Martin and Karen in the
front. Amy had been a shade disturbed by this arrangement

at first, thinking it would have been more seemly for her and Karen to share the backseat. On the other hand, she and Karen—and Martin and Charlie—were all adults. They could be trusted to keep themselves in line.

"Thank you." Feeling nervous, Amy blurted out, "Karen found this gown in a rack of clothes that are going to be used in Wilma Patecky's next picture." She felt silly afterwards and wished she'd left her remarks simply at *thank you*.

"Is that so?" Charlie sounded impressed. "That's sort of swell, isn't it?"

Swell. There was that awful word again. Amy tried not to be disappointed that Charlie had used it.

"Er, I don't think I know who Miss Patecky is, though," he added after a moment.

Amy turned to stare at him. Well, wasn't that something? Charlie Fox had never heard of Wilma Patecky. It had by now become perfectly plain to her that she wasn't the only person in existence who didn't understand the sophisticated life. Of course, Charlie was a cowboy, which explained a lot. He had more of an excuse than she did, if it came to that.

"She's a Broadway actress who's been working in some of the recent motion pictures," Amy explained. "I've read about her in magazines and newspapers."

"Ah. So she's sort of like Mr. Huxtable."

Silence bloomed like a spring blossom in the car. Amy thought it was interesting that the mere mention of Horace Huxtable's name should produce such a numbing effect on four grown people. She made an effort to dispel the uncomfortable atmosphere. "I'm sure Miss Patecky is nowhere near as awful as Mr. Huxtable."

"No," Charlie concurred quickly. "She couldn't be. Nobody could be that bad."

"He's in another machine," Martin muttered. "I wasn't going to have him cutting capers in my Pierce Arrow."

"No indeed," said Karen. "Anything but that."

Amy didn't think it was funny, since Horace Huxtable had given her a very bad time lately.

Martin chuffed impatiently and said, "I'm sorry, Miss Wilkes. Karen. You know, I'm sure, that we've had to set guards on him."

"Yes," Amy said, her voice clipped. "Unfortunately, they can't always be around on the set when the camera's running."

She thought she heard a growl from Charlie but couldn't be sure because the engine in Martin's motorcar was louder than the growl. Overall, Amy thought, automobiles were interesting, but if she were to go for a romantic ride somewhere, she'd as soon go in a buggy—as long as the gentleman with whom she was being romantic didn't have to drive the vehicle, too.

"I can't apologize enough for his behavior, Miss Wilkes," Martin said.

All at once, Amy felt a totally unfamiliar recklessness overcome her stodgy Pasadena attitudes. She burst out, "Oh, please, everyone, call me Amy! I'm so tired of being the only 'Miss' on the set."

She saw Charlie's white teeth gleaming. Karen whooped and clapped her hands. "I wondered how long it would take you to unbend enough to allow us mere peasants to call you by your Christian name."

"Goodness, I'm not *that* bad," Amy muttered, then added a somewhat horrified, "Am I?" She hoped she wasn't. Although she didn't care to be taken for a loose woman, she didn't want to have a reputation as a prissy miss, either.

"You're not that bad," Charlie assured her, picking up her hand and kissing it. The memory of the kiss they'd shared earlier in the day came back to Amy in a rush, and she felt her face flame. Fortunately, it was too dark for anyone to see. "You're wonderful, in fact."

Wishing she could fan herself, Amy muttered in a smothered voice, "Thank you." She wanted to add, *I think you are, too,* but couldn't make herself say such a telling truth aloud.

"I think Amy is a very pretty name," said Karen. "I wish my parents had named me Amy instead of Karen. I'm named after my Norwegian grandmother, though, and had no choice in the matter."

Martin laughed. "I'm afraid nobody has much of a choice when it comes to their own name."

"Oh, I don't know," said Amy, beginning to recover her composure. "Actors seem to take great liberties with their given names. And the Peerless Studio didn't seem to care for my name, so they changed it. Without even asking me if I preferred Amelia." She feigned outrage so well that Karen actually turned to peer at her over the motorcar's front seat. Amy grinned at her to let her know she was fooling.

"That was Mrs. Lovejoy's idea," said Martin uncomfortably. "She seems to think Amelia will be accepted more readily than Amy. She thinks it's more romantic."

"I don't know why," Karen grumbled. "If she wanted a romantic name, she ought to have picked something like Rosalie or Celeste or something."

"Celeste Wilkes." Amy shook her head. "I don't think so."

"Rosalie's kind of nice." Charlie didn't sound sure of himself.

"Well, you can call me Rosalie if you like," offered Amy. "But chances are I won't know who you're talking to and won't respond."

With a laugh, Charlie squeezed her hand. Amy knew she should withdraw it, but couldn't make herself do it. Her hand felt so good in his. And nobody could see, so it wasn't as if her reputation would be damaged.

It occurred to her that if her reputation remained undamaged through the remaining few scenes of *One and Only* it would be a miracle. Surely, sooner or later, Horace Huxtable was going to try again to injure her, and she wouldn't allow him to get away with it. And probably Charlie wouldn't, either. Her mind's eye pictured the bloody battle that might ensue between the two men, and her heart swelled with appreciation. Charlie was so gallant.

"I've always wanted to hear my name on your lips, Amy," he murmured into the palm of her hand, which he'd lifted to his lips.

Amy nearly fainted. "You have?"

"I have. I love the name Amy."

"Charlie's a nice name, too," she said, hoping Karen and Martin weren't listening. They didn't seem to be. Amy thought she heard something from the front seat about a version of *The Prisoner of Zenda* that Peerless wanted to film. Amy hoped they would film it, because she'd loved the book.

Merciful gracious, she was trying to distract herself from being made love to by Charlie Fox! She recognized the symptoms. Why was she doing that? She thought Charlie Fox was the most wonderful man she'd ever met. Why would she want to distract herself?

She supposed it was only that she was unused to feeling these tumbled emotions about a fellow. The good Lord knew she felt no particular emotional intensity when she dealt with poor Vernon.

Oh, dear, whatever should she do about poor Vernon?

Charlie didn't press her, however. He kissed the palm of her hand, seemed to sense her level of discomfort, and replaced her hand on the plush upholstery of the backseat. She shot him a quick, grateful smile, but wasn't sure if he saw it. Night had fallen, and the lamps affixed to the front of the motorcar, which didn't shed much light on the road, didn't shed any light at all inside the vehicle.

* * *

"I reckon Martin was right about this place," Charlie murmured to Amy as the car approached the portals of the Royal El Montean, a rambling facility that contained a hotel, restaurant, and nightclub. "You're much too pretty for it. You should be in a fancy nightclub in a big city somewhere."

"I'll run inside the hotel, check us all in, and bring back the keys," Martin said as he parked the motorcar. Charlie got out and held the door for Amy.

Charmed, Amy smiled up at him as she descended from the car and said, "Thank you. I believe you're exaggerating. After all, I'm a simple working girl from Pasadena. The closest thing to elegance I've ever been to is the Green Hotel." She sighed, recalling the night she and Vernon had gone to a dance there. "Now, that was something special."

"Is the Green Hotel in Pasadena?"

Amy noticed that Charlie's smile had faded, and she hoped she hadn't given him the impression that she was accustomed to the elegancies of life. She might *become* accustomed to them in the future, if she married Vernon. Marrying Vernon, however, was becoming ever more remote a goal for her. She wasn't sure if that was a good thing or a very, very bad one.

"Yes," she said. "It's where all the Eastern swells—you know, from New York and Boston and so forth—come to stay for the winter." Recalling Mr. and Mrs. Catesby, Sr., of New York City, she added, "If, of course, they don't already own their own winter home in Pasadena."

"Be right back," said Martin, and sped off into the dark.

"I'll go with you and help hold the keys," Karen said, taking off after him. Amy barely noticed they were gone.

"I don't expect there's anything as fancy as that anywhere in Arizona Territory."

Charlie sounded glum, and Amy took his arm as they began

walking over the uneven ground to the front door of the building. "I shouldn't imagine the lack of elegant hotels would be much of a hardship for a rancher."

She peeked up at him, hoping her facial expression conveyed the look of a woman whose greatest aim in life was to set up with a rancher in Arizona Territory and raise a brood of children. And cows, of course. She was pleased that Charlie didn't seem enamored of ostriches, because she wouldn't know what to do with an ostrich even more than she didn't know what to do with a cow.

She was disappointed when Charlie seemed to twist her words into something disparaging. "No, I reckon we're not awfully fancy in the territory."

His voice sounded cool, and she sighed. When one shoved all the romantic nonsense about a union between herself and Charlie aside, the fact remained that she and he were from two different worlds. Sometimes those two worlds appeared not so very far apart. But sometimes, like right this minute, for instance, she and Charlie seemed to belong on two entirely unrelated continents separated by oceans of unnavigable water.

"I don't much care about elegant living myself," she said as he held the door for her to enter the restaurant. The mouthwatering aroma of spicy, well-cooked food greeted them as they entered. "It's fun to dress up sometimes. Like tonight." She shrugged, trying to give her words the light edge she wanted him to hear.

"Is that so?"

She didn't get to answer because Martin and Karen walked up to them, Karen smiling and holding out a fistful of keys. "Here we are," she said. "Number four for Charlie, number six for Amy, and number eight for me. Martin already has his."

"Thanks," Amy said, putting the key in her small beaded bag. She saw Charlie drop his key into his trousers pocket.

Martin sniffed the air appreciatively, rubbed his hands together, and said, "We have reservations in the restaurant's main dining room. The rest of the cast and crew will be seated in a banquet room in back. Huxtable wasn't happy about that, but I don't care."

"You got Horace Huxtable to sit in a banquet room with *other people?*" Karen looked as if she might burst out laughing, restaurant or no restaurant.

"Yes. I told him in no uncertain terms that if he wanted to come, he had to sit at a separate table in the banquet room with Gus and Sam, both of whom have been sworn to absolute sobriety the whole night long, and Eddie, who doesn't drink anyway. But I thought the four of us should sit together in the restaurant. There will be dancing in the nightclub afterwards. It's right over there." He indicated a door on the other side of the dining room.

Amy didn't hear any music yet. She was eager to try the new ragtime steps Karen had taught her, and hoped she'd be able to test her skill with Charlie. Unless he was one of those clumsy men who didn't dance.

As if he'd read her mind, Charlie asked, "Do you like to dance, Amy?"

"Oh, yes. And Karen taught me some ragtime steps."

He smiled. "Great." Amy was happy to hear the enthusiasm creep back into Charlie's voice. "My sisters use me to practice on all the time, so I know lots of ragtime. And waltzes and polkas and stuff."

"I love to waltz." Amy sighed happily, and a feeling that the evening was destined to be a memorable one crept over her. She continued to hold on to his arm as they followed a waiter to a table. For such an out-of-the-way place, the Royal El Montean didn't have such a shabby appearance. Amy had expected something more along the lines of a tumbledown chophouse.

But the tables in the restaurant were covered with white cloths that were not too badly stained, there were barely wilted flowers residing in vases at each table, and the waiter looked as if he'd had a bath recently. Amy considered these circumstances indicative of an enterprise that was at least trying to achieve something in the way of style.

"Here, let me take your wrap," Charlie said as they drew up at the table to which the waiter had directed them.

"Thank you." She hated to give up the gorgeous gray silk shawl because it went so beautifully with Wilma Patecky's gorgeous gray chiffon dress. Since it was all pretend and dress-up and, in effect, the coach would turn into a pumpkin at midnight, she grinned to herself and relinquished the shawl. Then, after Charlie hung it on a nearby rack and came back to hold her chair for her, she noticed Charlie eyeing her as if she were some rare and succulent delicacy, and felt herself flush. She sat down in something of a flurry.

The waiter handed nicely printed menus to each member of their party, and Amy was glad she had something to concentrate on besides her acute awareness of Charlie Fox. Now, what, she wondered, should she order? She'd need to take the tightness of her corset into consideration, blast it.

"Oh, look!" Karen said, grinning. "They serve Mexican food. What a treat."

Amy noticed Charlie blink at Karen's enthusiasm and look uncertain. She eyed him over her menu. "Don't you care for Mexican food, Charlie?"

He turned her way. "What? Oh, no, I like it fine. It's just that we eat Mexican food all the time on the ranch."

"You do?" Karen's hazel eyes grew as round as pie plates. "Oh, my goodness, are there any jobs for dressmakers in Arizona Territory?"

Everyone laughed, and Amy's sense that this was a practically perfect gathering of friends grew ever larger. She hadn't experienced much of just plain fun in her life, but she expected this would be it. She was determined to enjoy herself.

"I wonder if they serve wine," Martin said, looking around for the waiter.

"I sort of doubt it," Karen said. "Although you never know about these places. I think there are some vineyards around here somewhere."

"Really? I thought they were all up north," Amy said in surprise.

"Ha! That's what the people up north want you to think. I'm originally from San Francisco, you know, and I know all about these things. They're real snobs up there when it comes to their part of the state."

Amy gazed across the table at Karen and felt something akin to awe for her new friend. "You are? From San Francisco, I mean?" It sounded romantic to her.

Karen nodded. "Yes, indeed. But when the movies began to move into Southern California, and I decided I wanted to be part of them—it seemed like the most enjoyable and profitable way to use my skills—I moved down here."

"Goodness, that was . . . well, awfully daring of you." Amy felt small all of a sudden, as if she didn't deserve to be seated among all of these interesting people who had done so much more than she with their lives. Her primary objective since early childhood was to achieve some kind of security for herself. That ambition seemed paltry in the face of this table full of adventurers.

"Daring?" Karen appeared truly startled. "Good heavens, no. I have family down here, and I had already secured a position with Madame Dunbar before I moved."

"Oh. I see." That didn't take much of the gloss off Karen's story for Amy, who greatly admired her friend for her adventurous spirit. Before she knew what she was doing, she blurted out the only interesting piece of her own personal history that she could think of. "Actually, I'm originally from the gold country. In Alaska, I mean."

She saw three pairs of eyes open wide, and wondered if they disbelieved her. But the story was true, although it was also true that her early years had been anything but thrilling or inspiring. They'd been uncomfortable and hungry, for the most part. And then her parents had succumbed, and she'd almost died, and . . . well, she'd never spoken of it to anyone before. She couldn't understand what had prompted her to speak of it now.

Since she could see they were all fascinated, she hurried on before she could become too frightened to do so. "Actually, my parents didn't go up there for gold. My father was a missionary. He and my mother were sent by the church to establish a mission for the Indians. The Athabaskans. Then other people, from the United States and Europe and . . . well, everywhere, I suppose, began moving up there, looking for gold."

"When was this? I didn't think the Alaska gold rush started until around 1900. I know you're not very old, but . . ." Martin smiled a question at her and said, "You're a little older than that."

Amy laughed nervously. "Yes, of course I am. And you're right about the big rush, but there were rumors before that, you know. It wasn't like California, where that man found a nugget in a stream and the entire East Coast flooded west. Alaska moved more slowly." She shivered suddenly.

"Are you cold?" Charlie asked with concern.

She wasn't cold. She was remembering. "No. Thank you. I was just . . . well, it wasn't a successful venture. That of my parents, I mean. I don't recall too much about it. I was a baby when we moved to Dawson, and only seven when my parents died. I'm not sure how anyone discovered the whereabouts of my aunt and uncle down here in Southern California. I—I suppose my mother had been writing to them regularly. I expect the Indian woman who found me with their bodies took some of the letters she found to town along with me. I . . . ah . . . don't remember much about it."

"Good Lord, do you mean there was no one else around when your parents died?" Karen looked horrified.

Which was nothing compared to the way Amy felt inside when she recalled that awful, miserable time in her life when she'd been so frightened, so alone, so bereft. She wished she'd never brought this up.

Pride. Foolish, foolish pride. She'd wanted her new friends to think she wasn't a simple stick-in-the-mud Pasadena girl. Although that was precisely what she wanted to be. People—herself included—could be very odd creatures without half trying, she concluded with bitter irony.

"I was pretty sick, too. As I said, I don't remember very much. I . . . well, I remember being confused and sad." Because she didn't want anyone to think she was fishing for sympathy, she laughed brightly and added, "But my aunt and uncle have been absolute saints. They took me in and have treated me as their own child ever since. They're wonderful. They're every bit as wonderful as my own parents would have been, I'm sure." What was more, they wouldn't ever haul a tiny child into an uncivilized wilderness where there was no hope of survival; Amy was sure of it.

The look of shock on Charlie's face might have been comical if Amy didn't feel so guilty for having caused it. Pickles. She wished she'd kept her mouth shut about her lamentable childhood. These people—Karen, Martin, and Charlie—could relate tales of interesting journeys and bold chances taken. Their stories weren't merely sordid and unhappy like hers.

"My gosh, Amy, I didn't know any of that," said Karen.

"Neither did I," said Martin.

Oh, good. Now they were *all* looking at her as if she were

a pitiable specimen of endangered animal life. Where was Theodore Roosevelt when you needed him? Maybe he could create a national park in her honor or something.

She said rather tartly, "It's over and done with, and I'm very happy now. Pasadena is a beautiful city, and I love living there. My aunt and uncle have a thriving business, and I enjoy working there, too. Well," she amended, her honesty getting the better of her determination to erase the bleak atmosphere she'd created, "except for people like Mr. Huxtable who occasionally come to stay at the Orange Rest."

Karen laughed. "Indeed!"

Martin smiled.

Only Charlie seemed to linger in the dismals that Amy had so foolishly allowed to get loose. Drat it, she ought to have known better. Her early life was too ugly to bring up at a dinner table—even in El Monte—and she knew it.

Fortunately for the state of her nerves, the waiter arrived with his pad in his hand. Amy hadn't studied the menu very hard, having allowed herself to become mired somewhere in Alaska for the past several minutes. She said, "You go first, Karen. I need to think a little longer."

She heard Karen order a chicken enchilada with frijoles and arroz con pollo, whatever that was, and decided she might as well be brave and daring and order it, too. She smiled at the waiter and said, "I'll have the same, please."

"I hope they serve mints or sprigs of parsley or something after dinner," Karen said with a laugh. "Otherwise, we'll drive everyone off the dance floor with our terrible breath."

Amy stared in consternation at her friend. Karen noticed the expression on her face and laughed again. "It's all the onions and garlic and chili peppers they use in the food. At least, that's what all the Mexican food I've ever eaten has been like."

"Me, too," agreed Martin.

"Yup," said Charlie.

Terrific. Amy had always longed to smell like a maiden in *Dracula,* strung with garlic to keep the vampires away. And here she'd been hoping that Charlie might move his lips up from her hand to her lips sometime during the evening.

Which shocked her. But she couldn't forget that kiss, and she'd really like to experience at least one more of Charlie's kisses before she had to give them up forever.

If she had to give them up forever.

Good gracious, there she went again, spinning dreams out of cotton fluff and nothing else at all. She shook her head hard, and could almost feel her fantastic fancies shatter and fly away on the spicy air.

"But it's probably going to be all right," Karen went on. "If that was the only kind of food they serve here, we'll all smell the same, so nobody can complain." She cast a cheery glance around at her tablemates, and Amy took heart.

The conversation drifted, as was natural, into the picture-making business, for which Amy was extremely thankful. She didn't want to dwell any longer on her own unfortunate past. Oddly enough—perhaps because of the garlic and onions—the topic drifted to Bram Stoker's book.

"I'm hoping Mr. Lovejoy will consider a motion picture about vampires one of these days," Martin said, sipping beer since there was no wine to be had. "Vampires are huge lately."

"So's the devil," said Karen nonchalantly.

Amy stared at the two of them. She'd never heard of the devil and evil nonliving creatures being discussed so casually. "Really?"

Karen laughed at her incredulity. "It's the truth. Nothing's sacred any longer."

"Now, that's not true, Karen, and you know it." Martin looked about as severe as a man with a beer stein in his hand can look. And he launched into an energetic speech about the wonders of the motion picture industry, how uplifting it was, and how it was going to break down barriers between cultures. Amy listened, greatly entertained.

Only Charlie, she noticed with interest, didn't appear to get caught up in Martin's enthusiasm. He kept sneaking peeks at Amy, and she kept feeling them, and wondering what he was thinking.

She hoped to heaven he wasn't contemplating the horrible story she'd told about her life in Alaska. Again she wished she'd kept her mouth shut. If there was one response she didn't care to generate in Charlie Fox, she realized with some surprise, it was pity. She could think of lots and lots of other emotions she'd like to inspire within him. Pity wasn't one of them.

Bother. This was becoming so complicated.

Fifteen

The dance floor was crowded, and the happy strains of "The Maple Leaf Rag" had everybody bouncing. Evidently, the entire city of El Monte, California, plus the folks from the surrounding countryside had turned out to gawk at the movie crew at the Royal El Montean. They were a friendly lot, too. Charlie liked them. He appreciated hospitality; it reminded him of home.

The entire crowd seemed eager to have fun, too. Charlie grinned when the band struck up "In the Good Old Summertime," and the dancers broke into song. The cast and crew of *One and Only*, not intending to be left out of the festivities, joined in.

That is to say, all of the cast and crew except Horace Huxtable, who huddled at a table in the back of the room, a shot glass in his hand and a bottle in front of him, glowering as if there wasn't anything in the world that could possibly please him. Gus, Sam, and Eddie sat so close they were almost in his lap. Charlie was pleased to see that the three bodyguards were taking their jobs seriously. Not that Huxtable's body needed guarding. It was the rest of the world that needed protection from him.

The notion of somebody preferring to sit and drink rather than dance and laugh and have a good time depressed Charlie, and he shook off the mood with a shrug. To hell with Horace

Huxtable. Tonight, if his luck was good, Charlie was going to reel in the girl of his dreams.

From "In the Good Old Summertime," the band rolled right into "Ida, Sweet as Apple Cider." The musicians were pretty good, and very loud, and Amy was a wonderful dancer. Charlie liked to dance, too, and they ended up dancing most of the numbers together.

"Oh, my, I can't remember when I've had so much fun," Amy gasped at one point, out of breath and shimmering with joy and perspiration.

She looked like a pearl to Charlie: immeasurably lovely, graceful, delicate, and priceless. She took to ragtime as if she'd been born to it, which he thought was very interesting. Adding this tidbit to the information he'd already gleaned about her, he deduced that she'd built up a wall of stuffiness and propriety around her on purpose, sort of like a protective layer. He could understand that, given her past.

His own life had been completely unremarkable. A loving mother and father, a big family full of aunts and uncles and brothers and sisters, lots of friends, and the wide-open, beautiful spaces of Arizona Territory. He recalled most of his childhood with humor and happiness. He couldn't even imagine what dainty little Amy Wilkes must have gone through when she was no bigger than a mite.

Hell, she was no bigger than a mite right now.

She sure was happy tonight. Charlie could hardly leave off staring at her as she danced around the floor with Martin to the music of "Hello, Ma Baby." It was a pleasure to watch her relax and have a good time with friends. When he first met her, he'd never have expected that this delightful, funny, good-humored girl lurked under all that stiffness.

The music ended. Martin took Amy's arm and walked her over to Charlie. Charlie appreciated the gesture, since it meant that Martin, at least, had Charlie and Amy paired up as a couple in his own mind.

Since he was feeling magnanimous, Charlie remarked, "You two look good dancing together."

Amy reached for the little fan dangling from her wide black belt—Charlie had heard Karen refer to it as a cummerbund—and fanned herself vigorously. "Oh, it's so much fun!"

"I think the nightclub is about to close," Martin panted, mopping his forehead with a handkerchief that looked much nicer than any of the raggedy old bandannas Charlie owned. He'd have to improve his wardrobe once he got Amy to consent to be his wife.

"Oh, do you think so?" Amy cried, disappointed. "I hope they play another couple of dances first. Although," she added with a laugh, "my feet are so sore I wouldn't be surprised if they fell off."

Martin laughed, too. "We can't have that."

"No, sir." Charlie looked down at where Amy's feet would be if he could see them, and wished he could take them in his big hands and rub them and then sprinkle sweet-smelling talcum on them, like his mama used to do to him when he'd run himself ragged as a boy.

Karen, who had been dancing with Benjamin Egan, a very handsome member of the studio's set-construction crew, gasped, "I'll run and ask them to keep playing for a while. I want them to do 'Frankie and Johnny.' "

Still fanning herself, Amy opened her eyes at that. "Mercy! Can you dance to 'Frankie and Johnny'?"

"*I* can dance to anything!" Karen declared, and dashed off to talk to the bandleader.

Martin chuckled. "I think Miss Crenshaw failed to attach herself to any of Dr. Freud's famous inhibitions."

Amy laughed.

Benjamin Egan, staring after Karen with overt appreciation, said, "By God, isn't that the truth!"

This time Charlie, sensing the same longing in Benjamin for Karen as he himself felt for Amy, laughed. Before Karen returned, the bandleader had directed his musicians through the first few bars of "Frankie and Johnny." Karen grabbed Benjamin, and the two of them folded into the crowd of dancers on the floor. Amy, Charlie, and Martin watched them go, smiling.

"Care to tangle with this one, Amy?" Charlie wondered if he looked as much like a moonstruck calf as he feared he did.

"Oh, there's Magnus. I have to talk to him." Martin took off after his chief cameraman.

"Poor Martin," Amy said, her fan losing some steam. "He seems to work all the time."

"Yup. He seems to enjoy it, though."

Amy nodded. Then she tilted her head back and peered up at Charlie as if she were trying to memorize his face. He wanted to tell her there was no need to do that; all she had to do was marry him, and she could see his face every day of her life. He lifted an eyebrow to prompt her to answer his question.

"You know," Amy said slowly, "I've had so much fun tonight, and I've never danced so much, but I'm hot and tired, and my feet are sore, and I'd really like to go outside for a minute or two. Would you mind that?"

Would he *mind?* Ha! Charlie said, "Wouldn't mind at all," and applauded himself as a master of understatement. "I'll get your wrap."

"Thank you."

Her smile was so warm and lovely and sparkled with the promise of so much untapped passion that Charlie very nearly forgot himself and swept her up off the floor and absconded with her. Fortunately for Amy—and himself—he controlled his uncivilized craving and only turned and headed for the cloak rack. He'd heard that big-city restaurants actually had special rooms to store coats and hats in, and special attendants to mind the rooms. He supposed a fellow would have to pay for that service, and spared a moment to be glad they were in the wilds of El Monte. Although he was far from stingy, Charlie was careful with his money.

During the course of the evening, folks had piled lots of coats and wraps and things on top of Amy's shawl, and it took him a minute to find it. When he returned to where he'd left her, he was horrified to discover her face to face with Horace Huxtable. Her face was bright pink. Huxtable's was sort of a washed-out ivory. Charlie ran the last few paces.

"Where are Gus and Sam and Eddie?" were the first words out of his mouth.

Amy turned at the sound of his voice, and the look of anger on her countenance instantly transformed into one of relief. "I don't know. Evidently Mr. Huxtable managed to shake them off. I told Martin to use chains, but he wouldn't do it."

"You damned bitch!" Huxtable slurred, wobbling slightly. "You think you're so grand. Well, you're not!"

"Oh, go away, Huxtable," Charlie muttered, helping Amy don her shawl. He didn't want any trouble in the Royal El Montean. Dammit, where were Huxtable's keepers? The music went on as if nothing untoward was happening, which he supposed was a good thing.

Charlie noticed that Amy's lips were pinched tightly together, as if she were having a hard time keeping some mighty hot words inside. He felt for her. He'd like to sock Huxtable in his filthy mouth, but he was holding himself back, just as she was.

"You think you're so great. Well, you're not. *I'm* the star!

I'm the one who will draw the crowds to see this picture. Not you."

"I'm sure you're absolutely correct," Amy said tightly.

She held her arm out for Charlie, and he took it and placed her hand firmly on his arm. He nodded at Huxtable. "You're the star, all right. We're a couple of nobodies."

Huxtable, apparently not having anticipated such complete agreement from two formerly obstreperous co-workers, blinked a couple of times and took a staggering step backwards. "Hunh," he said.

Spying Huxtable's bodyguards hurrying up to the star from behind, Charlie said, "Right," and left it at that. He and Amy began to walk away. The music was too loud for him to be sure that Amy giggled, but he thought she did.

The night air, which hadn't felt cold when they'd arrived at the Royal El Montean several hours earlier, hit them like an Arctic blast when Charlie opened the door for Amy. It felt good to him—fresh and clean after the stuffiness of the dance floor.

Amy pulled her shawl more tightly around her shoulders. "My goodness, I didn't realize it was so brisk outside."

"I don't think it's so much brisk as it is we're warm from being indoors and dancing," Charlie said, inhaling a lungful of fresh air. It smelled good—like Arizona.

"I'm sure you're right. It's actually quite refreshing." Amy's voice carried a happy overtone that Charlie was glad to hear. "Oh, look up there."

She must have forgotten her manners for a second, because she pointed at the sky. Although it was difficult for him, Charlie managed to drag his attention away from her and focus on the moon and stars. They really were pretty. The moon was almost full, and the stars were twinkling around it like a bunch of excited fireflies. "The sky's beautiful," he said, knowing the word to be inadequate. At the moment, though, all of his appreciation was entangled with the slight woman beside him. He didn't have much eloquence left over to spend on the scenery.

She hugged herself. Charlie wished she'd let him do that for her. "I just love seeing all the stars and the moon like this, out in the open. As much as I love Pasadena, the stars get tangled up in the orange trees sometimes. The vista's much vaster out here on the desert."

"Orange trees are nice," Charlie muttered since he couldn't think of anything more intelligent to say.

"Oh, yes, they're lovely. And the fragrance of orange blossoms must be the most intoxicating one in the world."

Charlie wouldn't know about that, having had little experience with oranges or their blossoms. Amy's own personal fragrance intoxicated him more than any other ever had. "I'll bet," he said, in order to be saying something.

She looked up at him quickly. "Haven't you ever smelled orange blossoms?"

He gave a little shrug. "At my sister's wedding. I think she had orange blossoms. Um, I think I remember them smelling nice." He remembered no such thing, but feared Amy would discard him as a worthless piece of nothing if he admitted it.

"Oh, you must come to my uncle's health spa in April. There are huge groves of orange trees surrounding it, and the fragrance is heavenly."

"Must be." Charlie cleared his throat. "Um, Amy, I've been wanting to talk to you."

"You have?" Again, she glanced up at him. He couldn't see the color of her eyes, but he could see the sparkle in them, and his heart gave an enormous twang, not unlike a banjo string being plucked hard.

"Yup." Oh, great, his mouth had dried out and his lips were sticking to his teeth. Not exactly romantic. He swallowed and blundered on. "Um, you see, it's like this . . ." It's like what?

"Yes?" Her voice was as sweet as the putative orange blossoms.

"Um, well, you know, I'm fairly well set up in the world."

The pause that ensued after this piece of information seemed to drag on into infinity. Charlie figured he was being fanciful, although it was a mighty long space of silence.

Evidently Amy felt it, too, because she said after a moment, "I'm glad for you. It must give you a grand sense of security to know that you're well set up."

"Yeah. It does." He shuffled and jammed his hands into the pockets of his new dress pants. If Karen Crenshaw saw him, she'd probably have an apoplectic attack. "Look, Amy, I'm going about this all wrong. What I'm trying to say is that I can support a wife and family really fine."

She blinked. "You can? How nice."

Shoot, was he a lamebrain or what? "What I mean is . . . well, there's the ranch in Sedona. It's not only thriving, but it's in the prettiest countryside God ever made. I don't know if oranges would grow there, but it's beautiful."

"Oh." Amy looked confused. "I'm sure it must be. How nice."

"Yeah, it's nice, all right. And you said you'd like to see it someday." He spoke in a rush, and realized he sounded as if he were daring her to deny it. What a damned fool he was.

"Yes," she said. "I remember. I would like to see it."

"Well, then, that's good."

"It is?"

"Sure. Because I can take you there, and you can see it all you want."

"You can? I mean, I can?" Her expression of confusion was giving way to one of irritation.

Lord, why didn't somebody just come along and shoot him?

It would be easier on him than this. "Blast it, Amy, I'm not saying this right."

"No?" She looked as though she agreed with him but was too polite to say so.

"No. What I'm trying to tell you is that I can support a wife really good. We might not be rich. Not at first, anyway. But I've saved my money for years now, and I'm getting a bundle from working in this picture, and when I put everything together I'll be able to start a family right and proper."

She stared at him. "Er . . . I'm glad for you," she said presently.

"Dagnabbit, what I'm trying to say is that I love you, Amy, and I want to marry you."

Her eyelashes fluttered like a butterfly for a second or two, and her mouth fell open. "You . . . you what?"

"I love you. I love you more than anything else on earth. More than my family in Arizona. More than the ranch. More than anything."

"You do?"

"Yes." He licked his lips, swallowed, cleared his throat, and fumbled forward. "And if you can find it in you somewhere to look kindly on me—the good Lord knows I'm not worthy of you—then I thought—mind you, it's probably a stupid thing to think—but I thought that maybe we could hitch up together and have a pretty nice life."

"You did?"

Out of words, Charlie could only nod.

"You . . . you really love me?"

She sounded incredulous, a circumstance Charlie didn't understand at all. "Lord, yes. You're the most wonderful female I've ever met in my life."

"I am?"

"Yup."

"And . . . and . . ." She hesitated, as if she weren't sure she should be speaking of whatever it was she wanted to bring up.

Charlie, wanting to encourage her in any way possible, as long as she was leaning toward a yes, said, "Ask me anything, Amy. I want you to know everything about me so you can make a decision."

She lowered her eyes and gazed at the ground. "I don't want you to think I'm a terrible, grasping woman, Charlie."

"What?" It was his turn to be incredulous. "You're kidding me, right? I know you better than that, Amy. You're wonderful. You're not grasping, and you couldn't be terrible if you tried."

When she raised her head, a crooked smile decorated her beautiful lips. "I'm not so sure about that."

"I am."

"Well, then, I guess I'll ask." She added quickly, "I don't care about wealth, you understand. It's only that . . . well, it's only that I'm scared of being left like I was as a child, Charlie. All alone and without resources. I swore to myself when I was seven years old that I'd never be alone and helpless like that again."

Thinking of his enormous family and all of his brothers, sisters, aunts, uncles, cousins, nieces, nephews, and everyone else in his orbit, Charlie shook his head positively. "If you marry me, you'll never have to face anything like that again, Amy. I can promise you that."

"Really? I mean, you have sufficient . . . well, re-sources . . . so that if the worst happened, I'd be taken care of?" She turned away with an impatient gesture. "Oh, that sounds so crass! I don't mean to sound like some kind of gold-digging harpy, Charlie. Honestly, I don't."

Good God, she was crying. Charlie was a man of enormous self-control, and he'd been taught proper behavior by his mother and father and a whole slew of interfering aunts and uncles, but he was a man nevertheless, and he could only take so much. "Here, Amy!" He reached out for her. "Please don't cry, sweetheart. Golly, I didn't mean to make you cry." He pulled her into his arms.

"I'm so stupid," she mumbled into his shirtfront. "I didn't mean to cry." She gave an enormous sniffle. "You surprised me so much."

"Did I?"

He felt her nod and heard a muffled "Yes."

"I'm surprised you're surprised. I figured everybody on the set must know how much I love you by this time. I can't stop staring at you from morning till night, and I'm with you every single second I can manage. Shoot, I figured you might be so used to me by this time that it would only seem natural to keep me around forever. Sort of like a puppy dog or something." He supposed that was pretty lame, but he was trying to lighten the atmosphere.

It worked to a degree. She gave a watery giggle. "Oh, Charlie, don't be silly."

"Is it silly?" It seemed like the truth to him.

He felt her nod again.

"So," he asked after a minute of nothing at all but holding her and feeling her and listening to his heart whack against his ribs in the night. "What do you say? Do you need time to think about it?"

She took a deep breath and a step away from him. He was loath to let her go, but knew he had to. "No, Charlie, I don't need any time to think about it."

"You don't?" He wasn't sure if that was good or bad and licked his lips. "So, um, what do you think? Is it the worst idea you've ever entertained in your life?"

"No, it's not."

Lord, Lord. Charlie didn't dare get his hopes up for fear the crash would kill him if they fell, but it looked to him as if she were smiling awfully prettily for a girl who was about to administer a death blow. He gazed down at her, holding his breath.

"I would be the happiest woman on earth if we were to be married, Charlie Fox. Yes, I accept your proposal."

"You do?" Charlie hadn't been prepared for failure, but he also didn't quite know what to do about success. He was thunderstruck. Knocked cockeyed. Stricken silly. Bereft of speech and coherent thought. All he could do for the next few seconds was stare at her like a complete idiot.

"I love you, Charlie," she added softly, in her orange blossom voice. "I love you very much."

It was too much for Charlie. He couldn't believe his ears. She loved him. She loved him? He stared at her harder, trying to catch her in a lie. He couldn't do it.

By God, she loved him.

Charlie let out a whoop that could almost have been heard over the band, and picked her right up off the ground. As their lips met and the band played "I Love You Truly," he kissed her the way he'd been wanting to kiss her for days now.

And she kissed him back.

For more than a decade, Amy had not expected a whole lot out of life. She'd never, for example, expected a thrilling romantic adventure to befall her, mainly because she didn't ever want to experience another adventure again for as long as life remained to her. Alaska had been a sufficient adventure for ten lives. The most she'd dared hope for was a tidy and secure life with Vernon Catesby in Pasadena, California. She'd never really expected love to tag along with the rest of the package.

But Charlie Fox loved her. And she loved him. And he could support her perfectly well. She'd probably never have the luxuries she'd have had with Vernon, but she didn't care about them anyway. She'd never been so happy.

"Oh, Charlie, I can't believe you really love me."

"You're joshing me, Amy. I know you are."

Laughing and crying, Amy shook her head. "I'm not. I can't imagine why you'd love me. I was so scared when we first met, I could hardly get my mouth open, and I acted abominably, and I know you didn't like me. You can't deny it."

He laughed—a huge, open laugh that went perfectly with the huge, open spaces around them. "Gosh, Amy, I thought you were such a prude. I didn't realize that . . . well, that you were protecting yourself."

Amy hadn't considered her prim manners in the light of protection before. But they were. And Charlie had figured it out. What a brilliant, marvelous man he was. "You're right. Oh, Charlie, you're so wonderful. I love you so much."

"Now, that," said he, "is what I can't figure out. Why a beautiful lady like you would ever love a big lug like me."

"You're not a big lug. You're my own special cowboy."

"Ha! I'm not really a cowboy, you know."

"You're not?"

He hadn't yet put her down, but Amy didn't care. In fact, she'd just as soon he hold her forever. At present, he was carrying her to the hotel entrance, where, she guessed, he aimed to take her to her door and leave her. She didn't want to part from him this evening.

"Nope. I'm a rancher. The cowboys are the hired hands on a ranch. They work for the ranchers."

Wasn't that nice? Although Amy wouldn't mind being married to a cowboy, as long as he was Charlie and his pay was sufficient to support a family, it sounded much nicer to be the wife of the person who owned the ranch. "That sounds so nice."

"What does?" He was nuzzling her ear and almost fell up the steps to the hotel entrance.

"Being a rancher's wife. Tell me about the ranch, Charlie." She sighed into his arms, feeling loved and protected.

"Well, it's real pretty in Sedona. There are huge rock formations all over the place, and big canyons, and the sky looks like magic most days."

"Magic," Amy breathed, trying to picture it. Her life had been deficient in magic, for the most part.

"The canyons and rocks look almost like they've been painted, there are so many different colors in lines and streaks and so forth."

"Are there Indians around there?"

She felt him shrug. "Oh, sure, but they're mostly on the reservations now. They're not a problem any longer. I'm afraid we've wiped most of them out altogether."

"Really?" Intrigued because he sounded unhappy about it, she asked, "Is that a bad thing?"

"Well," he said after a judicious pause, "I'm not sure it's a good idea to run over an entire race of people like we ran over the Indians. On the other hand, we wanted to use land they only sort of skimmed over, and it worked out the way it worked out. I suspect the same thing goes on all over the world. A stronger civilization will overpower one that doesn't have enough power to fight for its right to preserve life the way they live it."

Amy had never thought about the Indian situation in the United States along those lines, although what Charlie said made sense to her. She did not, however, aim to spend this particular night fretting about lost civilizations and murderous interlopers. "Is there a big city anywhere near the ranch?"

"It's not too far from a couple of fair-sized cities, although there are none the size of, say, Denver. Or New York City. Say, have you ever heard of the Grand Canyon?"

Amy felt her eyes widen. "The Grand Canyon? Yes. One of my uncle's inmates had some photographs of the Grand Canyon. It looked magnificent. I wish I could see it in person. And in color."

"Sedona's kind of close to the Grand Canyon."

"Oh, my." Amy could hardly take it in. Not only was she going to marry the most wonderful man in the world, but she was going to live in the most beautiful place on earth. "Do you suppose they'll ever pass a law to protect it, like Theodore Roosevelt is talking about?"

"I don't know. I hope so. It would be a shame for people to go in there and build buildings all over it."

"I should say so." A sudden fierce longing to see the Grand Canyon assailed her. She'd never felt much interest in travel before. It must be that she felt safe with Charlie. If she went to the Grand Canyon with him, she knew she'd be protected from all harm.

Somehow, Charlie managed to open the door to the hotel and push it wide with his back, still carrying Amy. He'd proceeded down the hallway for a few yards when he said, "Shoot, I'm going to have to put you down. I can't see to read the room numbers on the doors."

She laughed. "I'm sure I can walk on my own."

"Maybe, but I like carrying you."

Wasn't that just the sweetest thing? Amy's heart swelled so, it felt as if it might burst from happiness.

The hall was dark, and when he set her gently on the hall runner, they both had to squint to see the room numbers. "Um, does that look like a six to you?" she asked at one point.

Charlie leaned over and peered closely at the number on the door. "I'm not sure. Do you have your key?"

"Yes, but I'll bet the keys are all the same."

He chuckled. "You're probably right. If we open the door and it's not your room, there might be trouble."

"What a dreadful thought." She smiled, though. She couldn't help it.

"Let's see if there's a number on any of the other doors." He inched through the darkness to the next door. "I think this is a four. That's mine."

"Well, then, this must be either a two or a six, don't you think? Aren't all the even numbers on one side of the hall?"

"Beats me. Here, let me try your key. If somebody's in there and doesn't like it, he'll shoot me first."

"I certainly hope not!" Nevertheless, Amy fumbled in her tiny beaded bag until she found her room key. She handed it to Charlie and watched while he turned it in the lock. The door opened, and they both peeked inside with some trepidation. Amy brightened at once. "Oh, look, there's the bag I brought. This must be my room." They entered the room, searching for a lamp. Amy fumbled over to the bed and discovered a kerosene lamp on the bedside table. "Do you have a match?"

"Sure." He dug a sulfur match out of his pocket, struck it on the heel of his shoe, and lit the lamp. The light revealed a pleasant, plain room with a large bed. He sighed gustily. "Well, here you are. I reckon I'll have to leave you now."

"Do you have to?" Amy really, really didn't want him to go away.

"I reckon so." He appeared surprised at the question.

Pausing for only a moment to think about ramifications, Vernon Catesby, and her own sanity, Amy went on recklessly, "But I don't want you to go, Charlie."

She saw his beautiful eyes open wide.

"You, um, don't?" He swallowed.

She shook her head.

"But . . . but . . ."

"We're going to be married, aren't we?"

He nodded. It looked to her as if he were having trouble speaking.

"Well, then, I don't think it's improper for you to stay with me, at least for a little while."

It was absolutely improper, and Amy knew it. So did Charlie.

He stayed anyway.

Sixteen

Charlie hadn't meant to stay with Amy any longer than it took to get her settled into her room. He knew he should leave her, untouched and intact, here in her hotel room. He was a villain not to go.

When she walked up to him and put her arms around him and began kissing him with all of the passion he'd always suspected lurked inside her, his resolution faltered. When she whispered, "Please stay with me tonight, Charlie," he nearly fell over dead. When she ran her fingers through his hair, his hat hit the floor, and when she nipped his earlobe, he was completely lost.

"Amy, Amy," he murmured. "This is wrong."

"No, it's not," she murmured back. "We're going to be married."

"But we're not married yet."

"That was all right, Charlie. I love you so much."

"I love you, too."

How inadequate those words sounded. And how delicious was the notion of spending the night with Amy in this cozy hotel room. He knew it was wrong. He knew he was violating one of his own firm principles of proper behavior. But he couldn't seem to stop himself from continuing.

The sweet, elusive fragrance of Amy's perfume floated like an invisible cloud around him, and the feel of her hands on his body enchanted him, and her lips were like heaven, and the lure of her body was more than any mortal man could resist. And Charlie was nothing if not mortal. Every nerve in his body cried out for her, and his sex was already as hard as it could get and throbbed for her. Lord, how he wanted her.

And then she said, "Please, Charlie. Please make love with me. Please teach me how to love you."

The very last of his resistance floated away like so much dandelion fluff. He thrust aside any lingering notion that this wasn't the right thing to do and devoted his whole energy to making this experience good for Amy. He already knew it would be good for him.

"I've dreamed of this, Charlie."

"You have?" He had, too. He didn't know ladies had dreams like that. He picked her up and carried her to the bed.

"Yes. I never thought it would happen. I always thought I'd have to marry someone I didn't love and never experience this sort of thing."

He sat next to her on the bed, and she reached for his shirt buttons. He quickly wriggled out of his suit jacket so she'd have an easier job of it. "This sort of thing?" Great. His voice was going. He sounded like a sick frog.

"You know—making love with the man of my dreams."

He watched her as she maneuvered his buttons open. "Am I the man of your dreams? Honest?" He shrugged off his shirt, collar and all, giving a fleeting thought to the collar studs, but not really much minding if Amy dropped them. They could get lost forever, for all he cared.

"Honest. Of course you are. Do you think I'd do this with anyone who wasn't?"

Actually, it sounded to him as though she'd planned to do just that, if she'd assumed she'd marry somebody she didn't love. He didn't bring it up because he didn't care about that at the moment. He was too hot and too hard and too interested in seeing what she'd do next. "May I take your shoes off, Amy?" Above all things, he didn't want to spook her.

"Of course."

So he got off the bed, knelt before her, pushed a froth of chiffon and silk aside, lifted one little foot, and removed the pretty black evening slipper from it. "You've even got beautiful feet," he murmured.

"Thank you."

When he glanced up at her, he saw that she was blushing. Because he still wasn't sure if she really aimed to see this thing through, he was gentle when he ran his hand up her calf. His aim was to reach her garter eventually, but he was going to take his time in case she got scared. "Your whole body is beautiful."

"Thank you."

She put her hands flat on the bed, bracing herself. Charlie hoped that wasn't a precursor to flight. It didn't look much like it, but what did he know? Licking his lips, wondering if it would kill him to stop, he asked cautiously, "Are you really sure, Amy? Are you positive you want to do this?"

"I'm positive."

She sounded positive. After another moment's hesitation, Charlie decided to take her at her word. If she backed out, it might kill him, but he'd stop if she asked him to. He loved her that much. And more. "I'll, uh, just untie your garter, then."

"All right. Only they're hooks, not the tie kind."

Hooks? Good God. Charlie's hand stilled on her knee. "Um, I don't reckon I know what that is, Amy."

"A hook? Well, it hangs from the corset, you see. Here, I'll show you."

And, lithe as a newborn colt, she slid from the bed and lifted her lovely evening dress. Charlie stared, astonished. He'd sort of expected that it would take Amy ten or twenty years to overcome her reservations around him, but he guessed he'd underestimated her. Thank God, thank God.

"See?" she said. "It's a newfangled type of corset. I'll show you how these things work."

She did. She unhooked her gray silk stocking from the garter hook and began rolling the stocking down. Charlie, worried that she'd take all the fun out of his part in the enterprise, said, "Here, I'll do that."

"All right." She smiled at him sweetly and sat on the bed again.

He rolled the first stocking down and went to the other leg. Her legs were gorgeous. Not that he didn't already know that. He'd seen her legs that time when Huxtable had knocked the costume tent over. He'd never expected to be able to touch those beautiful legs, though. Or take stockings off them. But he'd be able to do those things for the rest of his life if she really planned to marry him. And she must be going to, or she wouldn't be allowing him to do these things to her now. His hands were shaking slightly as he unhooked the other stocking, but it didn't seem to matter; he got the job done, then rolled that stocking down, too, and licked his lips again.

"There," he said. "All done."

"What now?" she asked.

"What now?" He looked up and found her gazing at him with infinite love and amazing trust. He silently vowed that he'd never violate that trust. He would never, ever, if it was within his power, do anything to hurt her. "I reckon we have to get the rest of these clothes out of the way."

She smiled uncertainly. "So that nothing will remain between us, you mean?"

He nodded. "Something like that." He was uncertain, too.

"Well, then, maybe I should start." She looked him straight in the eye as she unfastened the wide velvet belt at her waist and it fell away.

Catching himself staring rudely, Charlie gave himself a sharp shake and said, "May I help with anything?" How polite of him, considering he was offering to aid in her deflowering.

If he didn't stop thinking things like that, he'd ruin the evening for both of them. So he commanded himself to pretend that they were already married, that this was the night of their marriage. This was their wedding night, and they were in love, and he was going to make it special.

"Help me slip this over my head, please," she said, taking him up on his offer with much more aplomb than Charlie himself could muster.

He did as requested, and heartily approved of the way Amy looked in her underthings. She was beautiful inside and out, and he loved her for it.

"Will you unhook this thing in the back, please? It's pretty tight. I'll try to suck in my tummy, but you'll have to pinch a little bit, I fear."

"I don't want to hurt you."

She'd turned her back to him so that he could reach her corset hooks. At his last comment, she turned suddenly and threw her arms around him. He obliged instantly with an embrace of his own.

"Oh, Charlie! I know you don't want to hurt me. That was what's so extraordinary about you. You actually care about how I feel about things."

Startled, he blurted out, "Of course I do. What man wouldn't?"

After kissing him thoroughly—so thoroughly that Charlie almost forgot he'd vowed to take things slowly and would have ravished her on the spot if he'd not caught himself in time—Amy said, "I can think of one or two." She sounded vaguely disgruntled about it.

It took him a few moments to catch his breath, and by that time Amy had turned again. His hands shook as he unfastened the hooks. He didn't have to pinch her. "I can't believe that," he gasped when he could.

"You can't believe what?"

"That any man who got to know you wouldn't care how you thought about things."

"Well, it's true. That's one of the reasons I fell in love with you, Charlie, because you actually seemed to care about my likes and dislikes and hopes and fears."

He shook his head, unable to imagine that any man worth his salt could ignore Amy's desires. Look at him, for heaven's sake, violating one of his most firmly held moral values and going to bed with her before the wedding. Of course, he was consulting his own desires in this particular case, too, but still . . .

The corset fell away, and Amy stood before him in her drawers and camisole. She turned to face him and, very slowly, slipped the camisole over her head. He swallowed hard.

"Lord," he whispered in awe. "You're so beautiful."

"Thank you. I'm glad you think so."

"Oh, I do."

She untied the tapes of her drawers and pushed them down, then stepped out of them as if stepping from a mound of snow. Then she stood before him, as naked as the day she was born, gorgeous, perfect—and his. He felt humbled for a moment.

The moment didn't last long. "It'll only take me a second," he said in a shaking voice. And he was almost right. It took him about a second and a half to rid himself of the remainder of his evening clothes. He flung them anywhere. He didn't care; he was in a hurry now.

He slowed down considerably when he realized Amy was staring at his engorged sex, which was standing at attention and saluting her smartly. He glanced down at himself and had to own that such a large masculine tool must look kind of alarming to a gently reared virgin. "I'm sorry, Amy. I shouldn't have gone so fast. Don't be scared."

"Um, I'm not scared." She sounded scared to death.

"I'm sure you must be. It's . . . strange at first, I reckon. But don't forget that people have been doing this since the Garden of Eden. It's how the race of man survives."

"How—how, um, interesting."

Charlie had never considered himself much of a martyr, but his next words elevated him in his own mind to the stature of absolute hero. With leaden heart and throbbing sex, he asked softly, "Do you want to stop now, Amy?"

He'd have done it, too. Lord above, he must really love the woman, because he was sure he'd keel over and die on the spot if she said yes.

She said, "No."

He shut his eyes and breathed a prayer of thanks. Opening them again, he said, "Here, Amy. Take my hand. We'll lie down, and I'll try to make you forget how strange it all is. It feels real good, honey. Honest, it does."

It wouldn't have surprised him if she'd said, *It had better,* but she didn't. She said only, "All right, Charlie," in a trusting little voice that about broke his heart—but didn't do a thing to diminish his lusting manhood.

He led her to the bed and carefully lifted her onto it. Her skin felt like silk and satin and all the other smooth and luscious things in the world. "Your skin is sure pretty, Amy." Lame. That was about as lame a comment as a man could make under the circumstances. "I—I like to stroke your skin because it's so silky."

Amy, bless her, only said, "Thank you. I—like to feel your skin, too. It's so rough compared to mine."

"It sure is."

With a combination of fear and excitement that was more potent than any combination of emotions and physical sensations he'd ever experienced before, Charlie began a tactile survey of her body. As he feathered small, warm kisses over her face, his hands roved freely. "I hope my calluses don't hurt you."

"They don't hurt," she assured him.

And since she was at the moment thrusting her breast into his palm, he guessed she meant it. He obliged her, rubbing his thumb gently over her nipple until it pebbled and hardened. Then he kissed her there, warming her breast with his tongue, taking the nipple between his teeth and gently tugging.

"Oh, Charlie!"

He stopped instantly, freezing into immobility, frightened nearly to death that he'd hurt her. She grabbed his head and bent it over her breast. "Don't stop. Oh, please don't stop now!"

So he didn't.

He'd been grazing on various parts of her for a long time when he became aware that she'd spoken to him. His concentration was so entirely centered on his sexual needs—and hers; he was always conscious of making her feel good—that he hadn't been paying attention to the sound of things. The first word that came through the sexual fog in his brain was, "Well?"

He blinked and lifted his head. He'd been maneuvering down to the curls between her legs, taking his time. "I, uh, beg your pardon?"

"I asked if you'd mind," she said, as if she were repeating something she'd already said once or twice.

Oh, God, was she going to make him stop *now?* He'd surely die. "Mind what?" he asked, perhaps too abruptly.

"If I felt your body the way you're feeling mine," she said sweetly—oh, so sweetly.

Charlie wasn't sure he should believe what his ears had heard, since he was pretty sure his brain was making it all up and she'd actually said something entirely different. He took a chance anyway. "Er, no. No, I wouldn't mind at all."

Thank God, thank God, she began to touch him. He hadn't misunderstood her. He groaned, unable to keep it inside any longer.

"Oh, did that hurt?" she asked, lifting her hand from his stiff sex.

"Lord, no, honey. That felt just fine." He groaned again when she replaced her hand. "Just . . . fine."

All right, he'd been a good boy. He'd gone slow. It was time to take a major step here, before he exploded. With a feeling akin to reverence, Charlie let his hand creep to the juncture of her thighs, to where the soft, springy curls hid her woman's most precious treasure.

Heaven—or something—rained its mercies upon him; she was ready for him. He could tell by the dampness he felt and the fact that her hips lifted to meet his fingers. Her cry of pleasure helped him reach the conclusion, as well.

"Oh, Charlie! That feels so good."

"It sure does, honey." His fingers stroked her slick folds for a couple of moments; then he carefully dipped one finger into her passage. He knew there would be a barrier to his sex, but he hoped it wouldn't be painful when he broke through.

And as there was only one way to find out, Charlie guessed it was about time. If he didn't do it soon, he'd disgrace himself, and he didn't think he could stand that.

"Um, Amy, do you think you're ready?"

She'd had her eyes closed, and was engaged in a blissful rhythm in time to the stroking of his fingers. Her eyelids fluttered once or twice, and her eyes looked unfocused when they sought his face. "Ready? For what?"

He closed his eyes, too, and sighed. "For me. For the act of love. For what this is all leading up to."

She blinked a couple of times. "Oh. Why, certainly. I guess

so." She gave him a brilliant smile. "You know more about this than I do."

True. He wasn't as experienced as lots of men, but he'd known a woman or two in his day. And since that was the case, he decided for her. With a brisk nod, he said, "You're ready."

"Good."

She reached for him, which made it easy for him to kneel over her. He hoped she could read the love in his eyes as he gazed at her. "Help guide me in, Amy," he said, and he took her hand and put it around his erect member.

So she did. With one more "Oh, Charlie," she guided him home.

He'd never felt anything like it. She was as warm and wet and smooth as anything. Her passage was tight and seemed to suck him in. He sighed deeply and kissed her hard. "God, I love you, Amy."

"I love you, Charlie."

He came to the barrier of her virginity and paused. He didn't want to hurt her almost as much as he needed to accomplish this deed.

"Keep going, Charlie. I know it might hurt a little," she said.

He silently blessed her as the most absolutely perfect woman in the world as he pushed past the barrier. She gasped, and he stilled, holding himself back with all the strength of character and body he possessed. "Are you all right, sweetheart?" If she wasn't, he wasn't sure there was anything he could do about it at this point.

"Yes. I'm sure I am. Just wait a minute."

So he did. Charlie had always known himself to be a man of patience; patience was a virtue in any kind of ranching operation. Cattle weren't known for their swift thinking or cooperative nature. The patience and restraint he showed with Amy, however, impressed even himself.

Through gritted teeth, he said, "Tell me when, sweetheart."

She was silent for a moment, then said, "All right. I think I'm all right now."

Thank God. With a huge exhalation of breath, Charlie let himself go. He didn't want to hurt her. He tried to be gentle. But he didn't stop again. Since he was so close to the edge, he reached between their bodies and found the nub of Amy's pleasure and began to stroke it gently.

She gasped. "Oh, my!"

He'd begun to drip sweat on her, and was sorry about it, but he was, after all, only a man. "Does that feel good?"

"Oh, yes." Her hips lifted. "Oh, *yes!*"

He felt her climax happen, and it surprised the hell out of him. He hadn't really expected it—not their first time together. Hell, he'd been under the impression that lots of wives only submitted to their husbands out of duty. He was so happy to find out that Amy wasn't one of them, he would have hollered his joy to the sky, except that his climax came almost as soon as he felt hers, and his voice box was occupied in crying out her name.

He didn't know how long they lay there afterwards, too enervated to move, but eventually he managed to move so that he wasn't crushing her with his weight. She was such a tiny thing. Delicate. Fragile. And he'd forced his big, rough self on her. Well, perhaps not *forced*.

When he thought he could speak without gasping, he stroked her stomach—which was damp with perspiration—and whispered, "Are you all right, sweetheart? Did I hurt you?"

She turned over and placed her hands on his chest. Staring into his eyes, her own as full of love as if she were speaking the words aloud, she said, "You didn't hurt me, Charlie. I'm fine. I've never been so fine."

That was a load off his mind. He grinned, hoping he didn't look too proud of himself. "Good. I'm glad. Um, was it all right for you?"

"All right?" She seemed puzzled for a moment; then her expression cleared. "Oh, do you mean did I enjoy it?"

Shoot, once she decided to open up, she really went at it with a vengeance, didn't she? He nodded. "Yes, that's what I meant." He'd been too shy to say it out loud.

"Oh, my, yes. I had no idea. Why, I think marriage is going to be perfectly wonderful. I never thought about the physical aspects of marriage before this minute. Well, except in the sense that I didn't want to starve to death or anything like that."

"Right." She was moving a little fast for him. Like his uncle Bill might say, she was talking faster than he could listen. But Charlie had never heard anybody speak of starving to death in connection with marriage before.

Then he remembered Alaska, his big heart turned sloppy and warm, and he drew her into his arms, sweat and all. If she could talk about sex so openly, surely she wouldn't object to his sweaty chest. "Sweetheart, I swear to you that I'll take care of you. You'll never have to worry about having enough food. And if we're lucky enough to be blessed with kids, they'll never have to suffer the way you suffered when you were little. I swear it."

"Oh, Charlie."

He could tell she'd started to sniffle, and hoped she wouldn't bawl. He'd never been sure what to do when females cried in front of him.

After a few minutes of that, Charlie's sex began to stir again, and he hoped he wouldn't shock her unduly—Amy pulled away so that she could talk. He kept petting her because he couldn't seem to leave off. He'd never in all his born days expected to have such an exquisite creature in his life. And she'd agreed to marry him. He could scarcely believe his luck.

"I can't wait to see the ranch, Charlie." She curled up next to him and put her hand on his chest. She seemed to like running her fingers through his chest hair. That was fine with him; he liked it, too.

"We can go to Arizona as soon as the picture's wrapped up, if you want to."

"Oh, I'd love it. Do you suppose my aunt and uncle can go, too, if they can get away for a little holiday?"

"Sure. I'm sure there will be room for them. I'll write my mother."

"Your mother? Will she put them up?"

"Put them up? Well, sure." He looked down at her. "She and my dad live there, and there's loads of room."

"They live on our ranch?"

Our ranch. That seemed like a funny way to phrase it, but Charlie kind of liked the sound of it. Made their life together seem like a sure thing. "Sure."

"Oh. I guess I didn't realize."

"Oh, sure. Heck, that ranch has been in the family for more than fifty years. A few of my brothers and two of my sisters live there, too."

A brief silence preceded Amy's, "Oh. That's a lot of people. Um, I thought it would be just the two of us."

Uh-oh. Charlie didn't like the sound of this. He tried to recall exactly what he'd told her about the ranch, and guessed he hadn't mentioned that lots of his family still lived there. Actually, he guessed he hadn't mentioned his family at all, except to say the ranch had been in the family for a long time. He hoped he hadn't given her the impression that the ranch was his alone.

Feeling foolish and a little desperate, he said, "Well, there will be the two of us eventually, because we'll set up our own operation. In the meantime, the ranch is plenty big enough for all of us to visit. It won't be our home after we're married, of course."

"It won't?"

"Shoot, no. I always expected to have my own place some-day. What with the money I'm making from this picture, I'll be ready to set us up right."

"Set us up? You mean you aren't set up already?"

The sugar in her voice seemed to be disintegrating. Charlie didn't like the sound of it. "Well, not yet, but you don't need to worry, Amy. Honest to God, I've got plenty of money. And I've got lots of built-in help to work on the place, too."

"Built-in help? I don't think I understand, Charlie."

Charlie was disappointed when she withdrew her hand from his chest. He was getting an uneasy feeling about this con-versation. "I mean my brothers. They'll be happy to help build us a house and start up the operation."

"Start up," she murmured. "I was under the impression your ranch was already a going concern."

"It is. That is to say, the family's ranch is about as suc-cessful as a ranch can be. I'm going to set up on my own."

"Oh."

Oh? Just oh? Charlie's heart began to shrivel in his chest, and he scrambled to regain lost ground. "And we don't need to do it in Arizona Territory, either," he rushed on. "If you prefer living in California, we'll just establish a ranch in Cali-fornia. Land's cheap here, and there's lots of it, and it's a great place to raise cattle and kids."

He saw her lick her lips. "I, um, didn't imagine that we'd have to start out with nothing, Charlie. I believed you had a ranch going full tilt already."

"The family ranch is," he said lamely. "But I don't even have the land for my own operation. Yet. I'm going to build a place and stock it as soon as possible after I get paid for this picture."

"I see."

She sat up. He did, too, and said, "Amy, I'm really sorry I gave you the wrong idea. Honest to God, I didn't mean to deceive you."

"I'm sure you didn't."

Her voice had gone . . . bleak was the only word Charlie could come up with to describe it. "Amy . . ."

"I, ah, think you'd better go now, Charlie. I don't want anyone to gossip about us."

"Amy, please, let's talk about this. It'll be all right. I swear to God, Amy, I'm well set up in the world. You'll never want for anything or suffer anything. Honest. Please, sweetheart, just talk to me for a minute, and you'll understand."

"Um, I don't think I'm up to chatting any longer tonight, Charlie."

He could tell she was trembling when she got out of bed. She went to her overnight bag and withdrew a big flannel nightgown. Her beautiful body looked white and forlorn and very small in the dark room. He leaped out of bed and ran over to her. "Here, let me help you."

"Thank you."

"Lord, Amy, I'm sorry. I swear to you, I didn't mean to give you any wrong ideas."

"No, I'm sure of it, Charlie. You're too honest to do that." He could almost hear the *on purpose* that she didn't say. She slipped the nightgown over her head and looked up at him as if she expected him to be dressed already.

"Amy . . ."

She shook her head. "Let's talk about it later, Charlie. I'm afraid there's been a misunderstanding."

A misunderstanding. Good God, he couldn't believe this. "Amy, I—"

"Please, Charlie. Just go to your room, if you will. I . . . need to rest."

"But—"

"No. Please."

Charlie gave up. He'd never felt so guilty and unhappy; his feet felt like lead and so did his heart when he closed the door of Amy's room and went next door to his own room. The vision of her standing there in her voluminous nightgown, looking lonely and forsaken, stayed with him all night long. He didn't sleep a wink.

Seventeen

Amy didn't cry, a circumstance that later astonished her. Her eyes burned and felt as hot as a scorching poker, but the rest of her was colder than she could recall ever being—except when she'd been abandoned in Alaska. She sat on the edge of her bed and contemplated the disaster of her life, wondering how she could have been so totally mistaken about Charlie. And about herself.

Wishful thinking. That's what had led to her downfall.

"It can't be true," she whispered into the blackness that seemed to have spread from the outside in until it enveloped her, body, heart, and soul.

Even as she spoke the words, she knew she was wrong. It *could* be true—and it was. She would never dream of accusing Charlie of deliberately misleading her, but she'd been misled nonetheless; perhaps because she wanted so very much to believe what she'd believed. Wishful thinking.

Perhaps she was being silly. Perhaps it didn't matter so much that Charlie didn't really have a ranch of his own, and that he and she would have to start an operation together. Out of nothing. She tested the possibility in her mind, and such an internal earthquake rattled her that she was soon shaking from head to foot and had to cling to the bed or fall to the floor.

No. She was unquestionably reacting strongly to the truth

of Charlie's situation because of her own personal background, but there was nothing silly about it.

For whatever reason, Amy couldn't abide the notion of going out into the world and creating something out of nothing. Not after what had happened to her parents. Not after watching them sicken and die from attempting to achieve an impossibility. Not for her the establishment of a mission from scratch.

A ranch. She meant a ranch. It was a ranch, not a mission, that Charlie wanted her to start with him. Ranches weren't as impossible to succeed at as missions, were they?

Mission. Ranch. Mission. Ranch. Both words and the images they brought forth whirled around in her brain like dervishes. It didn't matter what she called what Charlie wanted them to do together. The end result was the same: blind panic.

Amy Wilkes was unfit to *begin* anything, and that was that. She needed security like other people needed food and water. There was no use pretending otherwise. She'd been damaged early in life, and some scars were permanent.

"Oh, dear Lord, what have I done?" She stared into nothingness and contemplated the catastrophe of her night.

It had started out so well, too. Dinner had been fun, dancing had been thrilling, and making love with Charlie had been the most exciting, fulfilling experience of her life.

And then, after she'd built up in her mind the wonders of a life together on his thriving and prosperous ranch—obviously, she'd been foolish to do so—he'd told her he didn't have a ranch at all. Not one of his own, where he could bring a wife and raise a family.

Amy couldn't bear the notion of starting from nothing. She'd been avoiding anything even remotely insecure since the middle of her seventh year, and building a marriage from nothing sounded like the knell of doom to her.

She felt guilty about Charlie. Surely he was going through

agonies of doubt and misery that she'd misunderstood him, and he probably thought the whole thing was his fault. But it wasn't. Her own personal inadequacy had created this ghastly mistake; her deficiency; her shortcoming.

Unable to bear the thought of his pain heaped upon her own, Amy buried her head in her hands. She still didn't cry. Her insides felt as if they'd been sucked dry and wadded up into a tight knot. They throbbed and ached, but there were no tears in her. She was empty; devoid of spiritual nourishment. There was nothing in her that might assist her in facing or, better yet, overcoming this crisis.

"There's something wrong with me," she told herself. And she was right. There was something very wrong with her, and her moral defect was now spoiling what might well be her one chance at happiness with Charlie Fox. He was, as nonsensical as it might sound, the man of her dreams.

Of course, there was always Vernon Catesby. Amy groaned. She'd given herself to Charlie tonight, under the misapprehension that they were soon to be wed. If she now married Vernon, she'd be giving him damaged goods.

"I'm sure he's slept with other women," she said, feeling savage and scrambling for a way to make herself not wrong.

But his sleeping with other women, as she well knew, didn't matter. There were two standards prevailing in the world: one for men, and one for women. Amy had violated the standard for women tonight. That meant she'd either have to lie to Vernon or tell him the truth. If she told him the truth, he'd have nothing more to do with her. If she kept quiet, she'd be lying every bit as much as if she protested her innocence aloud.

So what did that leave her? The Orange Rest Health Spa, she supposed. Uncle Frank and Aunt Julia would be happy to have her stay with them forever and continue working with the inmates. And they'd never need to know what she'd done.

They'd wonder what happened to Vernon, but they'd never find out. Heaven knew, she'd never tell them.

Which meant she'd never tell Vernon, either, and he'd more than wonder. He'd press her to reveal her reason for backing away from him after she'd received his attentions, if not with eagerness, at least without distaste, for months.

What a mess she'd made of everything. What a calamitous, horrible, unhappy mess.

Amy slept eventually, but she tossed and turned, and awoke in the morning with a headache and with heavy, puffy eyelids. As luck would have it, she met Karen in the hallway outside her room. She'd been praying that she'd not meet anyone, but Karen was the least worrisome of the many people she might have run into, so she tried her best to smile.

"Good Lord, Amy, you look terrible this morning. Are you feeling unwell?"

How sweet of Karen to offer her an excuse. "I think I'm coming down with something. I don't feel at all well, actually. Sick. I feel quite sick."

"My goodness." Karen's brown eyes lit up. "Say, you and Charlie didn't go out drinking last night after the dancing was over, did you?"

"Drinking? Good heavens, no." Although, come to think of it, if she had been drinking instead of doing what she'd been doing, she'd probably feel better this morning. At least a night of drinking wouldn't have such detestably permanent consequences.

"Oh."

Feeling low and irritable, Amy snapped, "You sound disappointed. Do you want me to turn into a drunkard?" That wasn't nice, and she wished she'd bitten her tongue instead of saying it.

"Of course not. Golly, you really *do* feel bad, don't you?

You're never snappish except to Huxtable. Can I get you anything, Amy? Some water? Some juice? Anything?"

All at once, at Karen's solicitude in the face of her own irritability, the tears Amy hadn't been able to shed the night before gushed forth. She ran back to her room, with Karen following her and looking worried. Amy flung herself across the bed, which she'd made up herself, and cried like a baby.

Karen sat next to her and put a hand on her back. "Lord, Amy, maybe you ought to see a doctor." She pressed a palm to Amy's forehead. "You feel warm. Maybe you're getting a fever."

She'd had a fever last night. Charlie had cured it. Now she was suffering the consequences. She didn't tell Karen any of that.

"I—I'll be all right. I'm just feeling under the weather this morning."

The only thing Amy could hear for at least a minute was her own sobbing. She felt foolish and miserable and was torn between wishing Karen would go away and wishing she'd stay and offer the comfort of her friendship.

All at once, Karen said, "Did you and Charlie have an argument?"

Shocked, Amy sat bolt upright on the bed. Her face streaming with tears, she blurted out, "Why do you ask that?" Good heavens, Karen couldn't *tell* what they'd done on this bed last night, could she? Amy had scrutinized herself in the mirror this morning, squinting from all angles, trying to determine if her changed status from proper virgin to debauched hussy was in any way visible. She'd come to the conclusion that, as long as no one could read her heart, she was safe from discovery.

Karen shrugged. "Well, you were happy as a lark last night, and then you and Charlie went off together—"

"What do you mean, we went off together?" She brushed tears from her cheeks and stared at Karen, aghast.

"Well, I mean, you went for a walk outside. I figured you wanted to cool off. I know I did after the band quit. Benjamin and I had quite a nice little walk together."

Amy could scarcely believe her eyes when Karen—outgoing, bold, daring Karen—blushed. "You did?"

With a sniff of defiance, Karen said, "Yes, we did. So what?"

"Nothing." Amy shook her head so hard the French knot she'd made in her hair lost a pin. She stabbed it back in clumsily, not caring if the whole thing fell apart. The rest of her was falling apart; why not her hair?

"Benjamin is a very nice man. We . . . like each other."

"I'm sure of it." Blast it, why did her eyes keep leaking? Why couldn't she have cried last night and gotten it over with? Amy scrubbed her face with her fists again. "I'm sorry. I didn't mean anything."

"Well, did you?"

"Did I what?"

"Have a quarrel with Charlie."

What a good excuse. Even if it wasn't the truth. What was one more lie in her life? She might as well begin weaving the fabric of lies now, so she'd be in practice when she went home to Pasadena and had to face her aunt and uncle. And Vernon.

"Yes," she said. "We had a quarrel."

"Oh, Amy, I'm sorry." Karen hugged her, and Amy gave up any pretense of strength and sobbed on her friend's shoulder. She'd never had a friend to cry with before, and she appreciated Karen this morning more than words could say.

Karen, in an excess of empathy, perhaps brought about by her own newly tenderized heart, cried with her. Amy had never felt worse in her adult life.

Eventually, the two women dried their eyes, blew their noses, straightened their clothes—Karen twisted Amy's French knot up tighter—and tidied up. Karen persuaded Amy to wear a little powder to hide the swollen blue patches under her eyes. Amy figured she might as well wear makeup since she was already fallen beyond redemption.

Finally they were able to go downstairs and face the rest of the *One and Only* cast and crew. They were going back to the set today, and filming was expected to be finished shortly.

Amy saw Charlie first thing, and the shock was so great she turned away before she could stop herself. She'd meant to treat him with cool friendship and try to demonstrate no change in their relationship to the rest of the crew, but she'd expected to be able to warm up to it. She hadn't expected to see him standing there looking around as if searching for her.

Moving picture people lived in perilously close proximity to one another when they were filming in remote areas like this one. The fact had not especially bothered Amy until today. Today she wished she wouldn't have to deal with anyone at all connected with the picture until she was under better control.

But there was Charlie, and he'd seen her. He came over to her, his long strides eating up the ground, his expression one of grave concern. His expression irked her. She didn't want rumors and speculation to race through the cast and crew, as they were bound to do if people suspected anything amiss between them.

"Amy," Charlie said when he reached her side. "We've got to talk."

"For heaven's sake, Charlie," she said crossly. "Stop looking so obvious."

He drew himself up short, as if her words and the tone of her voice had slapped him. "But . . . but we really need to talk."

"Fine. But not here and not now. Please, Charlie, have some discretion."

"Discretion?" The word fell out of his mouth on a breath of air. "Discretion?"

"Yes." She glanced around. "Oh, Lord, they're all staring at us."

When she turned her head and peered up at Charlie, she found him staring down at her as if he'd never seen her before. She hardly blamed him; she'd never felt like this before. Taking his arm, she whispered, "Please, Charlie, let's talk about it later. I—I can't right now. Anyhow, we've got to get back to the set."

"I see." He took a step away from her and glanced down to her hand gripping his arm. "So, it's all over? Is that what you're telling me?"

Through gritted teeth, Amy hissed, "I won't talk about it now. I can't. There are too many people standing around."

"I see. It didn't mean anything—that's what you're trying to tell me, isn't it? You thought I was rich, I'm not, and it's all over now. I get it."

"Stop it!" she said. "I can't talk about it now!"

"I see."

She saw him lick his lips, and then she glimpsed an expression of anguish enter his eyes. She wanted to grab the knife out of his scabbard and stab herself. That couldn't hurt any worse than this.

He was going to hate her now; the only man she supposed she'd ever love—and who loved her back—was going to hate her. And all because she was a moral coward and a spiritual invalid. Because she'd allowed a childhood experience to ruin her life.

And she couldn't help it. "Charlie—"

"No. That's all right. I see it all now."

She sucked in air. "Good. I'm glad you see." Her voice had gone as cold as the blood in her veins.

Charlie turned and walked away from her, and Amy felt her heart crack in two.

It took two more days to finish the filming of *One and Only.* Charlie went through the motions as if he were walking in his sleep. Somehow he managed to convey the impression that nothing in the world was wrong with him, but it wasn't true.

He was crushed. Vanquished. Brought low. Made miserable by the one person in the world who he believed would lift him up and create brightness in his life forevermore.

Fat damned chance. He should have remembered that first impressions are often correct ones, and that he'd pegged Miss Amy Wilkes as a prim and prissy female who didn't care about anything but money and appearances the first moment he'd set eyes on her. His initial impression had been confirmed with a vengeance when they saw each other outside Martin's Pierce Great Arrow before Martin drove them back to the Peerless lot. She'd as much as told him she didn't want him now that she knew the ranch in Arizona wasn't his but belonged to his family.

Not for Amy Wilkes a young man starting out in life. Hell, no. Charlie Fox, whose prospects were as good as any man's but who hadn't achieved his goals in life yet, wasn't good enough for her. She'd probably go back to that rich banker in Pasadena and settle down. Or find one of those slimy lounge lizards from a big city somewhere; the rich, old farts who went after the chorus girls.

He knew he was being irrational. After all, while Amy might have pulled the wool over his eyes and made him believe she was really interested in him—hell, she'd said she was in love with him—she'd never given any indication that she'd succumb to anything but a proper marriage. At the moment, however, he was bitter. He couldn't seem to stop these unkind thoughts from holding sway.

As the last few scenes of the picture were shot, he watched her, trying not to be obvious about it. She appeared much as usual. That first day after the glorious hour of love they'd shared, she'd looked tired and down-pin. The next day, and the days following that, however, she'd looked just fine. She'd looked as if she'd never had anything more to do with Charlie Fox than a shared sandwich in the chow tent.

He could hardly stand it.

"Your scene's next," Martin said, startling Charlie, who hadn't heard him walk up. "Are you all right?"

He glanced at Martin and frowned. "Sure, I'm all right. Why? Do I look sick or something?"

Martin jerked back a bit at Charlie's tone, which was savage. "Er, no. Sorry, I didn't mean to imply you don't look well. There's just . . . well, it's only that you haven't seemed quite as happy as usual these past few days, and I wondered if it's anything I could help with."

Crap. The poor man, one of the nicest fellows Charlie'd ever met, was trying to help him out of his dismals, and Charlie'd snapped him off. Criminy, unrequited love was a real pain in the ass. In fact, it stunk, and Charlie hated it.

"Er, no. Sorry, Martin, I didn't mean to let my bad mood out into the open."

Martin eyed him for a moment, then shook his head. "If you ever want to talk about it, I'm right here. You're a good fellow, Charlie, and I hope nothing's gone amiss with you and . . . well, with you and any of your fellow cast members."

Dang, did everybody on the whole blasted lot know about him and Amy? Charlie thought about it for a second or two and decided they probably did. Super. He'd always wanted his deepest personal ordeals out there entertaining the masses.

He said, "Thanks, Martin," and took his place on the set. He did appreciate Martin's concern. He'd sooner poke out his eye with a branding iron than admit to how stupid, how utterly gullible and ridiculous he felt.

Taken advantage of by a city girl—and all because he'd believed her to be something other than a city girl. He'd thought she was a real, honest, down-to-earth person underneath her starch. What a blamed fool he was.

He even tried to hate her, but couldn't manufacture so much as an ounce of antipathy. Mostly, he just felt rotten. And, although it pained him to acknowledge it because the knowledge made him feel like an idiot, if he suddenly came into a fortune, he'd chase her down and propose again on the spot.

Which meant, he concluded, that there was no hope for him whatsoever, and the sooner he took himself back to Arizona Territory and got away from these blasted motion picture people, the better off he'd be.

It therefore came as an unpleasant shock when Martin cornered him on the final day of shooting and begged him to act in "just one more cowboy picture, Charlie. Please? You'll be doing me the biggest favor of your life. We need you, Charlie. There's nobody else we can use. There's nobody else as good as you."

Aw, hell. "I dunno, Martin. I'm not keen on doing another picture."

Martin pleaded. Charlie demurred. Martin pleaded harder. Charlie declined. Martin begged. Charlie, although his heart was weakening, kept his tone of voice firm, knowing he really didn't want to work in another picture. Then Martin made him one last offer.

"We'll pay you well for it, Charlie. We'll pay you three times what you made on this picture. Imagine it." Martin waved his arms in the air as if conjuring the studio's largess right then and there. "You'll be a wealthy man. And I swear to you, we'll never ask again—unless, of course, you want to be in more pictures. There will always be roles for you. You look better on celluloid than any other actor I've ever seen."

"Yeah?" Charlie felt his left eyebrow—the one that doubted everything—arch like a rainbow.

Martin said, "I know, I know, it sounds like I'm spinning moonshine, but I'm not. You haven't seen the daily rushes, but I have. You're going to be a star, Charlie, whether you want to be one or not. If you want to hide your light away in the deserts of Arizona Territory, so be it, but I'm begging you to consider making one more picture with Peerless."

"Well . . ."

Martin clutched at his arm. Charlie was too accustomed to the ways of movie folks by this time to mind. "It's financial on our part, too, Charlie. It's because you're so good. Mr. Lovejoy, who's a genius at this sort of thing, thinks *One and Only* is going to take off like no picture has done since *The Great Train Robbery*. He's sure it's going to be the making of Peerless. He's also sure that if you'll star in a follow-up Peerless feature, the picturegoing public will flock to see it. You see, this will set Peerless up better financially than anything else he can think of. You'll be doing Peerless a tremendous favor, and Peerless aims to pay well for your consent."

"Well, shoot, if you put it that way . . ." Charlie fell. With a heavy heart, he resigned himself to another month or so of living in California.

It probably wouldn't be too bad. They discussed the matter further, and Martin said the filming would be done in and around Los Angeles. That being the case, Charlie wouldn't have to run into Amy anywhere.

His heart gave an enormous twinge at the knowledge, and he wondered if he'd hurt forever or if he'd eventually get over being in love with Amy Wilkes. Or even, failing that, if he'd develop scabs over his open wounds that would protect him at least a little bit from the everlasting pain of losing her.

Not that he'd ever had her. She'd wanted a man well set up in the world and had believed him to be the one. He wasn't, and she'd scooted off like a spooked longhorn in a lightning storm.

The very last scene to be shot was one in which Amy and Horace Huxtable were supposed to ride off into the sunset together, staring at each other moony-eyed from the saddles of their respective horses. Martin was worried about the scene, but he hesitated to ask Charlie to keep an eye on Huxtable.

"Charlie's been acting really strangely these past couple of days," he confided to Karen, who looked worried herself.

"He's not the only one. Amy's been in a real blue mood."

Karen gave Martin a glance he could only consider significant. Unfortunately, he couldn't figure out what it was meant to signify. "Er, do you think they . . . had a fight or something?" He'd noticed that they'd become chummy and then that their relationship had cooled off since their stay at the Royal El Montean. "Um, a lovers' quarrel, perhaps?"

"Yes, I do," Karen said with none of Martin's hedging. That was one of the reasons he liked Karen—she never beat around the bush.

"I see." Martin realized he'd begun tugging at his favorite tuft of hair and let it go. He wished he wouldn't do that. "Well, I want somebody to watch Huxtable during this last scene. It'll be his last shot at Amy, and I don't trust him."

"Nobody trusts him," Karen said grimly. "I'll talk to Charlie."

Relief swept Martin from tip to toe. "Thanks, Karen. That'd be swell."

She marched off like a general aiming to give his troops a good dressing-down, and Martin grinned. Good old Karen. Nothing daunted her—at least not for very long. He hoped Benjamin Egan was up to her weight.

Charlie saw Karen coming, knew she was aiming at him with some purpose in mind, and wished he'd thought to conceal himself. She was bold enough to ask him about what had gone wrong between him and Amy, and he didn't want to talk about it. Not to anyone.

He hadn't thought fast enough to hide, though, and anyway, there wasn't much of anything to hide behind—not to mention the fact that hiding was the epitome of cowardice—so Charlie faced her with a smile. He trusted it didn't look as fake as it felt. He even initiated conversation, and gave himself a mental pat on the back.

"Howdy, Karen. Fine day." It was probably the worst day of his life, but he didn't feel like going into that.

"Hello, Charlie."

She came up to stand beside him, turned, and observed the scene with him. They both watched as Amy, in her split skirt, heaved herself up into the saddle after a couple of tries. No matter how much she practiced, she'd never be any kind of a horsewoman. Charlie tried to take some satisfaction from the fact, but couldn't drum up an iota. He sighed, and wished he'd controlled himself when Karen shot him a look.

"Listen, Charlie," she began. "I don't know what's happened between you and Amy, but I'm sure it's only a misunderstanding."

Like hell. He said, "Hunh."

"I know, I know, it's none of my business."

Right. He said nothing.

"But the truth is that I care about both of you, and I know Amy thinks the world of you."

Like hell she did. He didn't say anything.

She shifted irritably. "Oh, very well, don't speak to me about it. Amy won't talk about it, either. And that's your privilege—both of you. But if you'd only talk to each other, you could probably fix things in a minute."

"Like hell. She won't talk to me, either." Dagnabbit, he hadn't meant to say that. Charlie squeezed his lips together and wished his uncle Bill were here to toss a few oldtime adages at him. He could use a couple. Unfortunately, the only one that came to his mind at the moment was *Some things just ain't funny*.

"Oh. I didn't know that."

Charlie noticed that Karen's eyes were squinty, and she looked as if she were thinking hard. He didn't want to hear any more about Amy today. Or ever, for that matter. It hurt too much. Because he figured Karen was just winding up to spew more platitudes at him, he spoke first.

"Listen, Karen, I'm sure you mean well, but there's nothin' anybody can do about this. If you have something to say, please just say it and get it over with. I'm not going to talk about it, so you'll be doing a solo."

She looked up at him for a minute, frowning, then said, "I won't bother you, then, Charlie. I'm very sorry, though."

He nodded, unwilling to test his ability to talk. He feared he might cry, and then what would his uncle Bill say? He heard Bill say *A man can pretty much always stand more than he thinks he can,* but right this minute Charlie didn't think he believed it.

"Anyway, Martin was wondering if you'd be willing to watch out for Amy during the filming of this last scene. It'll be Huxtable's last chance to do something awful to her, and I suppose he'll try. Unless he's finally come to his senses."

"Naw, he ain't done nothin' so sensible as that." Charlie spoke with conviction. "I'll watch out for her."

"Thanks, Charlie."

He liked and appreciated Karen Crenshaw more than he ever expected to when she gave him one last searching look, nodded, and turned and walked away without trying to pump him. God bless her.

Eighteen

The last time Amy had been so glad to see the end of something was when she'd bidden good-bye to Alaska and gone to live with her aunt and uncle in California. She could hardly wait to get back home to Pasadena, to hug Aunt Julia and Uncle Frank, to go upstairs to her own room with the chintz curtains and bookcase full of novels, and hide away from the world.

She'd have to deal with Vernon, of course, but not immediately. She had some healing to do first. And before she could begin to heal, she had to get through with this odious picture. She wished she'd never seen Martin Tafft, as much as she liked him. Even more than that, she wished she'd had the strength of character to resist his offer when he'd made it.

She hadn't, and here she was. At the very last scene in the picture. Thank God.

Horace Huxtable was going to do something beastly to her; she knew it. And she was prepared. She'd even armed herself. If he so much as looked at her cross-eyed, she aimed to throw something at him. If he tried to hurt her, she was going to stab him with her letter knife. It wouldn't hurt him much, but it would stop him; Amy'd bet on that.

Oh, good grief, there was Charlie. Amy saw him leaning against the fence on the far side of the corral, and wished he hadn't come to watch the last scene being filmed. Was he worried about her still? He'd seemed very cold and distant during these last few days. She certainly didn't blame him for that. She deserved to be shunned by him.

Her heart gave a hard spasm, and she scolded herself for thinking about Charlie. She was a miserable coward, and she'd spoiled any chance of happiness for the both of them. So be it. She had a job to do now, and she'd better concentrate on that and not the mess she'd made of everything.

Concentrate on finishing the picture, Amy Wilkes, she lectured herself sternly. *Pine away for Charlie Fox later.*

She'd do that for certain—probably for the rest of her life.

"You have quite a faraway expression on your face, Miss Wilkes," an oily, snakish voice said in her ear. "Are you daydreaming about riding off into the sunset with me?"

She turned and looked Horace Huxtable straight in the eye. "I'm thinking about how happy I'll be never to have to see you again, actually."

She saw the ornery expression she'd become accustomed to during the past few weeks cross his face before it smoothed out and the actor took over. He smiled beatifically. "My, my, you're quite a bitch, aren't you? I had no idea you'd turn out like that. When I was in that dreadful prison run by your uncle, I believed you to be a kindhearted young woman. It didn't take me long to discover my mistake."

"Good." Amy, who could think of few worse fates than being liked by Horace Huxtable, continued, "See that you keep it in mind. If you do *anything,* anything at all, to hurt me today, you'll regret it."

"Is that a threat, my dear?" He drew himself up so that he loomed over her. His smile didn't waver.

Amy didn't care. By this time, he had no power to do anything more than disgust her—except when he got her alone, and she'd prepared herself for that. "Yes, it is. Try anything, and I'll do my best to see that you pay for it for a long, long time."

"Get on your horses now, Amy and Horace!" came Martin's call from the sidelines. He appeared worried, and Amy hoped for his sake that Huxtable wouldn't do anything too awful today.

Without another word to the man whom she'd begun to think of as her mortal enemy, Amy turned and walked to her horse. If things had been different between herself and Charlie, she'd have asked him to check the saddle cinch, bridle, reins, and other equipment that could have been tampered with. Since Charlie was unavailable to her—if she expected to keep what was left of her pride—she and Karen had performed that task. All of the riding accouterments had looked all right to them, although they were far from being experts.

She sighed as she took the reins, put her foot in the stirrup, and gave what she hoped was a game smile to the young man who was holding the bridle for her. She was so unutterably bad at this horseback-riding stuff. What an idiot she'd been to think she could actually have made a suitable wife for Charlie Fox, when she couldn't even ride a horse.

It took her three tries, but eventually she managed to get herself into the saddle. Although she hadn't intended to, she sought Charlie on the sidelines, hoping he hadn't noticed how awkward she'd been in mounting the beast. Her luck seemed to be running uniformly bad these days, because he was there, and watching her. She sighed again, resigned to having one last miserable day on the Peerless lot.

With another smile for the boy holding the bridle, she said, "I think I'm set now. Thank you very much."

His eyes held a vaguely worshipful expression when he gulped and said, "Sure thing, Miss Wilkes." Which just went to show how much attention people paid to things. If this lad had been paying any mind at all to the way Amy Wilkes went about her job, he'd know she was a failure at it.

Oh, for heaven's sake, buck up, she told herself sternly.

After all, while she might be a poor horsewoman and a novice actress, she'd comported herself well through the whole ordeal of making this picture. She didn't think she'd ever be able to watch it, though. It would surely play in Pasadena, and her friends would naturally want to go see it with her. Amy guessed she'd just have to catch something during those trying times, so that she could plead illness.

Coward, her innards fussed at her.

"Ready, Martin," she called, trying to ignore both her innards and her outers, which were uncomfortably sitting on a stupid saddle, and get this over with.

"Good. All right, Horace and Amy. Take your places on the set."

With trepidation, strained nerves, and severely flexed muscles—Amy was certain she'd never be able to relax on a horse, no matter if she were to ride every day for the rest of her life—she guided the animal to the mark chalked in the dust of the yard. Huxtable, who rode with ease and grace, was waiting for her with his customary sneer in place when she pulled her mount to a halt.

"Christ," he muttered. "Some people are absolutely incompetent."

He was talking about her. Amy knew it, and although she resented his words, she also knew he was only trying to rile her, so she didn't react but instead looked at Martin so that she wouldn't miss her cue.

Karen stood next to Martin, her arms crossed over her chest, watching Amy with concern. Amy knew Karen cared about her state of mind, but she hadn't been able to talk to her friend about Charlie yet because the wound was too raw.

Besides, Karen had made no bones about her feelings regarding Vernon Catesby and Amy's fear of trying new things. Amy was sure Karen wouldn't understand why she'd rejected Charlie's proposal. In reality, even Amy didn't understand. All she knew was that when she contemplated starting out in married life—even with Charlie Fox, the man she adored—with nothing standing between herself and death but one man, no matter how wonderful he was, her insides knotted up, her heart twisted, and her brain went into total rebellion.

She simply couldn't do it, and she knew it. What a worthless piece of female flesh she was. Charlie should be happy he was getting rid of her so easily. Before things got too serious.

Sleeping with him had been a very serious event to Amy, but she knew men were different. All at once the knowledge that she might be pregnant slammed into her brain, and she nearly fell off her horse.

"Good heavens," she murmured, aghast.

"What is it this time, my little sweetie pie?" Huxtable asked in his malicious smear of a voice. "Does your tender little bottom hurt?"

She turned the most vicious glare in her repertoire upon him. "I'm *so* glad the filming ends today, Mr. Huxtable. And I hope I'll never have the misfortune of ever seeing you again."

"No more do I," he said suavely. "Bitch."

"All right, Amy and Horace, quit talking to each other. We're going to get this in one take!"

"One take?" muttered Huxtable. "With this female who's pretending to be an actress? Absurd."

"I never pretended to be an actress," Amy said, forgetting she knew better than to answer his jibes.

He smiled a sugary smile. "It's a good thing."

"Quiet on the set!" Martin hollered. "Get set!"

He was beginning to sound a little frazzled, and Amy was sorry she'd had a part in making him so. She turned as much as she dared in her saddle and smiled at him to let him know she'd do her part, and she was ready. More or less.

Huxtable snorted.

Amy wondered why people like Horace Huxtable seemed to go on forever and good people like her parents died young. It wasn't fair. She'd have to have a chat with God about it when this was all over.

"All right," Martin shouted, a little more cheerful. "And—action!"

The cameras began to crank noisily, the sprockets began shooting out, and Amy's and Huxtable's horses began moving slowly away from the others. Amy took heart from the knowledge that this was the final scene in this horrid picture, and that she'd never have to work with Horace Huxtable again as long as she lived.

Facing the man she detested more than any other man on earth, Amy put on her loveliest, most adoring expression; an expression that, when viewed by the picturegoing public, would appear to be one of abject love. "You have made my life miserable during the past few weeks, Mr. Huxtable. I'm sure you know that and are proud of yourself, although you did fail to kill me, which I'm sure you wish you had."

"Nonsense. You had a few unfortunate accidents on the set, and they were brought about by your inexperience and stupidity. I had nothing to do with any of them."

"That's a lie, and you know it." If this had been any other man, Amy wouldn't have said such a directly hateful thing. Huxtable deserved it, however, and she'd cast aside her natural courtesy and let him have it.

"Balls," he replied, not at all contrite. "You don't know what you're saying, any more than you know what you're doing."

"I know what I'm saying this minute," Amy responded instantly. "I dislike you very much, Mr. Huxtable. You were awful at my uncle's health spa, and you're even more awful on the set of this picture."

"Bah. You're raving."

"Fiddlesticks. You know very well I'm not raving. I think you're probably less than human. I do believe you're a throwback to a lower life form. I never believed in Mr. Darwin's theories until I met you." To make her performance for the cameras even more believable, she held out her hand to him, as she was supposed to do, and batted her eyelashes.

"And you, my dear," Huxtable countered, "belong in that deadly place, Pasadena, serving up that deadly liquid, orange juice. You're unfit for a more sophisticated life."

"I'm sure you're right. And I'm sure that if you personify the sophisticated life, nobody with two principles to rub together would want anything to do with it."

"Good! Good!" Martin cried behind them. "You're looking good. If you can go a tiny bit more slowly, do it. This will be the public's last sight of you—"

"Thank God," whispered Amy.

"—and we want to make it good!"

"My sentiments exactly, my dear."

"You're squeezing my hand too tightly, Mr. Huxtable. Please loosen your grip." She hadn't meant to say anything to him about how much he was hurting her hand, but was finally driven by pain to protest. "I'm going to shout in a minute and draw everyone's attention to your childish antic."

"Nonsense. The scene's almost over. I'm only making sure you don't fall off your horse. You're no horsewoman, you know."

"Of course I know it," Amy ground out through her teeth. "Release me instantly."

"Make me," he said, sounding even more childish than before.

"All right, I shall."

"And ruin poor Martin's one perfect take? Tut, tut, wench. You're certainly no professional."

"No, I'm not a professional. Nor am I a martyr."

"Perfect!" Martin shouted. "Just a little more now, and we'll be all through."

"We're through now," Amy declared savagely. And with that, and with more athletic skill than she knew she possessed, she withdrew her dullish letter knife from the pocket of her skirt and stabbed Horace Huxtable on the back of his hand.

"Ow!" Huxtable bellowed. "You damned bitch!" He yanked her hand, pulling her right out of the saddle.

But Amy fooled him this time. She'd been expecting him to pull some stunt like this, and she didn't let go of his hand when she fell. Not only did she not let go, but she reached wildly for his leg as she went down. She managed to snag his calf and held on for dear life. If she was going to fall, so was he.

"No!" he screamed, and Amy had the satisfaction of seeing him lose his balance and begin sliding in his saddle before she hit the ground and somebody turned out the lights on the set.

She woke up in Charlie's arms, hearing his voice in her ear. "It's all right, Amy. You'll be all right. Jesus Christ, you'd better be all right."

His panic-stricken tone of voice puzzled her. She couldn't imagine Charlie Fox, the brave and noble cowboy who'd handled stampeding cattle and blue lightning balls, being panic-stricken. She wondered what was wrong. It must be something really bad to make Charlie sound like this.

Although it hurt to do so, she lifted her arm and brushed a strand of hair from his dear forehead. He stopped walking so suddenly that her body swayed in his arms and hurt all over. She couldn't suppress a moan of pain.

"Amy!" he cried, hurting her ears, which made it unanimous: Every inch of her hurt now.

Although her chest and lips and throat hurt, she whispered, "You needn't speak so loudly."

"Amy!" he cried again.

She'd never known him to be a blabbermouth, but she'd always believed he had more than one word in his vocabulary. Her eyebrows lowered a little bit—not too much, because they, too, hurt. "What happened?"

"Good God, he almost killed you."

She huffed impatiently. "Of course he did. But I fooled him this time. I stabbed him and made him fall from his horse, too." She couldn't understand why Charlie seemed so worried. Unless . . . "Oh, did I get hurt?" Stupid question, since she felt the answer even as she asked it. Because she didn't want to be considered unintelligent by Charlie Fox, of all people, she amended the query. "I mean, did I break anything?"

"We don't know yet. Be still. I'm trying to get you to your tent."

"Oh." That made sense. Curious, she asked, "What happened to Mr. Huxtable."

She was pleased to see a tiny grin lift his beautiful lips. "Before or after I beat the tar out of him?"

Had he really done that? Amy was so pleased she could hardly stand it. "Oh, I'm so glad. Thank you."

"You're welcome. He fell right on top of you, and the doc's going to see if he broke any of your bones."

"Ew." Amy didn't like the thought of Horace Huxtable on top of her. It made her feel queasy.

Charlie continued. "I think he busted an arm falling off his horse."

"Good." Satisfied with this initial report—she'd hear the full story from Karen later—Amy decided to close her eyes again. They didn't want to be open. From what seemed like far away, she heard somebody running up to them.

"How is she?" It was Martin. Wasn't that nice? Martin was worried about her, too.

Amy drifted off to sleep in Charlie's arms.

Without turning, Charlie responded to Martin's worried question. "I think she passed out again." He tried to hurry and be careful with her at the same time, incompatible actions that were frustrating him a lot. Add that mixture to the anxiety gnawing at his innards, and he was in a state.

"Oh, dear, oh, dear. I was afraid something like this would happen. I should have had her strapped into her saddle or something."

"That would have been worse. She could have broken her back."

"My God." Color drained from Martin's face. He murmured, "It's all my fault. Lord above, Charlie, this is all my fault. I should have fought Mr. Lovejoy. I never wanted to work with Huxtable again. I think the man's gone completely mad."

"You couldn't have predicted this. I only hope Huxtable's pretty face will never recover, and he'll never have another chance to hurt another woman."

"I'm afraid that's all taken care of." Martin didn't sound awfully happy about it, considering what Huxtable did to Amy. "His nose will never be the same. And Amy managed to mangle him pretty badly all on her own, even before you showed up."

"Yeah. She did a good job on him. I'm glad I was there to see it."

"Oh, dear, oh, dear. I hope we don't have to reshoot any scenes that he's in."

"Yeah. Me, too."

"He'll never look the same again."

"I sure hope not."

Obviously, Martin didn't share Charlie's happiness about the injuries Huxtable had sustained. Charlie didn't wonder at that, although he thought Martin should be more pleased than not. Huxtable was certainly no asset to any picture Peerless might make.

"I've sent Eddie to get the doctor. He'll be here soon," Martin said distractedly. "Maybe I'd better go help him." He veered off in the direction of the doctor's tent.

Charlie had almost reached Amy's tent by the time Martin left him alone with Amy. Karen had run on ahead and lifted the tent flap so that Charlie could carry Amy in and tenderly set her on the bed without fumbling with the flap.

"How is she?" Karen asked, clearly worried.

"I'm not sure. I think she's only woozy." Charlie prayed he was right. "Martin's gone to get the doctor."

"Good. Oh, Charlie, I hope she's going to be all right."

Charlie could scarcely believe it when he saw Karen wipe her eyes. He patted her on the shoulder. "I'm sure she will be." And if she wasn't, he was going to kill Huxtable for her, no matter how hard Martin tried to dissuade him. If he got locked up for it, so be it. He wasn't too keen on living without Amy for the rest of his life anyway. He didn't suppose it mattered where he did it.

He was appalled when he realized where his thoughts had drifted and gave himself a mental kick in the butt. "Ain't no woman worth gettin' het up for," Uncle Bill used to say. Quite often. And, while Charlie didn't really believe it, he knew good and well that any woman who wasn't willing to follow her man into hell wasn't the woman for him. And Amy wouldn't even follow him into a new ranch. She surely wasn't worth sacrificing himself for. No matter how much the notion of killing Horace Huxtable appealed to him.

As he peered down into Amy's face, which was at the moment as white as a snowdrop, he knew Uncle Bill was dead wrong. He also knew Amy was wrong to reject him for such a frivolous reason as the one she'd given him. If she really loved him, she'd marry him, even if he wasn't rich.

Because his heart was in a turmoil and because he didn't want to be around when Amy awoke—he feared her weakened state would weaken him, and he'd end up acting like a sick puppy and following her back to Pasadena—he waited only long enough for the doctor to arrive and shoo them all outside. There he paced up and down with Karen and Martin until the doctor pushed out through the tent flap. The three of them stopped pacing and stared at the man. Charlie bit his tongue so he wouldn't holler for information before the doc had a chance to get his thoughts together.

"She's going to be just fine. She sustained a minor concussion—"

"Concussion!" That didn't sound minor to Charlie, and he took a step toward the doctor, intending to shake the truth out of him. Martin grabbed him by one arm, and Karen grabbed him by the other, so he couldn't fulfill his intentions.

The doctor took a step back, and his eyes opened wide with surprise and apprehension. "She's going to be fine," he repeated. "The concussion isn't serious. Just be sure she's awakened every hour or so and given liquids. Don't let her get up and walk around, and you might want to check her vision occasionally to be sure there's nothing more amiss than I think there is."

After giving Charlie an assessing glance, the doctor continued, "I'll go check on Mr. Huxtable now—"

"Check on *Huxtable?*" Charlie roared. "You're not checking on Huxtable until you tell us more about Amy!"

"Charlie," Martin muttered. "Please try to calm down."

Tugging at his black coat, the doctor frowned and said, "Really, Mr. Fox, there's nothing more to be done for Miss

Wilkes. With rest, she'll be just fine. Huxtable, on the other hand, is in pretty bad shape."

"Good. I hope the bastard dies."

"Charlie!" Karen hissed. "Stop talking like that."

"It's the truth."

"I don't care if it's the truth or not. For that matter, I'm of a like mind, but we don't want anybody else to know it."

"Oh, dear, oh, dear." Martin started tugging at his hair.

"I must say, Mr. Fox, that it's not your fault Mr. Huxtable remains breathing. You did a good deal of damage to his nose and jaw."

The doctor's words cheered him. "Good."

Karen whacked him on the arm, and Charlie, realizing he was being unreasonable, shook himself and muttered, "Sorry, Karen. I'm all right now."

"I should hope so." She poked him in the chest with her rigid forefinger. "Now, I'm going into that tent, and I'm going to tend to Amy. If you want to help, stay out of trouble and don't hurt anyone else." And with that, Karen vanished inside the tent.

Charlie gazed after her, dismayed by her words. Had he caused trouble? He'd thought he was avenging Amy. Maybe, in the strange and mysterious world of motion pictures, that was considered trouble. He shook his head to clear it of the cobwebs that seemed to have taken possession of it.

"I'd appreciate it if you'd stay away from Huxtable, Charlie," Martin said. "The picture's wrapped up, and all I have to do now is the editing. The musical score's been written, and the titles are done, and now I've got to put it all together. I'm hoping against hope that we won't have to do any reshoots. I'd as soon not have to worry about one of my stars killing another one, if it's all the same to you."

His voice was gentle, but Martin's voice was always gentle except when he had to raise it to be heard over the grinding of the cameras. Charlie was suddenly ashamed of himself. "Right," he said. "I reckon I'll get going, then, since you don't need me anymore."

Martin's surprise was evident. "Get going? You mean leave the lot?"

"Yeah. I reckon."

"But don't you want to wait and make sure Amy's all right?"

"I trust the doctor." He wouldn't trust that doctor any farther than he could throw him, but he didn't suppose it mattered. He wasn't needed here, and he wasn't wanted here, and he experienced a tremendous need to be gone.

"But—but, Charlie, how can I get in touch with you?"

Charlie shrugged. "Darned if I know. Why don't I call you or something? I can probably find a telephone somewhere."

"Do you know where you'll go? Are you heading back to your brother's ranch?"

"No." By God, he was never going to punch ostriches again. It was long past time he set up for himself. Hell, if he'd had the gumption to get himself organized before now, he wouldn't have lost the girl he loved.

Dammit, he wished he'd stop thinking things like that. Obviously, Amy didn't care enough about him to take him as he was; ergo, he shouldn't mourn losing her. He mourned anyway. "I'll be in touch," he muttered, and began walking slowly in the direction of his tent.

"Please do, Charlie," Martin called after him. "Don't forget, I'm taking everybody in the picture to Chicago for the grand premiere. And you've agreed to do one more Peerless picture. Don't go too far away, and call within the month."

"Right." Charlie lifted his arm but didn't bother to turn around. "I'll be in touch."

He heard Martin chuff with frustration, and regretted having caused it. He liked Martin. But he couldn't abide another our in this place. And if he saw Amy again, he'd probably start beseeching her to marry him, and his pride couldn't stand that.

Gus, one of the men who'd been assigned to guard Horace Huxtable, agreed to drive Charlie to the small train station near El Monte. So Charlie packed his brother's old carpetbag, slung it over his shoulder, got into the car, and rode away from the Peerless lot in a cloud of dust. He looked back, although he'd told himself he wasn't going to, until the tent city disappeared from his sight. Then he sighed.

"You okay, Charlie?" Gus asked.

"Yeah," Charlie said. "Fine."

"I'm glad you punched Huxtable. He deserved it a dozen times over."

"Yeah."

"I hope Peerless never hires him again."

"Yeah."

Sensing the futility of trying to begin a conversation with Charlie, Gus subsided into quiet. All the way to the train station, the only noises Charlie heard were those of the car's engine and its tires throwing pebbles up to patter against the underside of the carriage. The pebbles seemed to ping out a rhythm, and he heard Amy's voice speaking along with them in his head. The voice was saying, "No, no, no," over and over again.

When they got to the train station, Charlie bought a ticket on the first train out without determining where it was headed. He shrugged when he read the stub and saw that the train's ultimate destination was Los Angeles.

Los Angeles was fine with him. He'd never been there. In his present state, one place was as good as another. As long as wherever he went didn't contain Amy Wilkes, he was satisfied.

He wondered if he'd ever be happy again, and decided it

was too soon to think about that. At the moment, his only goal was escape.

The prospect of going to Chicago, and of seeing Amy at the premiere of *One and Only* crept into his head, and he thrust it aside. Later, he told himself. He'd think about everything later, when he didn't hurt so much.

He had a feeling that later was going to be a very long time in the future.

Nineteen

Amy awoke and recovered in a world that no longer contained Charlie Fox, at least in her vicinity. It was, therefore, a gray world, a lusterless world, a world in which she could find nothing to interest her. The weather outdoors was sunny and bright and full of life. The weather inside Amy was wintry and bleak and totally barren.

The day after her fall from the horse, she lay in bed, plucking at the covers, as the Peerless set for *One and Only* was being dismantled around her. She heard the crew doing the work and thought about going outside so she could witness the activity. She'd surely never have another chance to see how a motion picture set was put up and taken down. In order to do that, however, she'd have had to expend some energy to rise from bed, put on some clothes, and walk to the flap of the tent. She didn't want to see the activity *that* much. She didn't want to see anything at all.

Except, perhaps, one tall, lean, lanky cowboy whom she'd pushed away and might never see again.

She sighed heavily and turned her face to the side of the tent. The blank side. The side where all she could see was canvas.

"Amy? Amy, are you awake?"

With another deep sigh, Amy turned her head at Karen's soft voice. She truly was glad to see her friend, even if she couldn't drum up any overt enthusiasm. "Hello, Karen." She tried to smile, failed, and decided it didn't matter. Nothing mattered now.

Karen's smile was big enough for both of them, although it looked as if she had to force it. She strode over to the bed, yanked off the big straw hat she wore, tossed it aside, and sat with a thump on the chair beside Amy. "Whew! It's a real mess out there."

"I expect so." Blast. This was no way to talk to her new best friend. With a massive effort, Amy managed to put a little—a very little—spark into her next words. "How long is it going to take to get the whole thing packed up?"

"I don't know. Here, I brought you some lemonade. It's not great, but it's wet, and I managed to finagle a piece of ice from the cook, so it's almost cold."

Lemonade. Now, there was something Amy could view with slightly more animation than if she were a dead cow lying on the desert. She was thirsty. "Thanks, Karen. That sounds good."

"Well, it's not, but it's wet."

"Thanks." With a good deal of struggle, because her muscles were still sore from the damage they'd sustained the day before, she sat up and took the lemonade glass. She hoped Karen would initiate a conversation since her own mind was a blank. The only topic of conversation that interested her was Charlie Fox, and he was gone.

"Martin said he'd drive us both home in his Pierce Arrow, so at least we won't have a miserable bumpy ride in the wagon with the rest of the cast."

"That's nice of him."

"He feels guilty about not keeping a better watch on that wretch Huxtable."

Amy would have shaken her head if she'd had the vitality. "That wasn't his fault. Huxtable alone is responsible for his actions."

"I know it. And I suppose Martin does, too, but he still feels bad that he wasn't able to prevent what happened."

Amy managed a tiny shrug. It hurt, but at least it spared her from thinking up a string of coherent words to say.

"But it's nice to know that Huxtable won't be fit to act in any more pictures for a while, so he won't menace any other poor actresses."

"Good."

"It *is* good. And it was Charlie Fox who did it, too. He ought to get a medal."

He ought to get more than that. He deserved the world on a platter, and if Amy were worth spit, she'd be there with him. She wasn't. She tried to tell herself not to be maudlin, but didn't have the strength of will or body. She lifted her glass and sipped instead.

The lemonade tasted good, although she was beginning to pine for some of her uncle's fresh orange juice. Soon. Her uncle was always telling people how beneficial and healthy orange juice was. Maybe a sufficient quantity of orange juice could cure the lovesick blues.

She doubted it.

Karen fidgeted in the chair for a second, then rose abruptly and began striding around the tent. Amy watched her, vaguely curious. Suddenly, Karen turned and spoke to her. "Listen, Amy, I don't know what happened between you and Charlie, but whatever it was must have been bad, but I can't imagine either one of you doing anything so terrible as to cause such a rift between you. Why, you're both terrific people, and you're perfect for each other."

Holding her lemonade glass to her warm cheek in order to capture some of its coolness, Amy again turned to the wall. Her heart hurt too much to talk about it. She heard Karen stomp her foot, and she sighed.

"Will you stop sighing and tell me what happened? For

heaven's sake, Amy, you can't keep everything inside of you. You're eating your heart out, and so is Charlie, and now he's disappeared, and you're lying here like Camille dying, and it's stupid! You're both intelligent people. If you had some sort of problem, certainly you can work it out!"

Tired, sore, and now feeling beleaguered, Amy turned her head and scowled at her friend. "My love life is none of your business, Karen Crenshaw."

"The hell it's not!"

Karen's profane outburst was enough to shock even the wounded Amy out of her lethargy. She gaped at Karen, who blushed. Astonishing.

"Dammit," Karen continued, stomping her foot again, and again shocking Amy, who wasn't accustomed to hearing young ladies swear. "It's my business because I care about you. Both of you. It's my business because I'm your friend. It's my business because I don't want friends of mine to be miserable— and you're both miserable!"

In reaction to this, Amy pruned up her lips. She was beginning to feel abused as well as wounded and beleaguered, and she didn't appreciate it. "Nonsense."

"It's not nonsense!" Karen exclaimed. "What happened, Amy? I swear to God, if you don't tell me, I'll track down Charlie Fox and make him tell me! Then I'll hog-tie him and haul him to you and make the two of *you* talk it out."

"Don't be silly."

"It's not silly."

And then Karen did something that so alarmed Amy, she could only gape in wonder for a second. She burst into tears. Amy said, "Stop it, Karen. Please."

"Oh, you're driving me crazy. Both of you! I care so much about you, and you're both so unhappy, and that makes me unhappy, and I *know* there's some bit of nonsense at the bottom of it that if you'd just talk about it, everything would be fine, but you won't talk to each other, and you won't talk to anyone else, and Charlie's run away, and you're lying there like some expiring heroine in a bad melodrama, and it's not fair!"

Although she could sort of appreciate Karen's point of view, Amy felt it important to point out the obvious to her friend—whom she truly did esteem. "It's my life, Karen."

Karen wiped at her cheek furiously. "I know it. But it's my life, too, and I value my friends. I don't have enough of them that I can afford to see one of them making an egregious mistake and not butt in."

Amy took in breath and let it out. That was indeed one of Karen's most notable characteristics, she supposed: assertiveness. "All right, I appreciate your concern. But I'm not really up to talking about it."

"Bother! What *else* do you have to do?" Karen threw out her arms in an extravagant gesture that dislodged her hat from the bureau on which it had landed. She caught it gracefully and replaced it on the bureau.

"Recover," Amy said dully.

"Right. And I'll bet you anything that you'd recover a darned sight faster if your heart didn't hurt so much."

Without realizing what she was doing, Amy pressed a hand over her heart, which did ache abominably. Karen, needless to say, saw the gesture and pounced upon it.

"There!" she said in triumph. "It's *exactly* as I said!" She rushed over and sat in the chair again. Taking Amy's hand in hers, she said, "Please, Amy, talk to me. I'm sure it won't seem so bad if you let yourself talk about it."

"Well . . ." Actually, it might feel good to unburden herself a little bit. Not about everything. She'd die before she'd admit she'd slept with Charlie Fox before marriage.

"Please?" Karen pleaded. "I haven't told you my news yet, but Benjamin has asked me to marry him."

"Oh, Karen!" Amy was actually able to drum up some excitement for her friend. She squeezed Karen's hand. "I'm so happy for you."

"I'm happy for me, too. And I want to be happy for *you,* too. What's more, I want you to be my maid of honor, and Benjamin wants Charlie to be one of his groomsmen."

"My goodness."

"But in order for that to happen, the two of you have to be willing to exist in the same space together—at least long enough for the wedding ceremony to take place. As it is now, neither Benjamin nor I feel comfortable about asking the two of you to be together in the wedding party, but you're the only two we want, besides my sister and Benjamin's brother."

Karen had a point there, Amy guessed.

"Please, Amy, won't you give talking a chance? I promise you—I'll swear on a Bible if you want me to—that it will go no further than the inside of this tent. I won't even tell Benjamin, if you don't want me to."

Horrified that her secrets might be spread about, Amy spoke before thinking. "Good God, no, don't tell anyone! Please."

Karen held up a placatory hand. "I won't. I promise." She crossed her heart. Amy remembered making that gesture when she was little and playing with her friends in Pasadena. The only things she could remember about her life before Pasadena were cold and ice and fright and misery. Which sort of prepared her for the coming ordeal.

She took an enormous breath, paused to gather her wits, and told Karen almost everything.

Karen stared at her throughout her recitation and for a long time after she'd stopped talking. After what seemed like a century, Karen said, "I see." Another stretch of silence ensued; then Karen said, "I hadn't realized how deeply your experience in Alaska had hurt you. It really left scars, didn't it?"

An all too familiar sensation of helpless dread began to creep through Amy. It always started the same way, with a sinking feeling in her stomach. It worked its way through the entirety of her body, not skipping her heart, until the whole of her felt like a lump of lead—cold, vulnerable, powerless, and unable to think. "Yes." She shivered in the smothering heat.

"I see." Karen tapped her chin with her forefinger. "I'm very sorry, Amy. I'm sure it was an abominable, frightening experience."

"It was."

"And it's certainly damaged you, if you're willing to give up Charlie Fox, who would never in a billion years hurt you, in order to keep protecting that little kid you used to be."

Now, there, Amy thought, was an interesting way of looking at it. She tried to resent Karen's assessment, but it sounded perilously like the truth. "I guess so."

Karen got up and slowly circuited the tent, pausing now and then to pick up and put down homey decorative items that Amy had set out here and there. She lifted an old photograph in a silver frame and peered at it closely. "Are these your parents?"

"Yes."

Karen nodded and continued her circuit of the tent, carrying the photograph with her and studying it as she walked. When she got to the flap of the tent, she stopped, lifted the flap, and stared outside. Light poured in, and Amy was surprised to see how bright it was. The coldness that had invaded her soul had tricked her into thinking it must be cold outdoors, too, even though it was around noon on a blistering summer day.

After several minutes of staring, Karen turned, dropped the flap, and held the photograph out in front of her. "You know, don't you, Amy, that your parents were a couple of darned fools."

So startled was she by Karen's words and tone of voice, which was quite harsh, that Amy jerked and stared at her. "Wh-what? What did you say?"

"You heard me. Any two people who would take a tiny child into the wilderness without the means to keep her safe are no better than idiots. What's more, they were lousy parents."

"Don't you dare talk about my parents like that!" Furious, Amy sat up in bed. She felt her face flame. If she'd had anything to throw besides the lemonade glass, she just might have thrown it.

"Why not? They've been dead for years, and anybody would think they'd already done their worst, but they haven't. Why, they just ruined your life!" Karen sounded angry, too.

"How dare you say such a thing! You don't know anything about it!"

"I do, too! I know *you!* If this is what your parents made of you by their bumbling, then I hope they're roasting in hell!"

"My father was a minister!" Amy was appalled to hear her voice shake with rage and tears.

"I don't care what he was! If he'd had the sense God gave a gopher, he'd have left you in some civilized place in the care of somebody with a brain instead of taking you to God knows where to do God knows what so you could watch him and your mother die of improper food and inadequate medical attention!"

"That's not fair!"

"It is so fair!"

"No! You're wrong!"

"I'm not wrong! My God, Amy, do you realize what you're doing? You're willing to give up a man who would treat you like a precious treasure—who'd treat you the way your parents *should* have treated you—because your parents abandoned you!"

"They didn't mean to!"

"Of course they didn't mean to. But any idiot would have known to take precautions. Evidently, they were absolutely alone on their iceberg, except for you, a little girl, to take care of them. What kind of planning was that?"

"They couldn't help it." Tears had begun to trickle from Amy's eyes, although she tried to stop them. She was furious, and she didn't want Karen to think she was weakling enough to cry. Unfortunately, she was a weakling, and she was crying. "I can't help it, either."

"Bosh! You're no milksop, Amy Wilkes, whether you want to pretend you are or not. And you're not a fainting maiden. You're not a little kid any longer. You're a strong, accomplished woman, and you have the ability to take control of your life, which you couldn't way back then. Can't you tell the difference between you then and you now?"

Through a film of tears, Amy glared at Karen, wishing she'd just go away. She didn't like hearing these things from her friend. "I know I'm not a little kid, Karen Crenshaw."

"Well, you're still acting like one!"

"That's not fair!"

"Bosh! For heaven's sake, Amy. You're an adult female American citizen. If Charlie Fox ever did anything to hurt you—which he won't, because he worships the ground you walk on—you can get up on your hind legs and leave him. You have friends and family who can help you if something goes wrong. You're not all alone in the world and too young to make decisions anymore! Can't you tell the difference?"

Yes, Amy could tell the difference. She could not, however, control the panic that welled up inside of her when she considered doing what Charlie had asked of her. She cried harder, feeling trapped between two intolerable options. "But . . . but,

Karen, I'm . . . I'm scared." Her throat was so tight, the words were almost indistinguishable.

"Oh, Amy!" Karen rushed over to the bed, thrust the photograph aside, and took her friend in her arms. "I'm so sorry."

Karen's sympathy was the only thing Amy needed to complete her demoralization. She collapsed, weeping piteously, and ashamed of herself for doing it.

"I know you're scared, Amy. Anybody would be after going through what you went through when you were only a kid. But you're not a kid any longer. And the world's a different place now than it was back then. And you live in the great state of California, not the Yukon Territory or wherever Alaska is. We have telephones and doctors and medicine and streetcars and automobiles, and all sorts of things you and your parents didn't have. And you're all grown up. If you or Charlie or one of your kids gets sick, you can take care of it. You don't have to die for lack of medicine and freezing cold and starvation and stuff like that."

"I know," stumbled wetly from Amy's aching throat. "I'm sorry I was so mean to you."

Amy shook her head, knowing Karen had only spoken the truth, no matter how hard it had been for her to hear it. But, oh, how was she ever to overcome this blind panic that throttled her and rendered her immobile every time she thought about starting out in married life with nothing?

"Here," Karen said, her own voice sounding suspiciously thick. "Blow your nose. We need to talk some more." Karen handed Amy a handkerchief she'd hastily snatched from a bureau drawer.

Amy blew her nose. "Oh, please, no," she mumbled, sure she'd die if she had to go through any more of these hateful truth-revealing sessions. "I can't talk anymore."

"Oh, please, yes, you can so," Karen said, after blowing

her own nose in another of Amy's hankies. "Knowing what you're doing isn't enough, you know."

Indeed, Amy knew. Quite well, in fact. She only nodded, still weighed down by the feeling that all was lost and could never be found.

"I mean, it's all well and good to know that you're reacting like a seven-year-old to an adult situation, but there are still the terrible memories and fears that lurk behind everything and that keep you from making sensible decisions." Karen gave her nose another hearty blow.

"There's no need to be horrid to me," Amy said shakily.

"I'm sorry. I'm always blundering around and saying things I probably shouldn't. I try not to, but it always happens."

"Hmph."

"I think what you need to do is develop some sort of strategy to deal with your feelings. I mean, there's no law that says you can't be scared of something—after all, you *did* go through a pretty awful time—but there's also no reason for you to let fear keep you from a happy marriage with a man who loves you and whom you love." She eyed Amy hard. "You can't deny it. I know you love him."

"Yes," Amy said humbly. "I love him."

"Well, then, what you need to do is develop some sort of coping strategy."

Hmmm. There was a novel notion. Holding the handkerchief up to catch her dripping tears, Amy stared at Karen, curious. "What do you mean?"

"What I mean is that you need to overcome your fears." She bounced up from the bed and began pacing with her old vigor. "I mean, I'm sure you've read over and over again about stage fright."

"You mean when actors get scared before they go onto the stage to perform in a play?"

"Exactly! In other words, they're scared, but they don't let their fear stop them. They might perform scared, but they perform, and pretty soon they get involved in the role and the fear disappears."

"Merciful heavens." How intriguing an example, particularly since Amy had spent her first several days on the Peerless lot performing scared, and her fear had eventually disappeared. Could she do the same thing with other aspects of her life?

Why not?

By the time Karen left Amy's tent, the two women had discussed the matter nearly to death. Karen was thrilled, and Amy was so exhausted she barely had enough vitality to turn over and go back to sleep.

She was no longer feeling abandoned and alone, however. Nor was she unhappy any longer. She still harbored a vague sensation of uncertainty. Everything hinged on whether or not Charlie Fox would be attending Peerless's premiere of *One and Only* in Chicago.

It was a much cheerier Amy who arrived at her uncle's health spa two days later, pulling up in Martin's huge and luxurious automobile, with Karen seated next to her. All the guests at the Orange Rest rushed outside to see who could possibly be arriving at the spa in such a grand manner.

"Amy!" Aunt Julia rushed out to give Amy a gigantic hug. It hurt her various bruises, but Amy didn't even say Ow.

"It's so good to be home!" she cried, and gave her aunt a smacking kiss on the cheek. "Let me introduce you to my new best friend, Karen Crenshaw, who lives in Altadena and works for Madame Dunbar—"

"Mercy!" Julia slapped her hands to her cheeks as if the news of Karen's employer had stunned her. "Madame Dunbar! Why, she's famous."

Karen grinned and held out a hand for Aunt Julia to shake.

"How do you do, Mrs. Wilkes. Amy and I had a wonderful time on the set of *One and Only.*"

"Oh, I'm so glad." Julia shook Karen's hand enthusiastically.

"And you already know Mr. Tafft," said Amy, directing her aunt's attention to Martin. "He was kind enough to drive Karen and me home today."

"My goodness, Mr. Tafft, it's good to see you again. Thank you so much for taking such good care of our Amy."

The three picture people exchanged a significant glance. Martin said, "Miss Wilkes proved to be a wonderful actress, Mrs. Wilkes. She performed her role to perfection."

It wasn't true, and Amy knew it, but it pleased her to hear Martin say so.

He continued, "After the final editing of the picture's been done, the cast will be going to a special premiere of the picture in Chicago. If you can clear your schedules, I'd like to invite you and Mr. Wilkes to attend with Amy."

"Oh, my!" Aunt Julia went pink with pleasure.

"Thank you, Martin!" Amy exclaimed. "How very kind of you."

"He just wants to make sure you don't back out," Karen said in her humorous, downright way.

Amy frowned at her. Martin laughed.

"Won't you please come in for a few minutes and take a glass of orange juice?"

Karen and Martin looked at each other. Martin shrugged. Karen, grinning, said, "You know, I really want to get home, but I can't resist such an appealing offer. Amy's been extolling the virtues of her aunt and uncle's orange juice ever since she arrived on the Peerless lot."

Aunt Julia looked pleased.

Amy wrinkled her nose at Karen. "She's saying I was a dead bore, Aunt Julia, but don't you believe it."

They all laughed, and Martin carried Amy's bag up to the big white pavilion of the Orange Rest Health Spa. Julia, noticing all the inmates staring, straightened her shoulders proudly. Amy grinned inside. She knew exactly what her aunt was thinking. After all, it wasn't *every* family in Pasadena that boasted a moving picture star.

Not that she was a star.

She was, however, truly glad to be home. She couldn't wait to drink a tall glass of orange juice, carry her bag up to her room and unpack, and be among familiar surroundings.

Amy Wilkes was not an adventuress at heart. And that was putting it mildly. She'd had an adventure once, and it had killed her mother and father and almost killed her. Adventures could be disastrous, and she didn't trust them one little bit. She was, however, willing to attempt one last adventure in her life.

Now all she had to do was convince Charlie Fox that, although she might be uneasy, and although she'd already hurt the both of them, if he was willing to be patient with her, she was willing to try something new with him.

This was, of course, provided they ever saw each other again.

Chicago. He had to be in Chicago. Amy pinned her heart and hopes on Chicago.

Twenty

Charlie looked at himself in the mirror and wasn't sure it was him. The face bore a slight resemblance to the Charlie Fox he'd known all his life, but the rest of him looked sort of weird.

But his duds were new and well cut and had cost him a whole lot of money. Martin had gone with him to pick them out, and since Martin always looked as if he'd just stepped out of a gentlemen's magazine, Charlie trusted his opinion on sartorial matters.

So he guessed he probably looked good. What did he know? The only thing he knew for sure was that he wanted Amy to like what she saw—if she could recognize him beneath all this finery. He was ill at ease in city clothes, but Martin had told him that as long as he pretended not to be, he'd be all right. That was what he'd done in the pictures, Charlie supposed, so Martin must be right. That was what actors did, after all. And since Charlie had just finished acting in his second Peerless picture, *The Lone Cowboy,* he guessed he qualified as an actor.

Not that he'd spent the entire two months since the finish of *One and Only* playacting. Far from it. Charlie Fox was only acting for money. His real life belonged on a ranch, and he'd spent the rest of his time in Southern California fixing that up.

Now, if he could only persuade Amy to join him in his

new ranching endeavor, he'd be a happy man. If she wouldn't be persuaded, he'd at least be a successful one; he was determined of that.

He glowered at himself in the mirror and told himself not to think negatively. He needed to project confidence.

One good thing about this Chicago trip—besides the possibility of trying to win Amy over to his side—was that Horace Huxtable wouldn't be there.

"Thank God he's off making a picture in the South Seas. Another studio shipped him off to some island somewhere, and they aren't allowing liquor anywhere near him. They're hoping he'll shape up and do a good job for them." Martin sounded doubtful.

"As long as I never have to see the bastard again, I don't care what he does or what you tell folks."

But Martin was worried. "We can't let the picture-viewing public know what an ass he was to Amy or they'll never go to see another Peerless picture."

"They don't have to know that part," Charlie assured him.

"Right." Martin peered into the mirror and caught Charlie's eye. "Say, Charlie, are you sure you don't want to travel with Karen and Amy and me? Her aunt and uncle will be on the same train, so there will be lots of people around."

Just what he needed, Charlie thought glumly: a passel of fascinated folks to watch his wooing. Provided he could get close enough to Amy to do any wooing. "No, thanks, Martin. I have some business to finish up in Los Angeles, and then I'll catch the train the next day." If he had to share passage with Amy, and if she refused to talk to him or anything like that, Charlie feared he'd just throw himself under the train and be done with it.

Dang it, there went that negative thinking again. He shook himself mentally. "But I'll see you all in Chicago."

"All right." Martin didn't look as if he approved of Charlie's traveling plans.

Charlie laid a hand on Martin's shoulder. Six months ago he'd never have made such a gesture, but he'd been around picture people so much lately that he hardly thought about it twice. "Don't worry, Martin. I'll be there. I wouldn't let you down."

"I know, Charlie. It's only that I . . . well, I'd been hoping for a while there during the filming of *One and Only* that you and Amy would pair up. You . . . you seemed happy together."

Charlie heaved a huge sigh. "Yeah." He'd believed they were. Then Amy had told him she didn't want a poor man who hadn't established himself, and his whole life had gone straight to hell. That was before Karen Crenshaw tracked him down. He felt an almost imperceptible lightening in his heart.

Good old Karen. And what she'd told him made sense. Sort of. Charlie figured it was worth another try, anyhow, and he was going to give it in Chicago.

A balmy breeze blew through the Orange Rest Pavilion, gently scenting the air with the heavenly aroma of honeysuckle. Everything around the pavilion was green and gorgeous, and it was a practically perfect July day in Pasadena, California.

It would be perfect altogether if Amy Wilkes weren't dreading the job she had steeled herself to do. She knew she had to. She'd been putting it off like the coward she knew herself to be, but Karen had given her a pep talk the day before, and Amy was determined.

Thanks to Karen, too, Amy had also concluded that it wasn't shame that propelled her. True, she felt odd about having slept with Charlie Fox when she was all but affianced to

Vernon, but she wasn't ashamed of it. Sleeping with Charlie had been an expression of deep and abiding love, and she cherished the memory. If she had her way, she'd have the opportunity innumerable times to experience the exquisite sensations he'd evoked within her.

There was, however, no gainsaying the will of Providence, and Amy might not get her way. The notion made her insides cramp painfully. Nevertheless, she aimed to do what she had to do, and she aimed to do it now.

She fingered the sash at her waist nervously and bowed her head. She sat up very straight in the white wicker chair, because Vernon approved of good posture. She knew very well that she was going to irk him plenty, and she owed it to him not to look slouchy as she did it.

"I'm terribly sorry, Vernon, but I can't marry you."

She sneaked a peek at Vernon and immediately bowed her head again. She didn't want to watch him get furious with her; listening to him was going to be bad enough.

"Amy! How can you say such a thing to me?"

"Not very easily," she told him honestly. "But it wouldn't be fair to you if I agreed to be your wife."

"And why not? Do you think some other, more knightly man is going to come along on a white charger and carry you away to a castle somewhere?"

"Please don't be sarcastic, Vernon. This is difficult for me, too."

He huffed.

Amy licked her lips and tried to explain without bringing Charlie Fox into the room with the two of them. In this case, three would definitely be a crowd. "You see, I've given it a lot of thought, and I've come to understand that I could never be the sort of wife you need."

"I believe I am the best judge of that," Vernon said coldly.

"You're the best judge of what you want in a wife, Vernon, but I don't believe I'm it."

"Nonsense."

"Oh, dear." Amy had expected him to be upset, but he was clearly outraged, which was more than she'd bargained for. She guessed she'd forgotten that Vernon didn't like to lose. And, although Amy doubted that he loved her, he'd assuredly be angry about losing her. "I'm so sorry about this. But after pondering it and praying over it and worrying about it for weeks, I feel I must put an end to your hopes for a marriage between us."

"It is typical of a female," said Vernon in his icily controlled voice, "to feel rather than to think. I suppose it's because women are unable to think critically."

Amy tried not to resent that, because she knew she'd never given him any reason to think of her as a reflective person. She'd always agreed with him, no matter what trash he spouted. He surely never believed that she'd mount a rebellion or oppose his will. Until this minute. It must be a terrible shock to him to learn she had a mind of her own and a will of her own after all the time he'd spent thinking of her as someone he could mold to his wishes.

Overall, Amy believed she'd like him better if he got mad and hollered like lesser men did, instead of continuing his cold, rigid pose, which was quite off-putting. She sighed heavily.

Vernon's lips set into a tight line. "That being the case, I believe that you—all women—ought to be prudent and take advice from the men who have your interests at heart. You're evidently unable to determine those things for yourselves."

She eyed him slantways. *Did* he have her interests at heart? Amy doubted it. "Um . . . I don't think it's possible for you to do that, Vernon, since you don't really know me. You certainly don't know me well enough to be able to assess my best interests."

"Don't *know* you?" Vernon's light blue eyes fairly started from his head. "I've known you since you were a child! And I've never held your background against you, either, no matter how sordid it is. I've never once mentioned your squalid beginnings. You have to admit that, Amy, because it's the truth."

She blinked, astonished. "Good heavens, Vernon, I wish you had mentioned this before. I had no idea you thought I was so far beneath you."

He frowned. "Well, honestly, being impoverished and abandoned by one's parents is not something one chats about every day, as if it were nothing."

"My parents couldn't very well help abandoning me. They died, if you'll recall." Amy heard the acidity in her voice and hoped Vernon wouldn't.

He didn't. She ought to have expected as much. He waved her objection aside with his hand. "I discussed the matter with my parents a long time ago, and they agreed with me that as long as it's not an episode people are likely to talk about, it won't become a problem or interfere with our position in society."

Our position in society. Good grief. Anyhow, it was obviously a problem already. Amy sensed she could never make Vernon understand that. She merely said calmly, "I'm very sorry, Vernon. I'm sure you don't understand, and there's no way I can make you understand. Just know, please, that this hurts me. Know also that you will eventually be very glad that you didn't marry me, because I'm not the woman you need as a wife."

"I can't believe I'm hearing this."

Vernon did something Amy had never seen him do before. He put a hand to his forehead. Good heavens, her news must have come as a dreadful blow if he was becoming animated.

She began to wring her hands in distress. "I'm so *very* sorry, Vernon."

"I see." He stood abruptly, causing his chair to skid on the floor—another indication of his inner turmoil. His outer self looked perfectly controlled. "I shall have to think about this, Amy, and consult with my parents. I can't but believe that you must have lost your mind."

"If that will make you feel better," Amy murmured, and couldn't continue. She felt rotten. "I'm very sorry."

"Yes, well, I suppose it's best to learn now that you're given to instability and flights of fancy. Perhaps you're right that you aren't the woman I need for a wife."

"I'm glad you're beginning to understand that."

She watched him stalk away from her as if he were a duke and she a lowly vassal who had displeased him, and she felt heavy, alone, and unhappy. She'd hurt his feelings, whether he knew it or not, and she didn't like herself for it. She'd have liked herself even less if she'd married him while she was in love with another man.

"I guess this lets out the Tournament of Roses," she muttered to herself as she went inside to resume her duties at the Orange Rest. Soon the inmates would be arising from their afternoon naps, and she'd be needed to distribute glasses of orange juice among them.

She had a momentary mental image of herself as a white-haired woman with wrinkles and no family, clinging to her job at the Orange Rest Health Spa because there was nothing else in her life to cling to. A sharp pang assailed her.

"Stop it!" she commanded herself.

That scenario wasn't in the cards for Amy Wilkes. No, sir-ree. She and Karen had talked about it for hours and hours and hours, and, while Amy would never be as bold and daring as Karen, she wasn't about to let herself dwindle into an old maid, either. Not without putting up a darned good fight, she wasn't.

She hoped she was in suitable training. The good Lord knew she'd been practicing.

"Ha! Martin's the old maid!" Amy went off into a peal of laughter. Martin, Karen, and Aunt Julia joined in. Julia had never before played cards and still considered them a relatively sinful pursuit, but she was lowering herself this once in order to keep from being bored during the long train journey from Pasadena to Chicago. Amy appreciated her aunt's amiability and condescension. Aunt Julia always had been a brick.

"Phooey," said Martin, feigning discouragement. "It's because the only women I meet are actresses, and any man would be a fool to marry one of them."

"I don't think they're all so bad," Amy murmured. "Mr. Huxtable was a fiend, of course, but I'm sure the actresses who work in pictures can't all be that bad."

"Hmmm," said Karen, as if she weren't sure of it at all.

Julia, to whom the newfangled moving pictures were a miracle, gazed wide-eyed at her niece and Karen, and at Martin Tafft, who was the most elegant man she'd ever met. She'd told Amy so several times.

"I wish Charlie could have come with us," Martin went on as he shuffled the cards. "Then *he* could be stuck as the old maid a couple of times. You three are too slick for me."

Karen slipped Amy a worried glance, but Amy only smiled. "I'm glad he's not going to miss the premiere," Karen said, striving to sound casual. "He performed his role very well."

"Yes, he did," Martin said, dealing out the Old Maid cards. "And he said he'd be there. We even went out together and bought him some fancy new clothes to wear."

Karen murmured something under her breath. Amy was surprised, too. "My goodness."

"He'll look like a Greek god," Karen declared dramatically. Occasionally Amy wondered why Karen hadn't been asked to perform in the pictures instead of herself.

Martin chuckled. "I don't know about that. He's pretty nervous about it. He looks elegant in his new duds, but I think he's more comfortable in denim britches and plaid shirts."

"Are you finished with the filming of *The Lone Cowboy?*" Karen asked.

"Yes, we are, and he did a wonderful job. I wish I could get him to do more pictures for Peerless. He has a tremendous presence on the screen." Martin sighed. "But he's got other plans." He brightened a little. "You never know, though. The money's good, and he might soften eventually."

Amy's heart crunched up a little, but she didn't let it show.

"I'll be so glad to meet him," declared Julia, eyeing her cards and putting a pair down on the table. "I've heard so much about him."

"You have?"

Both Karen and Martin stared at Amy, who blushed. "I've told my aunt about everyone on the set," she said defiantly. "It was an exciting adventure for all of us."

"I'll say it was." Karen gave Amy a sly grin, so Amy kicked her—not hard—under the table.

Julia nodded energetically and drew a card. "It sounds like it. Especially that flood." Julia glanced, bright-eyed, at Karen and Amy. "Imagine my two girls cooking for an entire cast!"

"I wouldn't exactly call it cooking," Amy temporized, although she was happy that Julia had begun thinking of Karen as part of the family.

"It was, too," Karen said firmly. "I've never made so much cornbread in my entire life. And you made a whole rabbit stew. That's cooking, isn't it?"

"Sort of, I guess."

"Charlie shot the rabbits," Karen continued, slapping a pair down and shooting a triumphant grin around the table. "Bang! Right there in the wilds of the desert. And Amy cooked a very tasty stew with them."

Amy decided silence was called for here, so she didn't say a word.

"I'm sorry Benjamin can't join us in Chicago," Martin said, as if talking about Charlie with Amy had reminded him of the close relationship between Karen and Benjamin.

"He's doing another picture, so he couldn't come along."

Karen sighed dreamily, and Amy's heart snagged before she steeled herself, as she'd been doing for approximately two months now. She wasn't going to invite defeat this time. If she was to be beaten at this game, she would go down fighting. Karen had taught her that much, at least, and Amy wasn't going to let her coach down.

"If Charlie doesn't fall all over himself and propose to you tonight, there's no hope for him." Karen gazed at Amy with what looked to Amy remarkably like the pride of invention.

Amy couldn't fault Karen for any feeling she might possess of having created something out of nothing. Not that Amy was ugly to begin with, but she certainly did look dazzling tonight—more dazzling than she'd ever looked before, even when they'd stayed at the Royal El Montean.

Amy told herself not to think about the Royal El Montean. But she appreciated Karen's talent and energy very much as she stood in her evening gown, fashioned and sewn for *her* this time instead of Wilma Patecky, by Karen's own hands. The entire ensemble couldn't have been more perfect.

What's more, Karen had talked Martin into footing the cost of everything by persuading him that the glory of Amy would send people flocking to see the picture. Martin had taken the bait, although, according to Karen, he'd seen beyond Karen's blithe talk to the two women's true motive.

"He knows you're pining away for Charlie," Karen said as she gazed at her handiwork with an eye to improvement.

"I'm not pining away! He probably agreed to pay because we're giving him the jewelry and the gown after Chicago." Amy, embarrassed and beginning to heat up, turned so that Karen wouldn't be able to see her consternation.

Blast! She hated when Karen's glib tongue told the truth in such a bald-faced manner. Amy was accustomed to people sugarcoating ugly truths. Such fiddle-faddling ways were not Karen's, though, and Amy loved her for it, even if she also deplored it sometimes. Like now, for instance.

"Pshaw!" said Karen, with no remorse whatsoever. Not that Amy had expected any. "And Martin says Charlie's pining away for you, too—although, of course, men handle pining differently from women."

Amy would just bet they did, although she'd die before she asked. Besides, she wasn't sure she wanted to know. If Charlie's pining involved other women, she'd probably fall down screaming and tear her hair out. How embarrassing.

Amy's internal emotions and reluctance didn't matter to Karen, who never needed to hear questions before she answered them. "I guess he's been running wild all over Southern California."

"Oh, my." This was serious news, indeed. Had the poor man taken to drink from the agony of losing her?

Try not to be a total ass, Amy Wilkes, her inner guide told her with remarkable pungency. "What's he been doing?" she asked, steeling herself for the worst.

Karen shrugged. "I don't know."

My, wasn't that helpful? Amy tried not to resent her friend. She was right to withhold criticism, apparently, because

Karen immediately followed her disclaimer with, "He's been looking at land, I understand. And reading everything he can get his hands on about other stuff."

"What other stuff?"

Karen shrugged. "I understand he's investing in Peerless."

"Oh." Did that mean he intended to stay in the pictures? For some reason, Amy was disappointed.

She'd always pictured Charlie on a horse on a ranch somewhere, looking lean and sleek and absolutely masculine, in front of a flock of cows. Or was it a herd? Whatever. Something about acting in pictures didn't seem quite manly to her, although she allowed herself to be prejudiced by her experience.

"Of course, he's made a ton of money with Peerless, so I imagine he knows what he's doing by investing. As annoying as Martin can be sometimes when he gets to spouting the marvels of movies with all his boyish enthusiasm, I think he's right about the flickers. They're going to make a whole lot of people a whole lot of money."

"I suspect you're both right."

Karen made a dive at Amy and executed one last adjustment to the waist of Amy's gown. She stood back to view her creation as Amy gazed at herself in the mirror. She was quite a sight, if she did say so herself.

Lace the blue of her eyes and mounted on cream silk adorned her body as if it had been sewn to her skin. The gown featured a daringly low neckline, short cap sleeves formed by a scallop of lace, and a blue cummerbund. The flared skirt dipped into a long train at the back. With the gown, Amy wore long cream-colored kid gloves, and a necklace and drop earrings of faux sapphires. If Charlie still had any feelings for her at all, she hoped the sight of her in this incredible finery would push him over the edge.

If, of course, his pride didn't stand in his way.

Fear and pride. To Amy's way of thinking, those were the two monsters that stood in the way of a union between them. Her fear and his pride. She'd wounded his pride. She was ashamed of herself for it, because it was her fear that had made her do it. Well, she might not be done with fear, but she was sure aiming to battle it tooth and nail in order to secure Charlie Fox.

Which was a darned good thing, since she was at present scared to flinders.

In the meantime, Karen's gaze of appreciation had faded. She now sported a small frown and was tapping her cheek with her forefinger.

Amy said, "What? What's wrong?"

Karen cocked her head to one side. "Nothing's wrong, but something's missing. Let me think for a minute until I figure out what it is."

Amy, who had become accustomed to episodes of this nature during the filming of *One and Only* stood still and waited. At last Karen cried, "I have it! Your hair."

Amy's right hand shot to her hair, upon which she'd spent an inordinate amount of time earlier in the evening. "What about my hair?"

"You need feathers."

"Feathers?" Good heavens.

"And I think I have some right here."

To Amy's amazement, Karen pitched into her luggage and, after digging around for a moment, produced one of her ever-present boxes, this one evidently having started out in life filled with Cuban cigars. "What's in there?"

"Feathers." Karen gave a negligent shrug. "And some other stuff. You never know what you're going to need."

Up until she'd met Karen, Amy had never considered emergencies of an apparel-related nature. Emergencies to her had always been accompanied by some kind of danger or worry.

How naive she'd been. She blinked as Karen tossed several strands of fake jewels—neatly rolled and tied—onto the bed, followed by several yards of rolled-up ribbons and a couple of silk flower hair ornaments, and then lifted a variety of feathers out of the box. "Here they are."

They were indeed. Amy, guessing that it was safe to move by this time, walked to the bed to see what was what. Karen whirled around and held out two blue feathers and one black one. "The very thing!" she cried.

Amy trusted Karen implicitly when it came to clothes, so she said, "I'm happy to hear it."

"You just wait."

Karen tapped her shoulder, and Amy obediently turned around. She felt Karen poke the feathers into her hairdo—a new and creative arrangement she'd practiced for weeks at home—and prayed that nothing would come loose. It didn't.

"All right, go look at yourself," Karen said. The note of complacency in her voice encouraged Amy to do as she'd said.

"My gracious, you're right. They're perfect."

"Aren't they, though?"

Amy turned around. "Thank you, Karen. Thank you for everything." Since she was about to sniffle, she grabbed a hankie out of the cleverly hidden pocket in her skirt and blew her nose.

"Nonsense," asserted Karen. "You're my best friend." She, too, began to sniffle.

It was therefore a couple of watery lasses who went to Uncle Frank and Aunt Julia's room a few minutes later to bear them off for a spectacular evening of frivolity and entertainment. Martin was going to meet them all in the lobby of the hotel and take them to a magnificent restaurant for a bite to eat before the premiere of *One and Only*. He had warned them that photographers and newspapermen would be swarming around them all evening in order to capture pictures and quotes from the stars.

"Don't forget," he'd told them with patent glee, "this is the very first featured motion picture ever made. This is a huge occasion for the whole of the motion picture industry. For the whole world, even! The newspapers are going to eat it up."

Amy believed him, although she herself considered the amount of publicity being expended for something as trivial as a moving picture rather sad. She'd prefer it if the press kept its photographers and writers for important things. Like floods and famine and war and so forth. Sensing that tragedy shouldn't be the only thing to which the press paid attention, she added the discovery of ancient Egyptian tombs, breakthroughs in medical research, and great scientific revelations to her list of publicity-worthy ventures.

Tonight, however, she was it—she and the rest of the cast of *One and Only*. Which, since Horace Huxtable wasn't present—thank God—meant Charlie Fox. Amy swallowed nervously and she and Karen, along with her aunt and uncle, all splendidly attired for the occasion, walked to the head of the magnificent curving staircase leading to the hotel lobby.

Twenty-one

Charlie had declined Martin's invitation to wait in the lobby for Amy and her family.

"Karen'll be there, too, of course. Can't have an actress attend a premiere of a major motion picture without her dresser along." Martin had chuckled gleefully and rubbed his hands together.

Charlie was glad Karen would be there. And Amy's aunt and uncle. Their presence, not to mention the hordes of photographers and print men Charlie had glimpsed in the lobby, would postpone his intended purpose, and he was grateful to them for it.

Shoot, he'd never been a coward before this.

His life's happiness had never depended so completely on one evening, either.

Dang it, he had to stop thinking these things. Charlie had smiled and bidden Martin farewell. At this moment, he held down the table at the glorious restaurant to which Martin and the rest of the party would go as soon as they'd all assembled in the lobby of the hotel. He'd ordered a cocktail, because he didn't know what else to do, and fiddled with it as he waited. He was as nervous as a newborn calf facing a branding iron.

Would she or wouldn't she? He wanted to run his fingers through his hair, or bury his head in his hands and moan for a while, but didn't dare mess up his fancy new haircut. Shoot, he'd never before been to a big-city barber.

But he'd done it for Amy. And when he'd looked at himself in the mirror, all duded out in his fancy Los Angeles tailor's clothes, he hardly recognized himself.

Good God almighty, what if *she* didn't recognize him?

He gulped some of his cocktail—a concoction called a Manhattan and awfully sweet—and told himself to calm down.

Oh, good God, there they were. He saw Karen.

He saw Martin.

He saw an elderly couple who he assumed were Amy's aunt and uncle.

He saw a swarm of photographers, all calling out for the party to stop walking and turn to have their likenesses captured on film.

He saw Martin smile and speak to the reporters. "After dinner, fellows. Let the lady have a bite to eat first." Martin sounded cheerful. Charlie felt a fierce, sudden, and unexpected urge to hit something.

And at long last—when he'd almost forgotten whom it was he was looking for—he saw Amy.

His mouth fell open. His fingers, which had been fingering his Manhattan glass in a frenzy of nervous energy, stilled. He felt his eyes open hugely.

It was a *damned* good thing he hadn't waited with Martin in the lobby. It would have been too humiliating to have his knees give out on him there, and to fall to the floor in front of her in an attitude of worship.

He'd always considered her a pretty woman, and since he'd tasted the sweets of her love, he'd ached for her, but he'd never seen her lovelier than she was this evening. He hoped his heart would hold out long enough for him to beg her to reconsider and marry him.

Bracing himself on the table so he wouldn't keel over, Charlie stood politely. Once he was up on his hind legs, he balanced himself by grasping the back of his chair. Because he'd been acting for a while and had learned the rudiments of pretense, he forced himself to smile amiably.

"There he is!" Martin cried happily. "Gentlemen, you can have one shot of Peerless's newest cowboy star before you depart and leave us in peace."

An army of photographers rushed up to Charlie. He'd never seen such heavy equipment wielded so handily. Although he was mightily disconcerted by Amy's presence, he steeled his nerves and smiled for the cameras, hoping all the while that Amy was impressed.

Or maybe she'd be disgusted that he'd done another picture. Shoot, he hadn't thought about that before.

On the other hand, Charlie'd heard time and time again that females were beginning to swoon over moving picture cowboys.

Aw, dang it, Amy wasn't like any of those stupid women. She was special.

At any rate, it was too late to decline. He must have been caught on film a hundred times or more by the time Martin succeeded in shooing the last of the newspaper vultures out of the restaurant. The restaurant manager, not happy about the swarming mob of reporters, helped.

The time had come.

Well, not the time for his proposal, but the time to greet Amy. He'd considered at least sixteen hundred different ways to do it, and decided a warm smile and a friendly handshake would be intimate but not pushy. After all, they'd worked together for a month. He knew better than to remind Amy of what else they'd done together.

Dagnabbit, every time he thought about that night they'd spent together—that portion of a night, he meant—a jolt of desire shook him. He suppressed it with difficulty.

"Charlie!" Karen cried, and ran up to him and gave him a big hug.

That was Karen all over, he decided with a grin. He wished Amy had a tiny bit of Karen's effusiveness. "Howdy, Karen. Good to see you again. How ya been?"

"Just wonderful. And you?"

"Fine, fine."

"Here's Amy," Karen said with the air of a master of ceremonies introducing the starring act. She swept her arm out, narrowly missing Charlie's cocktail glass, and indicated Amy, who was standing there looking both gorgeous and a bit shy. She had a glorious smile on her face, though, and her eyes, which were by some miracle of chance or purpose the same color as her gown, were sparkling like the sapphires around her neck.

"Amy," Charlie said, and couldn't continue.

"Charlie," she said, and seemed to have the same problem.

"Oh, for heaven's sake!" Karen huffed. "Kiss each other!"

Such an outrageous suggestion appeared to jog Amy out of her trance. Charlie, who thought Karen's suggestion an excellent one, knew better than to act upon it. Instead, he walked to Amy with his hand held out. "It's really good to see you again, Amy."

"Oh, Charlie, I'm so glad to see you again, too!" She shook his hand warmly, even going so far as to put her other hand on top of the two clasped ones.

Mightily encouraged, Charlie leaned down a little. "I'd like to talk to you after the premiere, Amy. Do you think that's possible?"

"Oh, yes! I really want to talk to you, too."

If those weren't the sweetest words Charlie had ever heard, he didn't know what were.

Amy felt as if she were living in a dream for the rest of the evening. The dinner was indubitably delicious, although she didn't taste it, and the wine superb. As she ate and drank, she was conscious only of Charlie, who sat directly across from her. More than once, she failed to hear a question directed to her and had to ask the speaker to repeat himself. Charlie, she noticed, had the same problem.

After this had happened several times, it was Karen who finally muttered, "Oh, leave them alone. They're not fit for company this evening." She laughed when she said it.

Amy barely heard her. She suspected Charlie didn't hear her at all, because he only kept grinning at Amy as if she were the only other human being in the entire world.

After dinner, the party repaired to the brand-new, luxurious Bijou Dream Theater, the first and most extravagant motion picture palace ever built. They rode there in two huge, luxurious motorcars manufactured by the Benz Company in Germany. Amy would have been impressed if she hadn't been so totally absorbed in Charlie.

They sat together in the motorcar, and when Charlie's hand slid across the backseat—under the folds of her filmy lace wrap for propriety's sake—and found Amy's gloved hand, she didn't move her hand but clasped his with fervor. And love. A great deal of love. Her heart almost overflowed at this indication that he no longer despised her for her cowardice.

One thing did manage to pry her attention away from Charlie: the crowds of people lining the street leading up to the theater. Sure that something alarming, and probably disastrous, must have happened to have drawn such a throng, she exclaimed, "Good heavens, what are all those people doing there?"

"They're there to see you, my dear," Martin said with glee. "They're fans."

"Fans?" Amy used a fan occasionally during the summertime, but had never heard the word used with regard to people.

"Fans. I think it's short for fanatic," Karen explained. "They're people who like the pictures."

"For heaven's sake." She and Charlie exchanged a surprised glance. He smiled first. She'd never been able to resist one of his charming smiles, and she smiled back. The crowd roared.

"That's the way," Martin said approvingly. "They love a good show."

A good show? Another glance at Charlie told Amy that he didn't consider it a mere show, either, and she laughed, suddenly happier than she'd ever been. Feeling expansive, she turned toward the crowd and waved. They waved back and cheered.

Six huge spotlights were burning in front of the theater, their beams crossing in the night sky. More people crowded around the door of the theater, making it difficult to maneuver toward it. Fortunately, Martin seemed to have thought of everything, and he called upon several uniformed policemen to hold the crowd at bay.

Astonished, Amy walked up a red carpet on Charlie's arm, to the cheering of the mob. At the door, as if they'd been doing it all their lives, the couple turned, waved to the crowd, and almost caused a riot—although they didn't know that until they read the newspapers the next day.

One and Only was a delightful picture. Even Amy, who hadn't cared for very many of the movies she'd seen, had to admit to its charm.

Horace Huxtable was superb. Although she knew it was evil of her, Amy wished he weren't. It was irritating for a person she detested to show any admirable qualities. But he was a fine actor, and there was no denying it. She was pleased that the crowd didn't seem to miss him. She knew *that* was evil of her, too.

* * *

It wasn't until far into the night that she and Charlie finally had an opportunity to be private together. The festivities surrounding the premiere of *One and Only* never seemed to end. After the screening, Martin took his guests to another four-star restaurant, where they had a light supper and drinks. He evidently hoped the party would all stay for dancing, but since Aunt Julia and Uncle Frank were fading fast—they weren't accustomed to late hours—Amy pleaded exhaustion, too, and she and Charlie accompanied them back to the hotel.

Because reporters seemed to be lurking everywhere, Charlie didn't dare go to Amy's room. Just before he left her at Julia and Frank's door, he whispered, "Come to room 410 when you get a chance. All right?" He looked apprehensive, as if he feared she'd rebel at doing anything that might be considered scandalous.

But Amy was past being hampered by society's strictures or her own inhibitions—even if they still bothered her. "I'll be there as soon as I can," she assured him.

His smile of wonder and pleasure buoyed her out of her weariness, and she made short work of Aunt Julia's evening gown and chatter. "We can discuss it all tomorrow," she said, yawning. "Right now, I have to get to bed before I fall over."

Her aunt accepted Amy's excuse with equanimity, believing, Amy was sure, that Amy would never, ever do anything untoward. Little did she know.

Amy visited her own room first in order to rid herself of her finery, replacing her smashing evening gown with a plain but pretty white cotton wrapper with pink embroidery decorating it. She wasn't going to have corsets in the way tonight, should things go as she wanted them to.

She scurried down the hall and up the stairs to the fourth floor. She peered around the hall door to check for reporters before she dashed to room 410. She'd barely knocked once before the door swung open, and there stood Charlie in his shirtsleeves, looking eager and nervous and more handsome than a man had any right to look.

She took one assessing glance at him, and threw caution to the wind. She loved him. He loved her. She'd bet her life on that, and the fact that he'd do everything in his power to help her overcome her trepidation. And she flung herself into his arms.

His arms closed around her, and she experienced at long last that delicious feeling of being cherished. She'd experienced it only once before, and had missed it as if she'd lost one of her senses. "Oh, Charlie, I've missed you so much!"

"And I've missed you."

They demonstrated how much they'd missed each other for several minutes before Charlie pulled away. Amy was disappointed.

"We . . . we have to talk." He loosened his collar, which was not one of the removable kind but was sewn onto his dress shirt. Beads of perspiration dotted his brow. Amy could tell he was in a state. So was she.

"I suppose we do." Blast. She didn't want to talk. Words always seemed to spoil things. Nevertheless, she knew he was right. No more cowardice. She had to face these things. "I'm very sorry, Charlie. I allowed my childhood experiences to interfere with my adult life, and that was foolish and cowardly of me."

"Oh, no, Amy. I'm the one who was wrong. I didn't take into consideration how much your early experiences must have scared you."

"Nonsense. I was a child then. I'm not a child any longer—"

"I'll say."

Since the exclamation seemed both heartfelt and involuntary, Amy let it go with a smile. "But I was wrong to allow my past to interfere with our future."

"So . . . so do you think you might not hate marrying me, even if I'm not exactly established yet? I will be. I swear to God I will be, Amy."

Although she'd have given anything to prevent it, a stab of fear shot through her so suddenly that she was momentarily immobilized. She shook it off. "Yes. I think I might not hate it." Her fingers reached for the ribbons at her waist and she began stroking them nervously. "But—but, Charlie, I can't help being afraid."

"I know it, honey."

"But I'll try very hard not to allow my fear to interfere with our life together—if you still want me."

His smile was tenderness itself. "I still want you, Amy. A whole lot."

"Good." She nodded. Terror had begun to gnaw up from her stomach and into her heart. "In that case . . . well, in that case, you'd better hug me fast, because I'm getting scared again." She felt like a pure idiot.

But Charlie understood, and he made sure Amy knew it. When he had her securely in his strong arms, he whispered, "Gosh, Amy, don't ever be afraid and not tell me. I'll do anything I can to keep you safe." He sat on one of the plush wing chairs flanking the fireplace—Peerless had spared no money on rooms for its stars—and held her tightly. "I bought a ranch, sweetheart. Right outside of Pasadena."

Amazed, she pulled slightly away and gazed into his dear, dear eyes. "You did?"

He nodded. "Yep. And I planted a bunch of orange trees, too. And I've got stock arriving next week. My brother's going to help me get started. I hope you don't mind about that. But I've hired an architect, and they're going to start putting up the new house as soon as the plans are done."

"Good heavens!" Amy couldn't help it. She started to laugh softly. "Oh, Charlie, did you do all of that for me?"

He grinned at her. "Well, not exactly. I aim to be a successful rancher, Amy, with or without you at my side, but I sure as the good Lord hope it'll be with you. Because I love you, honey, and it'll be a whole lot easier on me if my heart isn't broken while I work my butt off to achieve that success."

"Oh, Charlie. I love you so much!"

"If that ain't music to my ears," Charlie said in his best cowboy drawl, "I don't know what is." And he kissed her.

This kiss lasted longer than the other ones of the evening, and ended with them tangled in the covers of Charlie's bed. He made short work of the covers—and the sheets, too. And Amy's wrapper. And his own evening clothes.

When he plunged his rigid sex into her hot, wet passage, Amy thought she might just swoon from sheer pleasure. When he drove her over the edge into bliss, she did swoon, but only for a moment. She was awake again when Charlie found his own release and then subsided into her welcoming arms.

"I'm so happy, Charlie."

"So'm I, sweetheart."

They dozed off under the influence of their happiness, and only awoke when passion aroused them in the early morning. They didn't open their eyes again until somebody knocked at Charlie's door toward noon. Charlie popped up in bed, suddenly worried for Amy's reputation.

"Who is it?" he called.

"It's Martin, Charlie. You all right? You didn't come down for breakfast."

Shoot. Although he was fuddled from lack of sleep and sexual fulfillment, Charlie thought fast. "Er . . . I'm fine, Martin. I'm just not used to these hours. I slept late."

"All right. Say, I don't suppose you've seen Amy, have you? Nobody can seem to rouse her. I'm thinking of getting a maid with a key."

This comment brought Amy out from under the covers, too.

Charlie glanced at her and grinned. His prim and proper Amy didn't look too prim and proper this morning, all naked and tousled and flushed from good loving. She yanked on his shoulder and whispered, "No!"

Still grinning, Charlie said, "Don't do that, Martin. I talked to her last night and . . . and she said she was going to sleep until noon." He lifted an eyebrow in question at Amy. She smiled gratefully and nodded.

After a significant pause, Martin said, "I see. All right. I'll wait until noon. We've got an appointment with the press at one. Um, if you see her, you might remind her."

"Shoot, that's right. I almost forgot. Okay, Martin. I'll tell her. If I see her," Charlie added quickly.

"Right. If you see her." Martin walked away.

"I think he's laughing," Amy said uneasily.

"Don't worry about Martin, darlin'. We have to worry about getting you downstairs without anybody seeing you."

They managed. With some of the acting expertise they'd learned in the last few months and some of Charlie's clothes, they managed. And they had an interesting announcement for the press when they all met at one o'clock for lunch and interviews.

The press was pleased. Karen was ecstatic. Martin was happy. Aunt Julia and Uncle Frank were tickled pink. Amy and Charlie's fans were delighted and wrote by the hundreds to tell the happy couple so.

Horace Huxtable, sourly slogging through the filming of a beachcomber-native-maiden picture on a remote island in the South Seas, was as bitter as might be expected when he heard the news.

Amy adored life on the ranch. Even before the main house was finished, she'd settled in. She adored her husband, too, and thought his younger brother, who blushed and stammered every time he saw her, was a darling. In truth, she had to face very few hardships, thanks to Charlie's good business sense, brilliant management, and ample capitalization of his ranching project.

For the first few months of her marriage, Amy was plagued by old fears, but they gradually tapered off. By the time she was about to deliver her first baby, she hardly thought about Alaska at all, and when she did, it was with the remoteness one generally associated with old legends and fairy tales.

Martin Tafft stood as godfather to the first Fox child to be born, a bouncing baby boy whom they named Martin Francis in honor of Martin and Uncle Frank. Their next child, Karen, was born a year and a half later, approximately two weeks before Karen's first child, Amy, was born.

The two little girls grew up together, drank lots of good, wholesome orange juice, wore only the most fashionable clothes, learned to ride and rope like regular cowgirls, loved the moving pictures, and both served as Rose Princesses when they were the right age.

Their mothers and fathers were thrilled.

Vernon Catesby, the local millionaire banker, didn't have enough influence to block their selection. He sulked for a while but eventually recovered. After all, he was rich.

But Amy and Charlie Fox, who didn't have half the worldly wealth of Mr. Catesby and his wife—the former Miss Luella Simpson, hand-picked by Vernon's parents who no longer trusted him to choose for himself—knew themselves to be far richer than the Catesbys.

If you liked COWBOY FOR HIRE, be sure to look for BEAUTY AND THE BRAIN, the next in Alice Duncan's "The Dream Maker" series, available wherever books are sold in May 2001.

Studious Colin Peters, Martin Tafft's new research assistant at Lovejoy Studios, believes their new picture's star, Brenda Fitzpatrick, would never be interested in him. Blond and incredibly beautiful, Brenda is hiding something, however—her brain. All she wants is to make enough money in the "flickers" to set up housekeeping and indulge her passion for books. But when Martin asks Brenda to loosen up serious Colin, they discover passion together first. . . .

COMING IN APRIL 2001 FROM
ZEBRA BALLAD ROMANCES